Quest for the Dark Blade

Morgan and Merlin's Excellent
Adventures:
Book Three

By
MALORY

MALORY

Copyright © 2025 by Malory

Published through The Legion Publishers Ltd

Editing by Anna Johnstone

Cover by Sergey Shikin

Typography by May Dawney Designs

Formatting and additional editing by Christine Cajiao

This is a work of fiction.

Table of Contents

For Josiah,

You're not allowed to read *any* of these until you are older

CHAPTER 1 - IN WHICH THERE IS A CHANGING OF THE GUARD.

King Uther had been dead a month.

Sadly, his passing had come as no surprise. From the moment he heard his brother – Aurelius Ambrosius - still lived, he had seemingly wasted away with every passing hour. Nothing anyone could do made a difference.

I'd tried to force a few of my better-quality Elixirs down his throat – I became pretty good at spiking his food – but you can't heal someone who has simply lost the will to live.

I'd spent quite some time with him near the end. He wanted to hear as many stories as I could remember about his son's exploits in the world of Camelot – which he had dedicated his life to bringing into being. He also wanted to talk to Merlin and reminisce about the old days, and I was happy to play Whoopi Goldberg to that particular unchained melody.

Even right at the end, I couldn't find it in me to like him.

He was a brutal pragmatist with enough blood to have drowned a decent-sized continent, but everything he had done had been in the service of a big dream. As someone who had never done anything for a better reason than "it feels good", I had to respect that level of dedication.

Nor did I, I am afraid to say, feel any tremendous paternal bond with him. I'd had my own challenges with my Daddy dearest, and if I couldn't unravel them through therapy, fucking every proxy I could find and self-medicating with epic doses of recreational drugs, I wasn't going to find enlightenment at Uther Pendragon's deathbed.

The end, when it came, was pretty bland.

He was holding forth about a particularly fruitful boar hunt when his eyes just slipped closed, and he stopped breathing.

The King is dead, long live the...

Well, now there's a story. And that is kind of where things seemed to have become a bit more complicated.

Arthur had not been idle since we'd returned from the Dark Tower. Alongside Bors and Lancelot, he'd pushed every Saxon still lingering around, back over the border. I'm not sure 'pushed' entirely does justice to the epic levels of dark age violence that had been visited upon the blue-painted men from across the border of Dumnonia. There had been some highly hairy battles - particularly against the West Saxons led by Cedric – but when the chips were down, the bodies were counted, and the victor was dancing around cheering; it was the Britons who had prevailed.

So, when Uther stepped beyond the veil, there was no doubt that Prince Arthur was right at the forefront of those to succeed him. However, it was turning out to not be quite the slam dunk that might have been hoped.

Firstly, despite the thawing of the relationship between him and Guinevere, there was still no little bouncing baby Pendragon on the horizon. I'd heard more than enough rumours that the Princess was barren to begin to get distinct Henry VIII vibes about the whole court. Fortunately, it didn't take me too many 'accidentally' dropped fireballs to persuade those peddling that viewpoint to keep it away from my ears.

Secondly, and this one hurt, I think some of the reluctance about a wider acclamation for the new King might have had something to do with the efficacy of the Court Mage.

It's not that I hadn't been trying to progress.

Even Merlin, at his most pernickety, would admit I was making impressive gains in shoring up my foundations. Compared to the big, explosive techniques people were used to seeing from me, I was trying to do things right and put in place the building blocks for my future. It's just that when you used to be able to summon the very trees to grab and shag your enemies, the ability to create softly glowing fairy orbs of light lacked a little something.

<Fairy Orbs> are an entirely classic cultivating waypoint. You should, my dear, be very proud to have unlocked that technique yourself. It speaks of subtlety with an Air and Fire Qi that you have not been able to master. And what is more, you did not cheat.

"I hear what you're saying, Big M; it's just I don't think my newfound talent to provide mood lighting is exactly overcoming Arthur's detractors with the power of my magic."

And, my word, were there some detractors. Almost from the moment Uther had breathed his last, the voices raised against him were many and various.

"Serious times call for serious leadership," one particularly grey face had spewed all over the throne room.

"Quite," Queen Igraine has said, her face a mask of icy politeness, "which is why anyone so profoundly ridiculous to ask for my hand in marriage during the lighting of husband's funeral pyre must be considered at the height of pomposity."

If looks could kill...

Well, actually, I had it on excellent authority - Lancelot loved gossip more than a teenage girl - that a particular northern lord and his entire war band barely made it out of sight of Tintagel before falling into a series of unlikely accidents. At night. At the end of spears.

But it was the internal wrangling, more than the unsubtle machinations of the outlanders, that was trying our patience. It felt that every noble family with even the smallest claim to the throne was jockeying for position. It was getting very, very wearing.

"We could kill them." Bors downed his mug of mead and gestured for another.

"Kill who exactly?" Guinevere was lying with her head in Arthur's lap, and her feet were precisely two and a half feet away from where Lancelot sat, sprawled with a customary dopey look on his film star face.

If he so much as moved an inch closer to her... well, he was getting a <Fairy Light> up the nose.

"Oh, I don't know," he waved his newly filled mug around airily, "start with anyone we don't like and work our way downwards. It would certainly make it a bit fucking quieter around here."

"And it is your considered opinion that will bring unity to the kingdom, is it?" Igraine was standing uneasily in the corner of the room. She was the one who had called for this little get-together, but it was clear she would rather be anywhere else right now.

"Fuck unity! If you ask me, a few heads on pikes would encourage a bit more loyalty from people who should know better. And what is more, it'd show that Arthur's not to be messed with."

"No," Guinevere said, "it'll show that Arthur is a tyrant. We want him to be acclaimed the Pendragon, not feared the length and breadth of the realm."

"Sir Rickon called me "Any-hole-is-a-goal Arthur to his knights yesterday. If I'm honest, I could stand a bit of fear from that direction."

"Sir Rickon is a noisy windbag. He never speaks, but bile spills out. Also," Guinevere added, "it's hardly like he's entirely out of line."

"Not recently," Arthur flicked wine from his cup at her face.

Honestly, I'm amazed I kept the vomit restrained at such an unnecessary display of matrimonial banter.

"So, that leads us to the most important of questions. What are we going to do? I haven't called you here this evening because I wanted your company," Igraine's voice was steady but with all the chilliness of a good white wine. "My husband is dead, and my son is yet to be crowned king. That is unacceptable to me. It would have been unacceptable to Uther, too. I want that situation resolved."

Lancelot chimed up. "Back home, those wanting chief being strip naked, paint themselves in their death masks and enter the golden circle. Whoever standing left is chief. Until next challenge."

"If I thought that would work, I'd do it tomorrow." Arthur was shaking his head. "But this isn't just about fighting. It's politics, too. Everyone says they support my claim, but no one will be the first to call the Witan to acclaim me as such. I'd call the damn thing myself, but if I do, and no one shows up..."

A quest? Merlin popped into my head.

"Yeah, we fucking tried that with the whole 'chase me, chase me' thing with Guinevere. Didn't work out too well for us, did it?"

I was aware of several pairs of eyes suddenly looking my way. Sometimes, I forget that not everyone else can hear the voice in my head. "Sorry, Merlin was suggesting we needed a quest."

"What sort of quest?" Guinevere sat up. She remained two and a half feet away from Lancelot.

"Yeah, Big M What sort of quest?".

The other British Kings are never going to acclaim Arthur to the throne. They don't trust him, do not fear you, my dear, and each fancy themselves as the next Pendragon. They will be happy to allow Arthur to lead the charge against the Saxons whilst ever praying he will catch an arrow in the throat. I fear the longer success continues, the likelihood of one in the back grows.

"Let them fucking try," Bors growled after I'd shared the wizard's words.

"They have been trying, Sir Bors." Igraine's voice was grim. "I haven't been so busy foiling assassination plots since the first few weeks of Uther's realm. Please, and as much as it pains me to say it, let's hear Merlin out."

They may not be willing to acclaim you as Pendragon, but not one of them will be able to resist joining you on a quest. You just need something suitably epic to grab their fancy.

"Does the old goat have a suggestion?" Igraine – ever since the wizard had helped Uther carry out the Dark Age version of catfishing, she had not been Merlin's biggest fan. "Or is he just speaking for the sake of being heard? Not that we can hear him, of course. Which is a profound quality of life improvement for me."

You know, my dear, I once spent a very profitable weekend enchanting every single reflective surface in this castle so that Queen Igraine looked fifty pounds heavier whenever she looked into it, and with a complexion an Italian pizzeria would market as extra pepperoni. I call them the good old days.

"And you moan at me for frivolous uses of my Qi!"

Yes, but back then, I was at the peak of my power. You're barely in the foothills.

"And at your most potent, you decided to spend the time not creating world peace or ending all hunger but making a middle-aged woman feel fat and ugly. I must tell you, mate, we're perfectly capable of doing that all on our own."

"The quest?" Arthur pressed. "What could unite the other kings to follow me?".

I relayed Merlin's suggestions as they came in.

The Holy Grail, of course. But we're about twenty years early for that, and - honestly - I worry about the Pythonesque quality Morgan would bring to proceedings. (Hey - that's unnecessary and also 'Ni!') We're lacking in a Gawaine to go after the Green Man. 'We could seek to retrieve various Treasures of Britain, but I think the most obvious quest would be for Caeldfwch.

By the shocked expressions of those around me, you'd have thought I'd suggested fucking a giraffe in the throne room.

"Caeldfwch. That's real?" asked Guinevere. Lancelot and she were about a foot apart. I had a <Fairy Orb> ready.

"I don't even know what that is. Big M?"

Apologies, my dear. I thought you'd recognise its real name. You know it by its more familiar title. Excalibur.

CHAPTER 2 - IN WHICH I SING OF ARMS AND MEN

A short while later, the little gathering broke up, and I returned to my room. When I say 'room,' I mean massive fuck-off suite of rooms which I now occupy in Merlin's Tower.

The Big M had been a little bit leery about letting me move in here when I first settled into life at Tintagel. Apparently, he was worried that my tendency to "touch everything without thinking "might cause a timeline-concluding event or some such silliness. As I'd once had a T-shirt printed with those very words emblazoned across my chest, I didn't think I was in too much of a position to argue.

However, since the rather epic confrontation with Aurelius and, more importantly, the mammoth amount of time I had spent locked in a time loop, Merlin seemed to think I may be a little less trigger-happy.

To be clear, I wasn't necessarily sure that was the case, but I appreciated the vote of confidence.

Merlin's Tower - well, I guess, my tower now - stood at the far corner of the castle overlooking the sea. Compared to Aurelius' Dark Tower, it was pretty average in height - *it's not the size, my dear* - but had far greater girth. The inside was divided up into three floors, up through which a stone spiral staircase reached towards the roof, which was open - via a wooden shutter - to the elements.

I thought of Floor One as "random shit which a hoarder would baulk at". It seemed Merlin had never seen an unusual-looking rock or piece of weirdly shaped wood without scooping it up and then putting it on a shelf. At first, I'd assumed everything must have some sort of special Qi-related significance, but as far as I could tell, it was all just, as my grandmother would have said, "fucking tut". Even Merlin was a little hazy about the details when I tried to pinpoint why he kept some of this stuff.

Life is long, my dear, he said airily, *and you never know when—* he considered the bunch of twigs I was brandishing*— the hair of a giant lamprey may be useful.*

The Second Floor was much more pleasant - in that, every available surface was not cluttered with millennia of piles of crud. Here was what I charitably referred to as my 'living quarters.' As I did not really require food, drink, or even sleep much anymore, it was all still fairly spartan.

However, there was a comfortable chair that I'd learned was the focal point for all the Qi the tower channelled from the atmosphere, and that was a pretty decent spot to while away the evenings undertaking some cycling.

You know I died in that chair?

"Yes, Big M, I do."

Don't you feel awkward? Sitting in it?

"Not especially."

That's where I died, my dear. Surely you have some sort of... what do you people call it? An ick about taking up the same space as a dead body.

I opened my mouth to explain that - when you'd spent a fair bit of time eating out of bins, sharing needles and always sleeping on the wet patch - the idea of sitting on a chair someone died in a few months ago really didn't register on the old gross-out-metre. In fact, I'd be amazed if I'd owned a single item of furniture someone hadn't died in, on or under before I... acquired it.

Also, you know, I was *literally* squatting in the hollowed-out body of a Saxon spearman who had passed away just before I took possession. I don't know. Maybe it was just me, but it would have felt a touch arch to feel icky about a fucking chair when I was happily rocking this skinsuit.

However, with the power of my newfound cultivator maturity, I was learning quite how fucked up was my previous view of the world. So, I settled on, "It makes me feel close to you, Big M," and left it to that.

By the warm glow I felt down our connection, I sensed this was the right answer.

Personal growth, motherfuckers.

The Third Floor could be opened to the sky via a trapodoor if I so wished. Now, I know that sounds lovely, and if this were California, I'd be sunbathing topless with the best of them. Sixth-century Cornwall? Not so much. I'd opened it once, and it was like enacting a scene from the Titanic. It was also wall-to-wall books and scrolls, which seemed to be treated with some sort of water repellent.

If I thought my inventory could hold some shit, if it was nothing compared to these bookshelves,

Spacial storage, my dear. Each shelf cannot quite hold an infinite amount of material, but it's not too far off from that.

"Cool. So where do you keep your porn stash?"

My dear, I am a legendary cultivator. I do not need such things such as a 'porn stash. I am shocked you even suggested it.

"So, there's no reason at all while you're trying to pull my attention away from the top right shelf in that corner?"

There was a pause. *Would you like more information about Caeldfwch?*

"Sure, why not horn-dog?"

Caeldfwch was another of the Thirteen Treasures of Britain. It was also the one most associated with the legend of King Arthur and - in many ways – could be seen as the embodiment of his rise to power.

In my own timeline, there were various ways in which it was supposed to finally end up in Arthur's possession, but I was a particular sucker for the tale of The Sword in the Stone.

It was quite a downer when Merlin poopooed that.

And it was just lying around waiting for someone to pull it out?

"Well, no. Only the 'true' King of England could free it, so when he could, it was a key sign that Arthur was the right guy."

So, did it flame-fry anyone who pulled it and failed to release it?

I looked down at the quiet form of my own sword. Since failing to destroy Aurelius, it had been extremely reticent of late. Even lending it to Lancelot for his daily sparring seemed to do little to get Drynwyn's heart racing. I was worried I might have broken it.

No, Excalibur didn't hurt anyone who tried to draw it from the stone. It just wouldn't be pulled out.

What's the point of that?

I sensed I wasn't going to be able to get Merlin on board with the mystical joy of the tale of the Sword in the Stone. "What about Caeldfwch? How is it supposed to be recovered?".

Ah, just a standard Neriasl-gifting ceremony. You find her, ask for it, and providing she doesn't take against you, you are suddenly the proud owner of a Treasure of Britain. But what's interesting about Caeldfwch isn't how you get it. It's what it can do once you own it.

"Which is what?"

Caeldfwch destroys Qi.

***

In the dim and distant past, when the world was still young - or *my early twenties*, as Merlin put it - a tribe of giants became fed up with the way in which cultivators were throwing their weight around.

I chose not to ask Merlin to fill in the blanks around exactly what he meant here. We had an understanding that the adventures of "young Merlin" were not going to be made into a heartwarming Children's BBC special anytime soon.

So, in order to buy themselves a bit of room to - you know - not be slaughtered, these giants sought to forge a weapon that would even up the score somewhat. They took the metal from a meteorite, quenched it in the blood of as many cultivators as they could round up, and crafted a sword.

They called it Caeldfwch - Mage Killer - and when drawn from its scabbard - which they imbued with significant healing properties - it would create a void around its bearer that no Qi or Qi-empowered technique could breach.

Now, when I was the only cultivator of substance around, it was obviously not an ideal implement to have floating around.

"But with Aurelius Ambrosius kicking ass and taking names, it suddenly seems a more attractive option?"

I see we are on the same page.

"So how do we find it?"

Caeldfwch has a bearer. She'll be a water-based nymph, a Neriad, and if I know anything about that particular sword, she'll be desperate to hand the snotty cow over to the most righteous man she comes across.

"And we want that to be Arthur, I guess?"

We do. But it needs to be more than just Arthur riding into Tintagel swinging around a nice, shiny new toy. If that was all it took, we'd have given him Drynwyn, my dear, and called the Witan a month or so back. No, we need the other British kings to go on this quest with him, so when Arthur obtains Caeldfwch, we can show he has been chosen above all of them. That's how he becomes the Pendragon.

"And how do we ensure the... the Neriad gives the sword to Arthur and not one of the other Kings? Assuming they ever agree to join the quest."

That's easy, my dear; we cheat.

And so, the call went out to the other British Kingdoms that still resisted the Saxons. To Gwent. To Powys. To Deheubarth. To Gwynedd. The message went out far and wide, but it was to those four that Merlin insisted on the most persuasive messages of missions.

We get those four Kingdoms behind Arthur, and it won't matter what anyone else thinks.

"And they're not behind him already?"

In theory, sure. All pledged fealty to Uther, which included that they would honour him as the Pendragon and accepted Arthur as his heir. However, my dear, since the Saxons destroyed Isca and reached Tintagel's gates, there is disquiet. I may be a spectre of what I once was, but even I can sense the ambition of the rest of those sworn to follow Arthur. They will not be able to resist a chance to unseat him. And a quest for Treasure of Britain? That is a very good chance indeed.

It was three weeks before messengers returned and another month on from that before we saw clouds of dust in the distance that spoke of the arrivals of entourages.

For a Witan had been called. And it looked like we had visitors.

CHAPTER 3 - IN WHICH THE CORE CAST GROWS

So, I liked King Owain of Gwent.

He was this big Santa Claus-looking dude with a dirty laugh and a twinkle in his eye. He was old enough to be my grandfather, but that didn't stop him from leaving his hands where they had no place to be when we hugged.

"So, you're the new Merlin?" he boomed, "Far easier on the eye than the old one! Softer arse, too!"

"And you're from Gwent?" I replied, moving his hands above the water line. "I heard you had a bad harvest. What happened? You ate it all, you fat fuck?"

There was an awkward pause while all his bannermen drew swords and pointed them at me. Arthur's' men did the same, and, for a few moments, we had quite the Mexican stand-off. Nope. That doesn't quite work. Cornish face-off? Until Owain's belly laugh - and my, what a belly. It shook like a bowlful of jelly — decreased the tension.

"Ha. l like her. She is, what, what do you call it?"

"Suicidal?" Arthur glowered.

"Moronic?" Igraine chimed in.

"Foolish?" Added Guinevere.

"A bitch!" Owain finished. "A bitchy cultivator. I like her." He turned to me. "And if you ever need a roll in the hay with a big man, you let me know. Once you go fat, you don't ever go back..."

As I said, I liked Owain.

King Beric of Powys, on the other hand...

There's a type of man that you just know hates women. Like, **hates** them. Sure, he'll fuck us, but it will be through gritted teeth and only to show he has the most enormous, hardest cock in the room. His wife had a look about her I'd seen far too many times in the various shared accommodations I'd spent time in. There were no marks on her face - because even in this culture, it wasn't the done thing to beat the shit out of your women - but the way she held herself, and the way she moved, told me everything I needed to know. He was very lucky *<We want our Entwives back>* had been torn out by Aurelius Ambrosius.

I shook his hand when we were introduced, and it took every ounce of self-restraint I had not to crush his fingers to mush. "Morgan Le Fey, I understand? I was expecting someone... more powerful."

"Beric of Powys. I'd heard you were -"

My dear, let us not try the patience of another Monarch this morning. There are bigger needs in play than your desire to be a smart-arse.

"Here," I finished lamely.

His cold eyes fixed on mine momentarily, and then the bastard winked. As if he knew exactly what was going through my mind. "So, is it true?"

"Is what true, Your Majesty?" I hissed the honorific through gritted teeth.

"That you've studied hard and can make pretty lights appear? Truly, the enemies of Arthur have much to fear from such mighty a cultivator."

"Well, you know what they say. From small acorns, mighty things grow." I glanced downwards at his trousers. "Although, apparently, I hear that is not always the case." I might, or might now, have wiggled my little finger at this stage.

"Beric, you fucker!" Bors pushed past me and wrapped the King in a headlock, leading him away. "How's life in the valleys?"

My dear, unless you can keep your temper, it may be wise for you to steer clear of the King of Powys. He is famously thin-skinned, and you, apparently, have no ability to control yourself.

I bit back a reply and took in the last two major players that had been invited to Tintagel; Mark of Gwynedd and Corys of Dehuebarth. Their Kingdoms were far smaller than Gwent or Powys, but they continued to successfully hold the Saxons at bay, which was no mean feat.

Mark was even fatter than Owain, so much so that he was carried everywhere on a litter. It took absolutely everything I had not to call him Jabba the Hutt, at least not to his face. However, I was with Winston Smith that nothing was your own except the few cubic centimetres inside your skull. And inside my head, this dude was Jabba Desilijic Tiure.

On the other hand, Corys was the life and soul of the party. He was tall, powerfully muscled and had the knack of making everyone he looked at feel like they were the centre of the universe. When we were introduced, Guinevere gave him an appraising look, which really had no place on a married woman's face.

Awesome, so I now had *another* target for my cock blocking efforts.

A woman's work was never done.

Each of the Kings had brought a decent entourage with them, so the castle's banqueting hall was pretty packed when it was time to eat. I'd not really experienced a full-on feast at Tintagel since I'd arrived, and it was an awesome experience.

Look, give me a McDonalds and a large drink, and I'm anyone's. So, the idea of hundreds of courses that just kept on coming - plus every version of drink known to man - was something else.

With just a little injection of Qi, I'd found that I could pretty much keep eating as much as I wanted. As long as I burned it away, it never seemed to touch the sides.

Fourteen-year-old me hovering over the toilet bowl with her fingers down her throat approved.

"I love a woman who enjoys her food", Owain banged the table beside me approvingly.

"Just trying to keep up with you, big man!"

The King of Gwent patted his belly contentedly. "All bought and paid for, love. Sign of strength, you see? My people look at me and go, 'Look at that fat bastard. He must be really rich to get that big. Probably can afford some serious men-at-arms. Better do what he says."

He sat back and gazed around the room and I took the opportunity to follow his gaze.

We'd been seated at the far right of the royal table, with Owain wedged next to me. Presumably because he was immune to my insults.

Or maybe he just liked me.

It was sometimes hard to tell.

"What do you think of all this?" he asked, his voice nothing like the jovial tone I'd become used to.

"All this?"

He gestured to encompass the banquetting hall. "I don't know what Arthur thinks he's playing at. He's a nice enough lad, deadly on the battlefield, but he's no Uther." He nodded over towards Guinevere. "And she's no Igraine."

"And you are, I suppose?"

Owain's laugh was genuine and heartfelt. "Of course not, love. It's all I can do to keep my table full and the damned Saxons out of my land. I don't want the responsibility of leading the charge against them. Never have. Uther was the man for that. Besides, I wouldn't have the votes. No more than Arthur will."

"So, why did you come?"

"I hear there's going to be a quest for Caeldfwch. Fat as I may be, you can be damned sure I will be at the forefront of that." He looked at me, and I understood just how much of his former behaviour had been a front. I could see how this man commanded the loyalty of his people. "We all lived under the fear of Merlin razing our cities to the ground. If there's a way out there to stop that ever being a factor again, you can bet I'll seek it out. My people would expect nothing less from me. You seem like a nice enough girl, but I don't trust cultivators. None of us does. You tell me there's a sword out there I can kill you with? I'm after it."

"And if Arthur finds the sword first?".

"Well then, love. He will have the most powerful Cultivator in the British lands *and* the only way to protect himself from the magic you wield. I'd think that will be enough to get the man my vote at the Witan."

Something about the way Owain said that did not sit well with me.

Arthur had envisaged this quest as a way to build bonds with these Kings. To hear Owain speak, it was less about that and more about doing whatever was possible to stop Arthur from finding it first.

"Do the rest of the Kings feel the same?"

"Who knows? We don't have any sort of secret communication system. But Uther was the Pendragon because we knew he'd kill us if we didn't acclaim him. Either with spears through the door, a thunderbolt from the sky or," and Owain glanced towards Igraine, "a knife in the back in the dark." He refilled his glass with a nod to a serving girl. His hands were pretty free with her, too. "But then Isca happened, and none of us are too sure anymore that Dumnonia is the power it once was. Not with Uther gone…"

"For someone without a secret communication system, you seem pretty well informed about how everyone else is thinking. Arthur couldn't have done anything about what happened at Isca."

"Then what's the point of us having a Pendragon? If the Saxons can rampage with impunity across your lands, what help can we expect from you when they attack our holdfasts? More than one of us wonders if we would do better to treat with the Saxons for peace than rely on Arthur's strength to keep us safe."

"I thought the British didn't deal with Saxons..." My voice was tight.

"And I thought all you could do was cast pretty lights?"

I looked down at my left hand and was surprised to see a little ball of lightning crackling and arcing in the palm of my hand. At the same time, I became aware that all the talking in the hall had stopped, with everyone's eyes on me.

"Big M, what's going on?"

I could be mistaken... sorry, that's just me being self-effacing. I am never mistaken. I know exactly what has just happened. You have finally raised your various resistances to such a level that you have been able to unlock one of my favourite techniques.

"Which is?"

Well, I call it <Ball Lightning>, but I'm sure you will come up with some different, pithy title that will make me wince every time you say it. Essentially, if all aspects of your Qi are perfectly aligned - and you have the right emotional impetus - then lightning is literally at your fingertips. Just a couple of things I probably should make clear.

"Okay..."

Firstly, the last time I checked your Metal Qi was significantly behind your other aspects, so it is a touch surprising you have closed that gap this evening. If I did not know better, I would assume that someone has slipped something fairly viciously nasty into your wine.

My eyes searched out a serving girl who seemed to have slipped away. "I've been poisoned!"

Relax, my dear. There's nothing of it left in your system — it has all been burned away in the formation of that little lightning ball. Think of it as a mark of respect. We'd have known they were not taking you seriously unless at least one of them had tried to kill you.

"You said there were 'a couple of things'?" I couldn't help but feel Merlin was being a touch blasé about – you know – my attempted murder, but I sensed there was not going to be much more sympathy coming my way on that front.

Yes. Maybe I should have led with this. Unless you make use of <Ball Lightning> in a very short period of time, it has a tendency to explode.

I raised a hand to the ceiling and let a stream of energy lance out to strike the ceiling. It blew a hole straight through the stonework.

A second ball of lightning appeared in my other hand and I emptied that one closer to Beric than I truly needed to. To be fair, I barely singed him, and I was fairly sure that wanker was the one who'd tried to kill me...

"Sorry, guys. Apparently, I just levelled up. Talk amongst yourselves."

Hundreds of eyes stared, appalled at the smoking holes I'd blown in the walls and ceiling; Owain leant over and whispered loud enough for everyone to hear. "If everyone in the room didn't want a Qi-deadening sword before, I can guarantee they do now. Arthur will quite certainly have his quest."

Arthur raised his cup and saluted me. Looking at the expressions of people who I sensed were suddenly very motivated to kill me, I wasn't sure whether I'd truly helped or hindered.

CHAPTER 4 - IN WHICH LANCELOT GETS TO SHOW US HIS MOVES

"'Thank you all for agreeing to join us here this evening."

Arthur moved to the front of the royal table and addressed the largely silent room. My eyes scanned over the little pockets of inattention distracting from the stillness.

Mark and his ... the only word I could find was 'handmaidens' feeding him tidbits (I wanted to say 'titbits' but then I realised I wasn't a thirteen year old boy) from the table were being unnecessarily rude, and there were a few other minor chieftains and warlords who hadn't quite sensed the mood. Most, when I caught their eye, shut the fuck up. The King of Gwynedd, however, met my eyes and bit down on the grape that had just been placed in his mouth. Juice went everywhere

Not for nothing, but I absolutely rock a gold bikini. The dude needed to watch out.

"This is the first time a Witan has been called since the death of my father. I thank you all for the tributes sent in Uther's name."

A general rumble of approval for Uther went out around the Hall. Igraine's face momentarily crumbled, and then her flat mask came back.

"I had, however, expected that my fist Witan would acknowledge me as Pendragon."

Well, that was a mood killer

If I listened hard enough, I was sure I could make out a tumbleweed roll through the hall. "But I acknowledge that some of you have enough concerns that you would withhold your vote if it were called."

"Ballsy," Owain murmured next to me. "However, I am not wholly sure it is wise to announce this to a massive hall of warriors. You know, that they all think you're too weak to lead them..."

I agreed. In fact, I'd argued long and hard against this course of action. I was more in favour of a "King Kong got nothing on me" approach, but I'd been hushed. Sometimes, being the only person with pop culture literacy is a burden.

"And that is a hesitation I acknowledge I have earned. For too many years, I have not taken the responsibility of being Uther's heir seriously." He paused, perhaps hoping for denial from the floor.

An awkward silence greeted him.

"And yet," a hard tone entered his voice, "for all those justifiable fears about the maturity of my behaviour, I doubt anyone here would deny my successes in the field. The Saxons have been thrown back, time and time again. I have sent them running the length and breadth of my lands and have, at the same time, eased the pressure on each of you."

"I do not deny you have been active of late, Prince Arthur." Beric of Powys was on his feet. I went to stand to take issue at the 'Prince' title, but Owain stilled me with a heavy hand on my shoulder. "Your king needs to stand on his own two feet here, lass. Beric is a pain in the arse, but Arthur will need his vote. He won't win that respect hidden behind his pet wizard's skirts. No disrespect."

"None taken, lard arse."

Beric was enjoying holding the floor. "After all, it was not so long ago there was a Saxon warband at these very gates. I hear Isca still burns to this day. Would that you had been able to arrive in time to save all those British lives, I doubt any here would hesitate to name you Pendragon right now."

Prick.

Arthur observed him for a long moment. "That is true, your majesty. However, whereas I hear Powys buys peace from the Bretwalda with grain, livestock, and gold, I slew those on Dumnonia land and avenged Isca a hundred times over. In fact, now I think of it, I may well have looted some of your craven protection money from the corpses of their spearmen. Would you like some of it back?"

Beric coloured, even as the rest of the room started to show signs of warming up. "We fight the Saxons as much as any kingdom."

"Come off it, Beric. Everyone here knows you haven't called your banners in the last year." It was Jabba that added these thoughts, much to my surprise. From what Merlin had told me, he and Beric were tight. "Not that I blame you," he added, "I have often argued we need to find a way of living with these invaders. They've been here, what, twenty, thirty years? Maybe there is an accommodation we should be seeking, not finding yet more spears to throw at them. Who needs constant warfare?" Ah, there it is.

"They're Saxons!" Owain bellowed, standing and hitting both fists down on the table. "We don't make 'accommodation' with them! We kill the fuckers!"

Beric waved his hand, dismissing the Gwent king, "My people deserve a little peace."

Arthur raised his voice above both of them. "And here I thought the hesitation about naming a Pendragon was due to uncertainty about me! I never dreamt that a Witan would be called and there would be talk of appeasement. There will be no peace with the Saxons in my lifetime!"

I noted that, of the kings present, only Owain and Corys joined in the roar of approval that echoed around the room.

Arthur stilled the crowd. I have to admit, I was impressed at his showmanship. This shit might just work... "But we are not here to acclaim a Pendragon this day. I am instead asking for those of courage and resolve to join me in the search for something which will ensure the Saxons will no longer pose a threat to our lands. We all hear that their Bretwalda is a cultivator of extraordinary power - maybe even one to equal Merlin. Having faced him in his own fortress, I can tell you that is true."

The silence was of different type now. He had them.

"However, through the combined efforts of those in this room," all eyes flicked to Lancelot, Bors, Guinevere, and finally, to me, "we overcame that threat. However," and now his voice was as loud as I had ever heard it, "even now, the Bretwalda is recovering his position. We have retaken land that has not been in British hands since before my father's time. But we are at a critical point. Unless we come together and devise a way to destroy this cultivator's might, all we have achieved will be lost."

"My spies tell me the Bretwalda is your uncle! How do we know you are not planning to throw in your lot with him?"

Oh, had I mentioned Beric was a colossal prick?

But it was Lancelot, not Arthur, who answered. "I from long from here. But if you accuse my chieftain of two-faced double-dealing again, there will be blood."

Beric sneered back. "Prince Arthur, control your barbarian".

Lancelot was up on his feet. "And now you are rude being. If you would be so kind, your arse I will be kicking."

Boom. It was on.

Beric's eyes flicked to his champion, Eolgef, who grinned confidently back and nodded his head. "In the civilised world, barbarian, kings do not condescend to brawl with the help. Although, I will acknowledge that considering the conduct of your master in recent years, I can understand your confusion. I will accept your apology gracefully, at which stage we can go back to listening to our host's dreary monologue, or I'm willing for my champion to bring you to heel."

The hall rowed approval. Speeches were all well and good, but after a good meal, what you really wanted was a bit of blood-letting.

Owain leaned over to me, confusion on his jolly face. 'Why's Arthur allowing this' We're all on board with the quest. He doesn't need to alienate the men of Powys like this. Or is he sacrificing this barbarian to build bridges?"

I didn't answer the King of Gwent, giving him instead my best Mona Lisa smile.

Because this was exactly as we had planned... no, let's be honest, this was all about Igraine. I'm not going to lie, while all of our little leadership group had their own skills to bring to the party, the Queen Mother was the only truly devious mind amongst us. This little bit of tonight's entertainment against the gathering storm was all her.

It isn't enough for this Witan to agree on the quest for Caeldfwch. The only chance we had of defeating the Saxons was for all the kingdoms to unite, and as the Big M had advised, nothing brings unity as quickly as power.

My display of <Unnecessary Sequel Trilogy> had helped concentrate minds that I wasn't just a table decoration. Arthur had reminded them of what he could do at the head of an army, and now we needed something a little more visceral as to what was in the near future of anyone who didn't want to get on board the Pendragon train.

"In the interests of fairness, I should probably say my champion will only fight three", Lancelot coughed, "four on one."

"Not worth my shirt taking off for less," Lancelot said, ripping his shit open in an entirely unnecessary but aesthetically appealing way. I think even his pecs had pecs. I sharply looked towards Guinevere, but her eyes were fixed on Arthur.

Beric laughed humorously. "Well, if you're anxious to be rid of your mad dog, the men of Powys will oblige." He waggled his fingers towards Eolgef, who instantly picked three mean-looking motherfuckers to move to the centre of the room alongside him.

Tables were cleared, benches moved, and, by the time Lancelot jumped to the floor - I could swear it looked like he'd covered himself in baby oil in the hiatus - a serviceable fighting ring was set up.

The warriors from Powys arranged themselves in a wide-semi circle. Each of them was easily the same size as Lancelot and carried themselves with all the confidence of veterans. I felt a momentary pang of worry - if our dude was stomped to the floor here, that could well be it.

The end of Camelot before it even began. There's no way Arthur could come back from having his champion slain in his own feasting hall.

Then I remembered seeing Lancelot wade through rank after rank of Saxons in the battle before the Dark Tower. He was going to be okay.

"This is not a fist fight, dog," Eolgef drew his bastard sword, and his men did likewise. "We fight to the death in the civilised world." I wanted to make a gag about no fighting in the war room, but realised there wasn't anyone about to enjoy some Strangelove related humour.

Lancelot cocked his head. "Understanding, I am. But I like to be fair. And he wouldn't let me try ten at once. So barehand I be."

And, with no further ado, he attacked.

The first thing to note was that Lancelot was fast. Not 'fast for a big' guy, but genuinely, scarily, 'did I miss something?' quick. He moved with such casual grace most of the time that it was easy to overlook his capacity for explosive momentum.

Like a tiger made flesh.

Eolgef barely began his downstroke before Lancelot's hand was on his throat, sweeping his leg away to crash Powy's champion to the ground. It all happened so quickly that Lancelot had given him three massive, clubbing blows to the head before the other three even reacted. By the time they did, Eolgef was not getting back up any time soon, and Lancelot had a weapon.

And that leads to the second important thing to know about Lancelot. You really, really, really did not want him to get his hand on a sword.

"Fucking hell, where did you find this guy!" Owain breathed as Lancelot blocked a wild swing from the first henchman and disarmed him with a flick of his wrist, pulling him close and dropping him with a headbutt.

At this stage, the remaining two put some distance between them, seeking to attack from the sides simultaneously.

This did not help.

The fight was over in a few more seconds, during which time I'm sure I saw Lancelot yawn. He'd managed to avoid killing any of them - we'd thought slaughtering Beric's bannermen might be making the point too forcefully - but he was barely out of breath.

And they were fucked.

Arthur cleared his throat. "Well, that was instructive, I think? After that little diversion, shall we return to my... what did you call it, dreary monologue?"

The room was wholly with him now. Men moved to remove Beric's fallen champions and, cautiously, clapped Lancelot on the back.

All eyes were locked on Arthur as he spoke. All, that is, apart from, those of Guinevere, whose were resting on the glistering muscles below her. I could be wrong, but there was some colour to her cheeks

Shit.

CHAPTER 5 - IN WHICH I AM DEFINITELY NOT A WIZARD, HARRY

Funnily enough, it all went quite smoothly after that.

Of course, Beric and Mark moaned and whinged a bit, but Owain, and to a lesser extent, Corys agreed with the course of action Arthur outlined. So, in pretty short order, the four Kings - along with enough men to make each feel comfortable - would set off in pursuit of Caeldfwch and the first amongst them to claim it would have the right to return with it to their home kingdom.

You'don't have to go, you know, my dear. With the number of swords and spears on this little jaunt, I can't imagine they'll be in much need of you.

To be honest, I didn't disagree.

It was clearly going to be of far greater benefit for me to crack on with my studies. I was finding <Unnecessary Sequel Trilogy > to have all sorts of cool applications – I could literally channel the lightning energy through Drynwyn to produce an epic fire/lightning combination that fulfilled all my Thundercat's fantasies - which I needed to play with to get best value from.

Also, my Qi Core water feature was now filled to the very top, and I was sure just one more big push would tip me over the edge. "When it does, it'll move me into Harry, right? That's what the whole thing represents, doesn't it? It tracks my progress to the next level of cultivation?"

This silliness isn't going to go away, is it? Hey ho. A small price to pay, I suppose. As I am sure you are aware, it's not quite as simple as that, my dear. But, once your... water feature overflows it will begin the process of remaking your body into that of a... Harry. Just to check, you're sure we must use these infantile names for rather complex notions?

"Look, I've told you before, if we're going to play this game, then I'm not going to do it with a straight face."

And describing yourself and your ungodly powers in terms of hormonal teenagers helps you maintain your sense of poise and dignity, does it?

"Fucking A. So, what do I need to do to tip the water feature over the edge?"

There was a pause, and then I was pulled into my Artist's Studio. The Vitruvian-Man-As-Me filled my vision, and I could see my Qi paint moving around my channels in a smooth flow with my every breath; little tributaries branching off to my various mana stores, my armour, Drynwyn and the most recent addition, my cauldron

What do you see, my dear?

"Oh, you know. Just me being awesome. Crushing the Qi cycling thing like a legend."

Quite. As we've discussed - many times - you have had some experiences that have leapt your level of cultivation significantly further forward than would be expected when your actual knowledge is

considered. Your channels - following the incident with Vortigern's Dragon and your subsequent... enthusiasm with the mana stone - are capable of moving vastly more Qi than they are currently doing.

I wrinkled my nose at that. After months of relative calm, I felt I was probably as full of Qi as I could possibly be. My newest addition - the cauldron - had never stopped slurping my Qi down like a teenager with a lifetime's supply of Prime.

"I'm not sure I have all that much more room in here, Big M."

No, of course not. Your Qi levels are about as high as they are ever going to be. I'm talking about concentration.

I sensed there was a lecture coming on. "I mean, I'm happy to ask the question, or you can just go off on one."

For form's sake, I quite like it when you ask.

"Fuck's sake. Tell me, oh great Merlin, what is it you mean by 'Qi concentration?'"

Are you sure you are interested? I cannot help but notice a certain amount of - shall we say - shortness in your tone.

"Dude..."

Fine. It would be best if you thought about progression in quite a linear way.

First, you're a Neville (I'm hating myself.) You had significant potential, but no workable channels and relatively little Qi to move around them in any event. Secondly, with luck, you move into Ron territory. This is a substantially larger category which will probably cover most cultivators alive at any one time. At this stage, most Rons will have techniques that can move Qi around their body and, perhaps, expel it in specific quantities. A Ron's body will have enhanced mental and physical properties and the cultivator will generally be a menace to regular society.

Now, this is where it gets Interesting.

"Oh, good. I was hoping for an interesting bit..."

As you reach the threshold of ... Harry, you will begin to form your Qi core.

"That's my water feature, right? It appeared when I learned <Personal Space Invader>."

My dear, I cannot tell you how reductive it is to describe a Qi core as a 'water feature.' If you seek immortality, this feature will carry you there. It needs more respect.

"I'm barely capable of seeking tomorrow's breakfast, let alone eternal life. You're telling me it does something more than just spin around when my paint sloshes through it?"

Yes.

I sensed I was getting on his nerves more than usual. I did my best to dial down my 'me-ness'.

As your capacity to cycle increases, more of your Qi will be stored in the core until it is complete.

"Which is where I'm at now. So, are you telling me I'm a wizard, Harry?"

No. And I can promise you, I will never use those words. This is where your swift progression bites you, as it were, on your arse, my dear. Because most cultivators at the Ron stage have very limited channels through which to cycle, the concentration of their Qi naturally increases. Over the ten to fifteen years most will spend at this stage, they will need to focus on improving the potency of their Qi.

You, on the other hand, have twice blasted hugely unlikely volumes of high intensity Qi through your channels, resulting in the sort of cycling capacity that would not be out of line was someone three, maybe even four, levels of advancement higher. And, of course, you've had me reordering and reconnecting things, which an ordinary Ron would never do. So, you're now at the point of the threshold, but...

"You're Saying I'm a Lager Shandy when I should be Jack Daniels."

Merlin paused. *Whilst that is not a wholly inappropriate metaphor, can I again stress the deeply complex nature of cultivation, which should not be reduced to...*

"Yes, yes, yes. So how do I increase the potency. Is there an Elixir I can brew?".

There are any number of alchemical products that can increase your Qi concentration. I am sure you will eventually be able to reproduce then. Particularly as you have a Treasure of Britain. However, with things being as they are and your oft-repeated desire to reach for the quickest solution, I am not against allowing you to consume a natural treasure.

"You're sounding all a bit White Witch with Turkish delight here, mate."

Do you want my advice or wish to be delightfully irreverent?

"To be honest, I'd quite like to get laid, but considering my options appear to be limited to Father Christmas or Jabba the Hutt, I'm willing to give a... what did you call it? A natural treasure, a whirl."

Merlin guided me down to the lowest floor of his tower and over to a row of shelves packed with various odds and ends. He'd explained the nature of the unique storage that operated on these shelves, which did sound like colossal bullshit.

Apparently, all I needed to do was put my hand on the shelf and bring what I wanted into being.

"Earl Grey. Hot."

What are you doing, my dear?

"Just trying something out. You can't tell me you've got a replicator in here and not expect me to at least give it a go."

It is not a replicator. It is a storage device for everything of use I have collected over the years. If I had put a cup of hot tea in there, it would have been produced. However, as I tended to take my responsibilities as the land's foremost cultivator a little more seriously than that, all you will find here will be historic and deeply significant magical items.

"So, just checking, no chance of a bag of coke?" I sensed I was probably starting quite close to the edge. "Just joshing with you. So, what am I looking for?"

The most effective natural treasure of which I am aware - and, as you can imagine, I am aware of quite a lot - would be the root of the Erobes plant.

"You clearly just made that up."

Merlin ignored me. *Put your hand on the shelf and imagine a brown root about four inches long. It has rough skin, not unlike ginger.*

"Dude, tell me this game of 'What's in the Box' isn't going to be your cock, because I tell you, I've had this done to me before, and the description is easily similar."

I managed to banish the image of dicks of Christmas past from my head and tried to visualise what Merlin was describing. After a few heartbeats, something popped into my hand, and I removed it from the shelf.

It was pretty much. as Merlin had described - and if I didn't know differently, I would have thought it would have been nothing more exotic than a really dried-up knob of ginger. Maybe something more like cinnamon bark.

"So, what do I do with it now?"

Erobes root is deeply, deeply toxic.

"Awesome."

So, we need to prepare it with care. Even the slightest sliver can purge you of your Qi in the most dramatic of ways.

"Explosive diarrhoea?"

Explosive, certainly. We have to reduce its effectiveness to just the right level so it will distil and filter your Qi but not wholly expel it.

"Okay. And how do we do that?"

Well, you have a cauldron of unusual power, so that will help. Most of the other ingredients to boil it up will be here somewhere. Oh, but the last ingredient may be a touch tough to come by.

"What? I'm going to need the blood of a virgin?" I joked.

Silence.

"Big M. Tell me I don't need the blood of a virgin for this concoction?"

Okay.

"Okay, what?"

Okay, I won't tell you.

CHAPTER 6 - IN WHICH THE STATUS OF MY VIRGINITY APPEARS TO BE A SIGNIFICANT PLOT POINT

"Dude, this sounds like some pretty dark shit."

Look, even in your own time, my dear; you have examples of bodily fluids being collected to create health products: blood drives, plasma banks, even the essence of reproduction...

"You can't ever say the word 'sperm' can you?"

My dear, that's not really the point right now...

"Spermy, Spermy, Spermy, Sperm. Go on, say it."

What I am trying to say is that whilst, on the face of it, you may be right to note that there is something superficially distasteful about the idea of including a virgin's blood in an Elixir, it is not something that is as entirely insane as you are suggesting.

"Okay, so I'm not going to argue that with you, but... you know, virgin's blood?"

Look, my dear, I'm not suggesting we snatch a baby from its mother's breast and slit its throat over the cauldron.

"Well, clearly!"

I'm sure a peasant woman will be too happy to sell us one. The first thing to learn in the alchemical trade is that children are a growth industry.

There was a significant pause.

Obviously, I'm joking.

"Really?"

Unless you're up for it, of course.

"Merlin!"

So, we're drawing a line on infanticide. Good to know. It's important that we establish where we all stand with such things. However, this does not solve the problem for us. It is vitally important that we can raise the concentration of you Qi, therefore we are going to have to plow onward. The recipe calls for about half a pint, which isn't so much in the grand scheme of things. There's no easy way to ask this politely, but are you still a virgin my dear?

If the power of laughter could have been harnessed into some sort of superweapon, I'm pretty confident we could have wiped the Saxons off the map during my response to that question. "Mate, that horse has not only bolted; it's started its own little stables down the road and accessed funding to open a little chain of wayside cafes. It's not much, but it's keeping the foals well-fed and he's happy he will have something to leave to his growing horsey family."

Quite. Sorry, I don't think I'm being clear. Since your resurrection, my dear, have you lain with a man. Or a woman? After all, it is not for me to judge.

The face of the most beautiful woodcutter in the world swam into my mind. There had been potential there, certainly. Of course. Drynwyn beheaded him rather smartly after we made eye-contact, so that limited things a touch. There'd been a couple of others who had aroused my interest since then, including, interestingly, Corys of Dehuebarch. I'd have to consider that later.

Always fancied being a princess.

"No, Big M. Since returning to this veil of tears, I have found myself in a somewhat colossal dry spell."

Okay. Well then, I think we have found our virgin.

***

It is surprisingly hard to gather half a pint of a cultivator's blood.

For a start, my skin is mainly imperious to a little prick - oh the jokes, I am sparing you right now - so I had to spend a fairly traumatic ten minutes with a dagger slashing away at my wrists and squeezing.

Yes, in case you are wondering, this triggered any number of flashbacks.

Let's move right along.

Eventually, I had to go and find Lancelot to help me out.

"You want me to stab you?" If he found anything remotely troubling about the request, it didn't show.

"Yes, please," as he drew his sword with rather more of a flourish than I thought truly necessary, I backed away, "but just a little bit, mate. I just need to collect some of my blood for a spell."

"Blood sacrifice," he nodded approvingly. "My people big on this are they being. Most usual for prisoners to use? But, pretty-hair, your ways are strange and mysterious."

And with literally no further to-do at all, he stabbed me in the thigh.

"Fuck. Hang on! I don't have ... Fuck!" My femoral artery sprayed blood into the air for a good few seconds, before abruptly stopping and the wound healed up. I sighed, glared at the new Pollock-inspired artwork around my Tower and went to collect my cauldron and sat back down.

"Right, mate. I appreciate the enthusiasm, but that was a touch of premature exsanguination there. Let's take a breath. Maybe have a drink. There's absolutely no rush. We've got all night."

It took four more efforts to collect enough blood for Merlin to be happy we could make the spell work. To be honest, after the second time, I began to suspect he was just enjoying me being stabbed.

"So, we have the blood, what's next, Big M?" I tried to keep the wince out of my voice. No matter how quickly you heal, it doesn't remove the pain of the injury.

Now, we start gently boiling your blood and adding those other materials you've gathered, finishing with half-an-inch of Erobes root.

I'd collected eight or nine other ridiculous things from the spacial storage on his shelves. It wasn't quite the whole 'eye of newt' and 'toe of a frog' situation, but it certainly wasn't a million miles away from it.

When all this was added, I managed to coax Drynwyn to ratchet up the level—**I'll do my best, but my heart's not really in it. I'm so sorry, I don't know what's wrong with me**—and in no time, the dark red liquid changed it to a somewhat frothy, luminous pinky/purple foam.

It smelt and looked like nothing less than Calpol—eight years out-of-date Calpol.

"How much of this crap do I really need to drink, Big M?"

All of it, my dear.

Lancelot hung around after the stabbings—he really did not take social cues. Or even outright 'do you not have anywhere else to be?'—and looked down into the cauldron with interest. "And this will make you all berserk, yes?"

"No, mate. It's not that sort of potion. I need to..." I wasn't sure I could explain what I was doing in a way the barbarian could understand. He wasn't stupid but had an incredibly simple way of looking at the world that could be mistaken for it. "It's a training aid. It will make me stronger. In my magic."

He nodded affably. "Ah. Mother gave me such. When baby being. Make me strong."

That interested me. "Your mother was an alchemist?"

He laughed. "My mother is mad witch. Every day with the 'drink this man's blood, make you tall', 'eat this one's liver, he has strong hands' 'swallow these eyes, see in the dark'." He thumped his hand to his chest. "Mother helped me be leader of our tribe. Even day since born with the potions. And the elixirs. And the body parts."

Fuck me. I guess we were lucky the dude had turned out reasonably sane. Whenever he talked about his childhood. he sounded like he was one motel purchase away from being a full-on shower killer.

Tearing my mind away from the image of Lancelot in a wig and his mother's dress, I looked down at the bubbling mixture in the cauldron. And, well, it wasn't going to get more appetising by looking at it.

I downed it in one.

Merlin had talked me through what to expect once the Erobus root got into my system, so I dropped into my Artist's Studio to witness the effect. However, except for a growing feeling of intense nausea, I didn't see any notable changes to either my Qi or the way it moved around my channels.

From what I understood, this concoction was supposed to act like a giant diuretic, essentially sucking out at least two-thirds of the amount of Qi I had available whilst exponentially increasing the power in the amount that was left.

I had been looking forward to the show.

But no. Nothing

"Big M, this is all a bit anti-climatic. What's going on?"

I'm not sure, my dear. The effects of Erobus root should be almost instantaneous. Indeed, we've had to boil it down entirely due to its overwhelming potency. Bear with me for just a few moments.

I felt Merlin take hold of my Qi and direct it towards the ingredients around the cauldron.

Although I was happy to have him back in my head, I found the moments when he took control of my Qi—even in the extremely limited way his spirit could access it —rather distasteful. It wasn't exactly painful, but neither was it entirely unlike being roofied and steered upstairs with a guiding hand.

Ah, I think I see the problem.

I snapped out of some pretty bleak memories and refocused on the current issue at hand.

"So, what do we do? More blood is it?"

Lancelot's sword was in his hand in an admirable display of readiness that, in other circumstances, I felt I would be able to put to more fruitful use.

No. Well, at least not yours.

"How do you mean?"

My dear, there's no particularly delicate way to say this, so please do not take offence. It would be seen that your essential... non-virginess has managed to transmit across the barrier between the eras.

"I'm sorry?"

You may have abstained in this world thus far, but it seems a quality of your being that simply defies resetting has led to your lack of... purity being somewhat deeply imprinted on your soul.

There was a silence.

"Dude, that is some next-level Scarlet-Letter-Handmaid's-Tale, slut shaming. You're saying I'm too much of used goods to get a do-over in my second life?"

To be clear, my dear, it's not me saying that. It's ...

"What, the gods of body count? The special shag investigation squad?"

No. Regardless of what the religious will have us believe, there is only one person who has the right to define the nature of our souls, and that's each of us. If anyone has decided you are not to be allowed to start afresh, as it were, I am afraid it's you.

"Well, fuck me." *Or don't. I think that's kind of the issue here.*

There really was not enough therapy in the world, was there? I was pondering this latest example of how truly screwed up I was when the big dude piped up again.

"You need the blood of a virgin, yes?"

I nodded at him mutely; I'd thought I was doing much better of late. It was somewhat disconcerting to find out my soul still found me deeply distasteful.

"Well, easy, that is"

And, with a swish, he opened the veins of his forearm

CHAPTER 7- IN WHICH I HAVE THE FACTS OF REPRODUCTION EXPLAINED TO ME BY A LEGENDARY CULTIVATOR

Say what you like about Lancelot, but he's a gusher. Once I'd gathered enough blood for another whirl at making the potion, I forced him to have my last Inferior Elixir of Wellness before we spoke further. It was quite frightening how quickly people without access to Qi bled everywhere.

Like, seriously, how are these guys even staying alive?

"Dude, how is it possible you are still a virgin? I mean, have you seen you?"

"My mother," he said as if that explained everything.

I remembered some things he'd said about his mum when we were locked together in the Dark Tower. "She made it difficult for you to have girlfriends?"

His ridiculously handsome face opened into a guileless smile. "No girlfriends for me. Too important. After mother killed a few, rest stayed away did."

"'Too important?' What does that mean?"

"Mother said needed to save my essence."

See, it's not just me, Merlin chimed in. *I think you'll find most of us prefer a less crude expression for the male part of the cycle of life.*

"What had your mum got you saving your spunk for?" I was rewarded by Lancelot's horrified expression and a somewhat tired 'tut' from Merlin.

"I have to give it all to a great Queen." Lancelot's face took on a dream-like property. "There will be a time of great warfare, and I must put it right."

"To be fair, mate, if you've been saving it up for the best part of thirty years, that will probably do it. Nothing puts the damper on a battle than a water cannon."

He ignored me. "Mother had vision. After the great ends, when peace it is, I must give Queen the gift of my essence. Mother foretold it. And what she sees, is."

Awesome. No prizes for guessing who the Queen is going to be. But, looking on the bright side, at least it sounded like I didn't need to keep such a close eye on them right now. End of a great war? At the very least, I had to have after Arthur's coronation before they'd be getting it on. Assuming that we could get things that far, of course.

And speaking of which, my Qi wasn't going to increase its concentration all on its own.

I mean, it will, my dear. That is kind of the point. However, what we are seeking to do here is...

I switched off the sound of the Big M wittering, and turned to watch the cauldron bubbling away. The colour was definitely a bit more vibrant this time, and the smell was actually quite attractive. It was smoky, like something with paprika on the hob.

Then something occurred to me. "Merlin, If he's got that much ... essence backed up, there's no chance any of it will have leaked out into his blood, is there?"

My dear, we occasionally have days when you do nothing but impress me with your work ethic, intelligence, and impressive behaviour. Then we have these little moments when you ask me a question like that, and it reminds me that you really were quite a spectacular mess.

"So, I'm assuming not?"

I can absolutely reassure you that there is no possible way that any little Lancelot's have entered his bloodstream due to a... 'backing up' of his essence. Moreover, before you ask a further question that is likely to embarrass us both, I can also guarantee that drinking this potion will, in no way, risk you carrying his child.

"From your tone, I am assuming this was a really stupid question?"

Drink the damn elixir, my dear.

***

So, when Merlin had said it was going to be a bit like a diuretic, he'd not been kidding. I'd barely finished slurping this stuff down and switched to my Artist's Studio to watch the concoction drop into my Vitruvian Man before it sucked up all of my available Qi like the driest sponge in existence.

This was a bit freaky.

I was used to seeing my Qi represented as paint. From the very first steps I had taken as a cultivator, that is how it had manifested itself to me. I understood from talking to Merlin that each cultivator visualised their Qi in an entirely personal way. For me, it had been like watercolour paint, moving around my channels in a fluid, clear manner.

Ingesting the Erobus root, though, did something fairly spectacular.

From the second I swallowed it, my Qi thickened up, taking on the consistency of the most viscous of oil paint. It was still a liquid, of course, but now it was much more happy just staying in place rather than running free. Whereas I had become used to it whizzing around my channels with barely a thought, it took a considerable effort to get it moving, and what is more, it now did not seem to have any momentum behind it whenever I actually did get it moving.

If I stopped concentrating for a heartbeat, the whole slow ground to a halt.

"Fucking hell, Big M. Cycling has become a struggle..."

As it should be, my dear. The whole point of being a cultivator is that you are supposed to struggle. Without all your various shenanigans, this is what it was supposed to feel like right from the start of your journey as a cultivator. Think of it like 'desirable difficulty.'

But the thicker Qi wasn't the only change caused by drinking down a few pints of Lancelot's finest plus random herbs. My water feature, which had been so close to overflowing, had emptied to about a third full, with the Qi within it now of the same sticky consistency as elsewhere in my channels.

"So, I guess I'm not nearly a 'wizard, Harry' anymore?"

You are exactly where you were before drinking the potion, my dear, but now your potential is exponentially richer. As I tried to explain, you could have pressed forward into ... Harry if you'd wished, but the limits you would have put upon yourself would have been significant. Our original plan, when you first reincarnated into this world, was simply to put on a good show and make it seem like you were an epic cultivator. Therefore, it did not matter that your Qi was reasonably thin gruel. But now we know just how strong Aurelius is, you are literally the only game in town we have that could possibly compete.

"But Caeldfwch..."

Sure, that will help Arthur and anyone in his immediate vicinity. And maybe even a good portion of his army, should it come down to that, as he learns how to control the power of the sword. But the only way to truly combat the growing threat of the Saxons having an epically powerful mage is for you to become the biggest, baddest cultivator you can. This is a significant step toward that.

I could hear what the Big M was saying, but it did feel like I had taken somewhat of a backward step in my own journey. Cycling was such a struggle now, I was feeling out of breath just being in here. So, I popped out of my Artist's Studio and found Lancelot standing about an inch from my nose.

I wasn't quite sure how the time dilation worked when I was inside my Studio, but I'd never come back out before and had the situation in reality change.

Lancelot was fast...

"Dude, unless you're tweezering my eyebrows, step the fuck back."

"Peaceful you were looking; I was just making sure you were okay."

He was so close I could just lean forward and kiss him. Who knows, for the first time in my life, an impulsive snog might end up saving the fabric of a nation?

But no.

The moment quickly passed, and he was stepping back and looking at the various paraphernalia on Merlin's shelves. "Lots of stuff you be having, no?"

I packed my libido away for another day - and I still needed to think more about why on earth my psyche wanted to cling to being a good-time girl (and, when it came down to it, were the times ever really any good?) - and stepped forward to join him.

Or I would have done it if the moment I tried to walk, my legs didn't crumple up beneath me.

Oh, yes, my dear. A slight after-effect of Erobus root is that you're likely to be flat on your back for the next few days. And not, apparently, in a way you deem such an essential aspect of your personality.

"Oh, fuck off, Big M."

***

Igraine had returned to her room long before the feast had ended.

When she was Queen, such a thing would have been unthinkable. Uther would have insisted she stayed until the last guest was dragged from the drinking benches.

But now, she was little more than an ornamentation.

She sat at the royal table because -other than a grave - there was nowhere else for her to be.

Uther.

Who would have thought his loss would make her feel this way? When he was alive, she would have acknowledged that she was, at times, less than affectionate towards him.

Passion - neither love nor hate – could not stay at that white-hot intensity for thirty years of marriage. It was understandable that they had both drifted apart as the years went by. So why this wound in her chest? Why did her eyes keep cascading torrents of water down her face?

Igraine walked backwards and forward across the cold flagstones of her bedchamber, trying to push down a pain that threatened to overwhelm her. Wildly, she tried to think about something else and cast her mind to the kings who had arrived at the castle that day.

She knew them all of old. With them, she had played the role Uther needed - even if he remained naively unaware of her part in it all.

For example, she had directed men to 'visit' Owain's son when word returned to her of brewing discontent in Gwent. The boy - ha, he was twenty if he was a day - had his eyes on his father's throne and was making moves to displace him. Uther needed a strong arm to his north, and every indication was that Gryff ap Owain was not likely to be that. The boy's allies were too close to the Saxons for comfort.

Officially, it was a hunting accident - weren't they all? - but she had always suspected the King of Gwent knew the truth. After all, he had allied himself even tighter to Uther after that - either in gratitude or fear, Igraine did not know.

To be fair, she did not think it much mattered which it was.

King Mark was different, she reflected as she paced. His power over his small kingdom was absolute and so manifest that there was little for her spies to report on that wasn't already common knowledge. There had been rumours of some strife with one of his boys - he had so many, and by so many different women - it was never easy to keep track. Igraine frowned and pressed the issue in her mind for a moment, the fog of grief receding momentarily.

Tristian.

That was what the boy had been called. He'd fallen in love with one of his father's... Igraine assumed 'slave girls' was the only appropriate term. It was something Celtic she was called ...

Isolde. That was it. Who knew what became of them?

Ingrain made a mental note to find out - and then stopped, her knees sagging. Why? That was not her role anymore. Arthur had not once spoken to her about her network nor asked for her input on how to handle each of these very different men. She was, for the first time in her life since arriving at Tintagel, redundant.

That thought pushed her to the last of the two kings – Beric and Corys. On the face of it, those two could not have been more different. Powys, one of the remaining great kingdoms, easily capable of its King pushing to be considered for the position of the Pendragon should Beric have the drive. And then little Deheubarth, still holding out despite being almost wholly surrounded by Saxon forces. But the two men themselves?

They didn't associate with one another. Their temperaments were wildly disparate - Beric was all spice and vinegar, whereas Corys was affable and had a mouth filled with honey. And yet, and yet and yet …

Igraine stopped her pacing. She didn't know what role she played in this kingdom, but she was damned if she would let her son go on a quest with these men without being in possession of all the facts.

She turned to her door. There was a figure there, observing her.

"How did you get up here? What do you want?"

The hooded shadow shut the door behind him as he entered the room.

CHAPTER 8 - IN WHICH WE LEARN THERE ARE, APPARENTLY, TITS AND THEN THERE ARE TITS

Arthur, Bors and Guinevere remained behind after all the guests had left. The detritus of the feast lay around the hall, and various servants bustled hither and tither to prepare the space for the morning.

Two of Bors' giant wolfhounds lounged by the fire, both too old to be used in a hunt anymore, but, he thought, both deserving of a good night out.

"It went well, I thought?" Guinevere said, stretching upwards to release the kinks in her back. Although she had entirely healed from the wound inflicted on her by Cedric - thanks to Morgan and her Elixiers - she was pushing her training hard. Her body constantly felt like the ocean had tossed her around for a week. And that was without the... intense exercise of the evenings.

That thought brought colour to her cheeks, and she glanced over towards Arthur. Intellectually, she understood that his newfound ardour was not just because he was suddenly back in the grip of the flush of their first weeks together. After all, he had sworn off from using the brothels and the serving girls and, for now, seemed to be sticking to it.

Likewise, since his father's unexpected death, the need for an heir had increased tenfold - a hundredfold, really. As much as a mythical quest for a magic sword and continued success on the battlefield against the Saxons, it would be the announcement of her pregnancy that would most securely lead him to the Pendragon's throne.

Sadly, Nimue had confirmed she remained without a child just this morning.

Bors rumbled a response to her words, dragging her from her sad thoughts. "The other kings haven't made up their minds about how to jump yet. None of them really wants the throne for themselves. There's too much fighting with Saxons in our future, and no one wants an enemy army arriving on their lands. But not one of them wants to be the first to back him. Having the Qi-killing sword will be the key."

"Morgan scared the life out of them with her new skill." Arthur smiled grimly. Having experienced Drynwyn's fiery embrace firsthand, he did not need to imagine what it would feel like to be hit by that lightning. He rubbed his bald head and stopped once he realised what he was doing.

"Frightened men don't always act the way you expect. Especially not when they are kings used to getting their own way," Guinevere warned. "We'd be wise to ensure she's well protected while all these men are about."

Bors spat out his mead. "If there's anyone with the wherewithal to put a dent in her day, then that guy should announce his candidacy as Pendragon right now. I'd fucking vote for him. The girl is a force of nature."

"True, but Aurelius was apparently able to bring down Merlin, and, for all her undoubted strengths, Morgan is certainly not anywhere near his capabilities yet. Guinevere is right; we should remember that she will be a target."

"Lancelot's with her right now", Guinevere said, then blushed. She honestly did not know why.

"Then there's no power in the world to hurt her." Arthur placed a comforting hand on his wife's wrist.

Bors picked up a half-eaten chicken carcass and threw it to his dogs. They snarled and yipped at each other, but it was mostly for show. They did a decent enough job of ripping it in half and sharing the food equally. "We need to discuss the Marchegyon," he said abruptly.

Arthur nodded. "I know. It just seems disrespectful to those we lost to seek to rebuild so quickly.

"Fuck that!" Bors was never one for sympathy. "We're asking the other kings to put their faith in us, and we've got probably the smallest standing army of the lot, and that is before you consider that – even ignoring your Marchegyon – we'd filled Isca with most of our Fyrd's competent spears. So far, between me, you, Lancelot, and Morgan...

Guinevere cleared her throat meaningfully.

"Sorry, Gwin, everyone knows you've done more than your share. It's the tits, you see, it blinds a man."

"Morgan's got tits, too." Guinevere raised an eyebrow sceptically.

"Well, kind of. But there's tits," Bors made a small hand gesture, "and then there's tits," a more expensive gesture. "And you, quite definitely, have TITS", a much bigger gesture. There appeared to be honking. "With what you're packing behind your breastplate, it's easy to forget you're handy with a spear. Although, as my room is just down the corridor from yours, I can attest that you sound like you know what you're doing with all sorts of weapons and implements. If you know what I'm saying..." There was a pause. "I've had far too much to drink, haven't I?"

Arthur took a breath. "You were talking about the army?"

Bors grasped that conversational life-jacket like a drowning man. "Basically, we're punching massively above our weight. And that's fine when we're facing the odd war band here and there. But numbers will tell eventually. We need to be able to put three or four times the men in the field than we are at the moment to be comfortable with winning. At least without all of us lot being there and picking up the slack."

"What do you suggest?"

"A tournament"

"I'm about to go on a quest; I can't hold a tournament at the same time!"

"We divide our resources." Bors blushed as both Guinevere and Arthur looked his way. "So, this is Mrs. Bors's idea, not mine." The big man rolled his shoulders. He hadn't been looking forward to this discussion. It's why he'd been drinking so much. "When you go off on your quest, I think you should leave me here to run a tourney. Nothing grand, just a 'your country needs you' sort of thing. I'll grab the likeliest of the lads and then train them up. See if I can get us a reasonably solid shield wall for next time we need to kick some ass—Saxon or otherwise."

Arthur was frowning. "No. I need you on the quest for Caeldfwch."

"Mate, you really don't. Lancelot is a fucking menace. Most of the time, I can tell he's holding back because he's trying not to make me look bad. On my best day, I can't carry that guy's water." Bors stroked his beard, which Arthur was shocked to see had streaks of white in it. "If I thought you needed me, I'd be there instantly. But I fear we're not too far away from me starting to be an active hindrance."

Arthur sat back and took a deep breath. After the disaster of the battle against Cedric - following the shambles at Isca - the last thing he could imagine was going into battle without his oldest friend. He would rather face down a Saxon host unarmed than do so without the big man at his shield arm.

And yet...

He looked at the two old dogs in front of the fire.

Both had years ahead of them, but perhaps the days of being at the forefront of the hunt were behind them. And the big man was right; Lancelot was the incarnation of death in a scrap.

"You'll never be a hindrance," Arthur's voice, when it came, was soft. "But I see the merit in what you say. If I can't have you on my side, I can think of nothing better than for you to build up our forces. Lancelot, Morgan, and I will pursue Caeldfwch."

Guinevere's eyes widened. "You would leave me behind, my lord?"

Arthur smiled back. "I would have you assist Bors in the creation of his tournament. Without casting aspersions as to his motivational qualities, I cannot help but think we need some... some 'tits' to encourage people to give of their best." He made the same massive gesture Bors had earlier. "But seriously, it would do well for everyone to recognise you as a ruler in my stead when I am not here!"

Guinevere scowled but could say little to disagree with his assessment. It would not be brilliant tactical planning for her to be gallivanting around the woods without the succession being assured. But, on the other hand, it would be pretty hard to change that situation without being in the same place at the same time...

There was, though, a second bittersweet emotion about the quest: Lancelot would be going with Arthur. She was both sad not to have the company of that disarmingly honest man and yet... well, she was also a little relieved. A bit of space in that quarter would certainly not be amiss.

"I hear what you are saying." She looked up at Bors and winked. "Me and you then, big boy. You think we can run a tournament to sort the men out from the boys?".

"With your magnificent assets on display, Gwin, I am sure we will be able to make men out of the shyest boys." He licked his lips. "I really am very drunk, indeed. Mrs. Bors is going to have my guts for garters. And not the sexy sort, either!"

They laughed and prepared to go their separate ways when a messenger, face white, ran into the feasting hall.

"Sirrah, what ails you?" Bors was quick to stand and intercept the man. None of his supposed infirmities of age showed in stopping the messenger before he got more than a few steps into the room.

The two spoke for a few moments out of Arthur and Guinevere's earshot. Then the big man reeled back, his face a mask of grief.

"What is it? "Arthur was on his feet.

Bors shook his head, as is mute, and pushed the messenger forward. The young man's eyes were wide.

"The Queen, my Lord." The messenger paused, seeking to collect himself, then started again. "The Queen, my lord. She's dead."

CHAPTER 9 - IN WHICH MY JEDI MIND TRICKS REPERTOIRE INCREASES

I missed Igraine's funeral rites. Such as they were. From what I heard, there was not much appetite for another 'celebration' so close to Uther's, so the tail-end of one was folded into the other. Like in 'Hamlet', and with almost exactly the same amount of the feeling that something rotten was in the state of Tintagel, I couldn't help but feel she deserved much more. Of course, the uncertainty abound her passing did not help.

"My mother did not kill herself," Arthur had told me, "she didn't have a sentimental bone in her body. She missed my father, of course, but we had plans... we had..." And he had abruptly left my bed chamber.

Bors had visited later that day. He was taking it hard and was obviously worried about the impact on Arthur. As he said, to lose one parent was tough enough. "To lose the second -"

"May be thought of as carelessness," I supplied. There was a pause during which I wasn't sure whether he was going to cry or punch me in the face. I did my best to forestall either. "Sorry, mate, the Big M has me on some very strong Elixirs."

After a moment, Bors blinked and then continued as if I had not spoken. "But I do agree with what he is saying. There's absolutely no way in the world that Igraine killed herself. Just no way. If she was that way inclined, she'd have done it years ago when things between them were grim. It makes no sense for her to have done it now."

"Look, there's no argument from me here. But what's the alternative?" From the bits and pieces of gossip that had reached me, I understood that the Queen had taken a long trip from a short tower without the benefit of loading up on several hundred Elixirs of Wellness. As someone who had done something similar recently, I was happy to testify you had a long time to regret the choice on the way down. "Had she drunk too much at the feast?"

Bors wrinkled his nose. "Some. We all had, hadn't we? Only way to put up with some of those fucking kings. But was it enough to fall through an open window? Doubt it. The woman could hold her drink."

"Dude, she either jumped, fell or..."

"Yeah. I know. It's the 'or' that's keeping us up at the moment."

"I imagine there are guards to be questioned, Servants to - you know - torture horribly until they falsely confess to things they had never even dreamed of."

The big man stood and began pacing around my room. The bits and bobs from off Merlin's shelves that were lying around didn't quite wobble as he walked, but they weren't a mile away from it. The dude had gravity. "I've tried. No one knows anything." I opened my mouth to speak, but he met my eyes and shook his head.

"I'm not good for much in this world, Morgan, but when I ask a question, I get an answer, Sooner or later."

He sat down again on the edge of the bed, and I momentarily took flight. "I miss her."

I understood where he was coming from. Queen Igraine had not been especially kind to me during my short time in the Dark Ages. But she was clever, funny – in a bitingly satirical way - and took absolutely no shit from anyone. Seeing the way she'd collapsed in on herself in the days following Uther's death had been hard, but - as Arthur had said - she'd been central to the plans for the kingdom that we had discussed.

It was inconceivable she'd have abandoned the vision for the British lands that she had been so instrumental in plotting. But, on the other hand, was it any more likely this icy, controlled woman would have stumbled drunkenly through her window and crashed to her death?

Bors was wringing his hands again, his eyes downcast, shoulders slumped.

This might be a good moment, my dear, to try what we've been practising.

I should explain.

Since taking the Erobus root, Merlin has been trying to broaden out my Qi sensitivity a touch. I was proving pretty adept at pulling it in - *although, as you convalesce in my tower, it would take a cultivator of unusual incapacity not to be* - but I was still a bit of a blunt instrument in pushing it outwards.

Massive, sonic booms of Air Qi and arcing flames of lightning are not really the sign of a subtle and understated power, my dear.

"Mate, 'subtle' and 'understated' are not words that have been especially present in my life to date."

Old life, my dear. The new you has the potential for far greater things.

So, we'd been practising, during my enforced recovery from epic Erobus poisoning, on just trying to nudge people into taking actions I wanted. Now, I know that doesn't sound like the most altruistic of things for a cultivator to do, but Merlin had convinced me there was merit in developing the skill, and to be honest, the process was quite simple.

All I needed to do was take the thinnest threads of my newly super-concentrated Qi and load it up with a suggestion. Then, I simply pushed that little string of Qi into the other person's brain, and my suggestion would flow into their mind.

But when I say simple...

It's a suggestion, my dear. Not an imperial command backed by twelve war bands, a company of elephants and a phalanx of ninja werewolves.

I watched as the serving boy brought me my tenth tray filled with glasses of water, his panic-stricken face not unlike that of a horse being swallowed whole by a Komodo Dragon. Again, I reflected that subtlety was not a skill I seemed to possess.

It'll wear off shortly, but the art to this technique is to ensure the subject does not even realise they have been influenced. You will not be able to get much done if other people notice someone behaving bizarrely.

My serving boy bowed and scraped his head on the floor. "I'll be right back, oh enchanting mistress. I'm sorry for this one's slow response to your command."

"Too much?" I asked Merlin. His silence was the only required answer.

The thing was, if I made the suggestion too subtle, it slipped off my questing thread of Qi before it even reached its target. Likewise, if I made the thread too thick, I was rewarded with a range of confused, angry and puzzled faces as they brushed my intrusive thoughts aside.

The strength of mind of the person you are seeking to influence will also be a factor. It is very unlikely a cultivator, for example, will allow themselves to be influenced in this way. I should also mention, my dear, that it is seen as... uncouth to try to pressure a fellow Wizard in this way.

"So, I shouldn't try it on another cultivator?"

That's not what I said, my dear. Merely, that if you do, you should do everything you can not to get caught.

Over the last few days, I'd quickly realised who around the Court was open to this type of manipulation and who wasn't. I could, for example, get Lancelot to remove his shirt with the merest hint of it being slightly warm.

Whilst there is not a 'dark side' per se to Qi cultivation, my dear, I would merely note you would look askance if you caught me encouraging pretty young maidens to remove their clothes in my presence.

"Which you obviously did, right?"

Of course, and now you're judging me for it, correct?

On the other hand, Arthur and Guinevere were completely closed doors to me, no matter what I tried or however subtle my suggestions were.

Some people just know their own minds, my dear. I doubt either of them has ever done something they didn't wish to in their whole lives.

However, having Bors in front of me, clearly filled with guilt and grief, I felt this was actually a moment where I could use this technique for good. So, I pulled out the thinnest strand of my Qi as I could and gave a slight flick of my thick, glossy paint between the two of us.

To begin with, it didn't look like the connection would hold. However, after a few heartbeats, it stabilised. I let the link sit between us for a moment, just to make sure it wouldn't immediately fray. When it didn't, I was able to push the suggestion I had especially prepared just for him.

"It wasn't your fault."

Pleasingly, the effect was almost immediate. Bors sat up a little straighter, and the deep frown eased somewhat on his forehead. Don't get me wrong, he still looked utterly downcast, but I was pleased to see that the burden had lessened somewhat. I held the thread for just a beat longer and then pushed out a follow-up thought to follow it.

"There was nothing you could have done." Again, the tension eased somewhat around his shoulders, and I received the notification that I had developed a new technique.

There was dearly only one appropriate name for this one.

You know, my dear, there is no need for hand gestures when you channel this skill. Qi manipulation is an entirely internal process.

"True, Big M. But when <These Aren't the Droids You're Looking For>, it just feels right, you know?

***

It was the sixth day before I was able to put weight on my legs and walk about.

Merlin thought that said more about my levels of physical fitness prior to becoming a cultivator rather than any miscalculation in the formula he used to calculate the volume of the Elixir.

You have to remember, my dear, most cultivators will have spent years, if not decades, seeking to increase the physical limits of their bodies- I had hoped by putting you in Wulfnod's body, you would be able to inherit his foundations. However, as with you clinging on to your pre-reincarnation view of your sexual history, it does seem, somewhat, that your previous physicality has — infected is too strong a word, but you take my meaning - your current form.

"So, not only is the core of the problem my being a slut, you're saying it's a being a lazy one at that?"

To be clear, my dear, I am not saying that at all. You, however, seem determined to hold on to aspects of your previous personality that you yourself found distasteful. Your core, your soul, is as beautiful and inviolate as anyone else's. I would hazard I have had a hundred, two hundred times the sexual encounters you have, and they do not weigh on me one bit. You seem determined to cast yourself in a dim light. In the same way, there's no reason you have needed those extra three days in bed other than the fact you believe you did.

"Should I <These aren't the droids you're looking for> myself? Maybe with a motivational slogan to be less of a sad sack?"

You joke, my dear, but I have heard worse suggestions. There are few great cultivators who are wracked with self-loathing.

"To be fair, mate, I think I've made some pretty decent progress on that store. Sometimes, hours go by, and I barely hate myself at all." I thought back to my conversation with Zizzie in Aurelius' prison. I was doing my absolute best to let the past be the past. The fact it was, in reality, the future somewhat fried my noodle, but there was nothing to be done for that. Great Scott, and all that.

I don't disagree, my dear. The fact that we have largely been able to keep the timeline secure despite the appearance of a legendary cultivator who appears in no version of Arthurian legend of which I am aware speaks volumes for your success. But this is now the critical moment.

"With Uther dead, you mean?"

Indeed. If we can get Caeldfwch into Arthur's hand, if Bors can reinstitute the Marchegyon, if we can keep increasing your power and if we can get the remaining kingdoms to acclaim Arthur as the Pendragon, we will have - in the vernacular of your time - a ballgame...

"There's an awful lot of 'if's' there."

My dear, my vision still stands. I can see it as clearly now as I did on the night I received it: King Arthur, in his throne room, overseeing a land of peace and prosperity. He has the sword at his side, a happy wife, and a united kingdom behind him. While that vision holds, your timeline is secure.

We were interrupted by the sound of trumpets. I cursed and threw the last few of the things I thought I might need during the expedition into my inventory.

Arthur's quest was about to get underway. And to listen to Merlin, the stakes could not possibly have been higher.

CHAPTER 10 – IN WHICH I GET A CERTAIN

KING'S JUICES FLOWING

This was not going to be a lowkey quest.

It turned out that when you put five kings on the road, a certain degree of pomp and circumstance came with it, which was targeted at generating attention. If we had any hopes of starting this journey on the down low, the number of trumpets, banners, musicians and general hangers would thwart that.

I couldn't help but feel this would be less of a road trip and more of a very slow-moving rolling invasion.

By agreement, each king was allowed to bring fifty troops with them to ensure their safety – but it seemed that this didn't cover anyone whose purpose was 'miscellaneous.' There were several suspiciously buff and attentive 'servants' in each king's retinue making me think not everyone was studiously following the agreement

That made it pretty hard to swallow when there had been a little light to and fro about me joining Arthur's contingent. But Lancelot had lazily drawn his sword and yawned, and those worries appeared to evaporate. Although, that decision did seem to encourage a growth in tall, bearded cooks and cleaners with poorly hidden swords, so it wasn't all gravy.

"Besides," as Beric had charmelessly added, "as soon as one of us has the sword, she'll be as useless as a newborn killer."

"There is a lot of water to flow under the bridge before then, girlfriend. Might be wise to make sure you don't drown yourself in it."

"My lord!" Beric turned to Arthur, appealing, "Can you not control your tame magician? I will not continue to suffer her threats and slanders."

Arthur stared at him blankly. If possible, the grimness of his expression had increased since the loss of his parents. The silence stretched out until the King of Powys took a hesitant step back, running into the rather solid chest of Lancelot, who had come up behind him.

"To clarify, happy I am. Pretty hair did not threaten you." He rested his hand on the hilt of his sword. "I, however, will chop you up into teeny tiny pieces if you ever speak disrespectfully to her again." He turned his head to eyeball the men whose arses he had whipped in the duel back in Tintagel. "Fifty men, the stretch may well be. But this barbarian could never count too well."

"Prince Arthur!" Beric's tone was scandalised.

"King." If Lancelot was going to play this game, I was damned if I wasn't going all in. I let a like flicker of lightning play at my fingers.

"What?" he snapped back at me.

"Pardon," Lancelot said, drawing his sword a few inches more.

I always loved that guy. "You will address my lord as 'King'. While he may yet to be acclaimed as the Pendragon for reasons only pantywetters like you can understand, he is still the King of Dumnonia and will be treated as such by you. I can tattoo that on your forehead if you like?" For shits and giggles, I tried to hit him up with a suggestion that he really, really needed the toilet. Other than a brief frown, nothing really changed in Beric's demeanour.

"My apologies, *King* Arthur. It will take some getting used to. Your father was a great man who was much respected across the land. Whereas you are..."

I hit him with everything <These are not the droids you are looking for> had and was delighted to see a small puddle begin to form at his feet.

Arthur looked down and then up to the shocked-looking man. "Panty-wetter indeed," he said, just loud enough for everyone in the area to hear. Beric was bundled away by his men.

I was aware of eyes fixed on me and turned to see Mark and Corys whispering towards the back of the group. That felt less than ideal.

I'm not sure how helpful making one of the key allies we need against the Saxons urinate himself in public truly was.

"He won't know it was me. He's an older guy; these things must happen all the time."

The different factions had, finally, drawn themselves together outside Tintagel's walls. On the other side of the bridge, which had been recently so vigorously defended, Bors and Guinevere rode hallway across to see us go.

"Surprised to see you staying behind, old man!" Owain called back good-naturedly.

"Ah, you know how it is. You've been on one quest for one legendary blade; you've been on them all. Besides, think there are enough swinging dicks on this expedition without needing me around to make you all feel inadequate!"

Guinevere's horse trotted forward a few more steps. "We wish you well in your quest. Our gates stand open to welcome you on your triumphant return."

"From what I hear, getting her gate open is a task beyond Uther's boy."

There was an outraged hum as all in Arthur's party sought out the speaker. But other than smirks and disguised laughter, we didn't catch who was now living on borrowed time.

Guinevere sat taller, ignoring the noises. "We wish you good hunting, and may the bearer of Caeldfwch rise on to rule these lands."

The gathered host drew their blades and signalled back at her. There were no further comments from the cheap seats.

And then they were returning to the castle, and we were underway.

***

Guinevere returned to her room before letting the humiliation of the shout from the gate reach her face. She knew this was how she was perceived, as an icy maiden who had driven her husband to find his relief elsewhere.

The impression was not eased when so many of Arthur's bastards kept showing up. It hardly took complex, deductive reasoning to suggest the reason why the succession remained unsettled rested on her shoulders.

Or between her legs, she assumed.

Nimue, the minor cultivator her father had dispatched with her when her wedding was agreed, smiled at her from above her knitting. She had known this wrinkled old woman for as long as she'd been alive, and she had been tasked with identifying the moment Guinevere fell pregnant.

Leodegrance, her father, had promised Uther ten thousand spears the second the news that his daughter was pregnant was confirmed, and—to a certain extent—that expectation had kept the Saxons from pressing the issue against Dunmonia too closely.

But the years had rolled by, and Nimue's sad little shake of the head had become as much part of her morning routine as washing her face. After so much time and with such little success, she and Arthur stopped trying – the Prince moving into his own bed chamber in recent years – and then, soon after, they were not even speaking.

Much less...

Guinevere had hoped that the thawing of their relationship might bring about a change of luck, but thus far, despite some rigorous and thorough assaults on her gates, it did seem somewhat that the fortress remained resolutely unbreached.

A noise from behind her spun her around, twin daggers already drawn from their holsters at her wrists.

"My lady!" a nondescript man in grey stood there, arms raised in surrender. "My apologies; I did not mean to startle you."

"How did you get in here?"

The man looked around him as if unsure how to answer. "You are the queen!"

She restored one of the daggers to its hiding place and crossed the room to slam into the man, pinning his back to the wall. Her forearm rested against his throat, and the dagger pressed into his side. "If my question had been 'who am I?' then that would have been an acceptable answer. However," she roughly pulled him off the wall and then slammed him back against it, "as I wanted to know how you entered my room, your response leaves me unsatisfied."

The bland man was reddening under the pressure of her grip around his throat. He tried and failed to croak out an answer.

Nimue made a soft tsk noise from her corner of the room. The sort of noise she had made countless other times over the years. Such as when Guinevere refused to tidy her room or perhaps was caught sneaking out of a window at night. The queen instinctively released her hold.

The man sucked in air, the colour fading from his cheeks to leave him – what appeared to be – his natural pale, off-milk complexion. "My apologies, my lady. We have clearly got off on the wrong foot. I should have presented myself to you in a more formal way, but the late queen had ever a preference for quiet solitude when we spoke. It was my foolish assessment that you would seek to continue that tradition. May this be my solitary misstep in your service."

"That was a lot of words." Guinevere released the man and pointed at an empty chair. "Why don't we try this again? Who are you?

The man sat, casually crossing his legs. She realised he wasn't quite wearing grey: it was a patterned material that helped him blend into the background. The deconstructed shapes helped him vanish into the dark wood, much as he had in the shadows in the corner of the room.

"My name is really of no consequence, my lady."

"Humour me."

"The late queen was never much concerned with such things. She was happy –"

"Well, she's not too happy anymore, is she? She's fucking dead, and I don't have conversations with strange men that break into my chamber without knowing their names." Guinevere did not shout, but her voice had a tightness that brooked no dissent.

"Blæk, my lady. I am known as Blæk."

"Well then, Sir Blæk," his eyes popped for a second at the uncalled-for honorific, but he was wise enough not to interrupt, "am I to assume you served my late mother-in-law?"

The unassuming man – she kept having to glance at his face to remind herself what he looked like – nodded. "Indeed. We of the Grey have forever served the Queen of Dumnonia. My own father was honoured to have acted for King Uther's mother on more than one occasion. He was very proud when I went into the family business, as it were."

"I'm sorry, I'm still a little unclear. What was it you did for Queen Igraine? Or, perhaps more pertinently, what are the 'Grey'?"

"Everything, my lady."

Guinevere growled in frustration and tapped the dagger against her thighs. "Blæk, it has been a long and tiring day. My parents-in-law are both dead. My husband has left on a damned fool idealistic crusade for a magic sword. Four other kings – and who knows how many men – have had a good laugh at my fertility issues. No matter how often and in what position I fuck my husband, *that* particular issue doesn't seem to be going away. And now I am having the most frustrating conversation I have ever had since trying to engage Nimue in a talk about the birds and the bees. Who the fuck are you, and what the fuck are the Grey?"

Blæk cocked his head, not unlike a bird, and then his eyes twinkled. "We are spies, my lady. We are assassins. We are the hidden dagger behind the curtain. The king may have his knights, but the queen has her rogues. We are yours to command and will die in your service."

Guinevere paused for a moment, then sat back, a wide grin spreading on her face.

"Interesting, Sir Blæk. I find my day is improving."

CHAPTER 11 – IN WHICH THERE IS A DEEP, DARK WOOD.

When I was on my last quest—albeit the pretend one for Guinevere—I couldn't help but think we'd made more initial progress than was the case at the moment. If I squinted quite hard, even after two full days of travel, I reckoned I could still make out the top of Tintagel Castle in the distance.

Part of the problem, of course, was the group's size and its disparate makeup. All in, we were probably the size of a big warband but without the clarity of purpose of such a unit. For a start, Beric remained a monumental dickhead and refused to ever be at the back of the formation. He appeared to have it in his head that the other kings would screw him out of his chance at Caeldfwch unless he were with them at all times. Obviously, the fact that he was probably correct in this assessment did nothing to lessen the low esteem in which he was held.

Then there was the issue that Mark's retinue moved slowly. Like, fuck me, 'there speeds by a passing snail' slowly. His insistence on being carried in his ridiculous carriage – with a man at each corner – meant we were only ever a few minutes from a call to halt and swap over litter bearers. Like Beric, he was jealously concerned about the quest finding success with him left behind, so anytime it looked like the rest of the group was pulling ahead, we had ten rounds of 'I'm a very fat and important king and I will be respected.' Which, let me tell you, was a real treat.

In fact, the only remotely reasonably behaved of the kings was Corys, who seemed perfectly content to go with the flow and wait and see what happened next. I still haven't gotten a handle on the guy from Deheubarth. Whilst he'd done nothing to make me suspicious of him, neither had he endeared himself to me the way Owain had. Speaking of which...

"Where the fuck has he gone now?" Arthur yelled, standing high in Llameri's stirrups.

Owain of Gwent was being a pain. He had no interest in being part of a stately column, riding slowly through the countryside, and instead had volunteered for him and his men to undertake 'scouting'.

While, in theory, this might have been reasonably helpful in the circumstances, in reality, it meant that Arthur had a fifty-strong war party roaming around his land with very little oversight. No one was saying Owain was up to anything nefarious, but neither were we comfortable with his regular disappearing trick.

"Morgan, can you get a sense of his position at all?"

Before we had set off, I'd had a play with my map and been able to get a lock on the four kings. This meant I had a little aubergine showing for wherever Beric was, a slug for Mark, a question mark for Corys and a jolly little reindeer for Owain. They'd each had to agree for this to work – we'd explained it in case of an ambush, and I needed to be able to offer the fiery death sort of support – and right now, the reindeer was indicating that Owain was showing to the extreme left of our slow-moving column.

"He's just there," I pointed towards a thickly wooded area. "Probably after deer again." It had not gone unnoticed that the men of Gwent were eating significantly better than the rest of us.

Arthur blew out his cheeks. "This is not how I imagined this going."

Having been on quite a fair few school trips in my time, this was pretty much exactly how I had expected this thing to shake out. The journey was basically like herding cats through a maze. When some of them were dogs. And at least one was a shark.

Arthur continued, "Does Merlin have any sense of how much further we may have to go? At this pace, I cannot see us getting anywhere for weeks."

And this brought us to the final – and to my mind, probably the most significant – of our problems. We didn't really know where we were going. Of course, Arthur hadn't told any of the other kings this nugget of information. He hadn't outright lied, but he'd definitely leaned heavily on the 'strange and mysterious are the ways of cultivators' card.

"Merlin is clear he can find the sword?" Arthur had asked when we were putting the plans for the quest into place. "Because if I invite these very powerful men to my land and then have to shrug and say I have no earthly idea what I'm doing, there's a chance that this might make me seem less than ideal Pendragon material."

You can reassure him, my dear, that I will have no difficulty locating Caeldfwch. The sword projects such a strong negation field that I will not need to be too close to it in order to pinpoint its position accurately.

At the time, neither of us asked the critical question – which now tumbled from Arthur's mouth. "He's not intending for us just to stumble around in the woods for as long as it takes to get a sniff of it, is he?"

"Sounds like a decent question, Big M…"

There was a long silence. A much longer silence than I really wanted to experience, with Arthur glaring at me. Finally, his answer came.

I wouldn't want to quantify what we are doing as 'stumbling', my dear. In many ways, this is a reasonably professional grid search we are currently conducting.

Arthur could obviously read my expression. "Fuck's sake. This is a shambles. How have I allowed myself to hazard my throne on such a ridiculous endeavour."

"Is there anything for us to go on other than blink luck?" I asked the wizard.

Again, I take issue with that being a fair or accurate characterisation of what we are doing. However, moving past that, I am working on the principle that there are a few precedents, scrolls, and examples I am using to guide us in the right direction.

So, that seemed a little more promising. "And they are?"

Firstly, Caeldfwch never appears in the same place twice. So, we are not heading towards any area where it has already manifested itself. Secondly, we know the bearer will be a neriad, so we are trying to locate an appropriate water source. Thirdly, it would appear that being unrelentingly lost is a crucial aspect of the starting moments of the search.

Once we do not know where we are, other signs will appear. Merlin's voice changed as if he were now quoting from something before him. *There are three steps to finding the lake. The first is of blood, the second is of faith, and the third is a betrayal of all that is good.*

I relayed all of this to Arthur. "And he didn't think it would have been wise to share some of this before we set off? Call me cynical, but 'a betrayal of all that is good' sounds like something it would have been wise for all of us to talk over before setting off on a fucking quest in the woods!"

Tell him to stop his whining. There was a time when he would have lived for a mysterious quest. I miss 'fun' Arthur.

I sensibly declined to tell King Arthur that Merlin considered him to have become somewhat of a mood hoover.

We were – finally – on the move again. Mark's latest litter-bearers seemed to have a bit more oomph about them, and the break had been much less than had been the case recently. As we turned a bend in the path, there was a palpable change in the density and height of the trees. It would be fair to say that, before long, it felt like we were comfortably in Hansel and Gretel territory.

Although it must still have been mid-afternoon, the reach of the forest blocked out the sun, and we were moving in almost total darkness. If it wasn't for the torches that had been hastily lit, I doubted we'd have been able to keep moving too freely.

My dear, Merlin began and then stopped.

"What?" I don't know what instinct was speaking to me, but I'd drawn Drynwyn.

I'm reflecting on the wording of 'if you do not know where you are'. It's pretty interesting, really.

My heart was suddenly racing and a sense of overpowering wrongness was filling my every sense. It was like I was under assault from all sides. "Is now the time for a semantics lesson?"

I fear it might be. You see, in reviewing the information I have gathered from various sources, several essential things come to light. Although most largely agree that the way to find Caeldfwch is first to 'get lost,' it occurs to me that this may have been a lazy shortcut of a translation.

Something flew above my head, wings flapping in the dark. "Dude, if you've something to say..."

It's just that the rune for 'lost' is actually pretty distinctive. And, now I look at it, that's not actually what is written in the original. However, when you think about it, what is 'original'? It could be seen that what is there is just as wrong as in later sources. We should not become hung up on the veracity of primary sources. Indeed, at times, those who have come after have a great context and understanding of...

"Mate, I'm this close to exorcising you again."

How rude. Look, my dear, what I'm saying is that "do not know where" has a number of different interpretations. And I'm no longer confident that 'lost' is the most accurate. Indeed, in other circumstances, the rune would mean 'foreign', 'alien' or even, and I'm sure this will turn out not to be the case, 'fae'.

I was all ready to give him a mouthful and probably would have held forth at length over not recognising the possibility that our first step towards recovering Caeldfwch was to journey into the realm of the fae.

It was one thing to embark on a quest around Cornwall for a wet fairy carrying a sharp and pointy sword. It was quite another for us to deliberately seek to enter a different – and from everything I had read – malign plane of existence.

Arthur, Bors, and I had spent a very uncomfortable time in the Enchanted Forest when seeking to recover Guinevere, and I don't think any of us would have been especially gung-ho about this quest had we known that we might encounter the supernatural again.

Arthur, in particular, had been rather – shall I say 'intimately' – disturbed by the experience.

Merlin would have heard all about this – and more – if I had not become rather caught up in events.

Namely, being knocked from my horse by a dragon attack.

CHAPTER 12 – IN WHICH WE LEARN THE DIFFERENCE BETWEEN A WYVERN AND A DRAGON

Don't be so dramatic, my dear. That wasn't a dragon.
Clutching my mauled shoulder, I rolled as I fell from my horse and came up in a low crouch. All around me was chaos; the beating of leathery wings almost drowning out the shouts and screams of men and the terrified whinnying of the horses.

I couldn't make out anyone I recognised around me – where the fuck had Arthur gone? – but I figured that could be a problem for a me who survived the next few minutes. I flattened myself even lower as a massive fuck-off green reptile with wings flew overhead, an unfortunate spearman shrieking in its jaws. Although, on the plus side, not for very long.

"You're telling me that's not a bloody dragon!"

Hardly. You see how the wings are attached to the front talons? You won't see a dragon with that sort of body shape. Four legs and two wings all day long. And, my dear, whoever heard of dragons attacking in such numbers? Honestly, I have been quite remiss in your education.

One of these giant monsters swooped down to land on my horse, slicing its head off with one claw and opening its belly with the other. It was dark green and at least twice the size of my unfortunate animal. I'm not going to lie; it looked pretty damned draconic to me.

"So, what are they?" I could barely hear my own voice over the tumult of battle.

Wyverns, my dear. No fire and very little intelligence. I imagine they live on the border between our world and the land of the fae in order to feast upon unwary travellers. In fact, that's probably why we do not have better records, especially since the dividing line is so thin here.

"What do you mean?"

He means they'd eat anyone that came this way.

It took me for a moment to realise Drynwyn had spoken. I don't think I'd heard more than a few sentences from it in weeks. By the fire glowing around its blade, it seemed it may have got a bit of its groove back.

Fucking hate wyverns. The intensity of the flame increased.

Good, good, let the hate flow through you. The wyvern in front of me had almost finished eating my horse – it had swallowed it whole, and there was just a leg remaining sticking out of its mouth – and it was clearly casting around for its next meal.

By the bellows and shouts of orders, it sounded like some form of organised defence was being restored – now the initial shock had worn off. I probably wanted to start being part of that. I tried to send a Qi suggestion to the monster.

Sorry, my dear. There is not enough intelligence to push in this way. You're trying to influence something without any conscious thoughts, just instincts.

So, no <Those aren't the droids you're looking for> then. No worries. I still had plenty of tools in the old Qi shed. <Unnecessary Sequel Trilogy> channelled through a pissed-off Drynwyn, for example. A beam of fire lightning shot from the tip of my blade to completely engulf the creature. It screamed in a rather disturbing manner as its flesh went first red with the heat of the strike and then black as the monster was reduced to ash.

The whole immolation took barely a few seconds.

I was aware that, with the shrieking and the fire and the lightning etc, I'd gathered quite a bit of attention from the other combatants. At this juncture, a quip seemed appropriate.

"Yippiekayyay, motherfuckers!"

Not your best, my dear. Perhaps something more contextually amusing? "Now we're cooking with gas", for example, might have been better.

"Fuck off, Merlin," and I moved to help the rest of the beleaguered defenders.

***

Guinevere had spent the last couple of days having an awful lot of fun with the Grey, and Blæk in particular.

There had always been rumours of shadowy figures operating around the throne, and it was quite a thrill to realise that not only did these people exist but that she was now very much in charge of them.

The amount of information she had at her disposal was colossal. If she was interested in how much tribute a certain lord had paid in the last year, she could access that. If she wanted to know how much that lord *should* have paid and where he had hidden the excess in order to avoid detection, she could see that too.

There seemed to be no limit to the range of gossip, scuttlebutt and rumour that the Grey had collected, catalogued and prepared for her inspection. It was all quite overwhelming after a bit. And then there was the temptation to look into things that, just plain good sense, suggested she'd be wise to keep away from.

"And what do you know about my husband?" she asked lightly.

Blæk simply cocked his head in that strange, bird-like way he had. "Queen Igraine was most clear that every care should be taken to keep abreast of his movements. Especially around breasts. That was her joke, by the way, not me trying to be flippant."

"Please take it as read that I will assume any attempt at humour is you quoting someone else. What does it mean, though? That the queen wanted Arthur watched?"

"Everything, my lady. We know everything about King Arthur."

The destructive desire to reopen old wounds was overwhelming. She knew he had been spectacularly unfaithful over the years—it was an open secret across the court—but she was comforted by not knowing the precise details. Did she really want to know more now that they were trying to turn over a new leaf?

"You will know," she began carefully, "that my husband has not always been true throughout our marriage."

"I have the details of every brothel he has ever visited. We also track each of his bastards and have substantial records around each woman – peasant or noble – that we can confirm he had lain with."

Guinevere felt the colour come to her cheeks. "Goodness. Okay. Well, let's ignore all of that for now. Tell me, since our return from the Dark Tower…" She hesitated. Did she really want to know this? Things were so much better between them. Was it worth sabotaging that?

Blæk regarded her with his bland eyes. "My lady?"

Oh, well. Fuck it. Might as well know everything. "Has my husband been unfaithful since we returned from the tower of Aurelius Ambrosius?"

Blæk blinked once, then twice and cocked his head the other way. "We have no examples of the king conducting any such activities in that time frame."

"And you would know?"

Blæk smiled humourlessly. "We would know, yes."

A weight she did not know she was carrying lifted off Guinevere's chest.

"Right. Excellent. Well, now that's done with; let's focus on which thegns are not quite being full-throated in their support for the king."

***

Turns out, Drynwyn really hates wyverns.

By the time I joined the fray, though, things appeared well in hand. After the initial shock of the ambush, the various different sections of our group coalesced into the sort of professional, dogged defence you would expect from elite warriors.

Without panic blinding our eyes, it became clear there were only about ten wyverns, minus the one I had incinerated and a combination of sheer numbers and some well-aimed arrows and javelins were keeping things on an even keel.

Enter Morgan.

Or, to be fair, Drynwyn and my current coolest technique.

It took a few minutes, but in no time, I'd napalm-deathed six of the buggers, and a combination of Lancelot and, annoyingly, Beric's men, finished off the last few.

"How are you feeling, big man?"

Fucking hate wyverns.

"Glad you're feeling a little more like yourself."

Wasn't going to let you down again. Especially around fucking wyverns.

"Good timing," I said, ramming it back into its scabbard.

Arthur appeared, slapping me on my back in a very manly way that, in a different context, would have been tantamount to assault. "That was all very dramatic!" His face was a mess of cuts and scrapes, and I was alarmed to see his left arm was hanging uselessly by his side.

I tossed him one of the rare Elixirs of Wellness I'd started to be able to produce. He took a sip and quickly looked as good as new. Although still with no hair.

"Do you have any idea what happened? Or where they came from?"

I decided now wasn't the moment to share Big M's sudden realisation about alternative rune translations. It didn't really feel like the time. Instead, I looked at the chaos caused to our convoy. "Many casualties?"

Arthur shrugged. "Some. Not as many as it would have been without your intervention. I think we will have made a good impression on the others with your little display."

I mean, sure. In a leading-you-into-danger-and-then-saving-you kind of way.

Lancelot joined us, inexplicably shirtless. I swear, this dude went full Hulk Hogan at the slightest hint of trouble. His muscles glinted oilily in the firelight. "Of this place, my people speak."

Arthur and I turned to him. "Mate, we'll take all the info you've got at this stage. The Big M is basically making up as he goes along."

I resent that, my dear. This is a quest. It is not supposed to have a step-by-step how-to guide. There will always be an element of risk.

"Tell that to the guys who just got eaten," I called over the quartermaster, a heavily tattooed man called Karl. "I'm going to need a bigger horse."

We indulged in a few minutes of quality Jaws-related banter. This was only slightly ruined by the fact only one of us had seen the movie. Or was even aware of the existence of sharks.

"So, what do your people say about this place?" I asked Lancelot, who had fallen to the floor and was pumping out press-ups.

"We call it Niefeheim – the place beyond the pines."

"And what can we expect here, beyond wyverns?"

"Death. Death and pain." There was no glimmer of humour in his eyes.

Which wasn't exactly a great introduction to us realising we'd lost Owain and all his men.

CHAPTER 13 – IN WHICH BLÆK IS FLESHED IN SOMEWHAT

Bors stroked his beard thoughtfully.

There was apparently much more to organising a tournament than pulling a bunch of guys together, giving them a pep talk and letting them get on with it. Whilst he was not, by any means, a stupid man - he passed the fucking Trial of Thought in the Enchanted Forest, didn't he? - he could not help but think that this sort of organisational competence was somewhat beyond his skill set.

He looked at the list of suggestions prepared for him by Tasko, the man Pallemedias had recommended handing the whole business to. Like that dark-skinned swordsman, Tasko was from somewhere far away from Tintagel and seemed to possess all the various bits of knowledge of which the big man felt himself so short. He also talked—a lot.

After what felt like most of his adult life, Bors raised his hand to stem the tide of words. "So, to summarise, what you're saying is that this thing should - ideally - run over three days?"

"Not at all, my lord. I am just suggesting that in order to maximise the profits from the various stalls and concession outlets you will doubtless be commissioning, my research and experience would suggest that three days is well positioned in the sweet spot between novelty and consumer fatigue."

Bors blinked. "I didn't understand most of that."

Tasko smiled back. "I know, my lord. And that's why my second recommendation would be to hire me to take care of the minor details for you. That way, you can be reassured that all of the complicated, insignificant details are handled, and you can concentrate on the fighting and suchlike."

"He's a crook," Pallemedias had told him the night before. "An absolute, stone-cold-robber-Baron of the highest order. But, as far as these things go, he's an honest one. He's been connected to my family for years, and my father has yet to lop off any of his limbs, so I guess that probably tells you everything you need to know. My advice would be to let him scam you for an amount you can live with, and he'll solve more headaches than he'll cause."

Bors pushed the scroll back towards Tasko and glowered at him. Tall, lean, and with thick, black hair that he kept in a tight braid, the man certainly looked like a wealthy merchant. If Pallemedias had not given him the head's up, Bors would have been none the wiser to his... less salubrious habits. Fake it until you make it, he guessed.

"Here's the deal. For me, this ain't about the money."

Tasko opened his mouth, gold teeth flashing in the light, but Bors pressed on before he could speak. "We need men. Good men. Men who'll stand a shield wall, day in, day out. We need men that bards will sing about and who live for nothing more than sticking the spear in the guts of Saxons. So, I need something that'll attract every swinging dick in the land. And possibly across the sea, too. I want this to be the greatest tournament in these Isles. But I need it to happen quickly.

"I understand," the wheels behind Tasko's eyes were already whirling. The abacus too...

Bors pressed on. "I can sort the categories for the bouts and everything like that - the gods know I've fought in enough of them over the years - but for everything else, I'm looking for a likely lad to hand it all over to. I ain't got a head for numbers so I won't be looking too closely at that side of things." If possible, the merchant's smile grew even wider. "But I'm going to be all about the results."

Bors stood and rested his hands on the wooden table that separated the two. "I believe I have a reputation for a certain single-mindedness. My men will tell you that when I am happy, there's no one better to share a mug of ale with. On the other hand, it's been mentioned that my displeasure can be" - the table groaned as he pressed down on it – "intense. My best mate has asked for a tournament to swell our army. I've never let him down in my life. If you tell me you can make this happen, and you do," Bors opened his arms and beamed, "then we're all good—friends for life. I'll name my next kid after you. But if you overpromise and underdeliver..." He brought both hands down on the table, reducing it to kindling.

Tasko jumped backwards and pressed himself against the stone wall, eyes suddenly huge.

"So, what do you think? Do we have a deal?"

∗∗∗

"I hear you have been giving the 'I'm either your best friend or your worst enemy' talk again."

Bors turned at the sound of the familiar voice. He was standing on Tintagel's battlements, staring out over the narrow stone bridge that connected the island on which the castle stood with the mainland. He knew it was insanely early to hope to see the procession of Kings return - it wasn't like Caeldfwch would be a week's ride from these gates, but he lived in hope.

"You're hearing an awful lot of late, my lady."

Guinevere stood at his shoulder, that mischievous glint in her eye once again. It had been one of the real sorrows of his life to see that glimmer gutter and die over the last few years. "Hard not to when you need the Royal Carpenter every few days. Other intimidation tactics are available that do not require the demolition of furniture."

"True, but it's so damn satisfying."

Guinevere laughed and brushed her hair away from her face. She, too, gazed out into the distance as if wishing she could make the quest be completed faster just by sincerely hoping for it.

"I have a considerable volume of available information on this Tasko, if you are interested?"

"Unless any of it suggests he has a habit of risking his life when threatened in the most explicit of terms?"

Guinevere shook her head in response.

"In that case, I will rely on the old faithful of blind terror to get the job done. I hear he's already dispatched couriers?"

"Indeed. He appears to be working every hour the gods send to ensure this will be a tournament to remember. A fortnight, his missives say."

Bors' eyebrows shot up. "So soon?"

"Did I not mention he's running around like his arse is on fire? It would be tomorrow if he could portal everyone here. He is giving every impression of being very motivated indeed."

"Maybe I did lay it on a bit thick..."

They stood in a companionable silence for a while.

"My lady, do I need to be concerned about how you have access to so much information of late? For example, I hear it is not uncommon for cultivators to come late into their powers - particularly since the death of Merlin - but likewise, there are dangers there which make Morgan's absence a worry. If you think I'm scary, you should see what Arthur looked like when he told me to ensure no harm befell you. You going 'boom' would be pretty life-limiting for me."

Guinevere laughed. He was glad she was able to make that noise again. "No, Sir Bors, it's nothing like that." Then she paused, weighing him up. She liked Bors. She liked him even more after reviewing the information the Grey held on him. He was that rare thing - exactly what he appeared to be: a big, belligerent psychopath who was loyal to his wife, rabidly so to his friends and with absolutely no hidden depths, secrets or shadowy alliances. If she couldn't share her recent experiences with him, she doubted there would be anyone else she could talk with.

Certainly not Arthur. Blæk had been clear about that.

"Sir Bors, can I trust you?"

Bors shrugged his massive shoulders. "Depends. Can you trust me to royally fuck up anyone who crossed you? Absolutely. Can you trust me not to take the piss if you're going to reveal something kinky about your sex life? Probably not."

"I guess that's a pretty clear demarcation line. Okay, so here's the deal."

***

Blæk moved silently through the corridors of Tintagel Castle.

It was no exaggeration to say that he had spent his whole life in the shadows of these buildings. Should anyone have marked his passage, and he was quite sure that he was not seen, they would have dimly recognised him, just enough to accept his presence but not sufficient to note him.

It was a useful skill.

As he moved, he ran his hands into the various nooks and crannies in the stonework and the hidden recesses of doors and windows where those of the Grey left their messages. In a society where literacy was an exceptionally rare talent, it was not an inconsiderable matter of pride to Blæk that each and every one of his informants was capable of reading and writing in a variety of languages.

Had Merlin been aware of Blæk, he would have recognised him to be a cultivator of exceptional subtlety. Of course, that he - and others like him - had lived unknown under the very nose of that legendary wizard was a testimony to the potency of their abilities. Blæk would not have understood what was meant by Qi but would have been able to explain the process of wrapping his darkness around himself like a cloak and passing unseen through crowds of men.

What is more, Blæk, like his father before him, had a special connection with Metal Qi, which, although he would not have seen it in those terms, made him a frighteningly efficient assassin. His principal technique, <Wire in the Blood>, allowed him to coalesce all the iron in a target's body into one tiny sliver of metal, which, when it found its way to the heart, was inevitably fatal.

More than one visitor to Tintagel had failed to wake in the morning when the Queen deemed that their time on this earth was over.

Blæk had made quite a collection of slips of vellum when his hand reached for an alcove that had remained empty for many months. It was habit that made him check, rather than any expectation, so he was momentarily gratified that his fingers brushed parchment. As with all such unnecessary emotions, he squashed it down.

Retrieving the message, he slipped it into one of his many pockets and moved, with more alacrity than usual, to the dark space beneath Merlin's tower that he called 'home'. Although the entrance to his little room was wholly unhidden, anyone looking straight at it would find their eyes being tugged to the side and their thoughts elsewhere.

It was pitch black within Blæk's space, but that was no difficulty for him. He pulled the darkness around the letter inside himself, feeling refreshed by the action - he hadn't needed to sleep more than a few hours a week since childhood.

The message had only three words, but they made him snarl in an entirely uncharacteristic show of anger. How long had that message sat there? Had he neglected to check in on previous days?

He thought not.

But that was no matter. He needed to speak to his new mistress. In the swirl of darkness that marked his abrupt departure, the small message fluttered to the floor. A tiny flicker of light from a torch outside fell upon it so the words could be discerned just for a moment.

"Igraine was pushed."

CHAPTER 14 – IN WHICH BERIC IS, ONCE MORE, A COLOSSAL PRICK

So, misplacing one of the kings we were seeking to impress on this quest wasn't exactly Plan A.

Especially as we couldn't tell if Owain and his men were 'lost'-lost, or 'didn't cross over into the strange fae land with the rest of us' lost. Or 'eaten by wyverns' lost. Basically, that's quite a lot of variations on 'no one has a fucking clue where they have gone.'

"I thought you had some sort of... I don't know, magical tracking system set up?" Arthur's voice was a little too accusatory for my liking.

"Yeah, sorry about that, Your Majesty. In between saving everyone's arses from the massive flying reptiles and liaising with the legendary cultivator who forgot to mention that we'd be SWAPPING REALMS on this quest, I took my eye off the King of Gwent and his fifty bodyguards. My bad!"

Just putting this out there, my dear, but maybe don't point your finger, with electricity cracking around it, at the chest of the King of the Britons whilst shouting at him. It's creating a mood.

I looked around to see lots of open mouths, big eyes and hurriedly drawn swords. "Guys, relax. This is kind of our deal. I turned him into a flame-grilled Whopper *one time*. And that was a complete ballache to heal, so I'm not putting myself through that sort of pain again. At least, not this early in the quest. I'll give it at least a few more days before going down that road."

My charm and witty banter did not appear to ease tensions.

Then, Lancelot appeared, clapped his muscular arm around my shoulder, and led me away from the growing lynch mob. "Such a funny joker you are being. With the lightning. And the pointing. And the inappropriate shouting at our liege lord." His arm tightened, and I was suddenly very aware of how powerful this man was. "Probably best you laugh. Like great hoot, we are sharing."

I did so, trying to pull enough Qi into my hands to have a chance of doing... something should this all spiral out of control. In theory, I should be able to take Lancelot, no worries. But I was starting to worry that theory and practice would be very different where the barbarian was concerned.

"Remembering you will, that we need to show respect to Arthur. Like you, I do. Cut off pieces I wouldn't, pretty hair." With a final squeeze - which I'm sure cracked several ribs - he swung me around so we were walking back to the king.

I mouthed a 'sorry'. He just glared back. It was probably a fair cop.

"I don't know, my lord. When we crossed into this realm, Owain and his war band were scouting a little ahead of us. I don't believe I've seen him or any of his men since then, though. As tricky as the wyverns were to handle, it hardly seems credible he would have taken one hundred per cent casualties when the rest of us -" I looked at the crew currently digging a pit for the bodies - "got off reasonably lightly."

Arthur looked around at the defensive position we had taken up. We had enough archers between those of the groups that remained to be able to put a dent in the day of anything else that attacked from the sky. Now that everyone was deployed in a deep square, there would be no further sniping off an individual from a long column.

The king raised his voice above the background hum of men at work. "We need to give King Owain and his retinue time to catch back up with us. This seems a secure enough position for the night to wait, but we can reassess it in the morning. Sleep in shifts, quadruple watch. Flaming death first, ask questions later. All agreed?"

"Who the fuck put you in charge?"

Beric - of course, it was Beric - pushed himself forward. I'd seen his men in the thick of the fighting but didn't remember seeing him anywhere: his sword looked suspiciously clean, and his armour was undamaged.

Arthur turned to him; the contrast between his worn clothing and the gleaming appearance of the King of Powys could not have been starker. "I don't need to be 'put' in charge, my lord. Those are simply sensible instructions anyone could have issued. Anyone who had been in the fighting, at any rate. If you have alternative suggestions you would like to offer, perhaps drawing on your long and illustrious history of successful command in the field, I would be glad to hear them?"

Corys appears through the gloom, his gear battle-stained. "No need to be a prick about it, Ber. Let's take a breath, give the fat man a chance to get back to us and see where we are in the morning."

Beric retreated away back towards his men without saying another word. Corys winked at Arthur - or was it at me? Was he flirting with me? - and followed him.

"Kill him I can," Lancelot murmured. "In Niefelheim, all things are possible. His soul stolen in his dreams, maybe? Wouldn't come back to you."

Arthur turned and pushed the barbarian in the chest, snarling as he spoke. "He's a King! I need these men on my side. I have to unite our lands, and I won't do that over a pile of corpses." He turned to me, his temper not especially under control. I wondered if he would be interested in some meditation tips. Or a fireball to the face. "Find Owain. Stop antagonizing this alliance. And work out where we need to go next."

I held my curtsey until he and Lancelot were out of earshot. "Why don't you stick a broom up my arse while you're at it, and I'll sweep the fucking camp?"

∗∗∗

The first thing you need to know about the fae realm is that there are no rules.
"Like the enchanted forest?"

No, my dear, nothing like that. Within the enchanted forest, you are bound by a myriad of rules, precedents and contracts. Sure, you will most likely be horribly murdered, but there would have been some element of framework around your death. Once you passed your Trial, it would have been the height of bad manners for the forest not to honour the deal that had been made.
"And it's not going to be like that in here?"

I was sat, cross-legged, in front of a low burning fire. Drynwyn was laid across a bunch of wyvern bones and seemed to be enjoying the experience of gently roasting them. When asked for an explanation, he merely repeated: **I fucking hate wyverns.**

I was gently pushing my Qi hither and tither, trying to get used to its thicker consistency. As much as I hated the phrase 'desirable difficulty', I was actually enjoying the experience.

It felt like I had spent a lifetime trying to find something to do in the quiet moments of the night. A drink. A cigarette. A spliff. A line. A cock. Anything to fill the deep, dark void within me.

And now I had a process which needed all my attention. And it felt great to do.

The fae realm, Merlin continued, *is not like that. No, my dear. In some ways, it is closer to our own in its sense of chaos and unrestricted tyranny. There is only one rule here. The mighty take, and the weak are taken from.*

"And we're going to take Caeldfwch?"

Merlin paused. *That is a little more complicated. We are planning to take it, to be sure. But it is awaiting us. Should we be able to find it, it will be ours to take away.*

"After the steps of Blood, Faith and Betrayal?"

Indeed.

I thought back to the fight with the wyverns. "I don't suppose we've already achieved the step of blood, have we?"

There was a grim chortle from inside my head. *Not by any means, no. That was a very minor skirmish against a massively underpowered foe. Such things do not the stuff of quests make. No, the step of Blood will be soon, and we will need to be prepared.*

"And for that, it would help to know where King Owain and his fifty spears have gone."

I have an idea for that.

"A good idea, Big M? Or one of those ideas that inevitably leads to me in a battle for my life and racking up the PTSD points like a Vietnam vet?"

Life of a cultivator, my dear. Life of a cultivator.

***

I pushed outwards, trying to feel for a presence I would recognise as King Owain. *No, not like that.*

Sighing, I opened my eyes in frustration. "Dude, are you planning on being any help here at all?"

I am helping. I told you what to do, you did it wrong, and I told you. That's pretty much the definition of being helpful.

"HOW am I doing it wrong?"

Oh, I see what you mean. Subtlety. Softness. Caressing.

"Mate, am I carrying out a search and rescue operation or am I in a bad soft-core porn film?"

Quite. You don't need to do everything at a million miles an hour. Especially so, now your Qi is so much more concentrated. Not every problem requires you to blow the bloody doors off, as it were.

I pulled back on what I was doing - the Big M may have a point. I might have been going full beans at it - and let a single drop of my Qi hit the parchment. I visualised a palette of water and began to thin out that purple drop, spreading it in a smooth circle that would cover my internal map.

Better. You can obviously see the advantages of having chosen water as your Qi medium. No need to dilute that down, but I guess you are making the best you can from an inferior lot.

"Fuck off, Big M."

I worked the paint even thinner until I felt it could not have been reduced any further.

"Okay, now what?"

Use that as your model for seeking out King Owain and his men.

I did so and immediately felt the difference. Whereas, before, I had been inundated by sensory overload when questing out—I literally had been able to hear the grass grow—now it was much easier to see the wood for the trees, as it were. I retraced our steps to this point with my mind, trying to locate Owain. My hope was that they had done the same as us and held up for the night, hoping to follow our tracks in the morning.

But no. Nothing.

"Fuck's sake," I grimaced. "It's fifty men, twenty-odd horses and a lardarse of a king. They don't just vanish."

One second, my dear.

I waited. Then, I realised I had no idea what I was waiting for. "What is it?"

I appear to have stumbled across a strange overlap between the realms. It's not quite our world, and it's not the world of the fae.

I felt my attention being brought to a nondescript woodland area and could see what Merlin was getting at. On one side of the trees, it was definitely the mortal world, and on the other, it was Wyvern City. But at the place where the two intersected, there was a thin strip of land that was both.

And it smelled wrong.

I don't wish to raise undue alarm here, my dear.

I turned to the small group of spears that had accompanied me on this Owain-hunt and waved for attention, drawing Drynwyn and kicking Lancelot as the Big M was talking.

Because that strange patch of land didn't just smell bad, it reeked.

It reeked of blood.

CHAPTER 15 – THE STEP OF BLOOD (OR, 'IT'S BIGGER THAN IT LOOKS ON THE OUTSIDE')

"What. The. Fuck. Is. That?"

Slipping into what the Big M was describing as a pocket dimension was quite a thing. It wasn't like going through the wardrobe into Narnia, but neither was it a slap in the face with a wet fish.

The moment I crossed the dividing line, my perspective slipped and the land... concertinaed outwards. What was objectively about a ten feet square of land on my map, quadrupled in size to reveal...

A larder.

Yep. That was the only way to describe it. Rows upon rows of trees were adorned with sharp, metallic spikes on which hung hundreds of bodies. Wyverns. Deer. Boars. Some strange human/animal hybrids which made me think Mr. Tumnus got away pretty damn easy by being turned into stone.

However, that was nothing compared to the giant creature walking up and down the area singing to the corpses.

I believe that is a Shriket, my dear.

The monster was at least twelve feet tall and about half as wide. It's hard to know where to begin describing it because my mind keeps going, 'FUUUUCCK' when I look at it. Let's start with its lower half. There were legs. Yep, there were definitely legs. They were as thick as tree trunks and covered with a soft down of feathers. The thing had massive talons instead of feet with five claws as long as my leg on each. Fortunately, to stop it all looking too cute, the whole ensemble was splattered liberally with blood and pieces of flesh. Nice.

Moving upwards, the thing's torso was almost human—albeit magnified to a ridiculous scale. Its musculature put Lancelot to shame, even though much of it was covered by the same grey, blood-soaked feathers. The vibe was that I should be seeing some wings somewhere, and - sure enough - when it raised its arms to stroke one of the bodies, I made out a thin flap of skin that connected the hand to the thigh. It was something like a bat, but I'm not sure that gets across how disgusting it looked.

Think of that bit of chicken fat that never quite renders down in the pan and multiplied by - I don't know - raw effluence overrunning your toilet.

I guess that leaves the head? Yep, the Shriket had a head. Beak. Staring, insane eyes. Rotting flesh. Tick.

I vomited as noiselessly as I could manage.

I believe I have located our missing party members, my dear.

Wiping my mouth and flushing it out with a quick burst of Qi, I stared down the rows of the dead to where Merlin was tugging my attention.

Right at the far end were Owain's men. And his horses. The fucking thing had impaled them all on the spikes it hammered into the trees for this eventuality. And there they hung, helplessly, feet off the ground.

Blood pooled on the ground beneath them, and I could see it trickled down the bodies of men and their mounts.

"Big M, they're bleeding. So that means they are still alive, right?"

In answer, one of the horses whinnied and kicked its legs pathetically. The Shriket reacted to the noise and skipped - yep, I know - down to that point of its all-you-can-eat buffet.

It sniffed the terrified animal for a few seconds and then casually tore off one of its legs. The horse screamed as the creature chomped down on its prize. However, it was clearly not to its taste, as, in moments, it regurgitated the food down its front and tossed the half-eaten leg to one side.

"Ageing the meat, it is," Lancelot whispered at my side. "Not too rare, it likes."

Fuckadoodle do.

And then I saw him, right in the middle of a collection of dead and dying spearmen. King Owain. Sharp spikes protruded from his shoulder, and - presumably because of his greater weight - two others had been hammered through his thighs.

Owain's head was resting on his chest, and for a moment, I assumed he was dead. Then a cough racked his body, and his head roiled in agony for a heartbeat and then settled back down.

I looked around at the handful of spearmen that had followed me out into the woods. Without Merlin leading the way, I doubted anyone else would stumble upon this spot shortly. Assuming Arthur sent out scouts for us, they were never going to find us. I nudged Lancelot. "We need to do something."

Lancelot shrugged carelessly. "For sure. Plan you have?"

"Talk to me about Shrikets, Big M."

They are largely wysiwyg, my dear. Give or take. It can depend on their age, as—over time—they develop the ability to enforce temporary mental effects. Terror. Disorientation. Freeze. It is certainly not to be taken lightly.

What you see is what you get? A fucking giant carnivorous bird that had already defeated an elite bodyguard, not to mention all the other beasts and creatures it had casually strung up for next week's lunch.

"Drynwyn, tell me you have a horrifying anecdote about the time Ryhddrech Hael got a Shriket drunk and showed it a good time."

Funnily enough...

"You're kidding me?"

Of course, I fucking am. It's a giant monster. Rhyddrech liked to fuck around and find out. But even he had his standards. All those feathers, though? Motherfucker looks flammable.

Superficially so, I am afraid, my dear. Shriket have more in common with trolls than they do with birds. I doubt you will find fire and lightning will do too much to it. It'll have not dissimilar resistances to those you do. On the plus side, and I'm trying to look for an upside here, should you defeat it, I'm sure there will be vast amounts of Earth Qi for you to be able to absorb. There was a pause. *And you'll be able to save some lives, of course.*

I looked again at all of Owain's men, impaled and dying on the trees. Most of them were still hanging on - *that's a terrible pun, my dear* - but time was clearly running out.

The eyes of the handful of men I had at my disposal were like saucers. "We're going to need more men, my lady," one of them stammered out. I think he was one of Corys's warband.

"Nah. Owain had fifty spears, and it did him no good. We're going to do this the old-fashioned way."

Lancelot grinned. "Charging in without over-thinking?"

"I always liked you, mate."

***

I mean, things could have gone smoother.

It all got off to a pretty decent start when I gave the Shriket a nice double dose of <Unnecessary Prequel Trilogy> coupled with some of Drynwyn's finest. The monster went up in a very pleasing column of flame, and I was gratified to hear its insane singing turning into shrieks of agony.

Then Lancelot slammed into it, knocking it off its feet, and began hacking away at it while the other men ran to Owain and his bodyguard and started trying to heave them off the spikes.

Just as a head's up, my dear, it's about to...

And then the Shriket screamed. This, though, wasn't a noise of agony but rather an aural attack that ripped through our small assault group. I watched in horror as my plucky little group of spears collapsed to the floor, hands covering their ears, crying out in terror. Even after the Shriket's call stopped, they carried on reacting as if the noise continued.

Even Lancelot had been affected, falling away from his attack and clutching his head. I rushed forward to pull him out of the way of the flailing talons as the still-burning creature thrashed around.

"Big M?"

<Horrifying Call>, my dear. It has essentially, but hopefully temporarily, driven them insane.

Lancelot was clearly fighting the impact of the technique far more effectively than any of the others, and he was already groping around for his sword. "Nasty," he growled. "It's like Mother is hitting me with oar of canoe all over again." He shook his head a few times, his face white. "I okay now."

But then the Shriket shrieked again.

This time, Lancelot completely collapsed, his eyes rolling back in his head.

And I was one-on-one with the monster.

So, yeah, when I say things could be going better...

The Shriket was on its feet again; all its feathers burned away. If possible, with all its covering burned away, it looked even more horrifying than it did originally. The joy of my early childhood had been blunted by watching the Dark Crystal at too young an age. If you know, you know. Imagine one of those fuckers, the size of a rearing bear, and we will be on the same page.

I could swear the bastard grinned at me as it moved forward to attack. Having no other ideas, I let Drynwyn drag me into hacking range.

***

I'd been working really hard on my swordplay. There comes a time in every girl's life when she gets fed up with her magic sword having all the moves and just wants to bring a little something to the party herself.

I'm not saying I was ever going to be able to mix it with the best of them, but with all my cultivationy - *are you really creating that adverb?* - empowered speed and strength, I was better than most.

Will you fucking let me take the lead? Drynwyn disagreed.

Interestingly enough, our little battle of wills seemed to be working for us. The Shriket was doing its best to absorb most of my attacks on its forearms, which were taking epic punishment. However, Drynwyn was looking to pull off rather more exotic and complex strikes, so we were being the very definition of utterly unpredictable depending on who was in charge at any given moment.

We were not, however, doing much more than fighting to a standstill. As I ducked under a flashing claw, it occurred to me that it was taking everything I had to keep things this way. The Shriket only needed to connect with me once, and that was going to be that. And all the time I was dicking around, Owain and his men were bleeding out.

The Shriket shrieked at me again, and this mental attack stumbled me back a step, giving it just enough space to land a kick in the middle of my chest. It was like being hit by a car. Fuck it. It was like being hit by an entire motorway of cars.

I tumbled backwards, arse over tit, and crashed into one of the larder trees, the spikes tearing into me.

With a significant effort, I wrenched myself clear, tapping my mana stone earrings to repair the insane damage I'd received. I tried not to look down at where the kick had split open my ribcage, as my lungs had spilt out before my Qi kicked in and began rebuilding things.

It was time to take stock of where things were.

You know, if you make it through this, it will be one heck of a story.

"Cheers, Big M." And I charged.

CHAPTER 16 – IN WHICH MY ARSE CONTINUES TO BE KICKED

By the fifth time I'd been smacked away from the Shriket, I'd had enough. I was running dangerously low on Qi, and no matter how many times I thought I'd landed a decent blow on the thing, it made no discernable difference.

By any measure of how I understood these things, I was royally fucking this monster up, but it just kept Taylor Swifting my best attacks.

I'm not sure I understand the reference.

"Not the time, Big M. Is there anything you can suggest for me here?"

It's Trollkin, my dear. Once upon a time, I remember seeing one of them fighting headless. They simply do not have enough intelligence to know when they are beaten. Although looking at the state of you right now, I'm not sure it is the only one.

"Aw, shucks, dude. You and your motivational speeches."

I pushed as much Qi as I could spare into my armour. It was taking an absolute shellacking, and I was worried about what would happen if it finally gave up the ghost and fractured. This thing's claws were not fucking about, and I liked my organs right where they were.

"Is there going to be any mileage in <These aren't the droids you're looking for>?"

I doubt it, I'm afraid. As with the Wyvern, there is no true ruling mind here to make suggestions to. You might as well tell a rock to grow wings and fly to the sun.

Swearing, I hit the Shriket with my old faithful, <Personal Space Invader> and grimaced at how much of my remaining Qi it took to force the beast back just a few feet.

I took the moment of respite to look around for any good news at all. Unfortunately, Lancelot and the men who had followed us to what seemed like certain death were all still under the influence of whatever mental attack had been shrieked their way.

"How about those guys?"

How about what, my dear?

"Can I break whatever it is doing to them?"

There was a pause. *You know, that's an interesting point. I have always tended to operate alone - one of the drawbacks of being such a powerful cultivator. Besides my various apprentices, I've rarely had anyone beside me in battle. They just seemed like such a significant hindrance.*

"Dude, can I get them back in the game?"

I can see no reason why not. Your power of suggestion is significantly more potent than the base instinct the Shriket is appealing to.

I emptied my earrings and tapped one of the mana stone rings I kept for emergencies. The Qi in that was not my more concentrated type, but I'd not had a chance to fill them all up yet. It was going to have to do. I connected a thin line of Qi to Lancelot and the screaming spearmen.

It took me a moment to pick the right suggestion, but then I blasted out <These aren't the droids you're looking for> with everything I had.

Now I think of it; it might have been less than a suggestion and more of an order with all of the quiet fury of a mother ordering you to your room after you'd broken her most cherished porcelain figurine.

Lancelot reacted incredibly quickly. His mummy issues, I presume.

"Fuck up this giant chicken!"

When this is over, we will discuss how to sneak these suggestions in a little more under the radar, my dear.

I blocked a massive swipe of the Shriket's clawed hand on Drynwyn's crossguard and pushed again with <Personal Space Invader>. Unfortunately, I barely staggered it backwards with the lower concentration of Qi I was now forced to rely on. However, it was enough to give Lancelot a chance to jump on its shoulders and begin plunging a dagger in and out of its eye with all the fervour of a high school nerd getting lucky.

The Shriket screamed out its mental attack again, but the power of my suggestion held, and I was glad to see my men moving around Owain and the surviving spears of Gwent, lifting them off the trees on which they were impaled.

Then, my attention was very much back on the monster itself as it reached out and drove three of its claws straight through my chest and out the other side.

"Fucking hell!" I gasped, pulling out an Elixir of Wellness and tossing it down my throat, even as I was lifted straight into the air.

Well, that is less than ideal.

I realised I'd dropped Drynwyn when I'd been stabbed, which, again, did not feel exactly like it was from page one of 'Classic Battle Tactics'. Impotently, I battered against the arm holding me aloft, aware that my Elixir was fighting somewhat of a losing battle against the piercing damage that had taken out my liver and one of my kidneys and - in retrospect, I should have led with this - gone through my heart.

Blood gushed up my throat and down my chin as I tried to get another Elixir on board. In my slowly darkening vision, I could see Lancelot stirring his blade around inside one of the Shriket's eyes. I mean, it didn't much improve my situation, but it was comforting to know that this nightmare creature was also toast.

I have a plan.

"Is it a cunning plan, Big M?"

As much as I'd love to play the Baldrick here in this little skit, my dear, you are - in technical medical jargon - circling the drain.

"I'm all ears, mate. Well, actually, I'm all gaping wounds, but you get the point."

I had pulled Melehan's Curing Rock and had it in my hand, but it was - heroically - fighting a losing battle. The Shriket screamed again, and there was a finality to that sound. Lancelot was chopping away at its head and was, I'm sure, soon to have a fetching conversational piece to hang above his mantlepiece.

Unfortunately, that would not resolve my injuries, which were now on the other side of the catastrophic.

Consciousness began to drip away, and I concentrated on cycling my Qi. Maybe in the absence of a functioning heart, I could eke out a few more seconds this way. Doing so took up so much of my attention that I nearly missed Merlin's words.

... inside you.

"Sorry, mate. It turns out dying is loud. What did you say?"

Although it is usually understood you can only absorb the essence of a spirit beast once it has died, there's nothing manifestly impossible about doing so as it dies. Especially in the case of Trollkin, where this state can last a significant period of time.

"Fascinating. You should continue to discuss this with my corpse."

You need to absorb its essence. Now.

I switched on my magic eyes and saw a massive fuckton of Wood Qi just waiting to be gobbled down. I tried to breathe it in, but my lungs had long since stopped doing anything so facile as using oxygen.

It's not really breathing, my dear. That is just an easy way to help the young, the inexperienced and the stupid to learn how to absorb from spirit beasts. That's your Qi that the monster has there. Damn well claim it!

There was a note of panic to the Big M's voice - as well their might. This was pretty much game over. I switched off trying to maintain any flow to my extremities, and focused down on my core. As long as that was still alive and kicking, I was still in the game.

I focused on the Wood Qi. It sat right at the centre of the Shriket—about where my own water feature was. I pulled on it, and it was like trying to drag a speedboat up a beach. With dental floss. I simply didn't have the energy, and I certainly didn't have the time.

Come on. It's right there. Pull it into your core!

And then I was hit by a wave of energy. Or, more accurately, a wave of fire.

Fucking stop mooching around, bitch!

I absorbed Drynwyn's blast of Fire Qi and used it to force back the spiralling darkness. Then, twisting Drynwyn's energy into a lasso, I flung it over the Wood Qi and yanked it towards me. To begin with, nothing happened. I demanded more energy from the link Drynwyn was offering and felt the sword struggling to meet the request.

Get it done. I've not got much left. Fucking hell, you're needy.

With my last ounce of strength, I heaved on my lasso of Fire Qi, and then the Shriket's essence moved towards me. As if the release of this energy was its final resistance, the monster collapsed forward.

Lancelot lept clear, holding its head in one hand. I, however, hit the ground with its massive body on top of me, the impact driving the claws even further through my body, the talons cutting deep into the earth.

Oh, yeah. And the sudden movement ripped free my damaged organs, leaving me like a real-life version of Operation.

But that didn't matter. (Well, it did. I was fucked in about the worst way possible and - minor in the grand scheme of things, but it pissed me off - my cultivator armour was history).

But I had the Wood Qi.

The transformation this stuff caused was, in many ways, less dramatic compared to what had happened when I pulled in Voltigern's Dragon's Qi. Nothing exploded in my channels, and I didn't need Merlin to rewire my internal Qi systems to keep me alive.

On the other hand, the changes made to my actual physical body were profound. The piercing talons were forced out of my torso by the rebuilding of my organs. The Wood Qi swept up and down, strengthening muscles and flesh and purging the toxins out of my physical being. I knew Wood Qi was connected to healing - it was where Melehan had drawn from to keep Arthur alive after Drynwyn had toasted him - but the speed and breadth of the alterations were scary.

I'd benefited from being stuffed into Wulfnoð's body in ways I did not wholly understand. However, now, the space in which my soul inhabited was truly becoming my own. The Shriket's Qi reshaped everything about me so that I wasn't just a voice squatting in a body filled with potential for cultivation.

Now, I had a properly bespoke unit.

Opening my eyes, everything was suddenly more distinct - more vivid - than it was before. Zizzie had often spoken about how glorious it felt to wake up without a hangover and experience the dawn song as the first rays of sunlight appeared over the horizon.

For the first time, I kind of could believe it.

However, it was not just the Qi that I was sucking down. At Lancelot's disgusted cry, I looked down at the pool of water I was lying in. But, of course, it wasn't water. It was blood. Gallons upon gallons of blood from me, the Shriket, the animal larder, and Owain's injured warband.

And it was all being absorbed by my body.

I couldn't stand - not yet - but I could feel both the Wood Qi and the blood being overcome by my own Qi and then repurposed. My mana stones - all of them - were instantly refreshed, my link to Drynwyn and my cauldron were reestablished and made more substantial, and my armour was wholly reconstituted.

And as for my core...

"Say it, Big M."

I don't know what you mean.

"Come on, say the words. Don't ruin my big moment."

There was a pause. *Fine.*

"And it needs to be in the accent."

Merlin cleared his throat. *You're a wizard, Harry.*

And my water feature exploded.

CHAPTER 17 – IN WHICH BORS GOES OUT OF HIS GOURD

Tasko paused as he transferred one sum of money from a long column into a second, his quill hovering above the latter figure. He'd make a subtle change here in the usual run of things. Nothing massive. Certainly not noticeable to anyone without a significant grounding in finance. But a little difference here and elsewhere to the figures would equal a tidy profit for him when it was all added up.

He'd done it so often, was so accomplished at this sort of deceit, that he had to stop himself from doing it automatically during his calculations. However, mindful of his various conversations with Sir Bors, he'd never been quite so certain about the imminence of violent retribution.

"He doesn't expect you to be honest; he just wants the job to get done."

The merchant looked up at the speaker. His bodyguard, Pæps, had been with him as long as he could remember. He, too, came from a land far across the oceans and was a squat, strong block of a man with a shining black head above his thickly muscled shoulders. More than once over the years, his tactically cleared throat and shift of position had saved Tasko from a beating. Or worse.

"And just how sure about that are you? You weren't there when he crushed the table."

"Sure enough to offer the advice. Not sure enough to hang around if I'm wrong. I might not have been there for the exemplar, but I've asked around."

"And?"

Pæps wrinkled his nose. "Maybe keep the skimming to the minimum, now I think about it."

"That bad?"

"Worse."

Tasko carefully blotted out the number he had written and replaced it with a replica of the first. "This goes against my code."

"Fits perfectly well with mine. End the day with more money than you started. But end it alive."

"You speak the truth."

Tasko closed the ledger and stood, crossing to look out of the window. Queen Guinevere had insisted that he took a room within Tintagel itself while he planned the Grand Tournament. At the time, he had thought this was a tremendous honour. Now, he couldn't help but feel the pressure of the situation.

Two weeks was no time at all to plan an event of the size required. Fortunately, with money as no object, he'd managed to rope in a couple of minor cultivators he knew from the old lands to help with the transportation challenges. And, with various portals springing up across the country, he was now reasonably confident the bare bones of the plan were in motion. All things being equal, across the next few days, some flesh would start appearing and - please, by all the gods that kept him safe - this time next week, everything would be in place.

At least from the administration side.

Tasko looked down on the training yard, where Bors was trying to finish his fight categories. Groups of spearmen stood around him awkwardly as he divided them into different groups. Surprisingly, it was not difficult to eavesdrop on his frustrations.

***

"So, we've got the Heavy Spearmen category. The Lights. The Mediums with the potential to be Heavies. And the Lights who might be better as Archers." Bors ushered a few men around into different sections with a light tap. "Stop your blubbering; I barely broke anything. Next, we've got the Pugilists, the Royal Rumble, the Armed Melee and the Hunger Games..."

Over the next twenty minutes, Bors crafted a series of bouts, rounds, and round robins so intricate and complex that anyone still alive at the end of them was surely destined to be one of the greatest warriors of the age.

It was also fated to be one of the bloodiest tournaments in history.

He was pinning the ranking points per limb chopped off to the barracks wall when the Queen arrived to conduct a much-needed intervention.

She knocked gently on the open door.

Bors's face locked into a snarl as he turned. "I told you, no one was to—" the anger vanished as he saw who was waiting. "I am sorry, my lady. I did not know it was you."

Guinevere had taken a step back at the intensity of the man's rage, hands going to a sword her ridiculously elaborate dress did not allow her to wear any longer. Trying to slow her rapidly beating heart, she fixed a smile on her face. "Sir Bors, how goes the planning?"

Bors' own smile was a rictus grin. "Not bad, Your Majesty. Not bad. I was worried I was leaving some bases uncovered, but I think I'm getting there now. I'd made the mistake of treating the quarterstaff and the pike as the same weight class, but I've subdivided them now and I think I'm getting somewhere." He pointed towards the back wall of the barracks that, at first sight, Guinevere had taken to have been painted black. With a start, she realised it was covered with hundreds upon hundreds of tightly written lines of text.

"Are... are those the rounds for the tournament?"

Guinevere walked towards the writing, with Bors following close behind, anxious as a man at the birth of his first child. "Yes, my lady. I think I've managed to account for every eventuality and possibility. When all this is finished, and the dust settles, whoever is still standing will truly deserve to serve alongside your husband's Marchegyon."

"Right." Guinevere tried to follow the spiralling lines of intersecting text. "And how long do you envisage this process taking?"

A manic glint crept into Bors' eyes. When his wife had begged a moment with the Queen, she'd said that the big man had not been home for two days. "That's the beauty of it. In less than a month of constant fighting - providing we have enough of Morgan's healing elixirs, of course - we should be in a position to move into the second round."

"The second round?"

Bors turned and pointed to the opposite wall. Guinevere spun to look at the way she had come in to see an equally complex plan sketched on that surface too. "Fuck me," she whispered under her breath. "Sir Bors, why don't we take a breath of fresh air?"

***

It had taken every persuasive skill the Queen possessed to drag Bors out of the barracks and up to what she was beginning to think of as her 'office' on the battlements. Up high, and with the wind running through her hair, she felt like she could think much clearer. She hoped the bracing air would have the same impact on her big companion.

How should she play it? Softly softly? Try to slowly bring him to his senses. Or...

"What the fuck's going on with you? You have the whole castle convinced you've gone batshit crazy. You've put a quarter of our remaining spears in the infirmary during 'practice 'bouts' and, what is worse, you're making your wife worry. Explain. Now."

Guinevere watched Bors sag under the impact of her words, as if he were a bag of grain emptying from myriad cuts. He was silent long enough for her to open her mouth to speak again, and then she realised he had murmured a quiet reply.

"I don't want to let him down."

A thousand answers ran through her head, none of which seemed appropriate for the moment. Guinevere was an astonishing accomplished woman in most respects, but she'd never quite developed the skill of offering a soft shoulder to cry on. She was not too proud to admit his had played, at least a small part, in her marital difficulties. Thus, she went for a neutral: "How do you mean?"

"I was in charge when they all died. The Marchegyon. He'd trusted me to lead when he was hurt and I failed him."

From what Guinevere had heard of the battle with Cedric's West Saxons, the only reason anyone - including Arthur - had made it out of that clusterfuck was due to the extraordinary bravery and balls to the wall belligerence of Bors. He'd almost single-handedly kept the defeated forces together and led them back home.

But Bors was speaking again before she could set him right.

"And now I have a chance to redeem myself and I need to get it right. I can't trust myself to be at his side anymore, but I can make sure he has the very best men to protect him. I'm not letting anyone but a certified monster have his back."

Guinevere thought back to the infinitely complex arrangements of bouts she had seen on the walls of the barracks. "And if no one reaches the necessary standard..." she asked, gently.

Bors went to answer, then paused. His eyes focused on the path from which he hoped, any moment now, to see his friend return. "Then I'll just have to work harder until they do."

73

The Queen put some iron into her voice. "This is a lovely self-indulgent little fantasy you are participating in here. It would be wonderful if I had the luxury of humouring you. Really, it would. However, you have a job to do. Your King asked you to identify and train up an elite force, not play out some sort of sad sack redemption story arc. There will be three brackets. Sword, Spear and Bow. We will pair up competitors and the losers of each bout will be knocked out until ten are left of each. These will be the new Marchegyon. And it will be done in three days."

Bors spluttered. "But what about..."

"Am I understood?"

For a heartbeat, she thought he was going to argue. Bors' face went dark red, and his hands clenched and unclenched. Guinevere was not exactly afraid, but she was glad she had positioned herself so that, should he attack, the sun would be in his eyes, and she would be in a position to release a kick to send him over the top of the low wall and off the roof.

Then, Bors took a deep breath and all the angst vanished. He rolled his shoulders and the pained expression that clouded his face cleared. "I've been a bit of a twat, haven't I?"

"Nothing wrong with taking a command to heart, but if I hear you cause Mrs. Bors another night of no sleep, I will be kicking your arse myself."

"Deal."

Then, he suddenly spun around, plunging his hands into the shadow of the doorway. His fists reappeared, dragging a very startled, non-descript looking man into the light. "Fucking eavesdropping wanker!"

"My lady!" Blæk shrieked as Bors carried him to the tower's edge and prepared to drop him into the open sky.

"A moment, Sir Bors." Blæk dangled precariously over the battlements, Bors holding him by the throat. Guinevere frowned at the spy. "I asked to be left alone. I hoped you would honour my wishes! Explain yourself."

Blæk struggled momentarily and then, realised the hopelessness of his position, relented. In his dry, monotone voice he forced out, "I have taken a few days to confirm information received and to cross reference reports. However, I am now able to deliver news around the untimely death of Queen Igraine. And, what is more, I believe I know who killed her."

CHAPTER 18 – IN WHICH SECRETS ARE REVEALED

They retired to a more private part of the castle.

"No one will stumble across us here," Blæk murmured, slipping a key into the lock of a dark wooden door. Bors blinked at it. He was absolutely sure he had never seen this entrance before in his life. And he had grown up in and around this castle.

"My lady, I don't think you should... "

"If not her, then no one, Sir Bors. You are only here because she suffers you."

Bors reached out to bang the odd little fellow against the wall - nothing fatal, just a little light concussion to remind him of his manners - but he was astonished to see his hand pass straight through. Or, rather, his target wasn't there anymore but stood a few feet further back.

"Bors! Stop it. I trust Blæk."

Seemingly emboldened by the Queen's words, Blæk stepped back to the door, within range of Bors should he wish to repeat the maneuver and pushed open the unlocked door.

"Please. The sooner I can share my news, the quicker we can begin to plan... retribution."

They followed him into a small room. It was sparsely decorated, with just a few wooden chairs around a table. The edges of the space were clouded in darkness, and it seemed to Bors that if he gazed too long into that void, the blackness looked back at him. It was all very disorienting.

Blæk sat and indicated to Guinevere and Bors to do the same. They did not take him up on his offer.

"Queen Igraine. Speak." Guinevere's voice was level, hiding the emotions that roiled through her mind. There was a pause as the spy ordered his thoughts. When he spoke, his tone was utterly devoid of emotion, as if he was reporting the weather. "It is settled understanding that, following the feast at which King Arthur announced the quest for Caeldfwch, Queen Igraine retired to her room, at which time, either by accident or by design, she fell through her tower window. There has been speculation that the Queen was either in her cups or, perhaps, that the deep trauma following the death of her husband had damaged the balance of her mind."

He stopped speaking and looked at Guinevere expectantly. She was unsure how she was supposed to reply. Bors saved her the trouble. "And what of it? This is hardly news."

Blæk did his odd head cock, so reminiscent of an inquisitive bird, and began again. "Indeed. However, I recently received information that cast doubt on that story and set out to prove or disprove its veracity."

"What information? You mean one of the Grey thinks differently?"

"All in good time, my lady. Firstly, I sought to interrogate the initial assumptions. That the late Queen was inebriated and thus stumbled through her window. The serving girl who waited on the royal table that evening is unusually acute about such things and has a clear memory of how much each member of the royal party ate and drank that evening. Incidentally, Sir Bors, for a man of your age and temper, I feel I should recommend you be a touch more circumspect about your consumption of red meat and mead. It would go ill for the realm should you suffer the fate of the last three patriarchs of your household. Vegetables are food, too."

"The Queen, Blæk," Guinevere said, avoiding eye contact with a suddenly very self-conscious Bors who was trying to suck in his considerable gut.

"Of course, my lady. The Queen drank her usual water all night. Not a drop of alcohol passed her lips. So much for that aspect of the theory. But, of course, you do not need to be drunk in order to give into despair."

"And you have looked into that?"

"Indeed. I have it on good authority - and have interrogated numerous incidental sources - which are clear that although manifestly in mourning, the Queen was wholly engaged in plotting out the realm's future. Her detailed correspondence makes it clear that she saw herself as having a role to play in the new world order that you and King Arthur were seeking to establish. Just the very morning of her death, she issued a series of instructions for information to be gathered for a number of long-term goals. I submit that these are not the actions of a woman who feels she has nothing left for which to live."

"So, she wasn't pissed, and she wasn't suicidal." Bors was finding the atmosphere in the room oppressive and was anxious to get out into the fresh air. He was also smarting from being called fat and wanted to go and hit some recruits until he felt better. "But that doesn't mean she didn't just fall. Look, I liked Igraine, but when you hear hoofbeats, it's usually going to be horses, not men banging the shells of giant nuts together."

"To be sure, Sir Bors. And that is the final possibility that I have needed to explore most thoroughly. Do you know the last time anyone - let alone a member of the royal family - fell, and by this, I mean without question 'fell' to their death within Tintagel?"

"It must happen all the time. I mean, no, not *all* the time, but I'm sure it is not that unusual. There was a Saxon captive a few years back. Hansa, I think he was called?" Bors suggested.

"Jumped. Three eyewitnesses." Blæk's answer was instant.

"Lady Morraine?" Bors met Guinevere's confused expression. "Before your time. Long legs, but no tits."

"Helped on her way. She was becoming too friendly with the Queen. Igraine was most displeased."

"Fuck's sake, just tell us what you're hinting at." Bors was sweating now, and it wasn't just the rising heat.

"There have been thirteen defenestrations in the last one hundred years. My records go back further, but I thought this period was instructive. Three confirmed suicides. Two drunken mishaps. And eight... let us call them 'happy accidents'. There is not a single example of a sober, sane person falling to their death without aid."

"So the odds are against it. That does not make it impossible." Guinevere was not sure where Blæk was going with this.

"Indeed, but we must all agree it makes it an unlikely scenario. And now to the true meat of my report. There is incontrovertible evidence that a hooded figure entered Igraine's chamber around the time of her fall. I have been able to account for the whereabouts of every member of our own staff and the vast majority of the visiting retinues. I am confident that whoever entered the Queen's room did so for the purpose of killing her. However, I cannot narrow down the suspect list any further than that."

Bors was about to explode. "Who are the options? I'll get it from them!"

Blæk shook his head sadly. "I wish it were as simple as that, Sir Bors. The four suspects whose whereabouts I am unable to confirm are the Kings of Gwent, Powys, Deheubarth and Gwynedd. They were reportedly meeting together to discuss their reaction to Arthur's announcement. However, none of the Grey can find out where, for how long, or when they separated. So, to conclude. Queen Igraine was undoubtedly murdered - why I am as yet unaware - and it was by one of the four kings now on a quest with Queen Guinevere's husband,"

***

Beric of Powys stared into the fire.

He was unaccustomed to life on the road - it had been many years since he had needed to lead his own warband - and was finding it as unappealing as he remembered. The food was execrable, the company worse, and despite his vociferous argument, no whores had been allowed with his party. If he were not wholly committed to keeping Caeldfwch out of that young twat's hand, he would have refused to step outside of his lands.

"My lord wants to speak to you."

Beric's eyes snapped up into the face of one of Mark's litter bearers. She was young, comely and bore all the hallmarks of having just a few more months of... service ahead of her. As eager for action as Beric was, even he wouldn't dare dip it in that particular well. Who knew what he would catch?

Biting back his distaste at being summoned by a peer, Beric stood and followed the girl away from his own men and into Mark's enclosure. It irritated him how better prepared for this quest the other kings appeared to be. Mark, in particular, seemed to be especially well-provisioned for taking part in an extended road trip. Beric ran his hand down the canvas of Mark's pavilion - expertly put up by a team of spears the moment they made camp - and shook his head ruefully. Those of Powys had forgotten what it meant to be in the field during the years of tribute flowing into Saxon purses to keep the peace.

Leaving the girl at the entrance, he stepped inside and was surprised to see Corys sprawled on a chair next to Mark. This gave Beric a moment's pause.

"Mark. Corys," he nodded uneasily. He was all for shadowy alliances as long as he was included.

"Beric, thank you for coming." Mark's grossly fat face split into a smile. "And then there were three."

"You're sure of Owain?" Beric said, taking a seat opposite them.

"He's either dead or nearly so. The fat fuck always did like his scouting more than was good for him."

If either Corys or Beric felt it was somewhat hypocritical for Mark to comment on the weight of anyone else - at least Owain could walk under his own steam - now did not seem like the time to share.

"I'm less worried about Owain than I am about Arthur and his pet wizard," Corys added.

"It's the barbarian I am most concerned about." Beric could not lose the image of his men being humbled by that big man.

"It would be fair to say our lives would be an awful lot easier without any of Uther's court in our lives. And that goes double if the welp gets his hands on Caeldfwch." Mark tried to sit up straighter, and both Corys and Beric worked hard to keep their faces still during *that* little performance. "I will not accept Arthur as the Pendragon. So I swear."

The other two mouthed the same oath - a mirror of the one they had given a few days earlier in Tintagel. At the time, it had been a booze-soaked boast amongst old acquaintances. But now, in the fae realm and beset at all sides by challenges, the words were taking on a new weight.

"I worry," Corys began, "if we can prevent that from occurring, should Arthur claim the sword?"

"Well," answered Mark, "that would seem to be the crux of the matter." He waved to one of his servants, who slipped outside the tent. "I hope no one would think me presumptuous, but when I heard that dear old Owain had gone missing, I reached out to a few in my party with special skills."

Three hooded men entered the tent and stood before the kings.

Beric did not know why, but something about each of them both chilled and thrilled him at the same time. "What are you suggesting, my lord?"

Mark smiled again, and Corys joined him in that. "I'm not suggesting anything. I am being very clear about what is going to happen. Arthur will fall. His bitch of a wizard will die. And we will put down that mad dog of a bodyguard. After that, we can discuss who we choose as Pendragon amongst ourselves." Mark's grin suggested he had a pretty good idea of how that conversation would go. "But that can come after we bury the upstart."

Beric found himself nodding along. Perhaps expeditions in the woods were not so terrible after all.

CHAPTER 19 – IN WHICH IT TURNS OUT LEVELLING UP IS A VIBE

I'm not wholly sure I have the right vocabulary to explain the differences that came over me when I changed from being a Ron to a Harry.

In many ways, and from a certain point of view, there were very few changes indeed. I still had the same channels, my more tightly concentrated Qi flowed around them in the same pattern, and there were still a whole host of things that I could do that would make the average human's eyes pop out. I did not grow six feet tall, I did not develop the ability to fly, nor did my intelligence skyrocket. Neither did a shaggy, friendly giant turn up and give me my own wand.

So, yeah. All hail the new boss. Same as the old boss.

On the other hand, though, the change was so deep and so profound that it was like trying to compare Roger Moore to Timothy Dalton. Sure, they were both *technically* James Bond, but then so was Woody Allen and that way, insanity lies.

In every way - and I mean in *every* way - I was... just better.

Right at the end of The Matrix - and such is the colossal deluge of shite that is all of its sequels that I will fight to death for it to be known as the *only* Matrix movie - Neo stands in front of various Agents and is just **the man**. It's where he sees everything in code, and you know the smackdown is coming.

That's how I felt at this moment.

My dear, what is really important right now is that you recognise you are experiencing a post-threshold high. You will feel like there is nothing you cannot accomplish and that all of humanity is beneath you.

"Dude, I know Kung Fu," was about the most lucid thing I could say.

Ah, you see! That's exactly what I mean. You most certainly do not 'know' Kung Fu. You are, however, entirely secure in your confidence that - should you wish to attempt to - you could know everything about Kung Fu. And, to a certain extent, my dear, you are right to think so.

I looked around at the Shriket's pocket dimension. With its death and my claiming all its Qi, the world was already collapsing down into itself. I couldn't see Owain, but those of his entourage who still lived had been freed from their spikes.

"Mate, get those out to who needs them," I said, shooting a couple of handfuls of Rare quality Elixirs of Wellness to Lancelot. I paused and added in an Epic one. "That's for Owain."

"Sure," Lancelot was looking at me with concern in his eyes. "Okay, are you? Maggot food for sure, I thought."

I put my hand on my chest where the giant claws had pierced straight through me. There was no hint of soreness. My rebuilt armour had taken on a deep red colour where it covered the wound.

As well as all that Qi, you have also assimilated a considerable volume of blood, my dear. Alongside more mundane liquids, I note the presence of some reasonably exotic creatures in that... larder. I would expect that to awaken any number of unusual abilities. I am actually quite jealous!

As I turned my head, I became aware of little spindly lines that reached out from me to the other people, the ground, the trees... basically, to everything. "What's with all the strings, Big M?"

Ah, excellent. I was hoping that would fire for you reasonably quickly. As a... as a Harry, you are now more profoundly connected to the world than you were previously. What you can see are the threads of fate that bind you to all things.

"There's a thread of fate that binds me to that snail, is there?"

Indubitably. Should you decide to crush it, you will gather up not just its Qi, but you will now have access to all the impact it would have had on the world. All the lettuce it would chew, all the slime trails, all of it will become part of your story.

"That's epically sinister, mate. You're saying if I were to kill everyone in this clearing, I would gain not just their Qi but also suck down the power from all their future actions?"

Absolutely. Tasty stuff. You should, however, avoid saying such things out loud. It tends to make allies a touch nervous.

Everyone was staring at me with abject terror on their faces.

I imagined how I must look to them—a bloody, resurrected wizard discussing murdering them with her imaginary friend. I wish I could say this was the worst first impression I'd made on new people.

"Don't mind me. You keep drinking the very rare and expensive health potions I'm dolling out like candy."

The spearmen returned to work helping the rest of Owain's men off their trees and calming the surviving horses.

A word from the wise, my dear. Try not to get a name for yourself as a Lich—the decades I spent trying to live that down.

"Noted."

To avoid any further misunderstandings, I dropped into my Artist's Studio, which I could tell had received a subtle yet significant upgrade. I was used to encountering a blank page when I first manifested here, which I could flick to check on the Vitruvian version of me - with all my channels on display - and then a second page for my inventory, with the new one that had recently appeared for all my alchemy.

Now, however, the first thing I entered was a genuine Artist's Studio, like the one I always assumed I'd one day own. Or, more realistically, the one I'd break into when its owners were abroad and act like it was actually mine.

It was perfect in every detail to the place of my dreams. From the massive French windows looking out over the sea to the rows of easels waiting to be selected and used. Blank canvases were stacked against the one wall, with a host of unfinished and 'in progress' images mixed in with them. They were all by me, I was shocked to see.

On the opposite corner was a single sofa bed with a duvet carelessly thrown over it. It was the comfiest-looking thing I'd ever seen in either of my lives. Everywhere I looked was example after example of something I'd ever owned - or, more truthfully, coveted - arranged to create my perfect living space.

"What is this place?" I whispered.

The answer is both complexly psychological and reasonably straightforward. This is your—in the crudest of vernacular—'happy place'. Other religions may speak of Heaven, Nirvana, or the like, but this is your own personal version. What does it look like?

"Can't you see it?"

I'm afraid not, my dear. I am seeing my own, much missed, version. It is my dearest hope that... that when I died, my spirit - the rest of it anyway - simply slipped into a permanent residence here. I wonder if I even know I am dead?

We spent a few moments in silence before Merlin spoke again.

All the functions you are used to accessing will be available here. I cannot be too specific, but you should find it to be fairly intuitive.

"Like Apple products?"

Don't ruin the moment, my dear.

It took me no time to realise that the exposed copper piping running around the room was not just a charmingly rustic heating system but also accurately reflected the current state of my channels. Don't ask me how I knew that; I just did.

Likewise, on the shelf amongst a fairly definitive version of the collected works of Terry Pratchett, Neil Gaiman, and Tom Holt was a giant, leatherbound book called 'Inventory', another called 'Alchemy' and a new one called 'Techniques'.

I found I didn't need to do anything so mundane as actually go across the floor to collect one; just thinking about it was enough for it to be in my hand and open. The 'Techniques' book was a little short on info at the moment...

Not for much longer, my dear. My techniques were so numerous that I had to open a separate wing of my Mental Palace just to store the tomes.

"Mental Palace, Big M?" I smirked, looking around this perfect single room. "I doubt I'll ever need anything bigger than this."

You say that now, my dear. But Harry is the first proper step on a long journey. Should you progress as I would anticipate, you will be surprised at the changes you will need to make to your perspective.

That suddenly brought my mood down. "As soon as we stabilise the timeline, mate, I'm out of here. Zizzie and I have a lot of making up to do."

As you say, my dear. As you say.

There was a pause, and then he spoke in a more business-like voice. *There are a few last things that I should point out. Firstly, time dilation here is pretty spectacular. It's not quite 'drop-in, spend a year working out how to solve a problem, and then pop out, and it is the same moment,' but it is not too far away from that. You'll be able to get out of most problems if you keep your wits about you. Secondly, cycling here is much more efficient than doing it anywhere else. I'd recommend spending at least a few hours a day here - which will, in reality, be more like mere seconds.*

"That seems a bit cheat-codey, Big M."

Cultivation, my dear. The strong get stronger.

"Cool beans. And what about a visitor's policy? I'm assuming this is strictly a 'no boys allowed' kind of thing?"

My dear, if you can work out how to get someone here and make them stay sane, you're welcome to it. I wouldn't recommend it, though. It's taken you a considerable amount of work to get this far. Think how alien it would be to the unwary.

I popped out into real-time.

No one was paying much attention to me anymore. Or at least they were all so terrified I was going to kill them that they didn't want to make eye contact and volunteer to be first. So, I bent down and picked up Drynwyn.

You fucking made it through then?

"Just about. Thanks to you, I think."

I then did something I never thought I would ever do in my life. I hugged a sword.

CHAPTER 20 – IN WHICH I AM A MOTIVATIONAL SPEAKER

It took another ten minutes for the Shriket's pocket dimension to close. Merlin recommended not being inside when it did so, and judging by the fact that all the dead bodies vanished with a wet pop as it closed, he was bang on the money with that assessment.

But just by escaping, we weren't home and hosed.

Even with sinking down all my elixirs, Owain and his men were in a bad way. Although all their physical injuries had been repaired, there's something about being hung from a tree by spikes, slowly bled out and having to watch your comrades be eaten by a giant, monstrous perversion of a bird which leaves something of a mark.

I mean, I don't know that for certain. I'm just extrapolating from the available evidence.

I'd not yet had a chance to speak to the King since the rescue—his guards were more than usually clingy—so I took the opportunity of the journey back to our main camp to get next to him. I received a few glares in response, but a couple of 'you suddenly want to jump off your horse' suggestions demonstrated who was top dog.

Yes. Yes. Let the hate flow through you. There was a pause. *Sorry, my dear. I do not know what made me say that.*

"I'm happy that this isn't me slipping to the dark side, but stay on it, dude."

I was pleased to see that Owain was well enough to be riding his horse, but there were a couple of men in close proximity on either side, which suggested he was a bit wobblier than he looked. He looked at me for a few moments as if struggling to place me. Then his eyes swam into focus, and he grinned at me, some of his old humour returning. "Wizard, I owe you a great debt."

"Not at all, my lord. I'm just glad we arrived in time."

I walked next to him for a time, trying to hit him with a few probing strings of Qi. However, from everything I could tell, there wasn't really very much left wrong with him. I knew that my Elixirs of Wellness did more than just improve physical health, so if he still looked like shit with an Epic one on board, I was worried about how he was going to feel when the buzz ran out.

"I've lost half of my men," he whispered, his voice haunted.

"True. But there's still half of them needing you. I think they could do with seeing you're okay." I couldn't miss the nervous glances towards us. "They're probably thinking less about you letting them down and more about how they failed to protect their king from a monster. A bit of the old 'hail fellow, well met' would probably go down a treat."

"I'm not sure I have it in me right now."

I took a beat to wonder when I became the Agony Aunt for Dark Age monarchs who were having a crisis of confidence. I mean, you'd expect dudes at the beginning of history to have a bit more about them than crumbling into puddles at the first sign of trouble.

I dived once again into the well-plumbed depths of my empathy. "My lord, I think this is probably one of those occasions where you need to fake it until you make it. Did you lose some men in a horribly brutal way? Sure. Does that mean that it's time for you to pack up and go home? Well, only you can decide that. But, I'll be honest, there ain't many sagas written about kings who come, see, take a pasting and go home."

"Is this supposed to be a pep talk?" I was pleased to see a smile creasing the corner of Sad Santa's mouth.

"Dunno, mate. But if you still fancy taking part in a quest for Caeldfwch, you probably need to give the whole 'king' thing a little more beans."

Owain straightened a little in his saddle at that and forced out a simulacrum of a belly laugh. "Thank you, wizard. You are quite right. Where's Burford? Burford!"

A tall, thin man with an extraordinarily long beard and bald head jogged up beside the king. He was in dark leathers, with a bow in his hand and a quiver on his back. `He wasn't quite the definition of a poacher, but that was only because the dictionary hadn't been written yet.

"Your Majesty?"

"Good to see you made it through the staking and eating thing!"

"Not sure there's enough of me to be worth the eating, my lord." Interestingly, the man had a soft burr to his voice that I associated with cider and a combine harvester.

"Whereas I was clearly being saved for a special occasion," Owain slapped his belly and laughed again. It was a pretty decent facsimile of bonhomie, but I could see the lines of tension around his eyes. I doubted Burford was fooled, either. "I find myself somewhat peckish after our executions. How about you scare us up a few deer? Would be good to return to camp with more than just a story of woe and our tails between our legs."

The poacher nodded and peeled a few likely lads away from the main party to vanish into the woods.

"How was that?" Owain asked me softly.

"Spot on, my lord." I sent a few subtle suggestions of support his way. "You're the man," and such like.

"That pulling me more into the light side, Big M?"

Getting there, Padawan. Getting there.

***

We were carrying two deer and a giant wild boar when we reunited with the rest of the quest group. I was reassured that we were challenged by a bunch of sentries well before we were in sight of the camp itself. Regardless of the personal enmity between the parties, they could put self-preservation above petty grievances.

I left Owain and his men to reestablish their camp and made my way to find Arthur.

"Where the fuck have you two been?" I'd had warmer welcomes.

"We monster hunted," said Lancelot, throwing the decapitated head of the Shriket at Arthur's feet. "Was good. Saved Owain. She died."

Arthur turned to me. "You died!"

"Only a little. And it didn't stick. I might have tried to bite off more than I could chew. But it worked out okay in the end."

I quickly talked him through our little run-in with the monster. When I got to the bit about absorbing a pocket dimension full of blood, I saw something in his face change. "What did I say?"

"Sounds to me like you might have taken the Step of Blood, Morgan."

I paused, then nodded. "I think we can safely say that if that wasn't the Step of Blood, I will have to ensure I take a change of clothes when we finally meet it. What do you think, Big M?"

Arthur probably hit the nail on the head, my dear. I would be surprised if we have not completed the first of the Steps on the journey towards Caeldfwch. We, though, will only really know when - and if - we identify the Step of Faith.

"Any thoughts about that?"

I sat down heavily next to the king, unstrapping Drynwyn and respectfully passing it to the Quartermaster. The tattooed man went white as he received it and then ran to take it to our armourer sharpish.

Arthur glanced sourly over my shoulder to the tent where Mark had based himself. "The three of them have been conspiring in there all night. I'd say me being willing to have any of them anywhere near me was probably a major fucking Step of Faith."

Lancelot bristled at that. "They'll not harm you. Promise, I do."

"They significantly outnumber us if they band together. I doubt there would be much we could do - even with you two in full flow - if they decide betrayal is the only way forward."

I wasn't so sure about that.

Sure, there was a time - and not that long ago - that I would have agreed with Arthur. Lancelot was a nightmare with a sword in his hand, and I had no little game, but there were a hundred and fifty men under the command of those three kings - not counting Owain, who I kind of hoped would be at worst neutral in any confrontation.

That was a lot of arrows, spears and javelins that did not need to get lucky too often to take out the king. I was pretty sure I could bring anyone back from anything short of actual death. But three-on-one odds weren't ideal. Even then, Arthur being alive at the end of this quest was not the whole ball game. He needed these guys on his side too.

That gave me a good idea.

"My lord, can I grab your cloak for a moment?"

Arthur gave me a puzzled expression, unhooked it, and passed it over.

What are you thinking, my dear?

I held the cloak between my hands, examining it. It was soft, some sort of luxury material - who am I, a fucking weaver? -and was emblazoned with the symbol of the Pendragon—a giant, red dragon on a white background.

There was a faint, very faint line of Qi connecting me to the cloak, so I pushed some energy down it, but it disappeared into the air before connecting.

I pushed a bit harder, and the same thing happened again. It felt like there was some sort of block in the way.

It's not typical for objects not crafted with the intention of holding Qi to be retrofitted, as it were. It could well be that such a working is a touch beyond you at the moment.

You see, I've never really responded all that well to being told 'no'.

I gathered a huge dollop of Qi and shoved it along the thread of fate, not taking 'no' for an answer. Even with me giving it my full attention, I didn't immediately notice any difference.

But then...

There was a loud tearing noise, and I was through. My Qi flooded into the cloak, which promptly caught fire.

As it burned, I tried to make the idea in my head take shape. I took the dragon and gave it the firmest suggestions I could. Again, initially, I had no joy, but I had Qi to burn, and this would happen. With all the recklessness of a teenage boy beating one out to a poorly pixelated magazine he found in the woods, I forced the dragon to accept the suggestion.

With a nicely dramatic chorus of angelic voices, the cloak stopped burning, and light shot upwards. Morgan had done good.

I crossed to Arthur and fastened it around his shoulders. His eyes regarded me with a damn sight more respect than had been the way he'd traditionally looked at me. "What did you do?" he asked, with just enough reverential awe in his voice to make me feel pretty fine.

"Let's just say that if you think you need eyes in the back of your head to stay safe, I've been more than happy to oblige."

From behind him came a low growl and a "What the fuck are you looking at!" and a small ball of flame incinerated an unfortunate fly that wandered too close.

CHAPTER 21 – IN WHICH I BRING THE CONCEPT OF M.A.D TO THE DARK AGES

The rest of the evening passed without incident, and when the kings came together in the light of the morning, there were quite clearly some alliances that had been formed.

Beric, Mark and Corys had decided that the only way forward was to pool resources and be massive pains in the arse. On the plus side, Owain, since I had - you know - saved not only his life but the lives of half of his men, was Team Arthur. However, as he was down to twenty spears and a handful of camp followers, if push came to shove, the chances were this would get bloody.

With that in mind, I'd been to see Arthur first thing with a plan. I thought we were on the right track with his new battle cloak, but I wanted to push things a bit further. "In my own time," I explained, "there were these two... kingdoms who hated each other. It constantly felt that they would go to war, and the outcome of that for everyone else would have been catastrophic. So, to ensure the prospect of that fight was so awful, neither would contemplate starting it, they both tooled themselves up with the most insane weapons they could think of. It was called Mutually Assured Destruction - M.A.D for short. Basically, fuck with us, and we will fuck you up in return.

Arthur looked at me for a moment. "That is the most insane policy I have ever heard. You're telling me in over a thousand years the best diplomatic solution anyone could come up with was 'Don't try it, pal'?"

I shrugged. "At the time of my... death, it had worked for about fifty years."

Lancelot had joined us, squatting down to perform a complicated exercise routine. "On board with this plan, I can get."

"How do you see it working?"

I could tell Arthur was still not convinced, which was disappointing. "Look, I'm not saying we do anything overly aggressive. There's a line between 'don't fuck with us' and 'fucking want some?!' The trick is to be belligerent without inviting confrontation.

A servant approached with mugs of hot water, the movement causing Arthur's cloak to roar to life—literally. Then, a red claw extended to smash the tray to the floor, followed by a fireball burning it to cinders.

The king closed his eyes for a moment. "Somehow, I don't think we'll be lacking in belligerence."

***

"It therefore seems, my esteemed lord, that it would be sensible for us to, cautiously, proceed into the lands of the Fae. If the prophecy is correct, we have already taken the Step of Blood and are now seeking the Step of Faith. I can think of few more demonstrations of 'faith' than to continue on our current path without a clear direction... My lady wizard. Do you think you can stop that for a moment?"

"Oh, sorry. Is it bothering you?"

Lots and lots of scared, baffled eyes continued to regard me with horror.

"Too much, Big M?"

I pulled my Qi back inside and let the swirling vortex I'd conjured above our heads collapse down. I'd loaded it up with a touch of my aura and just let it flicker out little suggestions of "be afraid, be very afraid" to the rest of the audience. The little sparks of lightning it kept emitting, along with the rolling thunder, were creating a big mood.

I think if the idea was to cement in the minds of these kings that you are a terrifying presence, then job done, my dear. I am not sure, however, you have done a lot to convince them to trust you.

"Counterpoint. Do they trust that I will fuck them up?"

I realised everyone was still holding their breath.

They certainly understand the threat, my dear.

Arthur's voice shook everyone out of the silent terror. "I must say I agree with you, King Corys. It seems that the best way for us to take the Step of Faith will be to continue onwards and trust the alliance we have forged."

There were mutters of assent.

Then Owain piped up. "Do we have any sense of what manner of beasts we may be encountering? I understand you all were beset by Wyverns while I had... my own challenges. Can we anticipate similar monsters of power?"

Merlin had prepped me on how to answer this question. "We are in the borderlands of the Fae Kingdom, my lord. On the very edge of the territory, we can expect to come across all manner of renegade and exiled creatures. Scavengers, mostly, like the Wyverns, with the possibility of more powerful foes - such as you were unfortunate to confront."

"And as we go further in?" Mark's voice slimed its way into the discussion.

As he appeared constitutionally unable to address me with any sort of honorific, I just looked at him. We had quite the eye-fucking going on before Corys came to his rescue.

"My lady, do you have any thoughts about what awaits us as we leave the borderlands?"

I once again tried to size up the King of Deheubarth. I couldn't help but feel he was being the acceptable face of fuckwittery. He'd never been anything other than polite to me - a bit flirty even - but he was hanging around with two very unpleasant men. Dogs and fleas and all that.

But he'd been courteous, so I was happy to answer him. "Our chief concern will be stumbling across any of the Fae themselves. I doubt our expedition will be viewed as anything less than a hostile endeavour. We may find ourselves in conflict with them before we can explain our quest. This would be less than ideal. Beyond that, I would anticipate we will likely encounter goblins and orcs, especially around the edges of the territory. We may be able to earn ourselves some credit with the Fae if we exterminate any and all of these we come across."

"It would seem to me," Beric's expression was neutral, "we may be wise to stumble across some goblins and orcs, then, as a show of our good faith."

As he said that word, a little choral music sprung into life.

"Well, that sounds like we may have stumbled across our second Step, my lords,"

"Let's fuck up some Goblins," Lancelot added helpfully.

***

So, Goblins are precisely what you would expect.

If you are expecting something small, green and smelling of shit and blood. Oh, and there are fucking millions of them.

We'd decided to keep the integrity of the camp for the time being, with each of the kings organising a little scouting just to get the lay of the land. I'd accompanied Owain's troops while Lancelot had stuck with Arthur's. It seemed a touch like overkill for the two of us to stick together, and - privately - we were worried about any further reduction in the numbers of the men of Gwent. It was great to have his support, but that only mattered if he had the spears to back up the words.

We were being led by his poacher-in-chief, Burford, who - during the course of the careful hours we explored - I was coming to like. The search was so methodical I couldn't help but question how they'd fallen victim to the Shriket.

"The king thought we could take it," was the only response I could get from him on that topic. If he had any words of criticism to add there, he kept them to himself. Having gotten used to the non-stop torrent of moaning from my own side, I quite liked his taciturnity.

"Something - lots of somethings - up ahead." Burford suddenly appeared next to me. I hadn't heard him approach at all.

I followed the direction he was pointing and pushed out with my Qi, trying to sense what might be hidden in the woods. That's when the smell first hit me.

"Fuck me, there are a lot of them!"

We had pulled back to the main camp, and I tried to think of a sensible approach to deal with what I'd seen. If any of the other scouting parties had encountered a smaller group, then it seemed sensible to focus there. Annihilating an isolated warband or a largely empty village would be a much easier show of 'faith' towards the Fae than tangling with what seemed to be an entire clan on the move.

But then...

"Indeed, my dear. A show of faith needs to have significant weight behind it. If we are looking to earn respect from the Fae, then we are likely to need to do something that will cost us."

"Dude, that was a lot of green-skinned short-arses with axes and spears!"

And we are asking for a lot of faith.

***

And that's how, the following evening, I found myself standing amongst a shield wall, pushing out every suggestion of calm and confidence I could spare the Qi for.

We'd spent a long time trying to devise a better plan than 'charge in line—hold position—slaughter,' but, as Owain finally noted, "the classics are always the best."

The biggest worry was that the sheer numbers we'd spotted would flank us long before we killed enough to make a difference. That was when Beric and Mark

89

'volunteered' to act as flying sentries on the flanks with their heavy horse to keep any attempts to surround us unsuccessful.

"We all know that they're totally going to let us die, right?" I asked Arthur. "This is almost exactly the ideal double-cross scenario. They don't even have to do too much, either. Just be a little slow on the charge, and we'll be yesterday's toast."

"You need to have faith, Morgan." There was that choral music again. "Beric and Mark would have us dead in a heartbeat, but now is not the moment of betrayal. They need to pass this step first. They'll hold the flank."

Privately, I thought that was wishful bollocks. But I didn't want to create even more stress than we were currently experiencing. If Arthur wanted to trust to luck, that was fine. I just ensured I loaded up each of those kings with the heaviest of suggestions <These aren't the droids you're looking for> could manage: "You do not betray King Arthur."

A soft whistle signaled for us to step out from cover.

"Well, here goes fucking nothing."

And we crossed from the treeline to appear next to what I'm going to conservatively describe as five thousand goblin warriors.

It was on.

CHAPTER 22 – IN WHICH THE ARSES OF GOBLINS ARE HANDED TO THEM

As I quickly realised, the thing about Goblins is that they're stupid. This had advantages but also some pretty significant demerits.

On the plus side, it wasn't like we would be up against any military geniuses. And, to be fair, for all his personality defects, Arthur lived for this shit.

The Britons had long learned their lesson from the Romans. The days of gearing up for individual duels during a battle, undisciplined hordes running pell-mell at each other, had long since been beaten out of them. Too many warriors - and too many war chiefs - had found themselves being cut to pieces by carefully arranged, solid lines of shields and swords to ignore the example.

Thus, the shield wall.

Britons were a bit more attached to their spears to abandon them for short swords, but - in some ways - this actually made the British shield wall more lethal than the lines of Roman Legionnaires slowly grinding undisciplined rabbles to dust.

And, of course, every last man who accompanied their king on this quest – Beric's appeasing crew aside - was a veteran of countless encounters against the Saxons. In that sort of crucible, you got very good at this form of warfare, or you got very dead, very quickly.

The Goblins were no Saxons.

I was about three lines back from the front row, with the strictest of instructions not to work my way forward with the rotations. I'd argued, initially - I was stronger and faster than anyone else on the field (with the possible exception of Lancelot) - but I was left in no doubt that when it came to this sort of disciplined warfare, experience trumped anything else.

I was to watch, learn, and throw as much "devastating magic shit as you've got."

In an ideal world, my dear, you'd be hovering - beyond arrow range - above the conflict and just raining merry hell down on the little green buggers.

I added 'learn to fly' to my 'to do' list, all the time marveling that I even possessed a list that didn't just say 'get fucked' on it. Personal growth.

So, when our small force stepped out from the cover of the trees and the back rows opened up with arrows and javelins - modesty forbids the mention of the strong blasts of <Unnecessary Sequel Trilogy> - the Goblins predictably lost their minds and charged right at us.

Even as far away from the action as I was, I felt the impact of their attack hit our shields. Then the screaming started.

***

Arthur was on the back of Llameri with ten of Beric's heavy horses.

He'd wanted to be in the middle of the shield wall where his expertise with the spear would give the most value, but wiser heads had prevailed. It would have been too easy for a stray knife to find itself in his side - not even ordered by one of the other kings, but their men would understand what Arthur's death would mean to their master.

Instead, he found himself here. On the extreme left side of their formation, charged with killing any Goblins that got it into their heads to try to slip past and around the British shield wall.

Arthur winced at the impact of - literally - hundreds of green creatures flinging themselves on the spears in the line. He knew that the most significant danger right now was his men becoming overwhelmed by targets. That the sheer volume of attacks was too many for the barricade of wood, leather and iron to hold.

But then he saw the first of the attackers fall, the shield wall hold and pressure break away like a tide hitting a wave break.

By the gods, he loved these men. Even those from the other kingdoms. They were lost in an alien world; they were beset by creatures out of mythology; their leaders were in open conflict with each other. And none of it mattered. Nothing other than the shield, the spear and the warrior at their side.

His cloak hissed and snarled as someone rode up to join him. He wasn't quite used to Morgan's gift yet, but he could not deny it was proving to be useful. Certainly, no one was approaching him unseen while the dragon had his back.

He turned, it was Eolgef, Beric's champion. "They're spilling around the edge a little. Might be worth encouraging them away from that course of action."

Arthur nodded, ignoring the lack of a 'sir' or a 'your majesty'. That would come, or it wouldn't. Reaching up, he dropped the visor of his dragon helm, closing it over his face. "Nothing clever, boys. A quick in and out. Let's just let them know that we are here."

He kicked softly at Llameri's side, and the eleven giant warhorses were on the move.

***

I'd lost count of the streams of lightning and flame I'd launched into the press of Goblins. They were like ants boiling from their nest to assault our line, and nothing seemed to be bringing their attack to an end.

Then, from the corner of my eye, I saw Arthur's charge on the far side of the horde. I don't know about the little green fuckers, but the sight scared the shit out of me. Then Lancelot and the riders from the other side performed a mirror of the manoeuvre, crashing into the side of the column, such as it was, pinning us down.

The assault was perfectly executed, with all the mounted warriors bringing utter ruin to the Goblins and, at the sound of a horn, being able to pivot around and then back up the hill.

It was fucking glorious.

It was at this point, Merlin told me, that a human army would rout.

They were crashing against an unmoveable object; the death toll on Yoda's inbred cousins was catastrophic, and now they were facing heavy horses they were ill-

92

equipped to combat. And that went without mentioning the wall of Qi-death I was flinging out any which way I could.

And that's where the downside of fighting Goblins came into its own.

They had no concept of self-preservation.

We were kicking their arses every way until Sunday, and in any standard confrontation, they'd break and retreat, leaving us to open the victory mean and let the backslapping commence.

However, despite their losses and despite them being outgunned in any way that usually mattered, these dudes were simply going to keep coming.

And the men around me were getting tired.

I switched from blasting off beams of destructive lightning and concentrated on refreshing the stamina of those holding the line.

Be careful, my dear. Using your Qi in this manner substantially drains your resources.

"You know, there's something really fucked up about a process that makes it easier to kill people than it is to keep than alive. I feel I should write to someone about it."

Maybe another time, my dear.

"Look, I'm not sure how long they will be able to keep this up unless I help them out."

And how long will you survive if you drop out of Qi-exhaustion before this is all over?

I growled in frustration and halved the amount of energy I was directing into the men around me. It wouldn't be enough to restore them completely, but it was better than nothing.

And then - and I am not wholly sure how it happened - the man in front of me stumbled just as the guy in the front row looked to switch out for a break.

I'd watched these veterans perform this shuffle countless times during the fight and had been impressed by the smooth economy with which they achieved the swap during a pitched battle.

So, seeing it go tits up was a surprise. That's my excuse as to why, without thinking, I stepped forward to fill the gap, hauling the guy who was retreating backwards.

It was then I realised I'd made a couple of fairly significant errors.

The first was that I was at the front of a shield wall and had no shield. This is what was known in the trade as a 'schoolboy error'.

Fortunately, Drynwyn was drawn and was perfectly capable of fucking up anything that thought it was a good idea to come too close.

However, I sensed the second error was likely to prove a touch more costly. You see, the man in front of me had been one of Mark's retinue. And judging by the knife he had just slipped between my shoulder blades, his little 'fall' had less to do with unstable footing and more of, you know, a full-on assassination plot.

If that were the extent of the problem, we'd have been in gravy. Without wishing to brag, we'd long moved past the point where a little casual backstabbing was going to put me off my game. However, those men of Arthur's who were in the line alongside me were somewhat protective of their resident nuclear bomb.

They completely lost their shit and chopped the assassin to pieces.

This was, understandably, poorly received by everyone else in the shield wall who, not being privy to the half-arsed attempt on my life, could only see the men of Dumnonia going to town on someone under a different flag.

As you can imagine, this did little for unit cohesion.

The shield wall bent, bowed and then snapped - hundreds of green bastards flooding into the gaps. This gave me a terrible vision of the last time I'd witnessed a shield wall break - when Cedric had finally overcome Bors' defence on the retreat from Isca.

Men were fighting men. Men were fighting Goblins. Goblins - I swear - were fighting Goblins. As I might have mentioned, they weren't the smartest tools in the box.

And then a horn blew, and Arthur was with us, his horse rearing on its back legs and crushing Goblin skulls left and right. Trust me, it was a full-on 'Aslan off the Stone Table' moment.

Someone was shouting orders, and the melee was slowly pulling itself into order. Amongst the shambles and just on the edge of chaos, our formation shuddered, and a circle formed. Only two deep, but, fuck me, these guys had balls.

I'd have been feeling pretty good about things, knife still sticking out of my back aside, had not, at that precise moment, a second - equally as big - Goblin army not appeared.

Ah. Well, that's not ideal.

CHAPTER 23 – IN WHICH THE DANGERS OF PROFITEERING ARE EXPLORED

The first of the competitors were starting to arrive at Tintagel.

With just under a week to go before Guinevere opened proceedings, Tasko was faced with a dilemma. He had to introduce the newcomers to life in the castle and outline the various events that would be taking place, all while navigating the potential for profit and peril.

Fortunately, a number of the merchants and a decent cross-section of the entertainers had also arrived early, their excited chatter and laughter filling the air. The dark-skinned man reflected that maybe his announcement of the event may have been a touch more hysterical than intended - so there was plenty to do. And, more importantly, plenty to spend money on.

Tasko had tried to negotiate a cut of this action with Bors, but he found the big man extremely distracted. "Do what you think is best" was the only answer he got to his representations.

That is why he and Pæps were sitting looking at columns of numbers, trying to second-guess at what stage of skimming off the top they would start to lose limbs.

"It's a trick," Pæps said for the umpteenth time. "He's warned you to run a tight ship. 'Do what you think is best' sounds like a dare to see if you'll take the bait."

Tasko grimaced. The potential money on the table here was eye-watering. He didn't need to take too much of a percentage here to be set for the rest of his life. Providing, of course, he didn't take so much that it was the cause of his brutal and violent demise. The smart play was to lowball it and let the coins trickle in over the next few weeks. Sure, he wouldn't be coming out of things that far ahead, but at least he would still have a head.

On the other hand, neither he nor Pæps was constitutionally prepared to leave so much profit hanging there without at least trying to get *some* of it to drop into their pockets...

"Philosophically," Tasko began, "what I think is best is to maximise my cut. It could well be that Sir Bors is so impressed with our work that he is encouraging me to take my due."

Pæps let that idea flap in the air for a moment before shaking his head, snorting and directing his attention back to the ledger.

The Grand Tournament was shaping up to be spectacular. Several of the petty kingdoms of the north had clubbed together to organise their own portal, and a steady drip of fur-clad Celts from the hills, valleys, and glens was appearing at Tintagel's gates. As many were the size of Bors himself, this was starting to cause comment. Indeed, such was the buzz around the forthcoming event that had been generated, there were even Saxons appearing under a flag of truce.

If either Tasko or Pæps could have cleared these minds of their fear of Bors, they would have recognised they were achieving something quite unusual: a gathering of race, religion and creed rarely seen across the island. As it was, at a moment when they should have been basking in their triumph, they were scrabbling around in a fog of paranoia and second-guessing.

Tasko took a deep drag from a bottle of his finest wine. "So, what do you reckon? 20%"

Pæps head wobbled from side to side. "I don't know. Seems high..."

And so, they went back to going around and around - trying to parse Bors' words.

***

If the big man had any memory of speaking to the merchant recently, he honestly would not have been able to recall it. He was, of course, dimly aware that there was quite a lot of activity around him, but if you asked him precisely what was occurring, he would have had to beg forgiveness. The Tournament was coming along—anything else was noise.

If he had any impression of Tasko or Pæps at all, it was of two very useful mice that seemed oddly determined to avoid eating any cheese without checking with him first.

He hadn't given a fuck before he heard the news about Igraine, and he gave even less of one now.

It had been all Guinevere could do to keep him from suiting up and tracking down the quest party.

"What do you think you will be able to do?" she asked him.

"Arthur needs to be warned!"

"Warned as to what?" The queen dug her fingers into his arm as she was dragged along behind him. It was quite an unedifying sight, she was sure. "Do you think he trusts these men a jot anyway? He will be taking every possible precaution as it is. If you somehow manage to catch up with them - and how likely do you really think that will be? - what will you tell him? 'Hi mate, one of these kings murdered your mother.' How do you see Arthur reacting to that news?"

"He'll make sure he finds out which of them killed her. By any means necessary."

"Exactly. There's a bigger picture here, Sir Bors." Guinevere dragged herself past him and put both hands on his chest. "Will you stop!" He tried to take another step forward. "As your queen, I order you to stop!"

Bors finally caught up with her tone and came to a halt. "What bigger picture?"

"Arthur needs these men to support him; they don't have to do it with happiness in their hearts. They don't even need to do it willingly. But the outcome of this quest has to be that they support him as the Pendragon of the British. If you blunder in there, throwing around accusations, he will absolutely lose his shit and start taking heads. Any chance of building an alliance will be gone because he will fuck everyone up to get at the truth as to who killed Igraine. We need to be smarter than that."

Now the intensity of his white-hot anger had faded, Bors found himself looking at the queen with frustration. "They killed her, Gwin. One of those bastards came into the castle, her home, and threw her out of a fucking window. And they got away with it. That is not acceptable!"

"No. No it is not. And we will make them pay for it. But not in a way that destroys everything for which she worked so hard. She wanted Arthur as the Pendragon more than anything."

"So what do you suggest that we do?"

And wasn't that the problem? Because she had no idea how to make this right.

***

Tasko had a plan.

Between him and Pæps, they had settled on a sum that they felt was small enough to be acceptable payment for their services but large enough to have made all the stress worthwhile.

After they'd helped the latest arrivals settle in - three insanely buff Northmen that spoke no version of any language Tasko had ever heard of but had chests of gold to pay their entry fee to the Tournament - the merchant and his bodyguard had decided to lurk near Bors' accommodation to see if they were able to get a formal - or even an informal - nod on their calculations.

"What's the worst that can happen?" Pæps kept saying. "It's not like he's going to do anything more than tell us we are out of line and to rein it in a little. Then we negotiate. And, for what it is worth, I think we're offering a good deal."

Tasko was about to reply when he caught sight of Bors stalking their way. They hurried to his side and followed him as he walked. "Sir Bors, if we could have but a minute of your time. We want to clarify some things about the ancillary costs around the Tournament."

If Bors heard them, he gave no sign of it and continued to walk, muttering under his breath.

Pæps took up the conversational mantle. "We appreciate you are busy, sir, but if we can just get some clarity over percentages—nothing complicated, I assure you— it would be helpful for us to know where we stand before the Tournament kicks off proper."

Bors continued to stride forward, seemingly not hearing a word that was being said.

Puffing out his cheeks, Tasko made one last effort. "If you are too busy, my lord, we are happy to direct our proposal to the queen if that would help. After all, we do not wish to unnecessarily take up any of your valuable time."

At the word 'queen', the big man suddenly stopped and twisted to seize Tasko by the throat, lifting him and then driving him backwards to crash into a wall. Pæps grabbed hold of Bors' arm to try to break the grip, but it was like trying to dislodge a castle.

"It is not acceptable!" Bors bellowed into Tasko's face. "I tell you! The queen! Not. Fucking. Acceptable. There will be hell to pay!" And with that, he dropped the spluttering merchant to the floor and went through the door to his quarters, slamming it behind him with such force that the hinges snapped.

Pæps rushed to his master's side, pulling out one of the remarkably expensive elixirs he'd been able to procure since arriving at Tintagel. They were in a surprisingly plentiful supply in Dumnonia, and despite the eye-watering price, he knew that such things were vanishingly rare across the rest of their trade route. He figured he would be able to get four or five times what the crate of these things had cost him when they finally got back on the road.

It was, therefore, to the man's immense credit that he only paused for several heartbeats before pouring it down Tasko's throat. The choking man immediately stopped gasping for air like a captured fish, and a more normal colour returned to his face. His crushed trachea rebuilt itself in seconds- a not exceptionally comfortable feeling for someone used to physical brutality.

They sat together for a few moments whilst the adrenaline of the moment washed away. Then Tasko raised the scroll on which they had finalised their figures.

"Well, I guess he was clear enough there."

Pæps nodded, trying not to look at the door through which Bors had passed. To think, before he had met the man, he had heard that the giant warrior had a reputation for being somewhat naive in the course of business.

"Indeed. I suggest we revisit all of our numbers and ensure we are being as transparent as possible. If that were his reaction to proposing a little light profiteering, I would worry as to how he may view some of the other contracts which we have put in place."

The two had only just hobbled out of sight before there was a burst of raised voices from behind the door with the broken hinges—although it was mostly the female voice that was raised—and then Bors reappeared, red-faced, eyes cast down at the floor.

He cleared his throat. "I'm told that was rude. My apologies. My wife asks if you would like to come in for some supper, and you can explain what you wanted."

He looked up at the empty space in front of him

"Fuck's sake!"

Grimacing – Mrs. Bors could be tricky when things she asked for did not come to pass - the big man gingerly rehung his front door on its hinges and returned inside.

CHAPTER 24 – IN WHICH WE LEARN OF THE BALL-ACHE THAT ARE HOBGOBLINS

The funny thing was, our casualties were not actually that high—and those that were had largely been caused by our little internal security snafu.

"You holding up, pretty hair?" Lancelot removed the knife from my back and hurled it at an approaching goblin. The creature, with the blade embedded in its eye, was flung back into the advancing horde.

"Sure!" As soon as the blade was gone, my skin reknitted as good as new. "This doesn't feel like it's going as well as could be hoped?"

Arthur jumped down from Llameri and slapped Lancelot on the back. "Outstanding. The way you turned that group was a thing of beauty!" Lancelot grinned and offered his own congratulations for Arthur's own death-dealing. I felt quite left out of the sausage-fest.

Nevertheless, I took the opportunity of them tugging each other off to take in more about our current situation. We'd lost, perhaps, five or six spearmen, with another ten to fifteen in various states of mangled. The goblins were as focused on biting and scratching as using the makeshift weapons they held.

I made sure anyone from Dumnonia who needed an elixir got a sip or two, and then was also pretty free with the liquid with anyone who I felt had a positive rating on my internal 'dickometre.' By which I mean 'not a dick.' That's clear, right? Because, you might think a 'positive' rating on a dickometre meant you *were* a dick . . .

I'm babbling, aren't I?

Hey ho. Our losses looked pretty rosey compared to the goblins, whose fallen carpeted the field like the aftermath of a frog genocide. Like, they'd been properly done over. There had to be at least half of the original army lying dead and dying around us, the vast majority of whom had just ground themselves to mincemeat against our shield wall. Arthur and Lancelot's devastating charges had accounted for several hundred more squashed corpses. In any normal situation, these guys would be fleeing for some significant wound licking.

And yet...

The arrival of the same sort of numbers again in the second goblin wave was a bugger. The sheer volume of shrieking creatures we were now looking at was pushing things beyond Zulu territory and into the realms of 300. Don't get me wrong, I was all for the men oiling up and going full Leonidas here - Lancelot wasn't the only one who would really sparkle being filmed by Zack Snyder - but I'd rather hoped not to end my time in the dark ages being filled full of holes by goblin arrows.

Arthur brought me back into the real world with a slap on my back that I couldn't help but think was a little less fulsome than the one he gave Lancelot. "And I hear you caused no little damage yourself, wizard? The bards will sing of your deeds this day!"

"Sounds lovely. Of course, some of us need to survive in order to tell any stories."

Arthur laughed at that. I'm glad one of us was in a good mood. "We're fine. Our biggest challenge was going to be the flanking of the ends of the shield wall. And that nearly happened more times than we might have hoped. Fortunately, we had Lancelot to take care of that!"

"And you, my king."

"Not as impressively as you!"

"Too kind, sir."

The noise of my dry retching ended the collective love-in. Arthur appeared to sense my lack of being remotely impressed. "What I mean is that if I thought we could have established a ring formation in the middle of the field, this would have been my absolute first choice. We're golden here."

"Dude, we're surrounded. By thousands of goblins. And we just killed a significant number of their mates."

"Precisely, we've got them exactly where we want them."

I was about to reply to that little dose of wishful thinking when I realised there was a complete lack of panic in the men. Even the other kings, who could reasonably be assumed to be giving Arthur hell for the failure of his battle plan, were calmly going amongst their men.

Well, apart from Mark, who was leaning over his litter's edge, trying to grab the arse of his servant. I idly wondered if he had been responsible for the little assassination attempt against me. I assumed not. There was a lot of water still to flow under the bridge on this quest, and it struck me he was the type to want to be around for the final moment.

For what it is worth, I think you are right, my dear. I see little benefit for any of the kings in your death before the completion of the three Steps. That you were responsible for passing the Step of Blood should give anyone plotting your demise pause.

"Mind you, the fact that Caeldfwch's key purpose is to negate my power, it may be felt any opportunity to take me out would more than compensate for not getting hold of the sword..."

Good point, my dear.

I waited for Merlin to say more. Perhaps a few words of encouragement or solace. Nothing appeared. "Is that it, Big M?"

Sorry? Did you want more? I agree with you. It will probably be worth them killing you - by any means necessary - even at the loss of the sword.

"Fuck's sake, mate. Never take up a position with the Samaritans."

I was distracted from consideration of my impending death at the hands of three kings of England by Owain pushing his way through to me. "What do you think they're waiting for?"

The King of Gwent had clearly been in the thick of things, covered as he was in blood. I was assuming at least most of it was goblins. He saw me looking and grinned. "Had some tensions to work out."

I could dig that.

Lancelot pointed to a commotion at the back of the second goblin army. "Taking charge is someone."

I looked at where he was indicating and made out a goblin built on a slightly different scale than the others we'd been slaughtering. It shared the same general characteristics - green, hunched shoulders, spikey ears and sharp teeth - but it was the size of Bors.

"Oh, fuck," Arthur swore. "It's a hobgoblin!"

***

There is a long and undistinguished history to the race of goblins. Although they are primarily confined to the realm of the fae, they can be found in enclaves across the real world.

"Like Knockers?" I added helpfully.

Yes, thank you. I don't really need the colour commentary, to be honest.

"No worries, dude. I just realised I hadn't said that word lately. And I like it. Knockers."

Moving back to your imminent life and death struggle... Goblins are pretty much exactly as they say on the tin. Small, aggressive, and they tend to attack in large groups. They are not too dangerous to armed men unless they arrive in overwhelming numbers. Or - and this is where it becomes significant to your current situation, my dear - a Hobgoblin organises them.

"And that's what's about to happen here?"

Well, my dear, it does explain why the fae would view us removing this army as an act of good 'faith'. An undisciplined horde - no matter how big - would cause the fae as much challenge as a cloud of flies. Irritating, but entirely removeable. However, if they are led by a Hobgoblin...

"What? What change does a Hobgoblin cause?"

Arthur obviously thought the question was for him. "It makes me wish I had three times as many men."

I'd like to think that the affection Arthur had shown Lancelot earlier did not have too much to do with my following actions. But I think I'd be lying.

I drew Drynwyn and sighted down its length. "Say no more, blud."

And I let the Hobgoblin have it with <Unnecessary Sequel Trilogy> combined with added flame of pissed-off sword.

There was just enough time for Merlin to shout *"No!"* as the stream of arcing flame lightning leapt out to flash across the distance between the two armies. It struck the Hobgoblin in the centre of its chest and... did absolutely nothing at all.

My dear, goblins are eminently susceptible to Qi manipulation. Hobgoblins, however, by their very nature as mutated beings, have developed through an intuitive ability to harness ambient Qi. They feed on such attacks! And, at their worst, they are actually able to harness a Qi technique and... shield up, my dear.

I was just able to raise a thin dome of Earth Qi in time to deflect at least some of the energy of the returning strike away from me. The rest, unfortunately, I ended up tanking.

This was not a whole lot of fun.

It took a few minutes for me to regain control of my muscles - my first course of action was to swap in a pair of clean underclothes - but I felt this was an instructive lesson. "Okay. So, no flinging Qi at a Hobgoblin. Message heard and understood."

101

Arthur and Lancelot were looking at me with expressions of alarm. "What happened?!"

I retook my feet and subtly used a little flare of Drynwyn's fire to burn away the little puddle I was lying in. "No worries at all. Just a little light cultivator back and forth."

"Your arse he kicked," Lancelot said, grinning.

"Lulling it into a false sense of security, I promise you."

Trumpets blew behind me, and I was aware of a ramp-up in the general tension. Arthur began issuing a stream of orders I couldn't quite follow, but it seemed like his men were all over it.

The ring we were in seemed to contract as the press of bodies all moved in unison and then pushed outwards as the spearmen re-established themselves in a slightly different formation.

The little cavalry we possessed had spaced themselves around the ring, with little units of men - some with spears, others with bows and javelins - clustered around them. By the taut faces and white knuckles, it seemed to me that no one was any longer feeling cocky about how this was going to go.

And then Arthur's voice was in my ear. "Wizard, I need height. If we're stood here when the armies met, we'll be crushed flat. The Hobgoblin will ensure a much more disciplined attack pattern, and we will just be ground down to dust. I need to have higher ground."

"I can't portal this many people, my lord. Even at full power, that would be beyond me. And I'm nowhere near that!"

Arthur shook his head, but it was Merlin who answered.

Interesting. Arthur has formed up as if you were to receive an attack from below. It strikes me, my dear, he does not need you to transport the army out of here. He needs you to create a slope.

I looked at the flat plain that divided our small circle of humans from a large - fucking massive - mob of bellowing, green monsters.

"And I can do that?"

No idea, my dear. In theory, sure. You have the Qi sensitivity to achieve it. I think it would be sensible for us to find out.

Awesome. Because I'm always at my best under pressure.

CHAPTER 25 – IN WHICH I GET MY HORTICULTURE ON

What we think of as 'the ground' is actually an extremely complex endeavour. We can get a bit obsessed about the pretty bits we see—the flowers, the grass, the trees, and suchlike—but if we scrape the surface, as it were, there's a pretty convoluted arrangement going on down there.

I dare say I would have found it all fascinating if I wasn't trying to make the whole FUCKING THING MOVE!

Are you open to a bit of advice, my dear?

"No, not at all, Big M. I think it's much better I blunder around like a lost soul, twiddling at knobs and fiddling with dials, whilst a massive goblin army runs straight at me. Nothing like discovery learning, is there?"

You only need to ask, my dear.

I dropped into my Artist's Studio, hoping the time dilation would give me enough time to figure out, literally, how to make a mountain out of a molehill.

"So, spill," I asked, a touch ungraciously.

If Merlin took offence, he hid it well. Probably until the next time he planned to punish me in a strange and esoteric way. *You are trying to achieve your goal through brute strength. There will be a time - probably not too far in the future - when you can point at a patch of earth and tell it to rise into a column, and it will simply obey the force of your will.*

"I'm sensing you're about to say today is not that day."

I am afraid not, my dear. However, he had obviously seen my face drop, *we do tend to achieve more with honey than the stick, if I can mix my metaphor.*

Having had one rather... creative partner who very much enjoyed the use of both, I was unsure of the validity of this argument. Nevertheless, I was open to seeing how this would play out. "Go on."

Arthur does not need a massive column to rise. All that is required is a relatively small area of this plan to raise by perhaps five feet. It's the sort of weft and wain that would probably happen over the course of centuries. So, you're not trying to force the land into doing something it does not already wish to do, provided you can supply the energy it needs to do this.

"So, I should just ask it nicely?"

Of course not. That would be ridiculous. You ask nicely, give as much Wood Qi as you have into the area you are interested in, and probably add in a nice blast of warmth - via your helpful sword - to really get the juices flowing. Then, when it is all good and loosened up, shape it into what you want: preferably a reasonably sharp incline that a professional army can use to keep an onrushing foe at arm's length.

I took a deep breath, refreshed every bit of Qi by draining one of my smaller mana stones, took an Epic-tier Elixir of Wellness for luck and popped back to the battlefield.

First things first, I knelt down and placed the palms of my hands in the wet mud, reaching downwards in the earth, ignoring the rocks and dead vegetable matter I'd been trying to yank upwards. Instead, this time I found a bunch of root networks that seemed open to the suggestion of rapid and unrestrained growth. The idea was to go for some sizeable displacement upwards, which would lift the ring of soldiers straight up and give them Obi-Wan's favoured tactical position.

Next, I injected my Wood Qi. There's a chance I was a bit heavy-handed with it. I'm the girl who sees two teaspoons of garlic in the recipe and gets out the ladle.

Goodness me, my dear. Are we aiming for a hill or a new mountain range?

Under pressure from my Wood Qi, the roots I had identified swelled to twenty times their original size. God knows what trees they were attached to, but those motherfuckers had suddenly developed some hench foundations.

I felt the ground beneath my feet begin to shake and tried to calm the whole thing down. I was planning on smooth, gentle growth that would leave Artur's spears still standing, not lying flat on their backs.

A little bit of heat now. No, not too much. Just give the roots something to grow towards.

"You heard him, Drynwyn. Just a touch, though. We're literally dead if you scorch earth this field."

Your lack of fucking faith disturbs me, and the sword let out a soft, billowing heat that swam out over the plain.

The roots reacted immediately. Already swollen to a ridiculous degree, they now used all of that stored-up energy to grow towards the heat source, pushing dirt and rock upwards as they came.

Initially, this was all gravy. Through my connection to the source of their rapid growth, I could direct what was going on. It was not unlike an organic game of Tetris whereby I slotted in different growths to create the edifice we needed to make it through this engagement alive.

Slowly, we began to rise in the air. Various spears from each of the gathered armies cried out in alarm as they felt the push on their feet, but I was glad to see no one was dumped on their arse.

But it was taking everything I had to keep this as steady as possible. I caught Arthur's eye, and he nodded appreciatively at me.

I fucking hated that a little ball of pride flipped in my stomach. So, I was a poodle now, was I? I was just happy for a pat on the head? This flare of irritation caused a momentary lapse of concentration, which made us jerk upwards a bit too quickly, so I had to damp down on my emotions.

We were on a growing mound already six feet in the air, and the goblins were still not quite in javelin range. If they were surprised to see their target on a hill blowing up like a balloon, it didn't seem to cause them to pause. I wondered what the Hobgoblin was making of my success at geographical engineering.

We were ten feet up and looking down the sort of steep incline that would make a skier orgasm when Merlin started to fuss.

Cut off the heat now, my dear. It's all getting a little out of hand.

Drynwyn stopped as soon as Merlin spoke, but the roots did not take the hint, contriving to reach upwards. I was now at that stage of Tetris where you're just flinging blocks around in gay abandon, hoping something sticks.

"Big M! Ideas?!" I yelled, pushing down with everything I had, trying to keep the roots now seeking to break free from the bulging earth beneath the ground.

There was the most extended silence I have ever experienced, and then the wizard finally spoke.

Okay. Here's what we're going to do. In a not-unexpected turn of events, you've taken a subtle and intricate bit of cultivation and jumped on it with both feet. Far too much pressure is developing beneath our feet, so we will need to let it out or risk a cataclysmic explosion.

"Dude, if I let these roots burst from the ground, we're going to be seeing the sort of uncontrolled eruption that occurs when an incel finally tricks a girl with low, low standards into bed."

Thank you for that image, my dear. I would, in answer, direct your attention to thousands of goblins closing on our position and suggest that said eruption in their lives would be pretty detrimental to their goal of killing and eating us.

Sweat pouring from my face, I looked around at the goblins swarming up and around the base of my newly created hillock. It was what I was confident the American military would describe as a 'target-rich environment'.

I pressed down as hard as I could on the roots seeking to pop out under the feet of those on the hill, simultaneously releasing any control on the roots elsewhere around me.

To describe what happened next, I'm going to need to rely on the medium of YouTube. I need you to recall a video that I am sure you have seen. We're in a massive splash park, and a little kid is sitting on a giant inflatable in the middle of a pool. Their parent is at the top of a water slide. As the video progresses, they throw their massive body down the slide, careening downwards with all the grace and elegance of a falling meteorite. They reach the end of the slide and are propelled upwards, dropping to fall onto the inflatable.

Tiny little kid is then catapulted into the stratosphere. Much hilarity ensues.

The roots that exploded from the crowd amongst the charging goblins sent the little green things reaching for the sky like they were moonbound. Likewise, the level of impaling mayhem that took place would have made the Shriket's day.

In moments, the area around our hill had transformed into a Vlad-the-Impaler's-nightmare of thick, gore-encrusted roots that thrust to the sky like angry fingers. Some of the roots had four or five of the things spiked through.

"Fucking hell," Lancelot whispered from my side. "Piss you off, I would not like."

It seemed the wrong time to tell him that this little slaughter was basically a hotfix on top of a fucked-up plan. Especially as the rest of the spearmen were staring at me with a look of terrified awe.

I could see how Merlin might have ended up addicted to this feeling.

I'd moved the earth to save their lives and then obliterated a large section of an attacking army. Even I was pretty impressed with myself.

But then the drums restarted, the Hobgoblin shrieked orders, and the remaining goblins were climbing the newly-established hill to where our spears awaited them.

This is not over yet, my dear.

CHAPTER 26 – IN WHICH WE ARE ALL OUT OF GUM

Given a choice, fighting downhill is megatons easier than fighting uphill. And it's not just the fatigue of trying to work your way up the slope, although that, of course, is a major factor. If you're a skinny little green turd carrying weapons on your back, and you've been fast marching across the countryside to even get to the fucking battle, running up a steep incline is a bit of a stretch.

So, yeah. Knackered warriors are rarely the most effective.

But the key advantage is reach.

What had, a few moments before, been the reasonably inevitable slaughter of a plucky circle of spears just waiting for a goblin wave to wash over them was now something quite different.

At Arthur's command, the front row of spearmen planted their shields into the ground and braced behind them. In doing so, they abandoned their other weapons; their sole role in the battle to come was to hold the line. Whereas in a usual shield wall, they could expect to cycle in and out of position when exhaustion told, Arthur's plan for defending this hill was a bit different.

All of the fighting was going to take place above them.

I'd carefully positioned myself as far away from the Hobgoblin as possible. I'd launched <Personal Space Invader> and <Unnecessary Sequel Trilogy> down the slope for as long as my Qi held out, and I didn't want to accidentally supercharge that fucker.

"Hold!" Arthur shouted, circling Llameri behind the firm row of shields separating him from the goblins. They were finding running up the hill a bit of a ballache. And things would not become sunshine and rainbows when they finally reached us.

The rest of our mounted men were positioned at key positions, ready to stop any attempts to climb over the shield wall. Lancelot, for reasons that passed understanding, stood five feet in front of the rest of us.

Then I saw the bobbing head of the Hobgoblin opposite him. Ah, he was a barbarian with a plan.

"Men of Briton!" Arthur's voice carried easily across my newly constructed hilltop. "I feel it is time for these creatures to find out what it means to oppose us. What you say you?"

There was a satisfyingly unified roar of ascent.

"For Briton!" he yelled, lowering his helm and raising his spear.

I'm sure I was not the only one who heard the reply, 'For Arthur!' from a large majority of the troops. I had a second to wonder what the other kings would make of that, but then the green tide hit our shields, and I was suddenly pretty busy.

***

Lancelot had long understood that he didn't see the world in the same way as others.

He'd realised, whilst barely out of his crib, that he was different. But it wasn't until he had his first sword in his hand - a wooden toy made for him by an uncle - that he made that difference count.

Apparently, the rest of the world didn't perceive others in terms of how quickly you could kill them. When he'd mentioned to his mother that there were areas of people that seemed to call on him when armed, she had cackled madly.

Now he was thinking about it, he realised she did that disturbingly often.

After years and years of fighting, his ability to see to the heart of the matter - as it were - had been honed to such an extent that it often seemed that only he was moving in real-time. His opponents had long become all these flashing points of weakness, slowly arranging themselves into an easy-cutting position.

It had turned him into the terror of the group of islands around where they had lived. By his fifteenth birthday, his mother was the de facto leader of a whole heap of subjugated people, and he needed to explore the mainland for new challenges. The only time his extraordinary precognition in battle had failed him was in his fight against the cultivator in charge of the Saxons. He didn't know how that man had defeated him, but he was committing everything to ensure the rematch went another way.

It turned out Lancelot had quite a lot to commit to.

He didn't much care for fighting goblins, though. They were too fragile for proper training, and their bodies were essentially one big weak spot. It felt like he only had to look at them for them to fall down dead.

He'd positioned himself in front of the shield wall because he didn't believe there'd be anything left for him to do otherwise. His mother had explained to him that not everyone was as capable as he, but he simply could not believe anyone would have a problem slaughtering these squishy things.

He was, though, much more interested in the Hobgoblin.

That the creature had taken a full-on blast from pretty hair and returned it with interest was a very good sign. That suggested he might get a decent workout from fighting it. Maybe nothing to match the Shriket - that had been a good fight! He planned to have its head mounted and given to the other pretty hair back at Tintagel - but it was better than wasting energy scrapping with these other pathetic things.

Lancelot glanced back at Arthur, waiting for the signal he could attack. His greatest fear was that something would happen to the Hobgoblin before he had a chance to get at it...

***

It was going to be tight, Arthur knew.

Thanks to the wizard, they had a chance, which certainly had not been the case before the hill appeared. The roots exploding from the ground had further closed the equation, but it was all still on a knife-edge. Despite the confidence he was projecting to the men, it would not take much for the thin circle they'd salvaged to be overwhelmed.

107

It was his experience that quality often could overcome quantity. But there were limits. When you were this outmanned - or outgoblined, he guessed - it did not need too many things to go wrong for that to be that.

Looking down the hill, Arthur met Lancelot's beseeching expression and - with a sigh - nodded his ascent. The barbarian careened down the slope like a released arrow, aiming directly at the Hobgoblin.

They needed that commander down if they were to have any chance at all. Merlin had made clear, via the wizard, that the goblins would not rout while that mutant spawn still lived. Arthur sent a little prayer to gods he was not sure he believed in to speed Lancelot on his mission.

And then the two forces met.

***

I'd blown a couple of waves of goblins away fairly easily before I realised I was making things harder for the rest of the formation.

With so few battle Kermits willing to step into my cone of fiery death - even under the mental pressure of their Hobgoblin commander - it was adding pressure to those holding the line in the rest of the circle.

Puffing out my cheeks, I pulled back towards the middle of the circle to see if there was a different way I could support. It looked to me that Mark's men just to my left were struggling a little, so I joined their ranks.

The press of goblins here was so tight that the little buggers were able to climb over each other to get above the men holding the shields. As I watched, more than a few men were hauled bodily out of the line and back into the horde to be ripped apart.

I didn't think there was much even my strongest elixir could do in that situation.

To be honest, I wasn't feeling being in the middle of Mark's men - considering all the stabby action that happened last time - but if that portion of the circle gave way, we'd all be up shit creek in a chocolate teapot.

There's a chance the stress of battle is affecting my metaphor game.

Bracing myself for imminent betrayal, I muscled my way to the very front of the defenders.

What confronted me was an acrobat's wet dream. There was a leaning tower of goblins, six green bodies high, letting a constant stream of goblins clamber up and leap over the top of the shields. As I watched, more and more of them were avoiding being skewered by the defenders, jumping on top of the men, savaging anything they could get their teeth and claws into.

Little known fact about goblins, Merlin muttered as I slashed one through with Drynwyn, pivoting to boot one back over the shield wall and down the hill, *They are absolutely terrified of snakes. I believe it is some sort of primaeval, evolutionary thing.*

"Awesome." I ripped one of them off my forearm - on to which it had clamped down its gnashers whilst simultaneously jamming its sword into my guts - and used it to beat a few of its fellows to death before it fell apart in my hand. "Was that just some general trivia? Or was it the start of a plan?"

It just occurs to me that, when in a battle frenzy, I imagine you may be able to slip in a suggestion or two.

I stepped back through the thin line, allowing one of Merlin's men to take over my position, and concentrated on the whispy strings - thousands of them - that connected me to the goblin horde.

I decided subtlety would not be the order of the day here. Visualising that scene from the opening of the Last Crusade where Indy falls into the circus wagon, I pushed out the biggest 'Hiss!' I could make.

The impact was fairly immediate.

If you've never seen several hundred goblins shit themselves and run for it at the same time, it's going to be difficult to describe. But let's give it a go. Try imagining a mass of writhing squid blasting out ink in order to escape, and you still wouldn't come close.

The entire section of the battlefield I was facing cleared like someone had announced a sale at Primark.

I took the reprieve to check out how Lancelot was doing.

***

Lancelot was bored.

The Hobgoblin was built for absorbing punishment and had some decent mental attacks - it was how it kept the army in line, after all - but there was nothing of interest here.

He was pleased to see the rest of the defenders were getting a decent workout, though. How else could you hone the edge of a weapon without thinning it a little? Anyone who died fighting goblins was not someone he wanted around his king. Arthur deserved only the best. He was just toying with the Hobgoblin until he judged the war band had taken as much experience from the exercise as they could.

Lancelot focused on one of the glowing weak spots in the creature's leg and stomped his foot down on it. As expected, this caused the Hobgoblin to lose its footing, Lancelot spinning his blade to lop off its left hand.

That gave him plenty of time to spot the mass of green pressing upon the pretty hair's position to suddenly lose their shit and run away.

He laughed at the joke - they'd shit themselves. He was a pretty funny guy.

This was over.

He let his blade complete its outswing and leaned into its weight, spinning around in a circle and coming back with interest to chop the Hobgoblin in two. He thought about taking its head as a trophy for a moment, but the other pretty hair wouldn't like this one. It didn't have lovely feathers.

As soon as the creature fell into two separate piles of viscera, the spell it had over the other goblins broke. With a unified shriek, the little green monsters went into full retreat.

***

Llameri reared upwards and whinnied.

Arthur raised his sword to the sky, conscious that the sun was bound to flash off both his horse's armour and his own. It didn't hurt to take such moments to reinforce

109

his image. One of the things he loved about his horses was her understanding of the importance of visual branding.

"Britain!" he bellowed.

He was pretty damned gratified to hear "Arthur!" came as a response.

Only Morgan took the time to glance at the expressions on the rest of the kings' faces as their own men acclaimed the leadership of the man who would be Pendragon.

They did not look especially pleased.

CHAPTER 27 – IN WHICH I GET A LESSON IN REALPOLITIK

We stayed on the hill for a couple of days.

Merlin had explained that the world of the Fae-Fae had a time-dilation effect that meant we'd not been away from home as long as it felt like we had. It wasn't as strong as my Artist's Studio, but it still meant there was not really as much impetus to rush onward as might have been thought.

This was pretty good news, as our small force had taken quite a mauling.

I'd got a bit blase about taking fairly catastrophic wounds - I mean, I reckon I'd died at least once on this journey already - so I needed to remind myself that this was the Dark Ages and anything more serious than a splinter had the potential to be life-threatening.

Arthur had forbidden me from sharing out any more of my elixirs to the men of the other kingdoms – *to be fair, my dear, they are one of the great treasures of the kingdom -* and short of me giving every wounded spearman a turn with Melehan's Curing Rock, I needed to leave everyone to heal up from the battle as best as they could.

The only time I stepped in - Arthur could go fuck himself - was when I caught that look on a cutter's face that said, 'Not worth the effort.'

It was Owain's men I worried most about. They'd been bested by the Shriket and had been in the heart of the worst of the Hobgoblin's attacks. I was pleased to see the old poacher, Burford, still numbered amongst the living, but from the fifty elite warriors the King of Gwent had brought with him on this quest, only eight still remained.

"My son is going to be so pissed," Owain told me cheerfully, taking a massive bite out of a venison leg.

"How so?" I was doing my best to bind a massive cut in his leg to hide the fact I'd given him another one of my Rare elixirs.

"He told me this would be a fool's errand. I agreed, but as I'm not dead yet, I'm the one who decides what Gwent does, not him. If he'd not been so against it, I'd probably have stayed warm and safe in my castle. Fuck, that hurts."

"Sorry." It had been a long time since I'd taken a first aid course at school. "But he'll be pleased you're still alive, surely?"

"Not a bit of it. Cheeky sod packed my retinue with his own bastards." Owain drew his Santa Claus face closer to mine. "Not a one of them still with us, I'd have you know. Some loud voices often raised in support of his fucking ideas, all silent now. Poor him."

It was not the first time I realised that he might look like a jolly grandfather, but Owain of Gwent had quite the Machiavellian core running through him.

"So, what's the next disaster Arthur has planned for us?" Beric, on the other hand, was happy to wear his inner wanker on his face.

"I don't know, mate. From where I'm standing, I'm on the side of the king uniting the kingdoms by taking the fight to the goblins. I'm sure you could view that as a 'disaster', but only if you wanted the Saxons to win."

"Please tell me you just accused me of treason."

"I think I was focusing more on my king's awesome performance in the field of battle, which, from memory, everyone hailed as 'game-changing' leadership. I don't think I mentioned you at all."

We stared at each other for a moment. "You think you're clever, don't you?"

"Mate, if you knew anything about me, you'd know 'clever' is the last thing I think I am. What I do think is that you're looking suspiciously pristine considering the life-or-death struggle we've just been through, and I'm sure as fuck I've not been slipping you any elixirs. You know, if you want your men not to chant another king's name, you might want to draw that sword once in a while. The boys don't tend to go all doe-eyed over panty-wetters."

My dear...

I knew I'd gone too far. There was just something about his face that made me want to spit venom at him. That, and I couldn't help but feel indignant that the vast majority of his men still seemed to be fighting fit. Owain was down to a handful - even if he seemed pretty pleased with that outcome. Our numbers were in the low thirties, and even Mark and Corys had taken some fairly brutal losses. In the spirit of openness, I should note that the reduction in Mark's forces was due to the whole 'knife in the back' thing that, curiously, no one seemed interested in talking about.

On the other hand, Beric was now in possession of the single biggest force in our alliance.

The silence was quite awkward. All around us, men had fallen quiet as we snarled at each other, waiting to see what the king would do.

Will you just get on with it and fuck him or fry him. I'm bored of all the foreplay.

Beric's eyes widened at the voice that boomed from behind my back. I'd taken to wearing Drynwyn Witcher-style again, conscious that I probably needed its eyes - or what passed for its eyes, I could never work that out - watching my back. I reached behind me and drew the sword with a flourish.

"What do you say, big boy? It's been so long that my standards are almost subterranean. I'm easy to go, either way."

Eolgef was suddenly at his king's side and leading him away with talk of urgent business. I held the pose momentarily - because I am all about the drama - before resheathing the blade.

I think you may well have just put the final nail in the coffin of British unity there, my dear.

"Call me cynical, Big M, but I don't feel that me being a gobby twat is going to make much difference to that equation. If Arthur gets the anti-wizard sword, I don't see anyone doing anything other than bending the knee faster than a nymphomaniac in a brothel."

Tasteless simile, my dear.

"That depends on what the dude's been eating, Big M."

I turned to see if I could spot Mark or Corys anywhere, but, as usual, if they were out and about, they were avoiding me. I briefly wondered if I was worried about that but then filed the concern away. If Arthur got the sword, we were golden. If anyone else got their hands on it, we were fucked.

It was good to have such clarity in my life.

"Why didn't we just do this quest ourselves?"

Sorry, my dear?

"For Caeldfwch. The stakes here are fucking ridiculous. If any one of these guys can negate me, Arthur's fucked. He just becomes a guy with slightly fewer men than any of his allies."

It took me a moment to realise the noise in my head was Merlin laughing.

You've developed quite the healthy ego in the short time I have known you, my dear. It was not so long ago I found you wrestling with a wolf and being fifty-fifty about whether you could be bothered to live much longer. Now, you are apparently the whole ball game as to whether King Arthur keeps his throne. Should I be genuflecting?

I think even my ears blushed. "You know what I mean. Without cultivator support, Arthur cannot hold a British alliance together."

My dear, do not get me wrong. You are critical - in my stead - to the rise of Camelot. However, do not forget that I was at Uther's side when he first achieved the unification of these kingdoms and was pronounced Pendragon. Did I help? Absolutely. But there is no doubt that the kings would have rejected him if they did not think he had the power - on his own terms - to rule. I could have razed each and every one of their lands to the ground without thinking twice, but that was still not the reason they fell into line.

"No?" I couldn't help but think Merlin was soft-selling the terror in which he had been held a little.

No. And this time, the voice was firm. *Rulers do not need to be loved, but neither do they need to be feared outrageously. When Uther was acclaimed as the Pendragon, for sure there was one eye on me, but it was on his own merits that they cheered his name. This quest will have been worth it, even if Arthur cannot claim Caeldfwch. You heard the men during our battle with the goblins. He is proving, in a way none of the other kings can, that he is the true leader of the British. The fact he has a cultivator at his side that can change the very landscape of a battle and a champion who has single-handedly slain two mythical monsters...*

"I mean, I definitely loosened the lid on the Shriket."

Of course you did, my dear, he continued smoothly, *but the point still holds. You and Lancelot are terrifying, and you choose to serve Arthur. You would be surprised by how persuasive that will be in encouraging others to use our banner.*

"So, we'd still see this as a win if Beric claims Caeldfwch?"

Of course not. We'd have Lancelot chop him into kindling and take the sword from his cold, dead hands.

"But..."

Because that is what you do when you are the one in charge. We would not do it because we do not think we can carry water without you and your somewhat limited range of Qi techniques - as impressive as your impression of a snake was - but because Arthur is, unquestionably, The Man. And no one gets to mess with that.

"The Once and Future King."

There we go. I knew we'd get on the same page. If you want to keep your timeline intact and your sister well, we ensure that the Pendragon flag flies above Tintagel. Sure, for that, it'll help a lot for

Arthur to have a mighty wizard by his side and Caeldfwch in his grip, but those are secondary considerations. I know that man can pull all of this together. You must have felt the same during the battle?

I thought back to when Arthur's charge broke the first goblin army. There was something about that moment that made even me forget my issues with the bald adulterer. I could even see what people meant when they said things like, "I'd do anything for that man."

I opened my mouth to say something pithy about how I wouldn't do that, which doubtless would be wasted on a Meatloaf ignorant audience when I was rather rudely interrupted.

By the arrival of the Fae-Fae.

CHAPTER 28 – IN WHICH WE MEET THE FAE

As with all women of a certain age, there's a place in my... heart for Legolas. Don't get me wrong, I wouldn't do Orlando Bloom in any other guise or shape, but give me tall, blonde and pointy ears, and I will make any number of questionable life choices.

Every time Merlin had mentioned 'the Fae', that was the image I had in mind. At a pinch - hey, it's been a dry spell - I was even willing to climb aboard Noddy with enough sympathetic back-lightning and assuming Big Ears was around to finish me off.

My dear, some things do not need to be verbalised.

Thus, when our scouts reported the approach of a small delegation of Fae, my hopes were pretty high. If I tell you I went so far as to change into my cleanest set of undergarments and run my hands through my hair once or twice, you will appreciate the lengthy self-care routine I went through in order to make a good impression.

And first impressions were *good*.

I mean, seriously good. There were five of these impossibly beautiful things waiting for us when we reached the bottom of my hill. All the kings were there - Mark had even been bothered to walk, that's how important it was - and although there'd been an initial 'hurrumph' at me accompanying them, they'd seen sense.

Or I threw a massive tantrum and threatened to burn them all where they stood.

It was one of the two.

It was impossible to tell the Fae apart at first glance. Each was just over six feet tall and channelling some significant Scandinavian chic. Lots of white skin, lots of blue eyes and blonde hair, and lots of cheek and jaw bones that would have been effective offensive weapons.

After a few moments of ogling, though, I could tell there were some differences between them.

For a start, there were two men and three women. The latter wore a subtly different clothing style, with their overshifts a good half-foot longer, extending below the waist and belted in a thick leather cord. Likewise, the ladies seemed to favour bows, whereas the men appeared to be unarmed.

I focused on the men - *of course you did, my dear* - and had a brief moment of fantasy fulfilment. This continued all the way until the first of them stepped forward and made it clear he fucking hated us.

"You have profaned this sacred field with poisonous magic. Your filthy blood stains our precious earth, and your very presence throws the land into chaos. We wish nothing more than your immediate death!"

As openings go, it was a vibe.

We'd briefly discussed how to play this, but no one had expected the Fae equivalent of 'my name is Inigo Montoya, you killed my father, prepare to die.'

As if sensing our confusion, one of the women stepped forward. "Not that we are not grateful for your actions against the goblins. However, we had gathered our own forces to scourge them from our territory, and there are some of us -" she glanced at the first speaker - "who would advocate that we now fall upon you."

Her voice was high and musical, quite different from the first Fae's dark rumble and, oddly, she had a slight Irish accent. I was basically talking to Enya.

We all exchanged glances. We'd taken it as read that the Fae would be pleased we'd wiped out the goblins. It was our act of 'good faith' after all, and we were banking on it being the next Step on the quest for Caeldfwch. That our gift was being regarded in the saw way as if we were puppies proudly shitting in the middle of an expensive rug did not feel ideal.

A second of the female Fae added her voice. "We have been sent to discover your intentions and determine whether action is required."

The first Fae - who I was going to go out on a limb and say was not a fan of humans - immediately spoke up. "The Council has made clear their feelings. We are to destroy these vermin--"

"Maewyn," the third female raised a hand and placed it on the angry Fae's shoulder, "things are not always so black and white. We have been given discretion here, my son. Do not let your previous experiences cloud your judgement."

Son? The Fae who had spoken looked the same age as the man she sought to calm. It appeared Fae don't crack. Yeah, that was funnier before I said it.

Maewyn shrugged her hand off his shoulder and pointed an angry finger at me. "That was before they corrupted the land and twisted it for their own purposes. The only possible response is to cleanse them from the world."

I felt him channel a massive wodge of Wood Qi. He pulled it - no, that wasn't quite right. What he did was nothing as crude as 'pull'. It was like he simply asked the world around him to give him enough energy to nuke us back to kingdom come, and the land presented it to him in a nice shiny bow. It was the most beautifully elegant bit of cultivation I had ever seen, and I almost forgot to wade in with some countermeasures.

Almost. But not quite.

I felt his Wood Qi coalesce around him. I knew that if I let him do anything with it, we'd be history. Even if the other Fae were pissed off with him for jumping the gun, I doubted we'd rank too highly in the scheme of things for them to do much more than shake their beautiful, porcelain face in regret.

So, rather than become a sad little anecdote about the time Maewyn shat the bed at the next Fae dinner party, I did something about it.

I took the Qi off him.

Well, that's a ballsy move, my dear.

"Ballsy as in, 'well played Morgan. Another of your classic clutch moves, which once again saved the day.' Or ballsy as in 'fuck me, man the lifeboats.'"

A little early to tell. But good luck.

And I needed the wellwishing. This Wood Qi was weird. It tasted of newly mown grass and spring water when I dragged it into my Artist's Studio. It slotted nicely into my channels and cycled as smoothly as you like. But that's where the good news stopped. I was used to Qi acting like liquid paint, but Maewyn's stuff was hard. Like 'ice water from the top of a mountain peak', hard. There was no soft woodiness to it. It was like the thickest of thick peat bog and it was now completely blocking me up. There was literally nothing I could do with it. I had thought my Qi concentration had thickened up nicely, but this was evidence of how very far a Harry was from being a deal in the world of cultivation.

Even holding it in my Artist's Studio was painful. I could feel my body start to shake worse than my nastiest-ever detox.

Surprisingly, Maewyn did not react well to me interfering with his attempted death spell. This was odd, as he appeared so chill in all other ways. He was giving off the energy of someone who had never had anything taken off him in his life. His pale blue eyes opened in shock at the audacity of a lower form of life interfering with him and then narrowed in hate as I actually pulled it off.

Something told me I wouldn't be getting the Fae fucking I had hoped for in the near future. At least, not the enjoyable sort.

While I wrestled with what the hell to do with this massive block of ancient Qi sitting in the middle of my core going nowhere - I'd managed to absorb fucking dragon Qi! What on earth was this stuff! - a sword appeared in his hand and thrust straight at me.

It was at this stage that I'm willing to admit things went a touch awry.

Arthur whipped his spear around to deflect the blow, shouting in outrage at the unexpected assault. He obviously didn't know what had happened with my preemptive Qi gobbling, and it just seemed like this guy was whaling on me for no reason.

The spear was effortlessly chopped in two, but it bought me a second to whip out Drynwyn and bring it to guard position.

"This is going to need to be all you, mate," I said. I was concentrating too hard on figuring out what to do with Maewyn's Qi to fight as well.

Makes a fucking change, don't it? All our other duels have just been me sitting back and you showing off your hundreds of years of experienced swordsmanship. It's going to be nice to fucking do something rather than be a passenger in this relationship.

You know what? I think I preferred it when Drynwyn felt a bit down about things and wanted to make amends. Nevertheless, I was glad to hand over the reins, especially as I couldn't even follow the clash of blades that followed.

I knew I was fighting because both my arms were moving in a blur, but that was all I could see. I decided to concentrate on something I could affect.

"Big M, I'm looking for options."

Precious few I can think of, my dear. You will not be able to cultivate from this Qi. I doubt even I would have been able to. It's simply too dense.

"Can we focus on what I can do, rather than what I can't!" My arms were getting tired. If I was hoping for someone to step in and call a halt, I was destined to be pretty fucking disappointed. The other kings - other than Arthur - would be delighted for me to be chopped to pieces, and Arthur was now disarmed. I risked a glance at the other Fae, hoping for some help there. However, although they were watching with looks of disappointment on their faces, there was clearly going to be no interference from that quarter.

Two choices. You slowly let the Fae Qi diffuse out from your core, a little at a time until it is all gone.

"How does the longest fart in history help me right now?" I was drenched in sweat and couldn't physically keep the defence up much longer.

Fucking wuss.

Or you give it back to him.

"How is letting this bastard have a massive amount of Qi going to help keep us all alive?!"

I did not say give it back to him gently.

Sold. I gathered up the alien Wood Qi in my metaphorical arms - it weighed a megatonne - lifted it free from my core, and threw it back with everything I had.

It would be fair to note this gambit took him by surprise. His head snapped up at suddenly having full channels, and his immaculate footwork missed a step under the unexpected weight of Qi.

It wasn't much, but Drynwyn was a fucking Treasure of Britain. It twisted in my hands and sent the Fae's sword swinging away. As it then snaked upwards for his throat, I used the last ounce of my physical energy to turn the blade flat so that it blooted him on the side of the head rather than do something even I could tell would have diplomatic repercussions.

Maewyn fell bonelessly to the ground.

There was an awkward silence until the fifth Fae spoke up, his voice a pleasing middle ground between the women's alto and Maewyn's bass.

"Well, now that is over, why don't we talk properly?"

CHAPTER 29 - IN WHICH THERE IS SOME GOOD NEWS AND BAD

The second male Fae was called Tresaith and, all things considered, was a decent lad.

That is, when you realised that all of the things that you were going to be considering were that he was older than most mountains, could bench press our entire army for fun and was so many leagues above me in cultivation that Merlin suggested I thought of him as a Rowling.

Tresaith explained that his younger brother - the unconscious wanker at my feet - was ever the hothead amongst his people. He introduced the three women, Allavan and Bessen, and -as I had thought - Orwyn, the two males' mother.

"However, do not think that what Maewyn desires is not likely to be the will of the Council. We have long learned to mistrust those from your realm."

Probably a good time, my dear, to note I may have had dealings with Tresaith before. It would be diplomatic not to mention I'm still - you know - here.

"Dealings?"

As I have alluded to before, I have a long history of, shall we say, undistinguished conduct mixed in with my acts of undoubted heroism. The curse of a long life where not enough people are strong enough to tell me 'no'. Safe to say, I imagine my name would do little to smooth relations right now.

Arthur was speaking. "We mean to cause you no trouble, Lord Tresaith. My fellow kings and I are on a quest for Caeldfwch."

If those words meant anything to the four conscious Fae, they did not show it. Undeterred, Arthur pressed onwards. "We have completed the Step of Blood, and we believe that by eradicating the goblin army, we will have taken the Step of Faith. Our show of good faith to you and your people."

Bessen was shaking her head. "Which leaves only the Step of Betrayal of all that is good." Her face was grim. "Maewyn was right. We should kill you where you stand."

I was feeling pretty punchy after dropping the first Fae, so I took a step forward to cover Arthur. He put a restraining hand on my arm and was about to speak when Corys - surprisingly - took over.

"We understand your hesitation, my lady. However, the people of Dehuebarch have enjoyed a positive relationship with the Fae for generations. Whilst we know of the deplorable actions of the men of the South -" the dick's eyes flicked towards Arthur - "you must acknowledge that not all from the realm of men have been so disrespectful."

Allavan was smiling. "I recognise the set of your eyes, child. I spent an enjoyable afternoon with a Leofed of Dehuebarch. Do you know the name?"

Corys blushed under the Fae's rapacious regard. "My great-grandfather, my lady. He spoke often of the beauty and the grace of the Fae lady he once met."

"We did more than meet," the Fae gave a very unladylike snort and turned her head this way and that as if she were a snake hypnotising her prey. "I wonder whether the grandson would be as diverting as the ancestor?"

"Enough," Tresaith's voice was firm. "On behalf of the Moonpool Clan, I grant you guest privileges."

Bessen hissed - again with the snakes? - but he glared her into submission. "You will accompany us back to the Council, and we will follow their lead regarding what happens next."

Beric chimed up. "You cannot believe we will simply put ourselves in the hands of creatures who have already attacked us without provocation?"

Tresaith stared at him for an unbelievably long time before replying. I've heard of a withering stare before, but it was a real fill-up to watch the venomous pile of shit be brought down to size.

When Tresaith finally spoke again, his voice lacked any of the warmth that had been there before. "Beric ap Cronan ap Dresil. We honour the men of Powys and bemoan the stain that currently sits on their throne. You inherited a distinguished history which you betray with your avarice. Your presence is suffered but not welcomed. You are not a tongued one."

Mic drop, Merlin whispered in my head.

"What does that mean?"

Tresaith's basically said none of the Moonpool will recognise his right to speak. That's pretty funny. Especially as Corys appears to be a tongued one because his ancestor...

"Tongued one?"

I left the opening for that one, didn't I?

"Not as much as Allavan has."

Tresaith was looking at Mark now. "Our people know of your son."

Mark's face collapsed into a ferocious frown. "I have no son."

The Fae opened his mouth to speak, but his mother took over. "Our children are reflections of our better selves, Mark of Gwynedd. Their actions are shadows of the sun we have cast over them. Just as we should feel pride for good," Orwyn smiled at Tresaith, "we must take ownership of their mistakes." She didn't exactly look down at Maewyn and roll her eyes, but we could all get on board with that being what she meant. "Tristian should shine in your eyes."

"I have no son!"

I'm pretty new at this whole diplomacy thing, but I reckon shouting at the mother of the most powerful being you've ever met shortly after his brother has just had the shit kicked out of him is probably not on page one of 'How to win friends and influence people.'

Tresaith, though, barely reacted, turning next to Owain. "We recognise your right to speak for the men of Gwent." Owain obviously did not trust himself to speak and just nodded nervously back.

Then Tresaith turned to Arthur. "Arthur ap Uther ap Constantine. You seek to be the Pendragon of your people?"

Arthur nodded. Beric and Mark visibly bristled while Corys was too busy trying to avoid Allavan's lustful stare. "Your father came to us regularly."

Uh oh, Merlin whispered.

"Uh oh? What do you mean by 'uh oh'?"

"Uther made many promises and received many gifts. Some of those oaths were held, but many were not. We do not hold your father - nor his counsellor - in esteem."

"My father was a good man!" Arthur replied hotly.

"He was a man," Bessen spat. "And not to be trusted. The Council will have your head."

I drew Drynwyn casually and whistled a little tune. It might have been the theme song from Jaws. "I'm happy to go again if anyone is feeling up for it? Maybe I didn't make the lesson clear enough the first time?"

"You dare!" Bessen turned on me, fingers turning to talons.

"Listen up, buttercup. We're on a quest. As far as I can tell, the second part of that was to show you Fae fuckers we were on the level. To do that, we needed to take on an army of green shits many times outnumbering us. Lots of us died to make that show of faith. The first thing you guys did when you turned up was not to say 'thank you' but to throw hands. That's fine. I'm a big girl and I took care of business. But now we're in this ritual 'guest rights' bullshit, and you're still acting like we're the bad guys. I've sat one of you on your arse so far, and I'm more than happy to keep going until we all start acting friendly like. So, I guess what I'm saying is: are you next, bitch?"

Well... let's see how that goes down, shall we?

There was a significant pause, followed by an extraordinary sound. The Fae were laughing.

Tresaith wiped tears from his eyes and held out his hand to me. It took me a beat to realise he wanted me to shake it. Once I did, he turned back to Arthur.

"You seem blessed with a more straightforward advisor than your father. I like her. I may decide to keep her -" Excuse me! - "For her sake, the sins of the father will not be retained by the son. You will be a tongued one." But then, all levity dropped from his expression. "But you will have no latitude. Do not play us false."

Arthur nodded back gravely. "On my word, I will not."

Tresaith turned to his mother and held her eyes. She nodded. He did the same with Allavan and Bessen. Both nodded, Bessen noticeably more reluctant than the others.

"It is decided then. We shall recommend to the Council that the Moonpool Clan will not seek to impede you on your quest. We will report that you have done us service and will suggest past crimes," Tresaith's eyes flicked to Beric and Arthur, "should not inhibit current relationships."

With that, he bent down and lifted Maewyn effortlessly onto his shoulder. It was like he'd slung an empty backpack up there. This dude had game.

"I cannot promise the Council will accept what we say, but we will speak for you."

"And what happens if your Council decide we are more trouble than we are worth?" said Arthur.

Tresaith had already turned away and walked to the trees as Arthur spoke.

Bessen replied for him. "Gather your men. We will not wait on you."

She followed Tresaith, as did Allavan - who took Corys by the hand, dragging him effortlessly behind her. I sensed he might be in for a tiring evening.

Orwyn held back. Arthur, Owain and Mark were already issuing orders and men were hurrying back up the hill. I was sad to see quite how many still bodies were being left behind. I asked Arthur's question again to her.

"The ways of the Council can be mysterious. It may well be they rescind your guest rights."

"And if they do?"

Orwyn looked at me, her face completely flawless. Scerene blue eyes glinted in the daylight. "You will all be executed. But fear not."

"Hard not to let imminent death play on my mind! Why shouldn't we fear?"

"Because my son and I will die alongside you."

I took a moment, then asked the obvious, selfish question. "And how does you also dying stop me from being afraid?"

"The Council would think it gauche to torture us to death. So, if it does come to that, the deaths will be quick."

And with that, the queen of glass half-full thinking followed her fellows into the woods.

CHAPTER 30 – IN WHICH HANDS ARE THROWN

The first day of the tournament had not passed without incident.

To be fair, it had all started pretty much as expected. Guinevere had welcomed the three hundred and fifty competitors and encouraged them to make themselves at home amongst the host of entertainments, stalls, and merchants who had sprung up in and around the castle.

There was so much of this, in fact, that the road leading into Tintagel had transformed into a bustling market town, filled with the vibrant colours of merchant stalls and the lively chatter of visitors.

"How exactly are we paying for all this?" Guinevere had whispered to Bors as she had toured the various buildings that had, apparently, shot up overnight.

"No fucking idea. Last time I looked at the numbers, it was like they were paying us to be here. But that can't be right, can it?"

Bors had met with Tasko a couple more times since their last, rather fiery conversation. He'd done his best to put the merchant at his ease, but it felt like every time he thought he was making progress, it ended up with the royal treasury being enriched even further.

He eventually resolved to leave the man to his business and hope for the best.

Every type of service was available for those taking part in the Grand Tournament. Just as every decent warrior - or, more importantly, those that considered themselves as such - had scrounged up the money to get themselves portalled to the castle. And anyone who made their living selling wares to men - and women - with swords and spears had followed them.

"Do you not think that this might be getting a little out of hand," asked Guinevere the fifth time she had been offered a dress fitting using a material she'd never heard of. "Not that I'm saying you haven't done an amazing job," she added hastily. "Just that the point was to scare up a new Marghekyon, not create an entire feudal economy on our doorstep."

Bors shrugged. "Gwin, I'm as in the dark as you. But it can't hurt, can it? The lads are saying it's the greatest spectacle the land has ever seen." He paused. "You don't think Arthur will be pissed he missed it, do you?" he asked anxiously.

Guinevere patted his huge forearm reassuringly. "He'll be so proud of you. You've outperformed his wildest expectations."

But even as she said it, Guinevere's mind was whirling. Blæk's information about some of these people currently within shooting distance was not comforting. As soon as it got around that Tasko had spent the coin to have portals opened to Tintagel, the range and variety of possible competitors had gone through the roof. What had been conceived as a way of gathering together all the local British talent still resisting the Saxons seemed to have become a way for anyone with enough ambition and coin to show their prowess.

That was all well and good, but for each competitor, there were usually a few hangers-on. One guy, a Prince from some sundrenched land in the East had even brough his whole retinue.

"You cannot allow that many mailed horsemen within the walls!" Blæk was almost crying when he delivered this update to the queen. "I have nothing whatsoever on them. You must give the Grey time to gather sufficient material!"

"And how would you suggest I do that?" She had snapped, just about remembering that the more harshly she spoke to the man, the harder it was to see him or even recall he was there. More than once in their arguments about the seemingly never-ending flow of strangers through the gatehouse, she had found herself blinking into the dark, wondering what she was doing in the cellars of Tintagel.

"I do not know, my lady. But I cannot promise to keep you safe if you continue to so recklessly allow such freedoms around your person!"

"Queen Igraine was murdered in her bed chamber with you at full alert. Pardon me if I am not agog at your abilities." She'd barely said those words before she was wandering back to Tintagel's courtyard, feeling guilty but not absolutely sure why.

***

The first event, following Guinevere's welcome, was not of the official ranking bouts. Bors had been clear that they needed to demonstrate the strength of Arthur's kingdom so that they could attract the winners to join them.

"We might need them more than they need us, but we don't need to let them know that. We're riding high on the tales of Uther and Merlin. Arthur's got a decent rep, but we need to burnish that. Especially as he is not here."

Guinevere was not so sure but had gone along with it.

And, thus, the Grand Melee was born.

"Each man can choose to compete, or not, as he wished. There is no prize. There is no gold for the winner. There will be only the satisfaction of being the last man standing. No bladed weapons are allowed. And there are to be no killing blows. The goal is to be on your feet when the rest of the group is sitting on their arses. Nice and simple." Bors boomed out across the crowded field.

Silence greeted the announcement. There were lots of furtive glances as over three hundred warriors tried to work out whether it would be to their advantage or not to take part or if it would be more politic to wait for their own specialism.

Grand Melees were tricky. You could be an absolute legend and be tripped up by a farmboy with a stave - your reputation dented forever. Likewise, there was no better way to get your name known than to be amongst the last few standing.

"Are you taking part?" a voice shouted from the throng.

Bors had smiled. "I might. Arthur charged me with keeping you all honest. I'm forbidden from taking part in the other events," Guinevere had put her foot down there, "so I figured this was a good way of seeing who's the real deal."

And that sealed it. There weren't many in the crowd who didn't dream of joining the Marghekyon of King Arthur - and those who didn't had a very different reason for their presence at Tintagel. To help with that, Bors had come up with the best way

124

of identifying those who would be open for recruitment and those who had the sort of purpose that a certain non-descript man would be wise to keep an eye on.

"Make a note of who withdraws," he had said to Guinevere, slipping out of his best tunic and walking down from the speaking platform Tasko had arranged to be built.

Most of those below him began doing the same, divesting themselves of any swords or knives and passing off their various finery to servants. In no more than a few minutes, around two hundred men and not a few women stood in the centre of the courtyard, looking nervous.

Guinevere stood aloft, waiting for those who did not seek an opportunity for hand-to-hand combat to withdraw. Then she dropped the white handkerchief she was holding high, and the Grand Tournament of King Arthur began.

With a full-on, drag-out brawl.

****

It felt good to be actually doing something, Bors thought, throwing a small man with extremely ginger hair into a group of fighters. He wasn't cut out for administration. And he certainly did not have the talent for the kind of espionage Guinevere indulged in. What he was good at, though, was punching people in the face until they passed out.

The melee had been going for a good few minutes, and there was already a decent amount of space building up around him, which made sense. No one really wanted to test themselves against the big man, especially while there were still too many bodies about for people to notice.

Fighting Sir Bors was the sort of thing you wanted an audience for.

There were a few people he'd noted himself already. A tall, thin, wiry guy was holding his own over in the far corner. Parsifal, he thought he remembered the man introducing himself as. He didn't have Bors' brute strength, but by the gods, was he fast.

Bors nodded appreciatively as he caught a haymaker from a big Germanic-looking motherfucker, twisted it away from his body and kicked the guy in the head. Yep. That'll get the job done.

There were similar little pockets of studied belligerence that caught his attention. A squat, ugly man from the mountains of Gwent - Acanor, he thought - was just soaking up punishment as if he were being tickled.

Three guys were whaling on him, and it didn't seem to be making an ounce of an impression. His kind of dude.

And there was almost the complete opposite - a pale, slight lad who couldn't be more than sixteen. The boy seemed almost impossible to pin down. As Bors watched, idly backhanding a charging Frank away, the boy repeatedly dodged any and all attempts to grapple with him. He was jabbing out quick little punches and kicks, which seemed to cause far more damage to their recipients than was credible. Galahad, Bors thought he was called.

The numbers still stood in the middle of the Melee were drastically reduced. The rules were quite simple. You were still in until you were dropped to the floor, and large numbers of crawling men were getting away as fast as they could.

When there were just twenty of them left - all of those he had noted as likely lads were still up and kicking, he was pleased to see - they took a pause to allow the fallen time and space to withdraw. They also had a chance to get some mead on board.

"Well then. Here's a group of arse kickers and name takers," he grinned at a series of blooded faces and bruised bodies. "Who's up for the next go?"

He cracked his knuckles and headed straight for Acanor - he was interested to see whether he could do anything to the resilient fucker - when something else took his attention.

A flurry of crossbow bolts from the window of one of the towers hit him square in the chest.

He barely heard Guinevere's screams before the blackness claimed him.

CHAPTER 31- IN WHICH THE BEST LAID PLANS OF MICE AND MEN GET TRULY FUCKED

It takes a particular type of person to be a successful assassin.

Anyone can be a murderer. You just need enough white-hot fury - or booze - on board, and, well, people are squishy.

The thing is, and most people overlook this, is that murderers are stupid. The sort of choices you need to make that lead to hitting someone over the head with a log in a crowded place is not consistent with a sparkling intellect.

A murderer might not be caught today, maybe not even tomorrow. But, soon, thick as mince will out.

Unlike murderers, assassins face a constant threat, not just from the law but also from the families of their victims. Their success hinges on their ability to not only escape immediate capture but also to evade the wrath of those left behind.

This tends to mean that the careers of assassins are either extraordinarily short or worryingly successful. That Tenejalan and his little band of miscreants had been in the business for over ten years pretty much tells you everything you need to know.

That Blæk had witnessed Tenejalan and his crew infiltrate Tintagel without the observation triggering his usual warning tingles tells you even more. And the audacity of this group in managing to strike Bors with three crossbow bolts just as Tenejalan himself appeared behind Guinevere, slashing with a knife, really took the biscuit.

Unfortunately - well, unfortunate, where Tenejalan and his crew were concerned - that was pretty much where their good fortune started to hit the buffers. There are times when a decade of experience gets you out of trouble and others when it leads you to make a series of false assumptions.

For example, as a veteran of many a queen-stabbing, Tenejalan expected Guinevere to scream when he appeared. So, when she did so, it fitted well into the narrative of the events he had constructed in his mind and would recount to his employer. If he had been a touch more on his game - the quality of the refreshments available had been extraordinary - he may have recognised that the broad-shouldered woman he was attacking was not so much screaming in terror, as bellowing in rage.

Likewise, for his three fellows manning the tower with their crossbows, three direct hits were the best that could have been hoped for in the circumstances. Distance, angle, moving target - three from three was a job well done. Years of putting down recalcitrant knights for lords with money to burn on such things told them it was time to pack up and head for the rendevous point where the last two of their gang would be waiting with the horses. So, it was probably understandable that they were hightailing it down the tower steps rather than putting a dozen more shots into the man they'd been paid a large fortune to kill.

And finally, the whole gang probably overlooked the presence of a shadowy cultivator who was suddenly very motivated to use his considerable resources to bring immediate retribution for the castle's violation.

So, all in all, what looked like a pretty straightforward—if very lucrative—contract on paper was about to take a somewhat unconventional turn.

***

Guinevere put the sight of Bors collapsing to the floor of the courtyard out of her mind as the man in black thrust a dagger at her. She had no idea how he'd arrived on the wooden platform overseeing the Grand Melee, but that was a recrimination for another day.

She screamed her anger at him and flapped the heavy sleeves of her dress at the knife. The blade caught in the material rather than hitting her in the mid-drift, and she quickly yanked her arm back to try to disarm their attacker.

Tenejalan's eyes widened in momentary surprise, but then he ripped the knife in his right hand free from its entanglement in Guinevere's dress and added a second blade to his left. Not ideal, but none of the guards were reacting yet - they'd all run to the big man his crew had put down - so he still had time.

He prepared to run after the queen, who would doubtless turn her back and flee at any moment...

His head snapped back as the woman before him stepped forward and punched him in the face.

It had taken Guinevere longer than she would have liked to get over her fight with Cedric. On an intellectual level, she knew he had been bigger, stronger and more experienced. There was simply no way she would have been able to defeat him. That didn't mean her chest wound - and more importantly, the wound to her pride - didn't burn.

From the moment they'd returned from the Dark Tower, she'd thrown herself into her training with a somewhat excessive abandon.

The outcome was that Tenejalan had probably picked a bad day to try it on.

Guinevere followed up her jab to his face - the assassin's nose made a satisfying crunch at the contact - by reaching forward, putting both hands behind his head, and driving it downwards to meet her rising knee. His nose spread even further around his face. A thrust kick to his chest followed to push him - staggering - backwards. That gave her enough time to draw her daggers, tastefully strapped to her thighs, and settle into a fighting crouch.

Eyes streaming, blood pouring onto his chest from his broken nose, Tenejalan did the only obvious ploy left open to him.

He ran.

***

The three men from the tower didn't see their leader shit himself. They had their own problems. The difficulty with fleeing down a tower was that it allowed defenders to come up at you.

They'd discussed each taking up a different position around Tintagel, but having seen the sheer number of people and the various entertainment and food stalls, they'd figured it was just more straightforward to stick together.

The quality of guard they'd observed was execrable at best - Arthur had taken his best men with him - and there was no way any of them could stand up to the three of them together.

The truth of that was seen in vivid technicolour by the number of bodies that lined their descent from their vantage point. None of Tintagel's guards had made much impression on them as they sped past. They were just at the bottom and preparing to fall back to the stables and their escape route when three bruised and bloodied figures approached them.

They dimly recognised them as brawlers from the Grand Melee - none of them was affiliated with Arthur's castle - so they'd paid them no mind.

"Get the fuck out of the way," the first of the assassin barked at a spectacularly ugly man - more toad than human that was swinging his arms in an approximation of a warm-up routine. If he heard the order, it made no difference and continued to block their path to the stables.

The second assassin looked at the tallest of their three roadblocks. "You've got no weapons. What do you really think is going to happen here?"

Parsifal smiled back and then looked down at the slender boy who - bizarrely - seemed to be their leader. He raised an eyebrow, and Galahad nodded serenely back.

The final assassin, who had reloaded his crossbow during these social niceties, points at Acanor - the squat man looked the more dangerous of the three - "Back the fuck off, or you're dead!"

Things got a little intense after that.

***

The last two members of the death squad, the ones waiting in the stables, were dead before they even realised they were in danger.

It was rare for Blæk to feel such anger, but it had been decades since there had been any unsanctioned killings within these walls. The Queen Igraine and now the attempts on Guinevere and Bors. No. This was not acceptable. His father would have been devastated if he had lived to see what was occurring on Blæk's watch.

As the shadows receded to the walls, leaving two somewhat surprised skeletons collapsing into piles on the floor, he recognised that he had been a touch injudicious. Desiccated corpses did not tell any tales about who had hired them.

Likewise, it was unseemly that he had let his irritation at missing these snakes in the den - five amongst so many hundreds? There were limits even to his and the Grey's perspicuity - overcome his rational side.

Blæk took a breath, closed the stable door behind him - the Grey would deal with the bones - and stepped into the light of the courtyard.

He could make out a one-sided scuffle at the bottom of one of the castle's towers. Three men - well, one man, one hideously deformed man-troll and a young boy - he recognised from the Grand Melee were kicking merry hell out of three strangers. He assumed these were the assassins who had shot Sir Bors and that they were now having the error of their ways explained to them.

His expert eye suggested that no questions would be asked of these assassins either. So, that just left...

***

Guinevere tackled the fleeing man from behind. As she achieved this by diving off the wooden platform to do so, she struck him in the back with quite some vim and vigour.

Tenejalan crashed into the ground in the middle of the courtyard, kicking his legs to get free. He caught the queen on the side of the head and bought himself a few more seconds. Not that it mattered. He could tell he was fucked.

You got in, you did the work, and you got out. The game was over the minute you found yourself in a fistfight with your mark. He spared the men he'd put in the tower a quick, final glance as they were stomped to the floor. He assumed his men in the stables were similarly off the board.

Fuck it.

He turned to face Guinevere. What sort of fucking queen attacked the guy coming to kill her! She was up on her feet, and he was pleased to see his flailing leg had closed her eye somewhat. That would leave a nice legacy bruise.

"Who sent you?" Guinevere's voice was low and controlled.

Tenejalan attacked. Better to go down fighting than in a torturer's embrace. But it was like he was moving through sand. The bloody woman blocked and parried his every attack, returning blows with interest.

After a few heartbeats, they separated, and he was astonished to realise he was done.

"Perhaps you didn't hear," the queen said, barely breathless. "Who sent you?"

"What?" he spat, a stream of blood from his mouth. "I tell you, and I get to live?"

"Of course not. But you tell me, and I'll make sure they're dead soon after you."

That gave Tenejalan pause. He was a petty man and liked the idea of his revenge living long after he passed. "There's no way out for me?"

Guinevere looked down—they were almost standing over Bors' body— "No," she said harshly.

"Fair enough. Can't blame a man for trying. We were paid to eliminate you and--" he looked down - "Sir Bors. A thousand gold pieces a head."

An insane sum. Ludicrous. Who would have that sort of money? Well, she certainly knew of one person.

"Your client was Aurelius Ambrosius?"

Tenejalan's face crumpled into a frown. "The old Pendragon's brother? He's been dead for years. No, we were hired by King - "

And then a good thing and an unfortunate thing took place. First, Bors suddenly took a deep breath and sat up, regaining consciousness. He looked around wildly and, seeing Guinevere standing blooded above him, reacted in the only way that made sense to him.

He reached up and grabbed the man with whom she was obviously scrapping and, with a squeeze of his massive hand, crushed the man's throat flat.

"Oh, Sir Bors," Guinevere said after a slight pause, "your timing is not impeccable."

CHAPTER 32 – IN WHICH I GET MY POISONING ON

It took us two days of leisurely travel to reach our destination.

I say 'leisurely', but this was far from a leisurely stroll. It was a relentless battle for survival, where every hundred feet, we were bombarded by kamikaze attacks from the trees, each one more ferocious than the last.

Our path was littered with threats. Wolves, goblins, wyverns, and giant big cats lurked in the shadows, ready to pounce. Even the occasional Troll, with its massive frame and menacing growl, showed up to try and tear us a new one.

The relentless assaults forced us to move at a painstakingly slow pace in a perpetual battle formation. What should have been a three- or four-hour stroll became a gruelling march, with men carrying heavy shields and who were constantly under attack.

As we made camp on the first night, all of us thoroughly knackered from the 24/7 slogathon, Tresaith suddenly appeared beside me. He seemed to have a habit of doing that.

"I have come to apologise."

Considering he and his fellow Fae had been doing far more than their fair share of ambush slaughtering, I wasn't sure exactly what he was getting at. I tried telling him so, but he shook his perfect head regretfully.

"You do not understand. Our presence is drawing so much of the forest filth towards you. Your men are taking wounds meant for us."

That gave me a bit of a pause.

I had wondered what was causing the sudden upsurge in attacks, but figured it was something to do with moving towards the final Step of the quest for Caeldfwch. I hadn't thought the issue might have been that the Fae were shit-magnets.

Eventually, though, I shrugged my shoulders. "It's not like you're cowering behind our shields. You guys are more than pulling your weight."

I was probably doing him a disservice. Each and every one of the Fae was a moving death machine that made Lancelot look pacifistic. They were a massacre-on-legs, whether with bow, sword, spear, or just plain piling out Qi like it was on sale. Sure, the Britons were doing their bit, but I felt like he was wearing the hairshirt a little tight.

"Even so. We have discussed staying behind you and letting you reach the Glade without us drawing every dark soul in the vicinity upon you."

"Dude, as far as I understand it, without you guys there to smooth our entrance, we're going to be as unwelcome at the glade as a syphilitic stripper at a Women's Institute meeting."

Tresaith smitled. "Orwyn said the same. Without the incomprehensible simile, of course."

"Your mum speaks sense. Look, we're all shattered, but we're not taking terrible losses. And part of the deal with this quest was to bind the kings together. Nothing does that better than fire and blood." Even as I said it, though, the words felt pretty hollow. No matter how well disposed the average spearman in the column may feel towards Arthur, relations with their leaders - Owain aside - were pretty shit.

As might be expected, Beric had taken being denied being heard by the Fae really well. It was pretty funny to see him try to engage them in conversation. But not quite as funny as seeing these ancient, beautiful beings play an elaborate game of 'Can you hear something?' each time he tried it on. If a wolf didn't pick him off, the dude was a few more little chats away from stroking out, judging by his purple face each time it happened.

Corys was... occupied. In fact, if I had a complaint about the Fae, it would be that a) Allavan was not quite as present in the front line as her mates, and b) this was because she was having very loud sex with the King of Dehuebarch. I had the sense his retinue was feeling a bit put out as they were fighting for their lives while the king they were defending was being repeatedly, enthusiastically, screwed.

Of our detractors, that left Mark. I hadn't seen the fat slob since the whole 'I have no son' debacle, but Arthur reported the King of Gwynedd was in a particularly foul mood. He had forbidden his spearmen from working under Arthur's direction, which was nice, and any orders which impacted on his men needed to be approved by him before they were put into action. This was, as I'm sure the bastard expected, causing as many problems as any number of goblin strikes.

Tresaith cocked his head to one side. "Well, you know your people better than I. The apology has been made." He stood to make his leave, picking up a dark green leaf from the forest floor as he did so and popping it into his mouth as if that were the most normal thing in the world.

"What's that?" I asked, noting it was lit up by my alchemy skill as soon as I asked the question. Tresaith paused and then swallowed it down. "It's called Widow Weed. My people use it as a way of increasing our resistances."

I plucked a leaf myself and rubbed it between my fingers. The dark green surface released a pungent clear liquid when squeezed. "And eating it does something for your... motherfucker!"

My fingers suddenly felt like they were on fire. I looked down and could see bone.

Tresaith watched me dance around my campfire with a neutral expression. "You may want to be careful with the liquid the leaves contain."

"You think!" I pulled a bottle of spring water from my inventory and doused my hand in it, trying to ignore the fact my fingers were vanishing. Which is, surprisingly, pretty hard to do. When the water did nothing for me, I ordered Drynwyn to napalm the stuff off me.

It was disappointingly okay with that. I don't know; I'd have appreciated just a few follow-up questions before flame-throwing my hand. However, considering that this seemed to do the trick, I decided to let it go as I flooded the damaged area with Qi to grow it back.

I turned to the Fae. "You eat that shit?"

"Of course," Tresaith said, picking up another lead, squashing it and releasing what I was now going to think of as battery acid. "As your level of cultivation increases, you will find it increasingly challenging to progress. At the higher levels, you will need to actively seek out things outside your capabilities."

Tresaith held up his hand where the juice from the Widow Weed sat on his skin without burning holes straight through. "It has been several hundred years since I could coax a reaction on my skin. Hence why I must consume it."

I looked at him with undisguised horror. I couldn't even imagine what it would feel like to have that stuff go down my throat. And it goes without saying this was an area where I had some expertise.

He is speaking a lot of sense, my dear.

I didn't reply. We'd agreed Merlin would keep his head down as low as possible around the Fae. That he had whispered those words at all suggested he thought this was important to learn.

I - carefully - picked another leaf. "So, I should find a way to torture myself with something like this?"

Tresaith shrugged. "I am not of your race, little one. I would not like to offer advice on your own cultivation journey. However, if you seek to move things forward, I am not against stressing the importance of challenge to you."

I dropped into my Artist's Studio and grabbed a bunch of my alchemy books. I didn't recognise the words 'Widow Weed', but I thought I'd come across a picture of the leaf on one of the pages about poisons. "Any advice, Big M?"

Keep flicking. I'm unfamiliar with this particular plant, but the more toxic poisons will be towards the back.

I moved toward the end of a red book with a skull and crossbones on the front. After a few minutes of skimming, I saw the leaf I was looking for. "That looks right to you, Big M?"

My word, he said after a few moments. *It is, and I have to caution you about that potion, it is rather an advanced one.*

I scanned through the recipe. Along with the crushed outcomes of several bunches of Widow Weed, there were a couple of other unusual materials I had never heard of. "Any of the rest of this something you know about?"

The book containing my inventory started glowing, which I took as a good sign. I reached up, took it off its shelf, and let it open to the appropriate page. Did I mention my new 'happy space' is incredible? From what I could see, I already had several thousand of each ingredient in there. Voltigern's Dragon was quite the hoarder.

"So, I guess I have the stuff I need to make--" I squinted at the title of the recipe - "Potion of Agonishing Death. Catchy. These ancient alchemists really do know the secret of a powerful brand."

It is not a pleasant potion at all, my dear. There are really only two uses for something such as this brutal.

"Assassinations and skill-ups?"

You have the right of it. If you are wholly committed to this path - and I will grudgingly admit there is merit in what you suggest- you must progress very carefully.

I popped back into the real world - noting Tresaith was gone. The Fae did not seem to be affected by the time dilation within my Artist's Studio, which was weird - and swiped a bunch of Widow Weed, dropping it straight into my cauldron.

Grinding the leaves up, I had a moment of worry that the acid would eat out the bottom of the pot, but I guess Treasures of Britain are just built a bit different.

In no more than a few moments, I had a small depth of clear, thick liquid, which I was absolutely sure would chew through anything I put in there.

I took a couple of hours, and the sun was just starting to rise before I got to the end of the recipe. The liquid had turned a deep, disturbing red and smelt like the most overspiced curry I had ever encountered in the Balti Triangle.

I tried to dip one of my empty beakers in, but it obviously melted before it even broke the surface of the potion. This stuff was not here to play.

Encouraged by Merlin, I tried surrounding a drop of it with Earth Qi - *stable, solid, unreactive, my dear* - and managed to lift a small blob of it out of the cauldron and deposit it in a beaker.

The little sphere of brown Qi surrounding a malevolent red centre rattled around like a marble straight from hell. I gave it an experimental shake, but when it didn't do anything immediately traumatic, I felt safe spending the day's journey to the Glade carefully encasing little drops of the poison in Earth Qi and stowing them away.

By the time the cauldron was empty, I had over two hundred. According to my inventory, they were called 'Pills of Agonising Death'. However, despite that snazzy bit of PR, I hadn't yet been able to bring myself to swallow one of them.

Then Maewyn was suddenly breaking formation, calling ahead of him down the track.

"We return. And we bring guests!"

It appeared we had reached the Glade.

CHAPTER 33 – IN WHICH I GET ROOTED

The Glade was... exactly what is says on the tin.

As we passed through a tight circle of trees, my senses went through the roof at the number of eyes on us from high up amongst their branches. Then we came out into a wide clearing, probably the size of two or three football fields.

At the very centre was a massive pool with tributaries running off it to disappear into the trees. There were about ten of these, which gave the impression of the Glade being a gigantic wheel with liquid spokes running off it.

I couldn't see anything resembling houses in the clearing, but this wasn't surprising: Orwyn had explained that the Fae lived above the ground in the forest canopy. By the radiating hostility I was feeling from all the hidden eyes, I wasn't sure I would be invited to a play date any time soon.

The same could not be said for Corys, who was unceremoniously slung over Allavan's shoulder and spirited away into the woods. His men made some half-hearted argument, but he sheepishly waved them off. I couldn't blame him, to be honest. He appeared to have become the sex slave of 90s vintage Cindy Crawford. Sucked to be him.

A small group of manifestly older Fae were stood by the edge of the pool, glaring at us with barely restrained disgust. If Tresaith and the others who had come to see were ancient, then it beggared belief the age these guys must have been to look like this. I was not getting the impression we were a welcome addition to the community's social calendar.

"Tresaith Morningshot, explain yourself!" I wondered if that was the Fae equivalent of your mum using your full name when you were in some serious shit.

The speaker looked like one of those people who spent the whole of their retirement in Florida 'for the sun'. Its skin had turned to leather, and I could imagine, in another setting, demanding to speak to my manager.

Tresaith stepped forward. "As requested by the Council, we made contact with those from the mortal realm... "

"You were told to exterminate them, not bring them to tea!" A second desiccated Fae crouched out their displeasure. I made a guess this one was female, purely on the boob tube she was rocking. My word, she was old. Her eyes had sunken so far into her weathered face that I was amazed she could still see. I mentally flagged her as the 'Ur-Karen'.

"That is not so, Bresith, and well you know it!" Orwyn's voice was firm. "We were instructed to make contact and then use our best judgment on how to proceed."

The withered face turned to her. "You were given latitude on the assumption you had finally grown into good sense. We expected better."

Tresaith came to his mother's defence. "These mortals had dispatched the goblins marshalling to attack this place."

All of the Fae elders spat on the floor in an impressive display of phlegm synchronicity. "Trash that would not have lasted two minutes in our woods." The first speaker was back, spreading joy and sunshine.

"They then destroyed a second, newly arrived force led by a Hobgoblin."

Orwyn's words caused a little ripple of discussion. Then, a slightly less ramshackle elder pushed his way forward. He reminded me of nothing so much as Gandalf - right down to the flowing beard and giant staff. "You would have the Council believe that these mortals vanquished not just one goblin army but a second? And one under Hobgoblin command! You mock us."

"Their wizard bested Maewyn in one-to-one combat," Bessen said, having been suspiciously quiet thus far. She appeared to see humiliating her friend a notch above hoping for our imminent execution.

All eyes were suddenly on the Fae whose arse I had kicked - *recollections may vary, my dear* - who nodded solemnly. To be fair to him, since he'd woken up, he'd not been a drop of trouble. So much so, I had idly wondered whether - due to some ancient Fae tradition -whether he owed me some sort of life debt. I could do with my own Fae bodyguard.

I'd asked Tresaith about it, and he found it so hilarious that he couldn't breathe for several minutes.

"Not at all," he said when he regained control of himself. "He's just now understandably cautious around someone of your power. It has been centuries since he was bested in sword combat - much less via whatever dark art you used to appropriate his Qi."

This did not seem to be an auspicious moment to reveal that Drynwyn did all the fighting, and I had no idea how I'd nicked Maewyn's Qi. The words I told Owain not that long ago came to mind. 'Fake it until you make it', and all that.

"It is true," Maewyn said. "The wizard showed unusual martial promise."

Everyone turned to stare at me, including a bunch of kings who really, really gave the impression that they'd had enough of my shit. I did wish I'd stop giving them reasons to get hold of Caeldfwch and then use it to cut off my head. This quest was turning out to be less about keeping Arthur as Pendragon and more about ensuring my own survival.

"I have offered them guest protection," Tresaith boomed out.

"You had no right," Gandalf replied, his voice louder than the younger Fae's. "We have had no mortal in our Glade for an age. What you propose is the most egregious insult."

"My lords and ladies," Arthur pressed forward. "I am Arthur ap Uther ap Constantine. I have been granted the status of tongued one, and I would speak."

The response to this was silence. I didn't know whether this was a good sign or not. Neither did Arthur, who took a breath and then pressed on. "We are on a quest for Caeldfwch. We have completed the Step of Blood, and believe - in our destruction of the goblin armies - we have moved past the Step of Faith. However, I realise now that this cannot be the case."

Interesting," Merlin breathed in my mind. "*He's playing for keeps here.*

"Our people have been close before, and I understand now that, on occasion, my father may have played you false. I would ask for the opportunity to make amends. We have dispatched a threat to your lands, but I recognise that this has merely allowed us an opportunity to truly show you our good faith. What can we now do to show we are worthy allies? That we mean you and yours no harm."

"Hang on," Beric began, "we're not here for you to purge whatever sin your father inflicted on these fucking things. This is a quest for--"

"You are not a tongued one!" Tresaith stepped forward and punched Beric in the mouth. I could have kissed him. The King of Powy's eyes rolled to the back of his head and dropped like the veritable sack of shit.

The members of the Council completely ignored the show, eyes focused on Arthur. The Ur-Karen was the first to speak. "Harm? What possible harm could you short-lived things cause us? You are gnats around a stag. Irritating, but we will put up with your brief annoyance as we make our way through our lives. You ask the sun to make a pact with the clouds."

"The first metaphor was just about workable. The second... not so much. I expected better."

Everyone turned to look at the speaker. Who I realised was me.

Well, in for a penny...

"Dudes, look, let's not make this any more difficult than it needs to be. At best, this is going to be a side quest, isn't it? We've got to raise our reputation with you guys far enough to unlock the final stage of the main quest line. Don't get me wrong, I'm not anxious to begin the Step of Betrayal, but we've been on the road for a while, and I need to sleep in a proper bed and change my pants. Why don't you crack on and tell us what we need to do to make up for whatever grudge you're holding - it's kind of surprising slaughtering two goblin armies didn't make us quits, but, you know, whatever - and we'll get right down to it. I'm not feeling the whole vibe here."

"Fuck's sake," Arthur swore under his breath. "Don't you ever shut up?"

Mark was glowering at me, but at least Owain gave me a cheeky wink and a thumbs up.

Minor Karen was staring at me like I was a dog that had just shown him a card trick.

"You dare..."

"I'm a tongued one. Pretty sure that means I'm allowed to speak."

Gandalf banged his staff on the floor. "Enough. This is unseemly. Tresaith, you have granted these things guest privileges. However unwise this may have been, we will not profane that rite. These men and women - and their followers - will be kept safe for three days."

I did not like the implications that lurked, unspoken, in his words. Tresaith was likewise alert to the subtext. "Murrayin, what do you intend?"

"Just as I say!" He banged his staff on the ground once again, and roots exploded upwards, forming neat little cells around us. In an instant, we were all contained in little six-feet by six-feet lattice cages made of tree roots. If I hadn't been so pissed off, I'd have appreciated the smoothness of his cultivation work.

I went to draw Drynwyn to bring the fire when Merlin whispered caution.

Not yet. There will be time enough for escape. Let's not give them more reason not to trust us than they already have.

I looked through the gap in the roots and could see Tresaith and Orwyn - and even Maewyn - arguing with the departing Council. Only Bressen stayed behind, and the look on her face was the cat that had got the cream.

She sashayed close to me and gloated, "Three days. Then we'll see."

Oddly, that didn't seem like a promise to make daisy chains and swap make-up tips.

CHAPTER 34 – IN WHICH MY PILL-POPPING DAYS ARE APPARENTLY NOT OVER

I didn't take to captivity well.

It wasn't all that long ago that I'd spent an unspecified amount of looping time in a cell not that much bigger than I was currently in. That had not exactly been a high point of my life, and I could feel the rising panic the moment the roots closed over my head.

Of course, there were several differences this time compared to my experience at Aurelius' pleasure. For a start, I wasn't on my own with Drynwyn. Arthur, Owain, Beric and Mark were all similarly imprisoned, and I would be lying if the sight of the corpulently fat King of Gwynedd wedged into a cell barely wide enough for him to scratch his fat arse didn't ease my own suffering.

However, this enjoyment was undercut somewhat by the constant irritation of Beric's bitching.

"Just walked us straight here. Talk about naive."

Arthur just stared straight ahead, ignoring the King of Powys. Every time I felt the need to bite back on his behalf, Merlin nudged me as a reminder that our silence was probably pissing him off more than any *bon mots* I could come up with.

And that was the second major plus point about this lockup. I had Merlin this time. Obviously, I would pour boiling water on my tits and roll around in salt and lemon juice more readily than ever admit that to him, but something was reassuring about his presence.

When we were left to it, the first thing I did was drop into my Artist's Studio, but the Big M quickly persuaded me that this wasn't sensible.

You're going to be here for three days, my dear. You don't want to be dilating time.

So I popped back out again and did my best to tune out the whinging.

"Do you have any ideas?"

My experience of the Fae is that they are scrupulously fair. Nothing terrible will happen to you until the time of your guest right runs out.

"And then?"

They'll either be on board, or they'll kill you all. You were able to get lucky around a young, inexperienced warrior, but even he - without Drynwyn's assistance - would have wiped you out; there's nothing to be done worrying about the outcome of their deliberations.

"Easy to say when you're already dead, Big M."

Technically, so are you, my dear.

"Good point. Well made."

Beric and Mark were whispering together between their root cages, which didn't bode anything good for my future. But, on the other hand, Arthur and Owain were swapping legends about the Fae, which showed that - at least for one of the British Kings - the whole point behind this quest had been worth it.

Gwent was, strategically, pretty much the whole ball game when it came to keeping Cornwall and the Welsh tribes connected. If Owain closed his borders to us, Arthur would need to cross the Severn to have any credible wiggle room to launch an attack to push back the Saxons. And that would be, psychologically, a big deal. Sure, the other kings were important, but Gwent was pretty much the lynchpin to coherent British resistance to the Saxon invasion.

"So, what do you expect me to do for three days?"

"Funny you should mention that, my dear. I happen to have a couple of ideas."

***

There's an art to poisoning yourself.

If I weren't stuck in the middle of the Fae realm, trapped in a cell made of roots and contemplating taking a pull that was pretty much guaranteed to burn a hole through my guts, I'd probably be reaching for a Sylvia Plath quotation right now.

But, hey, you'll have to do the work. 'Lady Lazarus'. Google it.

I was holding the pill in my hand, rolling it between my fingers. The dark red dot in the centre was encased in a ball of Earth Qi which, by itself, I think I should have been getting more credit for pulling out of my arse. I wasn't especially talented with that stuff: it was only when I started to think of it as clay to be modelled that I began to get anywhere with it.

I'd taken a few pottery classes in my time - diversification, don't you know? - and could run off a couple of phallic pots with the best of them. In case any of you are harbouring fantasies about re-enacting Swayze and Moore around a wheel, let me do my bit for public service broadcasting. If you get clay anywhere... sensitive, you need to make sure you get that off before it starts drying. That was one visit to the waxing salon, and I'm not keen to relive it in the near future.

Back to the pills, my dear.

"Yep, I'm displacing, aren't I?"

So, the Pill of Agonishing Death. Absolutely guaranteed to positively fuck-up your day.

"Why am I contemplating swallowing this again, Big M? Surely it would be a net benefit for me to slip it to Beric as a treat?"

Now you are a wizard, Harry - goodness, I hate myself for humouring you with this - you need to take any opportunity to push beyond your limits. It's a very long journey to Hermione, and whereas at the lower levels, it's possible to progress by sheer, cussed determination, the improvements needed from now on are humongous. You will need to consume any number of natural treasures and absorb the Qi of countless spirit beasts to notice any improvement in your current situation.

"Dude, if you want to give me a magic mushroom, I'm absolutely here for it. I'm just a little leery about eating something that is specifically created to kill me."

First up, all cultivation is about risk. If you're not pushing the envelope, you're falling behind. Secondly, the whole point is to do something that <u>nearly</u> kills you. Then, when you come out the other side, you're that much more prepared against it. You have one hundred of these pills. Should you survive them all, you can pretty much guarantee you will make some sort of helpful advance in your skill set.

"Or I'll be dead... "

I refer you to my original point. Faint heart never won fair lady.
"I'm not wooing a damsel, Big M. I'm Socrates with a glass of hemlock."
There was a pause.
"Yeah, that's a pretty big reach, wasn't it?"
Just a bit,
"Fine."
And I downed the pill.

***

The second I swallowed it, the Earth Qi pulled into my channels. This gave me a nice little boost of chill - Earth Qi is nothing if not solid, good sense - which was swiftly overcome by the awareness of the drop of deadly poison burning its way down my throat.

I realise this might be a sensation you think you've experienced before - maybe you've sipped coffee that was a bit hot. Or took a bite of stew that was a touch warm as it went down.

Well, boo fucking hoo.

This was nothing like that. This stuff fucking seared my windpipe like it was a piece of burning sandpaper. I panicked as my airway closed and I reached for an Elixir of Wellness.

No, my dear. You must not mix the two. There's no knowing the interaction. It could well be catastrophic.

As I appeared to be having the mother of all anaphylactic shocks, I found that to be a touch fucking catastrophic, but I replaced the elixir in my inventory and took out a stiletto and a thin glass tube.

Trachyotemies are difficult in the best of circumstances, my dear...

I didn't give a fuck. I drove the knife into my neck, whipped it out and shoved the tube in the hole before my healing kicked in and sealed it. I could breathe again.

That was kind of where the good news came to an end.

The drop of poison - free from its Earth Qi case - was continuing its merry journey of destruction through my body, burning through my stomach wall, allowing all sorts of pleasant liquids to slosh about. I knew I had some decent health recovery since levelling up, but I doubted I was up to surviving something this spectacular.

I clung to Melehan's Rock of Curing and - mentally, at least - looked piteously at Merlin.

You need to cultivate that drop, my dear. If you leave it in your physical system, it will destroy you.

I didn't need telling twice. A small part of me, though - the part currently not screaming in agony - wished the Big M had pre-taught that slice of crucial information.

I pulled the poison into my core.

To begin with, my paint tried to treat it like any other drop of Qi. It wandered over to it and, with a gulp, consumed it. However, the moment this happened, my poor paint blob turned an alarming colour that I can only describe as 'gangrene'.

More paint hurried over, trying to overwhelm the rot, but no matter how much arrived or how big the blob became, it continued to go that terrible colour.

Okay. I was hoping that would do it. Hmmmmm. Bit of a pickle.

141

Awesome. The words you always dream you will hear from your legendary mentor while you are melting from the inside out are uncertain musings.

As Hamlet vacillated, my blob of paint collapsed. I sensed that if I left it in my core, the whole thing would be infected by this stuff. So, with an almighty effort, I began to cycle it around my channels.

I'd say this hurt, but I'm worried I'd undersell it.

Take the most unbearable physical and psychological torment you've ever experienced. Imagine that being ramped up a hundredfold and then narrated to you by Tom Hiddleston.

It was that bad.

Just as it had crucified my physical tubes and pipes, this stuff burned around my channels like a uranium enema. I kept pumping out my Qi in the hope it would dilute the fucking stuff, and then the store was empty, and I was emptying out my earrings. When they were done, I pulled on a bunch of my rings and drained their mana stones, too.

I was pulling everything I'd put into my cauldron out when I felt the destruction lessen. Not much, don't get me wrong. I was screaming my heart out, but the pain wasn't increasing anymore.

There we go, my dear. That's the sweet spot. That's the apex. All downhill from here.

The sun was just going down on that first day of captivity when I was finally able to open my eyes. My entire cultivation setup was fucked. My channels were burned, I was out of Qi, and I was a physical wreck.

And that was from one drop of the stuff.

I was aware of several pairs of eyes fixed on me. Arthur cleared his throat.

"Erm, you've been screaming for half the day, Morgan. Is everything okay?"

With some effort, I managed to flip him the bird before I lost consciousness, my hand still wrapped around the healing rock.

CHAPTER 35 – IN WHICH THERE IS A GREAT(ISH) ESCAPE

Arthur was unsure what to do. Morgan had been asleep—if that is what it was—for the whole second day of their imprisonment.

A number of the Fae had come to check on her during that time, and each had refused to answer any of his questions about her well-being. Neither would they tell him how the rest of the men were, nor what was planned for them at the end of the third day.

He was not taking this as an especially good sign.

Corys had made a few appearances, usually led around by Allavan. When he'd first seen the smug, satisfied look on the King of Dehuebarch's face, he'd wanted to reach through the roots of his cage and choke the man to death. But then, he reflected, was the man acting all that much different from how he had for the last ten years?

Have cock, will fuck.

"She's alright," Owain said for what felt like the hundredth time.

"Unless we've got fortunate," added Beric.

Arthur ignored them both. He needed a plan. He had been so sure that the destruction of the goblin armies would have been the Step of Faith. Everything he knew about the Fae was that they felt a powerful sense of honour over such things. He could not believe they would not acknowledge they now had a debt over removing that threat to their land.

What had his father done to piss them off so much?

But then he was shaken out of his reverie by Tresaith's approach.

"My Lord Arthur," the Fae said in his musical voice.

Arthur just glared back at him. Deep down, he knew Tresaith was not responsible for their current plight - indeed, he had argued vociferously against it - but he was not feeling especially charitable this day.

"I understand your anger. Once again, I apologise on behalf of my people who find this action to be distasteful. We have no history of misusing the guest privilege in this way."

"So glad that we can give such ancient beings an opportunity to experience something new." Mark's voice was harsh. Of all of them, with his excessive girth, he was suffering the most in the tiny cage; Arthur was almost - very almost - feeling sorry for him.

Tresaith's extraordinary eyes flashed Mark's way. "Should you not so fully reject your son, you would not be in this position. Unless you wish to offer apologies for your words and make amends?"

Mark, slowly and painfully, shuffled around so that he faced away from the Fae.

The story of Tristian - Mark's son - and Isolde was one Arthur was reasonably familiar with. If only because he had tried to bed that exquisitely beautiful woman himself and been shot down. With the intensity of a fiery meteor shower. Then, of course, Tristian had shown up and tactfully made it clear that if Arthur looked at Isolde twice again, there would be repercussions. Arthur had looked into that young man's eyes and knew there was no fighting with the scorching intensity of true love.

He'd heard a rumour that the two had killed themselves in the sort of self-indulgent act of childish monomania that he did not think suited either of the people he knew. If you loved someone as much as those two did each other, you didn't take your own life. And the way the Fae were talking about Tristian was very much in the present tense...

"How are the men?" Arthur dragged his thinking away from beautiful women with green eyes and intense young men in shining mail. He had an army to think about.

Tresaith's face went through a range of complex emotions before settling on something that was an approximation of rueful. "That's what I'm coming to you about. We may need a little help on that front..."

***

Lancelot stood amongst the shattered remains of his cage and ripped the bars off the one next to him. He'd been doing this constantly for the last forty-eight hours, and he could sense the Fae were beginning to get a touch pissed off with him.

At the very least, he knew he was taking a toll on their Qi reserves because a different old, old Fae had been repairing the damage he had been causing since the sun came up. It was the smallest of victories, but - as his dear mother always said - no one ever fucked a walrus by fiddling with its whiskers.

That had felt more relevant in his head. He was really quite tired.

Arthur's men had caught on to what he was doing almost immediately. If there was one thing spearmen understood, it was the value of being irritating. Led by the tall, tattooed quartermaster - Karl - they had begun systematically destroying their root cages in shifts.

Lancelot, though, was not interested in any downtime.

"For fuck's sake! Will you guys quit it? You're going to get us all killed!" One of Cory's men - the only group who hadn't bought into making constant escape attempts - hissed at him.

Lancelot walked over to that man's cell and ripped the door off. "Well done," he shouted so that the exasperated Fae running to - once again - rebuild the prison could hear. "Your plan is perfect being. Keep it up I will. Thanks to you for the sharing." He freed another few men of Dehuebarch and turned to confront the approaching Fae.

He had observed that it was only the really old ones that could create the root cells. The Fae who came charging each time he broke free were much younger - it was all relative, of course - and had obviously been told to restrain the prisoners as peacefully as possible until the slower-moving big guns arrived.

It turned out there was quite a lot of chaos he could wreak in that time gap, especially against opponents who weren't allowed to cause him any significant damage.

He'd freed enough of the men now and knew they would concentrate on freeing their fellows. There was no point in them trying to take on the Fae; regardless of how gently these beings were taking it, no normal mortal could hope to hold their own.

Lancelot, on the other hand, was treating the whole thing as an exciting training opportunity.

He ran straight at the nearest Fae and made to punch her in the face. She jerked backwards in shock and surprise at his uncanny speed, but not as much as the male Fae next to her, who was the one Lancelot actually clocked.

In a blink of an eye, he'd taken the unusually thin blade from that falling sack of perfectly proportioned bones before any of the others could react. And he was sweeping upwards to eviscerate the Fae arriving on his left a heartbeat later. It was only the superhuman grace of the thing that let it pivot on one foot and avoid the flashing sword.

Lancelot winked in appreciation of the move and headbutted him instead. Good in all realms, a classic nutting was.

There were four of five rather concerned-looking Fae left. None of them were old enough to bother him.

Wasn't this going to be fun?

***

"You're complaining my men are not acting fair?"

Tresaith grimaced. It was humbling enough that he was needing to ask the question, let alone explain why. The only reason he'd agreed to make the request was that he thought it might be more readily accepted coming from him. It turned out to have been a miscalculation.

"We are not allowed to hurt you while you have guest rights. Your men are taking advantage of that." Even to his own ears, those words sounded hollow.

"You've locked us up, lad," Owain said, the tone of his voice disbelieving. "You can't expect us to sit calmly and wait for the clock to rundown until you're allowed to hurt us!"

"But it's dishonourable!" Tresaith tried again. "We expected more... "

Arthur's laugh was bitter. "You speak to us of dishonour! Five Kings of the Britons are on a holy quest. Your reaction to this is to prostitute one of us, place the rest of us in cages and then complain when we do not meekly accept this treatment. The legends of the Fae are many and various in our lands. Some are good, and some are dark, but none of them are of you proving so false."

Tresaith bared his teeth in an entirely alien expression. "So, you will not help to restrain your men?"

Arthur spat at the Fae's feet. "You present to give us guest rights whilst imprisoning us, waiting for the moment you can slaughter us with a clean conscience. Fuck you and your request for calm. In fact -" Arthur knelt next to the sleeping form of Morgan and drew Drynwyn from its sheath- "I'm ashamed for not following their lead. Sword, light it up!"

With fucking pleasure.

***

It took the arrival of every member of the Council to restore a semblance of order. They were significantly less concerned with not hurting the Britons than the young Fae, and it was a relatively short amount of time before the root cages were restored.

Orwyn and Tresaith stood at the edge of the treeline, watching the finishing touches be added to the prison. Despite the cost in Qi, the Council had ordered a substantial increase in the density of the enclosing roots: there would be no further breakouts until the clock ran down on the third day.

"You know what will happen," Orwyn said to her son. "Murrayin will announce their death."

"If the Council wills it, who are we to question?"

Orwyn shook her head. "I raised you better than that."

"We can't trust them! You've seen the chaos they've wrought this day. And they knew we could not fight back. That was not the act of those I would consider as allies."

"You're looking for an excuse to do nothing. Two roads lie before you - one an easy stroll through light and fields and the other filled with orcs and thorns. There is no shame in wishing for the easy path, but there is in following it."

Tresaith watched as the man who would be the Pendragon hit the bars of his cage impotently. He knew his mother was right. He knew others amongst the Moonglade Clan were likely uncomfortable about this abuse of the guest privilege—let alone what all assumed would happen when the sun set on the third day.

"What would you have me do, mother?"

"Show a little faith, my son."

Although, alone in his cage, Arthur could not hear the Fae's conversation, he certainly made out the swelling choral music that suddenly announced itself in the grove.

CHAPTER 36 – IN WHICH BLÆK FINDS A SOLID LEAD

It was the start of the Grand Tournament proper, and there was a certain... tension in the air.

Of course, that was mainly because of the assassination attempts the day before. Security had been beefed up, which meant Bors had taken to wandering around with his arms wide open, asking loudly for anyone to "come and have a go if you think you're hard enough." As blood was leaking through a poorly tied bandage around his chest, his hair and beard were matted with sweat, and he had a somewhat wild gleam in his eye, this was proving to be a surprisingly robust measure.

Furthermore, most competitors found themselves in a state of unease, reporting a disturbed night's sleep as the shadows within their rooms seemed to roil and move. Had anyone harboured nefarious intent this morning, summoning the energy would have been hard.

Indeed, there was such a lack of festivity and general raucousness for the opening morning of the heats that Guinevere found herself summoning the merchants Bors had charged with organising things to see if anything could be done.

Guinevere noted that neither of the merchants looked well, and she didn't think that was just from one night's poor kip. Their clothes hung off them as if they had not been eating, and when Bors' voice drifted into the throne room from the courtyard below, they visibly flinched.

"Sirs, I thank you for the pains you have taken thus far with the preparations for this tournament. I have rarely seen the castle environs so vibrant and alive."

"Thank you," the smaller of the two men whispered. "Your Majesty," he added hurriedly at a nudge from his partner.

"Sir Bors assures me that this has all been achieved well within budget—" Did the bigger man start at that? "—and for that, you have my profound thanks."

There was a pause as the smaller merchant - Tasko, was it? - licked his lips and searched for the words he wanted. "If we could just return to the matter of the budget for a moment..."

"And if you want some, I promise I have it for you!" Bors' booming voice made the door tremble.

"Please, don't mind Sir Bors," Guinevere said, hoping to soothe these oddly anxious men. They had both cringed at the sound of Bors' voice. "He has some frustrations to work out after the events of yesterday. You were saying something about your budget?"

"No. Nothing at all, Your Majesty. All within budget. All exactly as agreed." Both men were alternatively nodding and shaking their heads. It was all very strange.

"Excellent. I am so glad to hear it because I have an unexpected request to make."

Was it her imagination, or did these men go somewhat weak at the knees? "I'm sorry, sirs. Are you both quite well?"

"Perfectly, Your Majesty. What request would you have of us?"

"I find the mood around Tintagel to be somewhat underwhelming this morning. It would seem sensible if we could get a little good humour going. How about we give mead away for free today? Just to get things going?" No, it definitely wasn't her imagination; these guys were flopping about all over the place.

"Free mead, Your Majesty? For everyone attending the first day of the tournament? That would be... wonderfully generous." Tasko said with all the enthusiasm of a man to whom it was suggested he set his testicles on fire.

"Can we achieve that and stay within our budget."

Both men laughed hysterically for a moment, then abruptly stopped as another incoherent threat from Bors was bellowed through the window.

"We can do that," the larger man hurriedly answered. His partner squeaked, then nodded.

"Excellent. Please let Sir Bors know if we need to increase the budget. I'm sure he will be willing to negotiate."

***

Sir Bors was currently negotiating quite loudly with no one in particular.

He'd been advised to spend a few days in bed following his wounds, but he was damned if a few little pinpricks were going to get in his way. He needed everyone to understand he was not going to put up with any more shenanigans and was doing that the best way he knew - by lots of shouting and offering to take it outside.

So far, no one was taking him up on it.

Thus, it was hardly surprising that Tasko and Pæps approached him cautiously. "Sir Bors, could we have a moment of your time?"

"Go for it," he said, looming over them, spittle on the corner of his mouth and blood running in rivers down his chest to drip to the floor.

"The Queen has asked for all mead on the first day of the festival to be free. We have agreed."

"Excellent!" Bors turned to the stallholder behind him and gestured. "Gimmie!" Once his mug was filled, he downed it and then held it out for another. Once that was replaced, he held it up and shouted, "The booze is on these guys! One day only! Get pissed while stocks last!"

The entire courtyard came alive. Everyone who had been nervously staying in their rooms whilst Bors rampaged around was now slightly more motivated to have a good time. Violent death was one thing, but a free drink? That was quite another.

"Very generous of you, boys. Very generous." Bors slapped Tasko and Pæps on their backs. "I know what people say about you merchants, but you both are stand-up guys."

"Thanks," Tasko said weakly, watching the queues line up at the concession stalls. "We aim to please."

***

After a morning's uninhibited drinking, it was perhaps not ideal that the first heats were archery.

A rather tipsy group of men and women congregated at the lists. Amongst them was Queen Guinevere, who had chosen not to partake in the free-flowing booze this morning.

"You know," Bors said as they watched a series of attempts fall well short of their targets, "a more cynical man than me would suggest you may have got everyone else pissed so you can win this bracket."

"Don't know what you're talking about," Guinevere said, abruptly loosing her arrow where it flew to sit dead centre of the first butt. "Just sorting the wheat from the chaff."

There was certainly a lot of chaff.

After just a few rounds, only ten competitors were left—including the Queen—who had been capable of hitting the first row of targets.

As the bullseyes were set backwards fifty more yards, Bors glanced at the large number of men who had been eliminated. "You know, your little ego cheat has probably knocked out any number of archers we would have been able to use."

Guinevere handed her bow to a lady-in-waiting and stretched. "And tell me, how much use are archers that are more interested in filling their skins when they should be shooting?" she nodded at the small group that remained in the competition. "These are your archers."

Bors looked uncertainly at them. "If you say so, Gwin."

Guinevere took back her bow and went to join those in the second round. "If they're going to have my husband's back, you better believe I want them more interested in their craft than beer. Now run along. Mama has a competition to win."

***

Blæk kept one eye on Guinevere, cheerfully showing up some of the craftiest and wiliest poachers across the land and the other on the crowds around the mead tents.

As the archery competition—or, more accurately, the lack of it—showed, the lure of free alcohol was rather overwhelming, and there were only a few sober souls around Tintagel by the time the sun was at its zenith.

Of those still upright, most were either castle guards—who had been expressly forbidden to imbibe—or those trying, ever so politely, to stop the Queen from running away with the shooting competition.

Blæk had his other eye on the handful of other teetotallers.

He discounted three of them as threats immediately. Parsifal, Acanor and Galahad had not gone near the flowing stream of liquor and were keeping themselves largely to themselves. The Grey had been clear they had equipped themselves admirably during the last assassination attempt, and all the reports suggest they had dedicated themselves to joining the new Marghekyon.

So, he only had a couple of dozen of his shadows watching them. You could never be too careful.

No, it was the other non-drinkers that were getting his personal attention.

His instinct was to kill them all. Better safe than sorry, and after what had happened the day before, he was rather keen to follow that path.

At the back of his mind, however, he knew that more subtlety was required if he wanted answers about who was behind these attempts.

149

So here he was, watching anyone who seemed to be still sober enough to be a danger.

These two men, in particular, had attracted his notice.

They were doing their best to pretend not to know each other, but their indifference was too studied to Blæk's expert eye. Both were expensively dressed but not ostentatiously so. And they were armed.

Of course, most of those within the castle carried any number of weapons. But few had knives hidden beneath their cloaks, strapped beneath long sleeves and against their thighs.

These weren't here for any of the competitions. These were assassins.

Blæk reached out with his Qi and took hold of the hidden metal. Blades of any type had always spoken to him, perhaps even more so than the shadows did.

He knew from where the original ore had been extracted, which had been used to forge them. He could feel the blows of the blacksmith that had shaped it into its current shape. And he could feel the echoes of the uses to which these knives had been put.

All this meant was that he had a reasonable sense of where the knives had come from.

Blæk's eyes widened - even as he pressed down on the metal to open up the veins and arteries of those that carried them. It was always handy when men kept their sharp things so near particularly gushing spots.

No one remarked on the two men who suddenly dropped to the floor - it had been that kind of day so far - and it was several hours before the pools of blood beneath their bodies were felt worthy of notice. Again, it had been that sort of day.

Forgetting their bodies immediately, Blæk made his way to the archery lists. Finally, he had some concrete news to share.

CHAPTER 37 – IN WHICH I TEST MY PAIN TOLERANCE

I know this will shock you to your very core, but I've experienced some hangovers in my time.

As I'm sure we're all people of the world here, so I'm confident you know what I'm talking about. Pounding headache, sickness and a bone-deep agony that is just screaming for a bacon sandwich.

I'm happy to report that a Pill of Agonising Death has an after-effect that is absolutely nothing like that. It was several million orders of magnitude worse.

I lay on the ground, unable to open my eyes in case the movement ripped open my face. Even breathing was torture; I could hear my ribs creak at each inhalation. Like, full-on, right on the edge of splitting if there was a hair more extension. The beating of my heart was a hammer blow to my temple, to the extent I was sure my brain must be exposed to the elements.

Ah, you are back with us, my dear.

I didn't have the energy to as much as think about telling Merlin where to go.

No, do not try to do anything yet. If my calculations are correct—and of course they are—you are still in the middle of an epic detox, and too much excitement could well be detrimental to your well-being.

"Tell me something I don't know, you patronising twat", I didn't quite manage to say.

I do not like to put pressure on you while you are in this state - I well remember my first time trying to increase my own resistances. Of course, I was up and about almost immediately afterwards, but we cannot all be me, can we? - but this is a very good opportunity we should not miss.

I tried to wiggle my toes and nearly passed out again. I was really not in a very good way here. I was, particularly, not going to be open to any of the Big M's bullshit right now.

You will remember, my dear, that the very first time you exhausted all of your Qi, it gave you an opportunity to add to your techniques?

I struggled to remember what I had for breakfast, so I just gurgled a generic response. My throat felt like a thousand pixies were scraping it clear with sheets of sandpaper.

It occurs to me that now might be the perfect moment to consolidate an early Water Qi technique of my own invention. You've thus far shown little ability with the medium, but in a state of complete mental and physical exhaustion, this is likely to be a good condition in which to have a good chance to flex those muscles, as it were.

"Can't... go... to... school... today... daddy. Dying."

Ha, you and your wit, my dear. Trust me, you will be recovering your faculties in short order. So, there's a reasonably short window here. Once your channels fill up again, the opportunity will be lost until the next time you find yourself at death's door.

Of course, you do seem to end up somewhat broken after most encounters with... well, pretty much everyone, so this isn't quite the 'one and done' it would be for most cultivators. However, being a... a Harry is all about taking your opportunities.

So far, my experience as a Harry did not feel all that much better than that of a Ron. However, it was beyond me to make that point right now.

No, no. There's no need to thank me. I understand how grateful you are, my dear. I see it as my role in life to smooth out your deficiencies. So, what we are going to focus on is developing a little something called <Ice Block>. I'm sure you will come up with your own pithy title, but that makes no mind. I want to ensure you have a few more defensive options than just healing up the damage.

I didn't disagree with him on this one, I just didn't see how I could possibly do anything right now. I know I'm not shy with the hyperbole, but I am genuinely dying. The very idea of doing any cultivation right now made me heave.

So, first thing first. You do not visualise your Qi as water, so we will need to develop a slightly different approach. For me, it was quite simple - of course, most things were, but that makes no mind - I just dropped the temperature, solidified my Qi and projected that outside my body in the form of a shield.

Yeah, I'm going to get right on that. I risked flicking an eye open, but the sun beating down was so bright I felt like it'd bore a hole straight through my soul.

So, the Big M was carrying on regardless, *We need to come up with a similar concept for paint. Is there a particular painting you feel instinctively secure behind?*

I very nearly ignored him. I absolutely was not on board with furthering my cultivator education right now. But then, something about his words stirred a pleasant memory.

There was a card that Zizzie had sent me for one birthday or another with the words 'Look familiar?' written on the inside. The image was Friedrich's 'Wanderer Above the Sea of Fog'. You'll know it if you saw it. It's the Victorian-looking bloke stood on top of a mountain staring off into the distance at the landscape. There's mist all around him, but he's just stood, facing away from the viewer, hand nonchalantly resting on his walking stick. It's the absolute embodiment of 'I don't need anyone' and, as she'd always done, my sister had hit the nail on the head completely.

On the inside of the envelope, she wrote, 'I hope you find somewhere to feel free,' with a couple of kisses and her latest phone number.

I'd never called, but I'd held on to the card. I don't know what it was about the anonymous figure standing defiantly out over the mountains. But I felt I'd found a kindred spirit. I knew exactly where that card was in my flat. Or, at least, where it would be in fifteen hundred years. This time thing was weird.

Ah, fuck me, the Big M was still talking, *I can see something appearing in your core. Well done, my dear, I wasn't sure you were listening.*

Oh, do fuck off, you sanctimonious wanker.

Annoyingly, though, he was right. I could feel the mist forming around me, with the smell of pine trees and the crisp snap of the mountain air. The pathetic droplets that were left of my Qi were slowly moving over the pages of my Artist's Studio, replicating the image.

I dropped into the studio proper, sad to realise I felt no better here than I did in the real world - with the added embuggerance that I wasn't recovering. I'd still need to feel shit for just as long outside, so this was - essentially - just torturing myself for no reason.

With an act of insane courage and resilience, I picked up a brush and helped my Qi make the picture. I'd painted versions of the Wanderer a million times, swapping the standing figure for all manner of things. I'd even sold quite a few: there was a surprisingly buoyant market for Victorian dudes up a mountain with a few additions. Oddest was a six-by-four feet canvass of a bloke's ex blowing the guy, which seemed to give the purchaser inordinate pleasure.

If you want to pay me cash for some artistic revenge porn, I'm absolutely not here to judge. At least not out loud.

So, even in my shambolic state, it wasn't that tricky to quickly knock off a pretty decent version. Don't get me wrong, it wasn't my best work, but considering I was somehow retching and hiccuping simultaneously, I felt I'd done a pretty solid job.

Well done, my dear. Thus, we have your Qi in a format that you feel offers you protection. What you need to do now is project it out in front of you. Imagine it like a shield.

Sure, and after that, I'll dance the Can-can while singing the opening aria of Aida while I do it.

I'm sensing some hesitancy, my dear. I should note there's a little bit of time sensitivity here. You must manifest this technique while absolutely at rock bottom to circumvent the usual consolidation period. You could always take another pill if that would help?

Fuck me, no.

I grabbed hold of the painting with two clawed hands - I couldn't imagine ever being able to stretch them out again - and tried to force it out of my studio.

Of course, nothing happened.

Come on, one last big push! The membrane between the real world and your studio is about as thin as it is ever going to be. You need to do this now, my dear. You do not want to know how difficult it will be to do this once your defences start to rebuild.

I gave a few more half-hearted pushes. The picture could not have been more than a few feet square, but it was too heavy for my overloaded muscles, and the distance between the external and internal world was simply too big.

I shook my head - which made me dry heave some more - and went to put the picture down. Then I felt the ghostly brush of Merlin's hands on my mind.

My dear, I am sorry to push you, but you do not have the luxury of giving up here.

I tried to speak, but my teeth were itching too much. I feared they'd sprout wings and fly away if I opened my mouth. There's just the chance I was hallucinating with pain now.

If what I anticipate is going to happen occurs, then you are going to need a decent shield spell. If not for you, then certainly for Arthur. I know you've been able to empty your channels in the past to block attacks, but you've got to be able to both defend and fight if we're going to complete this quest.

My vision was clouding over. The pain was simply too overwhelming. I tried to wrench my hands free from Merlin's control but, if anything, his grip increased.

This is your chance. You learn to do this now—when it will be relatively easy—or there will be months, if not years, of trying to breach the barrier. You are not lacking in resilience, my dear. Push this picture into the real world and secure the technique.

153

I kept my eyes closed and pushed everything I had into my hands, lifting my arms—feeling the muscles in both biceps rip—and with a scream, forced the Wanderer outside and into the real world.

As it went through, I followed it back into reality, seeing a blurry message appear before my eyes.

I was passing out again - I seemed to be becoming some sort of Bronte minor character -but not before the words **<Zizzie's Gift> technique created** - flashed across my vision.

Well done, my dear. I think it would be best for you to rest now. From what I can tell, tomorrow will be a very busy day.

CHAPTER 38 – IN WHICH WE GET OUT OF DODGE

I awoke to the sound of hurriedly whispered voices.

"The man's got no face!"

"Don't be ridiculous; he's just facing away from you."

"I tell you, there's no other side. You can't get around him!"

"Just pick her up! We need to get out of here."

I vaguely recognised most of the speakers, and if - as it sounded like - there was an escape, I was up for it. Provided, of course, I could move without my whole world falling apart.

Tentatively, I opened both of my eyes and was pleased to be rewarded with no white-hot burn of agony. I wriggled my fingers and toes and was likewise satisfied that my torture appeared to be over.

For now, my dear.

"Cheers, mate. What would I do without your help and counsel?" Glancing inside my Artist's Studio, I could see there was a decent stock of high-density Qi hanging around, so I - slowly - started cycling around my channels again. Everything was a bit sore - think more 'enthusiastic' new partner than epic cystitis - but nothing like I remembered the aftermath of absorbing Voltigern's Dragon. Nor my error with the mana stones. Or when Aurelius took me out to the woodshed.

Fuck me, I get battered on a regular basis, don't I? I might want to do something about that.

Interestingly, I thought the damage caused by that latest escapade was probably greater than any of those other events. I was just a tougher gal now. And that thought made me feel pretty decent.

I sat up and noticed three major things all at once.

First, I stank. Like proper reeked. I was rocking a lovely mix of a couple of days of total body sweat, vomit, blood and... various other things I appeared to have excreted from my body when trying to deal with the poison. I had just gone through a pretty seismic detox procedure.

This led to the second important thing. I felt pretty amazing. I mean, I was already feeling chipper since crossing the boundary into Harry, but this was how I imagine it felt for all those glamorous women on TV when they step out of a costly spa. Although I was willing to concede, they probably did so without being caked in *all* their own fluids.

I imagined Gwyneth Paltrow would probably market the shit - literally - out of my pills.

Everything felt better. I'd once sat through a PE lesson where the idea of 'fast-twitch fibres' had been explained. I felt like everything I had was now built like that.

At first, I thought it was just the difference from feeling so terrible, but no. It was like I'd taken another leap forward.

It almost made me want to take another pill.

Almost.

How are you feeling, my dear?

"Dude, I feel amazing. Will something like that happen each time?"

I am afraid not. As with all things, the law of diminishing returns applies. You have gone through a significant trauma, and your physical capabilities have improved commensurately.

Your next pill will have to fight against that improvement to cause damage, meaning the opportunity to develop will be much reduced. I imagine you will need to consume three or four next time to have anything like the same effect. After that, you'll need a couple of handfuls and then...

Well, we'll need to find something else to temper you. A cultivator's search for ways to cause themselves infinite pain is never at an end. However, can I draw your attention to a slightly more pressing issue...

That leads to the third important thing I realised when I woke up: I wasn't in my cell anymore.

***

It had been reasonably easy to achieve the first stage of the escape.

Of course, Tresaith recognised this was because none of the Council had anticipated one of their own freeing the humans. All of the previous escape attempts had involved lots of noise, fire, and general hubbub, which alerted the nearest Fae that something was up.

So, his simply and quietly encouraging the roots to retract into the ground was not the sort of thing that was likely to draw attention. He'd managed to gather the entire human army into decent order, ready to flee before it became clear nobody could wake their wizard.

Or, more accurately, no one could get close enough to their wizard to move her.

"Interesting," he said as the mist rolled towards him, seemingly coming from the human figure looking in the opposite direction. "And he moves to intercept any attempt to approach her?"

Arthur grimaced. Now hardly seemed like the time for a lengthy discussion about the oddities connected to his wizard. He realised it took a lot to get a Fae's blood pressure raised, but he couldn't easily relax when so close to powerful people who'd encaged them and were obviously planning to do away with them. "It's some shield spell, I think. She did something similar to my cloak."

Tresaith walked cautiously towards the wizard, and the man with the stick somehow moved between them. The Fae backed up and then darted to the left, and the faceless man was there again. "This is a quite lovely piece of Water Qi working."

"Glad you're impressed. Can't you just pick the bitch up and get us out of here?"

Tresaith carried out the odd pantomime all the Fae did whenever Beric spoke: frowning and looking around as if he's heard someone fart in church, but couldn't quite pinpoint who.

Arthur pressed the issue. "It's only a matter of time before one of your people's guards realises we're free. Is there nothing you can do to break the spell so we can leave?"

The Fae was looking at Morgan with an odd, faraway expression. "Of course. I said it was lovely work, not that it was resilient. It is such as one of our young children would cast to entertain its grandmother." Mark snorted at that, and Tresaith turned to him. "Which is to say it is a demonstration of power I have not seen from one of your people for many a long year. She is quite the find, your wizard."

"Ah, stop it. You'll make me blush."

And the wizard sat up, dismissing her shield spell.

***

I couldn't help but feel that escapes should have a touch more jeopardy about them. As far as I could tell, Tresaith had decided to save us, dissolved our cages and was walking the whole army out of the glade with literally no fanfare. I'd been on school trips that needed more detailed risk assessments.

We'd met up with the rest of those who had been trapped and were following a dirt path down and away from the centre of the Fae land. Corys's men had kicked up a bit of a fuss about leaving their king behind, but considering he'd fucked off to - well, yes. Literally - there was a general sense he could find his own way home.

"He will not be harmed. He has the favour of Allavan, and when she tires of him, she will not allow the Council to harm him. I imagine she will return him somewhere safe in your own realm."

"And I awoke, and found me here
On the cold hill side.
And this is why I sojourn here
Alone and palely loitering,
Though the sedge is withered from the lake,
And no birds sing." I said, quoting a nice little bit of Keats.

Tresaith looked at me and winked. "Something like that."

Arthur swung himself onto Llameri's back, his dragon cloak billowing in the air. Lancelot was at his side, and I noticed the other kings had fallen behind him. It was a subtle but important moment no one was talking about.

They're nearly there, my dear. They see him as their leader. Apart from the Big M, of course.

The king looked down at Tresaith, who seemed far happier being on foot. "What now? I thank you for freeing us, but what does that mean for you? Will there be repercussions for what you have done today?"

Tresaith shrugged. "A central tenet of my people is that we must always be true to what we think is right in the moment. Most of us felt Murrayin's decision was an error and that breaking our guest rite was unacceptable. However, she is head of the Council and made the decision honestly. I can disagree with her, but I do not blame her for her judgment. The seers have foretold great turbulence caused by allowing you to go free."

"So there will be no danger to you, lad?" Owain had ridden forward to listen.

Tresaith smiled. "I think most will be relieved. The Fae do not wantonly slaughter humans. We can barely raise ourselves to combat goblins. There will be some gnashing of teeth at my presumption. A war party may even be sent after you. But for me? No. Nothing."

"A war party?" I didn't like the sound of that.

157

"Do not worry, little wizard. I will deal with that. In fact," Tresaith said, looking at where the track we were on split in two, I think we're at the end of our shared journey."

"What do you mean?" I said, a touch disappointed. I was still thinking about that wink...

Tresaith pointed down one path. "If you follow that way, you will quickly return to your human realm. I am not that familiar with your geography, but there is a large river with settlements along it."

"Saxon or British settlements?" I could tell Arthur was tempted. The quest had taken its toll on our numbers. There would be attraction in re-equipping and refreshing in safety.

Tresaith shrugged. "You all look the same to me."

"And in the other direction?" Lancelot had already started walking down that way.

"Well, there is a legend in my people that if a trustworthy man takes that road, he will find exactly what he deserves in the pool at the end of the track."

Now we were talking. Although thinking about it, I wasn't wild about the semantics there. "And should an untrustworthy man walk that path?"

"Ah," Tresaith's teeth flashed very white. "That man will get what he deserves, too."

Arthur leant down to clasp Tresaith's forearm in the manly way men do when they're saying thanks for manly things. "What has made you help us, Lord Fae?"

"Let us just say, human, that I appear to have found faith that this is the right decision."

And there was more of that bloody choral music.

Our army set off down the road less travelled.

CHAPTER 39 – IN WHICH I AM RELIED UPON FOR SAGE ADVICE. WE'RE DOOMED.

To call the dirt track we were progressing down a 'road' would be stretching it somewhat. I'm sure after a hundred and fifty-odd heavily armoured men had lolloped their way down it, there was a little more to it, but for those of us near the front, we felt like we were navigating a little by guy instinct and guesswork.

The makeup of our column would be pretty interesting to a student of Machiavelli. Arthur's forces - which had only lost a handful in the battles with the goblins - topped and tailed the formation. Lancelot had argued against splitting our forces, but I could see the sense in what was intended. When the chips were down, it was only those who had the red dragon on their shields that we truly felt we could rely on. Basically, Arthur figured the others would be less likely to run if they had to do so past his men.

To be honest, I think the King would have liked to have added the double buffer of doing the same with Owain's men, but there were just not enough of them left. In lieu of their own leader, the King of Gwent had taken control of Cory's abandoned spears and had integrated his men into those. Owain held the middle of the column, and we had high hopes that this might actually work to install a bit of order.

"I've probably fucked enough women from Dehuebarch to be most of these guy's daddy," he had said with a giant, shit-eating grin on his face. But I could sense his worry. The single best service Corys's men could do him now - behind simply leaving him to fuck himself senile in a Fae glade - would be to ensure that the King of Gwent had a mishap.

I wasn't wild about leaving one of the few men on this quest that I liked in the middle of - at best - an ambivalent force, but Arthur was right. What choice did we really have? "He's not got enough men, wizard. I could hide him under my skirt tails, but he wouldn't thank me for it. You're only a king for as long as people feel you are strong enough to hold that title. Owain either earns the respect of the men of Dehuebarch, or there's nothing to be done for him. He wouldn't want it any other way. Ask him if you think I'm wrong."

I was pretty sure there were other options available other than crossing our fingers and hoping our staunchest ally wasn't merked by the men he commanded, but I was a humble twenty-first century wizard. What did I know about military strategy? The only time I ever played Total War, I used the cheat code to have twenty-thousand prime horse archers covered by several million cannons on turn 2.

However, the issues around Owain were minor compared to the headaches of Beric and Mark.

We'd spent some time determining how best to neutralise their threat. Having them next to each other in the column was a non-starter. Together, they had the single biggest number of spears. Even if Corys's men stayed out of any confrontation, it would still be ninety-odd against a little more than fifty. I was starting to have enough self-esteem to recognise I tipped the scales the other way reasonably effectively, and Lancelot was worth at least ten on his own. Still, if ninety men in the middle of the line acted up, there would be momentum behind that, which would get gnarly.

I don't care how good you are; an arrow through the throat was pretty compelling in any argument, and we couldn't be everywhere.

So, Arthur had popped Owain in the middle of them, splitting his two biggest detractors with the firebreak of the remainder of the spears of Gwent and Corys's abandoned men.

All that had been left to decide was who to put at Arthur's back and who to have a little too far out of observable range to keep honest. Neither was an attractive option, but it was Lancelot who decided it—or, rather, Lancelot's enmity with Beric.

Ever since the duel in Tintagel on the eve of the quest, Lancelot and the men of Powys had been niggling at each other. There's been nothing overt - you didn't prod a bear that could comfortably eat you whole without trying - but even I was aware of the tension. And I was about as oblivious to social cues and atmospheric undercurrents as it was possible to be.

As tempers were getting a little short post-captivity with the Fae and the whole 'not being a tongued one', Arthur had put Lancelot in charge of the men at the rear, bookending Mark's forces with Owain, and had Beric between the middle and the remaining Dunmonians at the front.

"Like it, I do not," Lancelot had said, flexing his pecs. "I can reach you in a crisis, but quick it won't be."

Arthur bristled at that. He liked the barbarian - hell, he liked him so much I felt like an absolute card not sharing more about what I knew was coming down the road - but he didn't want to give anyone the impression he needed babysitting. "In a 'crisis', Lancelot, you will stay in position and lead your men. You are not my spaniel to come running at the first sign of trouble. I was carrying my own water long before you arrived at Tintagel's gate."

They hadn't spoken much after that.

We'd been travelling in a column for the best part of the day without seeing or hearing another sound. There wasn't even the sort of noise I might have expected in a deep forest like this: the sounds of small children murdering old women in confectionary-based houses and suchlike. You know, just the classics.

I kept questing out with my Qi, but the sheer intensity of the Wood Qi around us overwhelmed my senses. Thanks to a few pointers from Merlin, I was just about able to keep my eye on the column, but it was like having to squint for the blobs of darkness in the middle of a neon rave.

"Do you think the Fae will follow us?"

Arthur's voice shook me out of my latest search for dangers. I sped up my horse and drew next to him. It might have been my imagination, but he looked... bigger, somehow. Not like he was physically growing, of course, But rather, he was more substantially filling his space.

I had a pretty complex history with Arthur - and, even as I say this, I know this is a crazy thing to even consider. I mean, me! A fuck-up from the mean streets of Brum having any sort of history with the Once and Future King was mental. But I did, and it involved a lot of fire, a fair bit of mental anguish and lashings of arse-kickings. It was, thus, a bit odd that I was feeling something like... was that respect?

I did say, my dear, when you get to know him, he is pretty impressive.

He did have a point, though. Ever since he'd crashed through those goblins, rearing high on Llameri's saddle, I was having this uncomfortable feeling in my chest. I kind of think I wanted to have his back.

Fuck me, I was getting sentimental in my old age.

I realised I was staring at him without giving any answer. "From what I understand of Fae culture," I said, "they won't be too motivated to pursue us. Merlin reckons anyone up for hunting us won't push it beyond where Tresaith is waiting."

Arthur nodded slowly. "Do you think we should have struck for home?"

I laughed at that. "Shit. I don't know. You're the boss."

My dear, he needs more from you than that. Part of the deal that comes with being a counsellor to a king, is that you need to - you know - actually counsel him. "Shit. I don't know," is not quite good enough.

"What do I say? I have no idea. We're still a fighting force, but I don't know how wise it is for us to keep pushing on."

So tell him that. He does not need you to agree with him, my dear. He needs to talk aloud with someone he trusts. Lancelot is all the way at the back of this disparate pack, and Owain is needed to hold the middle. I'm pretty sure if Llameri could talk, he would rather chat it through with her, but without that option, it is down to you.

"By which, I mean, of course," I added, silently cursing Merlin, "is that I'm not sure. My lord, we haven't achieved what we set out to do yet, and good people have died. I don't think there's going to be many spearmen back there damning your name because we're still on the hunt for the sword."

Arthur grunted, and we rode in silence for a little while. Then he said, "I'm worried about the Fae."

I waited for him to say more. Just when I thought that was going to be it, he continued. "They're too strong. If it had not been for Tresaith, I do not doubt they would have executed us all on the morrow. And there would have been nothing we could have done about it. Even their children had powers that dwarfed those of our mightiest warriors."

I rubbed my chin thoughtfully. That was what counsellors did, wasn't it?

"It's a bit like worrying about the tide, isn't it?"

He turned to me, eyes like still ponds. "Explain."

"Long ago - although, saying that, I'm probably talking about your great-great-great grandson or some time-whimey bullshit like that - there was (or will be) a king called Canute. He decided that the best way to prove his power was to test himself against the sea. So he wandered his royal arse down to the coast, sat down in the sand and told the tide not to come in."

"And what happened?"

"What the fuck do you think happened? Motherfucker got wet."

"I'm struggling to follow your point, wizard."

I flicked my hair back in what I hoped looked like a careless manner. "There are powers in the world we cannot do much about. I'd suggest that the Fae are one of them. Worrying about them won't do us any good. Just as ordering the tide not to come in didn't bother it any. As you say, they're too strong. If they want to wipe us out, the best we can do is choose the cloth they use. Worry about things you can affect; don't waste time on things you cannot."

I felt I'd just bastardised something my sponsor at AA had once said to me, but it seemed to do the trick. Some of the tension slipped away from the king's shoulders.

Well done, my dear. However, in the interests of fairness, I should note that Canute took to the beach to demonstrate to his court the limits of his power. He was seeking to make the very point you did and it's a travesty he's remembered as some sort of unstoppable moron when he was - in truth - a very wise and decent king.

"Yeah, my heart bleeds for him."

But then we all had much more to worry about than long dead - or long before being alive—one of the two - British monarchs.

Because the woods were suddenly filled with a familiar chittering and screeching.

The goblins were back for round three.

And this is time, it seemed like they meant for it to stick.

CHAPTER 40 – IN WHICH WE TAKE SOMETHING OF AN ARSE KICKING

Now, you may be thinking, "for fuck's sake, Morgan! You've kicked goblin-arse twice already; what is going to be different this time?"

And that would be a fair argument, well made.

As a counterpoint, I should note a few differences between meeting an army head-on when you have a plan and shield wall set-up and being ambushed from all sides when you are in a long, thin column through twisty forest paths.

I'd also highly suggest that these guys were gearing up to take on the fucking Fae. So, while they may not have exactly been Genghis' hordes sweeping majestically across the plains of Asia, neither were they a drone army of robots being wiped out by a bunch of frogs with magic, exploding rocks.

Even then, I agree we'd still be the hot favourites if everyone had acted in anything approaching a concerted manner. However, there was just too much suspicion going on now. In the few seconds before I got very busy indeed, I heard Arthur order one thing, Beric another, Owain's spears try something while Corys's men under his command did something different. Oh, and I'm pretty sure I saw Mark's forces turn on Lancelot.

But then I was involved in a scene that was not dissimilar to the climax, Gremlins.

I may suggest a shield would be useful in these circumstances, my dear. You are increasingly hardy, but it only takes one stray arrow...

I snapped out of watching four small figures streak towards me with 'lunch' in their minds. As a decent complement of ordinance came out of the woods behind them, I took the Big M's point and activated <Zizzie's Gift>.

And not a moment too soon.

The projected image of the painting whipped out in front of me, the figure's walking stick flashing left and right to smack the projectiles out of the air. Others followed, though, and the dude was quickly turned into a pincushion.

As he seemed fairly undisturbed by this development, I left him to it and turned my attention to the four little murder-kermits who were now on top of me.

I drew Drynwyn and thrust it at the lead attackers, three feet of ugly green knobliness carrying its own sword. Surprisingly, it did a decent job of parrying, which just made my sword angry. You won't like it when it's angry. A pulse of flame ended that little dust-up. I would have made a suitable comment - "a bit hot for you?" perhaps - if I hadn't found my hands a little full with the assault of the others.

They each attacked with some degree of coordination, taking advantage of my sword temporarily being engaged. Three spears reached for me. I <Personal Space Invaded> their arses but only succeeded in blasting one of them backwards, where it hit a tree with the sort of sickening crunch that suggested it would take more than a skilled chiropractor with a 'can do' attitude to sort it out.

The other two, though, recovered and got all up in my business. I was just pulling Drynwyn back towards a decent guard position when a bone-tipped spear took me in the shoulder. Don't get me wrong, I could probably have shrugged this off even before I was a cultivator. We were basically getting mobbed by off-brand Smurfs, and provided I kept my wits about me, there really should be little that could be done to cause me massive damage.

However, what the injury did do was numb my arm for just long enough for the sword to drop from my fingers.

For fuck's sake!

I pulsed Qi to the wound, and it healed instantly. I followed up by throwing out a nice couple of arcs of <Unnecessary Sequel Trilogy> at the goblins before me. I may even have cackled a touch as I did so.

I then took a step forward to retrieve my sword but then staggered to the side as a spearman I didn't think I recognised - I mean, something had bitten away half his face, so I wasn't sure that was fully competent identification check - crashed into me and, in the midst of the chaos, kicked Drynwyn away and into the melee.

Fuck.

I wasn't quite the helpless wee fawn I'd been before I found the sword, but neither was I going to be especially helpful to Arthur unarmed. I turned to follow the direction the blade had gone and grimaced at what I was looking at.

We were taking a doing.

I could see where little islands of resistance had sprung up the length of the column where someone had kept their heads long enough to pull men back into the formations that had served us well before. The thing is, there were thousands of years of 'mano a mano' juices swimming through each man's mind over which a thin layer of Roman discipline had been painted.

Arthur was golden. I mean, he'd clearly lost a few men we couldn't afford to in the chaos of the initial ambush, but there were still at least ten of his spears in a ring around him. I couldn't see Llameri, but I doubted Arthur had let anything happen to her. Goblins were still pouring from the woods, but they were breaking on that bulwark like a tide against a pier and then flowing further down the column.

And that was where the issues were coming.

I couldn't see Beric's men at all. I mean, I'm sure they were there. It was just that they were buried under a sea of green. It would be just my luck if that was where Drynwyn had ended up, too. I quested out down our connection with my Qi which confirmed it. Yep. Of course, that was where it was.

I covered my hands with the thickest of paint I could and checked my shield was still functioning - fuck, it had actually taken a shit-tonne of damage. The poor dude had lost an arm and a leg, and the mountain behind him was on fire. But hey, tis but a scratch. I refreshed him with a significant amount of my remaining Qi - and waded into the battle to reclaim my sword.

Now, the thing about goblins is not that they are hard to kill. It's more that both of you seem to be equally committed to their death being the outcome. They're like all those bugs that throw themselves at a speeding car's windscreen. One or two of them will have a negligible impact, but if enough block your vision, it will be a wipe-out city.

I was alternating between <Personal Space Invader? and <Unnecessary Sequel Trilogy> to try to clear a path, and there were hundreds of the little buggers going flying. I still wasn't seeing much in the way of Beric's men - or, at least, not in an uneaten state - but I was finding it tricky to give too much of a damn.

I was much more worried about the disaster happening around Owain.

I smashed two goblins foaming at the mouth at the prospect of my sweet, sweet cheeks on toast, shattering their skulls and using them as makeshift hammers to clear a bit more space to try to catch sight of the King of Gwent.

Compared to the mincemeat being made of Beric's men, there was at least some sign of life around Owain's position. All those seasons of peace with the Saxons had clearly led to the men of Powys being a touch soft around the edges. On the other hand, you could say what you liked about their king - and Cory's men had been saying plenty - but the men of Dehuebarch were showing some heart. The problem, though, was that the remnants of Mark's men - had they really tried to jump Lancelot? - were trying to force their way inside the defensive circle they'd established in the middle of our line.

That will get them all killed, my dear, Merlin whispered. *If Owain opens the circle to let Mark in, the goblins will pour in, too."*

"What do I do?" I opened the cone of <Personal Space Invader> to become a wide circle around me and activated it. This was a much more diffuse blast of energy, but it cleared me a few moments to think before the wave of green would wash over me again.

Me personally? I would slaughter Mark's men. This is now a salvage mission, my dear, and they are expendable. From what I can tell, they are running because they tried to attack Lancelot's men, which is a poor evolutionary choice.

"Okay. Well, I'll take that under advisement. Do I have any non-genocidal options? Just so I can say I've considered all sides, you fucking lunatic."

If you find that unpalatable, then you must find a way to significantly reduce the pressure on Owain's formation so that they can open their defences and let Mark's refugees in.

"And how do I do that?"

No idea, my dear. You will be wanting to refresh your shield, by the way.

I was being absolutely fucked up by arrows. I refreshed my poor Wanderer, who was just a pair of feet doing its best to intercept all the shit coming my way, and had a thought.

Merlin obviously had the same idea. *That would probably do it, my dear.*

I dragged all the arrows away from the Wanderer and, for good measure, gave a quick tug of Wood Qi to grab hold of any that were lying around on the floor. This turned out to be a lot.

"Just how many of these fucking things are attacking us?!"

You do realise what you are about to do is going to do a fair amount of harm to our own side...

"Dude, not two seconds ago, you were advocating for me wiping out a king's entire retinue. *Now* you are being squeamish?"

I am just here to offer advice. Like any well-meaning adviser.

"Well, be quiet for a minute. I'm concentrating."

I felt the shape of <Personal Space Invader> in my head. When Aurelius had torn out my other techniques, I realised they each had a particular position in my core. This was interesting as it suggested they had a physical presence within my soul. It would, therefore, seem to me that I could make some alterations with a bit of tweakng.

Holding on to all the arrows with the lightest of feathers of Qi, I brushed them against my <Personal Space Invader> technique and tried to subtly suggest it could do something else as well.

I scrabbled about for a bit and then felt Merlin take charge. I recognised the slightly frustrated noise he made before placing some guiding hands upon mine from a million... intimate encounters.

Then we were in business.

I triggered <Personal Space Invader>... or rather I didn't. This variety of the technique that clicked into being was called <I.E.D>.

All of the wood I'd packed against myself suddenly exploded outwards in a wide arc, turning a significant portion of the goblins into snot.

It would be accurate to say this turned the tide of battle.

CHAPTER 41 – IN WHICH MARK GETS SOME THINGS OFF HIS CHEST

It took a lot to surprise Lancelot.

His training, from the earliest days of his youth, was intense. The bloody battles he had been thrown into as soon as he could walk had seasoned him in ways few could understand. There were thus few gambits he had not experienced before.

Yet, even for him, the situation was rare. A goblin ambush with his 'allies' rushing him was not a scenario he had encountered often. But then again, life always had a way of presenting new, violently intense experiences.

"Spear pairs. Now!"

There were different approaches to take against overwhelming odds. Most people would opt for Choice A - *run for the high ground and signal for help.* Arthur had gone all in for Choice B - *turtle up and encourage them to hunt elsewhere.* On the other hand, Beric had chosen the ever popular Choice C - *be slaughtered to a man.*

Lancelot, though, was built a little differently.

He only had fourteen men available to him at the rear of the column. He'd spent a little time with each of them, explaining his philosophy of war and suchlike, and there'd been a chance to take them through a few manoeuvres that he liked to think of as 'old faithfuls.'

'Spear pairs' was one of the more accessible formations his people used and, he thought, the one that was likely to pay dividends in his adopted home. He knew the Saxons favoured overwhelming charges and frenzied hand-to-hand combat - in that way, not dissimilar to the goblins, now he thought of it - and the British mode of fighting behind a spear wall was a pretty solid response: tight formation, well drilled and heavy cavalry lurking around to mop up was spot on.

However, there was always going to be a place for warriors who tried something a bit different. His people called them hǫggsveit, but the best translation in this language was 'spear pairs'. Basically, you and your mate were an army unit on your own. When shit went down, you found cover; you located an appropriate target, and you fucking acted on your own initiative. Nothing else mattered but your pair. You had his back, he had yours, and fuck the rest of them.

As soon as Lancelot called for 'spear pairs', the entire rear of the column scattered for the trees, flowing past the startled goblins coming the other way and leaving Mark's men momentarily wrong-footed as the targets for their treachery vanished.

Lancelot stayed where he was.

There was a legend told around his people's campfire about a warrior who would hold a position single-handedly. Sometimes, it was a bridge. Others, the end of a valley. But the location really didn't matter. Everyone understood that the saga was a metaphor for their tribe's bloody-minded belligerence—everyone, that is, apart from his mother, who considered it more of a training suggestion.

He slowly drew his sword and tried to calculate whether it would be Mark's men or the lead group of goblins that reached him first. It was going to be close.

Or what his mother would call "a chance to be a man."

***

Mark swore as Arthur's men scattered like rabbits. He had gladly accepted the challenge of taking these men off the field. No matter how noble or how well Arthur was leading, without enough spears to press his claim, it would all come to nought. He had just been waiting for the right moment to dispose of the pathetic remnant behind him, and a goblin assault was as good as any.

Thus, as soon as he heard the beginning shriek of the ambush, he had thrown his men at the Dumnonian spears behind them, gambling they could wipe them out. Or at least fatally maul them and allow the goblins to mop up.

However, it turned out Lancelot was just a hair quicker.

Saying that, there was still just one irritating figure left on the dirt track. Maybe this wouldn't be a lost cause after all.

"What are you fucking waiting for? Kill him!"

***

The first spearman was dead before he even realised whom he was attacking. Lancelot had closed the gap between them and had thrust his sword through the man's throat in the blink of an eye.

The barbarian pulled his long blade clear and slashed to the right, low, severing the leg at the knee of the next closest attacker. He then pivoted, using the weight of his swing to twist in a wide circle, mowing down three goblins that were nearly on him.

He was back facing Mark's men just in time to block a downward axe blow on the cross blade of his sword. He smiled up at the attacker and winked. "Nearly got me, you did!"

Lancelot pushed upwards, far quicker than the axeman could respond, and ran him through. It was at this stage he stopped consciously thinking. He knew he wasn't the cleverest of men in the world - his mother told him that often enough - so he was much better at allowing his instincts to take over.

And what instincts...

The world shifted to that delicious, slow motion that made him feel invincible.

***

"Hold! Hold!" Arthur dragged a man back into line. The boy had wanted to chase after the goblin he was fighting, little caring about the hole he'd leave in their formation. "We do *not* pursue."

The man - blood lust on him - growled his assent, but Arthur appreciated the frustration.

Sitting behind a shield wall and watching your fellows be slaughtered was hard. Beric's men were gone. For whatever reason, they hadn't tried to form up, and the sheer number of goblins overwhelmed them.

Arthur had little time for the King of Powys, but over a quarter of their force was wiped away simply through incompetent leadership. And if what he could make out further down the line was accurate, it was probably a bit worse than that.

"Anyone have eyes on the wizard?" He asked. The lack of ostentatious fireballs of death was noticeable.

"Last I saw, she was making her way to Owain," one of his veterans replied.

"Fuck!" Arthur cast about, wishing he hadn't dismissed Llameri to the woods. He needed the height. He looked around at the men holding the tight circle. They were stuck. He didn't have enough to move safely, and breaking the formation would be irresponsible.

The dragon on his back let loose a low rumble. "I don't like it either," he thought back, "but we're going to have to wait this one out."

***

Mark's men were done.

There was no way they were advancing towards the maniac surrounded by bodies any longer. They were being battered by kamikaze goblins from each side, and Lancelot's men in the woods were being a colossal pain in the arse sniping from the trees.

They gave a collective 'fuck this!' and turned and ran towards the seemingly safe refuge of the sizeable shield wall behind them.

"What the fuck are you doing!" From his admittedly well-defended litter, Mark was watching in horror as his scheme failed. Lancelot stood - in fact, was standing much closer to their position than he was before - and his men were in full rout.

"Your majesty, we need to retreat!" The Captain of his guards was looking nervously at the approaching Lancelot. There really were not that many men separating them any longer.

"Fuck that. Help me up!"

His guard looked doubtfully at Mark's handmaids. He couldn't remember the last time he had seen his king standing on a battlefield. "I'm not sure this is the time, my lord. There are hundreds of goblins, let alone..." he stopped, not sure how to phrase 'let alone the man you tried to fuck up the arse who has now turned around and is looking pretty displeased at the attempt.'

"I didn't ask you to think. I asked you to help me up!"

Mark leaned heavily on the man, pulling himself to his feet. The men around his litter were somehow keeping the goblins off him, but it wouldn't last much longer. The chittering and screaming was getting closer and closer.

Seeming oblivious to the destruction around him, Mark pointed a chubby finger at the advancing Lancelot. "Fuck you. Do you hear? Fuck you! I know your sort. Just like my fucking son, aren't you? All honour and duty and brotherhood of the sword until it suits you. And then you'll fuck anything you want with pretty enough eyes! You're just like him, aren't you? You and my fucking son," Mark spat the word out

169

like it was poison in his mouth, "are two of a kind. Chivalry personified until you're not."

The guard captain went down, three goblin spears driven into his gut. Another stood to take his place, but the line was thinning. Lancelot kept closing in, chopping through goblins like he was scything wheat.

Mark stood there, continuing to shout insults. They were no more than thirty yards apart and closing. "And all anyone has to say is how honourable you are. How much integrity you have. Well, fuck him and his integrity. He stole my fucking wife! I'll be doing Arthur a favour by killing you off. You'll be up his bitch wife's skirts as soon as his back is turned!"

Another couple of Mark's men fell, and then Lancelot was in striking distance.

It wasn't clear what the barbarian had planned for the confrontation, and there wasn't a chance to find out.

Because some mentalist let off a giant bomb in the middle of the forest.

CHAPTER 42 – IN WHICH QI USAGE IS EXPLAINED THROUGH THE MEDIUM OF PREMATURE EJACULATION

There's something fairly liberating about being a suicide bomber.

I mean, I'm not advocating for it or anything. It's definitely a bad life choice, and trust me, the whole 'forty virgins thing', don't bother. If you're going to spend the rest of eternity fucking, make sure it's with people who know what they're doing. Now I think about it, I wonder if the call to jihad had promised 'forty slappers from Newcastle who know their way around a cock' as an incitement, the whole Middle East thing might have been resolved much quicker.

Was there a point you were seeking to make here, my dear?

"Not sure. I think I might have a concussion..."

That seems pretty likely.

"What I was trying to say was that I could imagine being a suicide bomber, when the 'suicide' bit was not a firm requirement, might be a touch addictive."

One moment, I was in the middle of a decently spicy situation, and the next... silence.

Well, not 'silence'. What I really mean is that the noise of battle was replaced by a sort of high-pitched whining noise, which suggested I may have blown out my eardrums. I pushed a lot of Qi that way - I really did not have very much left over at all.

I suppose being the centre of a Super Bomber Man-style explosion was pretty energy-expensive.

At an opportune moment, it might be worth discussing the 'less is more' approach to using your techniques. You do not always need to... I believe the correct pop culture reference would be 'turn it up to eleven'.

"I get the job done, don't I?" I muttered, looking around at the aftermath of the explosion. I'd certainly got something done, anyway.

Due to their lesser mass, I'd rocketed the majority of the goblins over the hills and far away. Those that had been hit by the fragments of the wood that had flown off me like shrapnel had been... shredded.

The silence sat like a malignant toad for a bit longer, and then spearmen started to drag themselves to their feet. There were some pretty crap injuries there too, but most of them seemed to have been caused by teeth, claws and spears rather than shards of flying, supersonic wood. I guess the sheer overwhelming mass of goblins had been a valuable bit of padding.

Before long, we had reestablished some sort of order and were able to work out where things stood. Good news: Lancelot and Arthur had salvaged most of their men, and the spears of Dumnonia numbered twenty-eight, counting the three of us.

That was pretty much where the upside ended.

The men of Powys were gone. Like, totally wiped out. Where they had stood in the column was just a mass of pink paste and bones with scraps of meat hanging off them. It was like they had been a field of corn, and the locusts had eaten their full.

"Anything you can do?" Arthur asked me.

"Think they're a touch beyond healing, mate. I'm good, but if you're looking for anything other than some serious necromancy, you're going to be disappointed."

He looked at me blankly for a moment. "I meant, can you not cremate them or something? We can't leave them like this."

Ah. Yes. That would make a bit more sense. I reached out for the long, thin line of Qi that connected me to Drynwyn. He was, of course, right in the middle of the goo. I pulsed a thought down our connected and was rewarded with a **Fucking remembered I was here, did you?**

"Dude, it's not my fault. I was stabbed. With a spear."

Do you have any fucking idea how bad it smells down here?

"It's not exactly the Garden of Earthly Delights this end either. You up for doing what you do best?"

There was a pause. **I'm a little short of the good stuff right now. Don't suppose you could do a sword a fucking solid, could you?**

I switched out my earrings, which were wholly drained and slipped on a couple of rings, which seemed to be about half-full. Maybe the Big M had a point. I did seem to be burning through my Qi at quite a rate since levelling up.

I dropped into my Artist's Studio, enjoying the neutral fragrance of the sea after the epic aromatic experience of the battlefield.

"I'm running through Qi pretty quick. Shouldn't the whole-increasing-the-concentration thing and then moving into Harry have given me more to call on?"

Did you notice, my dear, how much devastation that last technique you used caused?

"Sure, I mean, that was the point, wasn't it?"

It was indeed, my dear. But... let me explain it to you this way. Not that long ago, your cultivation power was the equivalent of a newborn kitten. Thanks to some spectacular mentoring and no little luck, you grew up to be a common or garden pussy...

"Dude!"

Don't worry, I heard it as soon as I said it. Let's switch metaphors. You were a puppy, and then you grew up to be a nice, yappy terrier. Pretty destructive to small rats and generally an irritating presence, nipping at ankles and suchlike.

"Is there a point to this?"

There is, indeed, my dear. In the blink of an eye, you grew from a terrier to a dire wolf, and you're still eating and drinking as a little rat muncher. You have all this extra power and capability, but you're pretty much constantly running on empty.

"I didn't think cultivators needed food?"

Metaphor, my dear. You need to dedicate some significant time to cycling. Because of... incidents, you were able to fill up your Ron tanks with fairly cursory meditation. But Harry is a whole different board game. You will still need to spend much less time cultivating each day than anyone else of your level, but it is now the time for you to take this seriously. You cannot keep relying on having a piece of mana stone jewellery to hand every time you bottom out.

That made sense. "So, I'm going to need to carve out some time to me 'Om' on every day."

Something like that, my dear. You could also, as I mentioned, dial back a little on giving every technique a hundred per cent. You should be able to have enough subtle control by now to have far greater sensitivity.

"I just hit the technique as hard I can. It's not like I ever reach for them in non-life-or-death situations, is it?"

There was a silence. *Sorry, my dear. I'm just trying to overcome my pain at one of my apprentices describing 'hitting a technique' as if they are playing some sort of arcade game.*

I wisely decided not to point out that was precisely what it felt like.

Since we've concentrated your Qi, it should feel much more solid in your perception. There was something of an excuse to spurt it all out at once at the lower levels, but now that you have more experience, I hope you have developed more control.

"You know, one of my first boyfriends had just that problem."

For the sake of my sanity, can we please not complete that line of thought?

"No worries. But you're saying I should be less 'letting it all out' and more 'thinking about my grandmother on the toilet'?"

I think Merlin might have gone for a walk at that stage.

I dropped back to reality and connected back up with Drynwyn.

"Okay, mate. Do you mind if I try just dribbling some energy into you? Merlin thinks I'm being a bit gung ho with it."

Couldn't fucking care less as long as I get out of here sharpish.

I wasn't wholly sure how to do what the sword had asked. I was getting reasonably good at pushing and pulling Qi around, but it was something of an all-or-nothing thing. I had a sense of how much Drynwyn needed to be... I don't want to say 'full' because that's not quite the right word, but to have as much of my Qi as it could hold.

I remembered that, when fighting the Shriket, the sword had poured stuff back the other way, so I figured I owed it.

But I didn't want to just spaff it down the connection – **that's a fucking horrible way to describe it -** and wanted to show the Big M that I was progressing.

I held a - metaphorical - handful of my Qi. It was undoubtedly thicker than the liquid I had started with when Merlin brought me back. I tried to drip a tiny quantity of it into my link with Drynwyn but quickly found it all being sucked up.

"Whoa, cool your jets there, D. I'm trying something here."

Sure. Take your fucking time. Did you know the stomach acid of a goblin has enzymes within it that, given enough time, will melt through anything? Absolutely no fucking rush at all. I always wanted to be a dagger.

Ignoring the snark, I gathered another handful and slowly began dribbling it down our connection. The experience was agonisingly frustrating. My instinct was just to let it go, but I understood Big M's point.

I have every advantage in the world right now. My channels were pristine, and after the generosity of the village above the Knockers—have I mentioned how much I like that word—I was able to call on reserves of Qi many levels above me.

But I wasn't making the most of these benefits. They were just filling in gaps caused by my not seeking to do things properly. Sooner or later, that was going to catch up with me. What I needed to do was get used to doing things properly so that when I did need to call on the big guns, they would push me over the line.

The face of Aurelius Ambrosius swam into my mind.

I was never going to be able to take on that dude without some serious effort.

Gradually, painfully slowly, I got more of a sense for what I was doing and the urgent pressure to get it done as fast as possible receded.

To be scrupulously fair to you, my dear, that's actually not too bad.

"My word. High praise, indeed."

Not being funny here or anything. But it might be working fine your end, but you're being a fucking Qi tease from where I'm at. Just finish me off, for the love of the gods.

I felt like we'd explored about as much sexual innuendo as could be extended from this particular situation, so I dropped in the rest of my Qi.

In seconds, Drynwyn burst into flames, vapourising the remains of Beric's men.

"Thank you," Arthur said. "At least that's one problem dealt with."

I turned to look where he was staring and swore.

To have lost Corys was bad. For Beric to be dead was less than ideal. But to see Lancelot stand over the bloodied form of Mark felt like it might well be a step too far.

It appeared that we were running out of kings.

CHAPTER 43 – IN WHICH WE MOVE TOWARDS ENDGAME

We set up camp to lick our wounds.

Lancelot's Rangers - yeah, they had a name now. Go them! - were hidden in the woods around our position, which at least gave us some sense we'd have a heads-up before getting mobbed again. I'm not sure Arthur was delighted to lose half of his men to this new unit, but I imagine he had wider issues with which to concern himself.

Two hundred fifty men had left Tintagel on this quest, but wyverns, Shriket, goblins, Fae, goblins again, and friendly assassination efforts had taken their toll. Every last man of Powys was gone. I wasn't all over this diplomacy thing, but I sensed that was going to cause comment. Especially as Beric had, very loudly, been anti this expedition.

We'd also misplaced the King of Dehuebarch and lost half of his men in our latest goblin entanglement. Owain was down to the last four of his own countrymen. I was pleased to see Burford's gaunt figure still in one piece. Worryingly, the amalgamated spears of Dehuebarch and Gwent were our single biggest contingent fighting under one flag.

To be fair, that little squad had held up pretty well during the latest dust-up, so it didn't seem right to cast aspersions, but I knew Owain was worried now he had so few of his own guys to watch his back.

Which left the issue of Mark.

"I mean, if we look on the bright side, what he did could represent the final Step for the sword?"

Arthur shook his head at Owain's suggestion.

Merlin agreed. *Attacking Lancelot was - and please beg my pardon - a dick move. However, it could hardly be described as a 'betrayal of all that is good.'*

"No cool choral music, either," I added.

Whether it had been the last Step or not, though, Mark's brainfart had brought our numbers down to the tragic range. "We haven't got the spears to keep him and his remaining men under guard," Arthur said aloud as if inviting comment, but I worried he had already made up his mind. "Anyone have any ideas?"

"Kill them," Lancelot said, not even looking up from sharpening his blade. "Dishonourable, they were."

"To be fair -" how on earth was I being the voice of reason here? –"his men would just have been following orders. I'm all for some brief and violent retribution against Mark, but are we really up for executing a bunch of men who did what their king asked? That's kind of a precedent to set..."

Owain nodded thoughtfully and stroked his Father Christmas beard. "We are looking very threadbare. I would worry how the men of Dehuebarch would react if we slay Mark's men. There are rumbles enough about keeping them captive."

"Kill them, too." Lancelot was nothing if not single-minded.

"I think if we're discussing executing over half of our remaining forces, we need to take a bit of a sense check."

Silence greeted my words, and I looked around our tight little camp. We hadn't really been on the road all that long, and we'd experienced some pretty shitty luck. At every turn, we'd been mobbed by creatures we were ill-equipped to defeat, regardless of our numbers. In fact, I wondered whether - even if we had another two hundred spears - we'd have been much better off right now.

Now, there was a thought.

"Big M, you know the whole 'Step of Blood, Step of Faith, Step of Betrayal of all that is Good schtick, where does it come from?"

There are many songs about the search for Caeldfwch. From my consideration of them all, those are the consistent features: Whoever wishes to gain the blade must walk those three steps.

"Do any of the source materials deal with how many people are supposed to undertake the quest?"

There was a long pause. I was dimly aware that Lancelot was holding forth at length on the various morale benefits of a good butchering. I suppose, as he had personally been the focus of Mark's betrayal, he was entitled.

Without spending too long parsing thousands of years of oral tradition, I think I know what you're getting at. Our current expedition could be seen following the course of a poem called Preiddeu Anwyn, in which a king enters a beautiful world filled with fantastical creatures. In many ways, this journey is echoed in the tale of Bronwen from Celtic mythology and...

"Dude!"

Sorry, this is actually quite interesting when you get into it. Most of the existing texts do make reference to the sort of travails that have met us thus far. In fact -

"How many people make the quest, Big M?"

It may be best if I quote the relevant section, my dear.

I don't speak of men of feeble intent
Who do not know the Step of Blood
Nor of the press of the green horde
Nor what it is to show faith to those of the woods
When we went with the man who would be the dragon
An encounter of betrayal
Save seven, none reached the sword"

I let that sink in for a while. Owain seemed to be quieting down Lancelot's blood lust somewhat, or at the very least, was getting Arthur on side.

"You know, mate, it might have been useful to quote that before, you know, we set out with over two hundred guys."

I am, of course, a huge fan of hindsight, my dear. However, I would note that Preiddeu Anwyn is just one small exxample of a massive collection of songs and poems.

But I wasn't too bothered. The poem wouldn't have made much sense until we'd actually reached this point anyway. Never had my new life felt more like a videogame than it did right now. We'd completed the various Steps of the quest and were now gearing up for - I presume - the Big Bad encounter.

And only seven of us were going to make it.

I cleared my throat, and all eyes around the fire turned to me. "If I may, I have a suggestion."

***

And that was how Arthur, Lancelot, me, Owain and Burford, Mark and his nominated guard - a massive bald fucker called Julka - found ourselves dismissing the rest of the army. Obviously, absolutely no one was happy with this, and I doubted any of them were going to do anything other than follow us at a discrete distance.

"You're leading us to our deaths!" Mark spat, stumbling over a root that a wag of wizard might have made engorge at just the right moment. The poor guy wasn't too steady on his feet, was he? Bless him.

As everyone else appeared to be ignoring him, it kind of fell on me to reply. "Look, if only seven of us are prophesied to make it to the sword, then we might as well cut the others loose and let them head for home."

"And, of course, the men of Dumnonia are in the majority of the seven!"

"Mate, there's one king here who has shown he cannot be trusted, and it sure as fuck ain't Arthur. If I were you, I'd be thanking your good fortune you're even being allowed to come with us."

We'd disagreed over that.

I might not have been entirely on board with Operation Kill Mark, but neither was I sure that cutting him loose and letting him bring a bodyguard was the smart play. Arthur, though, had held firm.

"This was a group quest to secure my claim as the Pendragon. We cannot do anything about the loss of Beric, and Corys made his own decision. But I will not further reduce our royal contingent unless I have no choice."

"He tried to kill Lancelot!" Owain was as uncomfortable with it all as I was.

"And failed. Spectacularly. Mark will come with us."

As far as starting the final step of a quest went, there was precious little fanfare. We simply gathered up our stuff and told the remaining men to retrace their steps back to Tresaith—who hopefully still held the crossroad—and take the other path to our realm.

It was manifestly clear Arthur's men were not going home - and I assumed Lancelot's Rangers would be hanging around unseen. I was sure Mark's remaining men might feel similar, but Corys's were basically legging it before we'd even finished speaking.

"You're sure that Mark's little backstab isn't going to count as the Step of Betrayal?"

My dear, the only thing to be sure of on this quest is to expect the unexpected. However, no. I do not feel that was the final Step. No one was surprised when Mark proved to play us false.

The quiet of the woods swallowed us up, and soon, we left any visible sign of the army behind us. If Lancelot's Rangers were out there, I couldn't easily track them: the strength of the Wood Qi emanating from the trees was too overwhelming.

The path we followed, though, was neatly cut through the forest. Indeed, the longer we rode down it, the greater the quality of the material beneath our horse's feet.

177

We'd been going for a few hours when each of us felt a change of atmosphere around us. It wasn't that the silence of the woods changed; it was more that it became epically expectant.

As if the leaves themselves had taken an inward breath.

My dear, Merlin whispered in my mind, as if he too was intimidated by the perfection of the quiet. *I think it would be wise to get ready.*

"For what?"

Anything.

Awesome. I love a good cliffhanger.

CHAPTER 44 – IN WHICH IT ALL GOES A BIT CTHULHU

We carried on in absolute quiet for a good hour. I say 'hour', but I don't think I was the only one of us who realised the sun hadn't moved for quite some time. If I was going to put money on it, I think we'd dropped into the Fae realm equivalent of my Artist's Studio.

Eventually, the track—which had now become a pretty robust Roman Road—broadened out, and we came out of the trees to find ourselves facing a giant lake with a small island in the middle of it.

Ah, this could be a touch tricky.

"Tricky as in 'funny bit of high jinx, all home in time for lashings of ginger beer' or tricky as in 'the wording of the prophecy saying seven reach the sword made no promises how many will live to find it'."

More leaning towards the latter, I'm afraid.

I jumped off my horse and strode forward to have a look around.

The lake was big. Like, if I couldn't see that it was totally circumscribed by woodland, I'd assume I was looking at a sea. This was a lot of water. I needed to sharpen my eyesight to make out the little island in the middle. It was impossible to judge its size - the scale was all off because of the water - but I could make out a cairn in the dead centre and what looked like a sword handle sticking out of the top of it.

"Fucking hell, we're really committing to *all* the myths here, aren't we?"

I walked to the very edge of the lake and squatted down to dip my hand into it. It was ice cold. Seriously, it was colder than anything I'd ever touched in my life. I had to hurriedly pull Qi into my fingers to stop them from developing frostbite.

"What are you thinking?" Arthur had moved up to stand just behind me.

"Well, unless this is an elaborate hoax, I'm guessing that's Caeldfwch just there. So, we've made it thus far. But I left my bathing suit back at Tintagel, so I'm going to stand right here while someone else swims over and claims it."

I would not advise anyone to get into that water, my dear. Merlin's voice lacked any humour whatsoever.

"The fuck are they being?" Lancelot pointed at some dark shapes moving at the very bottom of the lake. At first, I thought they were akin to dolphins as they moved so quickly and with such purpose. But, then again, I was being fooled by the lack of perspective to judge scale.

As they swam closer to the surface, I didn't need Merlin's shout of alarm to realise my mistake. These things were fucking massive.

"How about we all retreat to the woods?" I said, Merlin pretty much pulling on my soul to drag me away from the water line.

Mark was already backing off, covered by Julka and Lancelot, and I hastily shepherded Owain and Arthur that way before whatever the fuck it was in the lake broke the surface.

It seemed like the safest place in the world to be was wherever they were not.

We'd barely made it into the woods when I heard a water spout blast upwards and felt the icy bite of the spray stab into my back. Even Lancelot winced when it hit him, which scared the beejus out of me.

By the time we thought we were far enough into the woods to look back, there was no sign of whatever was in the lake.

"What the fuck were they?" Julka asked. And I realised everyone turned to look my way.

I didn't think a shrug would increase my standing in this little party. I dropped into my Artist's Studio, feeling much calmer once I was out of the creepy, silent forest.

"Okay, mate, what do we know?"

I've only heard of what I think they are; I've never encountered them myself.

"Which are?"

Kraken.

I sensed he was hoping for more of a reaction than the non-plussed expression on my face. "Oh no!" I moaned half-heartedly. "Not Kraken. Whatever will we do?"

You have no idea what I'm talking about, do you?

"To be fair, mate, that's pretty much a given 90% of the time. But, sure, I've heard something about Krakens. I remember a terrible Jonny Depp movie with a giant fuck-off Octopus in it. If you're telling me I will need to wrestle Jonny, I'm very much here for it."

A book started to glow and shake on the shelf in the corner of the studio. It was probably the most obvious contextual clues I'd had in my life. And I once had a member of a fairly well-known rock band look me up and down and then nod his head towards the door of a club's toilet.

I crossed the room and took 'Fantastic Beasts and How to Kill Them' by Rhyddrech Hael off the shelf.

It was a big book—biblically big—and the illustrations were like something out of Lovecraft's worst cheese-filled nightmare.

"Is there a particular page I should be looking for, Big M? Because flicking through this is giving me the willies." Seriously. If I had thought goblins were ugly fuckers, there was every type of mutated, horribly deformed shape I had never imagined on these pages. And more than a few of them bore passing resemblances to a couple of exes.

The book shifted in my hand and fell open to a page near the back.

I tried to look at the illustration, but my mind rebelled, flicking my eyes away to stare at the comforting landscape outside my window. I tried again, feeling vomit rise in my throat, and again, my eyes wouldn't take in the drawing.

"Big M, I cannot look at this thing."

No. I imagine not, my dear. I think, around your own time, a man named Nietzche described if you spend too long gazing into the abyss, the abyss gazes also into you.

"Meaning?"

Meaning there was a reason Rhyddrech Hael was a lunatic. You, however, seem to have a decent sense of self-preservation.

"Well, it's not much use if I can't even look at a drawing of the fucking thing! Is there anything on these pages that suggests how to kill it?"

I don't really want to look, my dear.

"Mate, you're dead. What's the worst that could happen?"

There are far more appalling things in the world than being dead.

"Look, if you're telling me we can't cut it and that we might as well pack up and head for home, I ain't arguing. I'm only here because you've made a big song and dance over getting Excalibur - sorry, Caeldfwch - for Arthur. If you want the story to be about Arthur coming, seeing the sword in the stone from a distance, but being spooked by overly rare calamari and fucking right off, I'm down with that. Just say the word."

There was a pause and then a sigh. *Fine. Hold the book open.*

There was another silence, and then a strained, *Turn the page.* I did so, and then there was another long gap.

"Seriously, mate, are there some words you need me to explain?"

When the Big M finally came back to me, he had the voice of a Primary School teacher after a day that contained both wet play and an unexpected wasp in the classroom. This dude had seen some shit and wasn't able to let it go just yet.

I think, my dear, if we ever had doubts about the insanity of Rhyddrech Hael, then that little entry puts them to bed. He did not just draw that but fought against them on multiple occasions. I would never have believed such a thing possible.

"Well, that's good news, isn't it? He obviously found a way to fight them. We copy that, get to the middle of the lake, Arthur grabs the sword, and we're home in time for the medal ceremony."

A plan with no flaws.

"Okay, come on then. Piss on my parade."

For a start, Rhyddrech Hael fought one of these things. I made out three within the lake.

"Okay, well, that mentalist was killed by a dragon I beheaded on my second day here. I'm not hating our chances right now."

I think we've discussed how spectacularly fortunate you were, plus the deviousness of my plan that led to that outcome. We probably should not view that as a standard approach. Three Krakens are going to be beyond us.

"Not sure I agree, but keep going. What kills them?"

Rhyddrech slew a Kraken by luring it out of its watery home, setting it on fire and hitting it with as many arrows as he could.

"Sold."

He had with him an army of three thousand bowmen who had spent six months specifically training themselves to pierce the hide of a giant monster.

I waved my hand carelessly. "So, it's just a question of scale. The theory holds, though."

They fired upon it for four days straight before it eventually died. He calculated that the number of arrows launched was... ' a lot'.

"Real details guy, Rhyddrech, eh?"

And even then, when burned to a crisp and without an inch unpierced, it still required Rhyddrech to cut out its heart to kill it.

"Okay, that's not so bad..."

From the inside. He had to cover himself in chicken blood and act as bait to get the thing to swallow him.

"Right." I gave that image a moment. "I sense what you're hinting at is that it's going to be a bit of a stretch for the seven of us to take down three of these fuckers."

I think we will probably need a different plan if we're going to get across the lake and get Arthur that sword. Your usual cavalier belligerence will not cut it on this occasion.

I dropped back into reality. "Okay, guys, here's the plan. We're going to need lots and lots of wood."

<u>CHAPTER 45 – IN WHICH LANCELOT AND I GO BALLS TO THE WALL</u>

My brilliant plan landed like a giant wet shit at a baby shower.

"Can I take it," Owain asked tactfully, "you have never constructed a bridge before?"

I shrugged. "How hard could it be?"

"Well, without wanting to pour unnecessarily cold water on your enthusiasm," he continued, "a little more difficult than 'let's chop down lots of trees, pile them on the lake and walk across'."

"But in theory, it could work?"

"In theory, you could stick a rod up my arse and use me as a punt to get across, but that doesn't make it a good idea." Mark seemed to have decided this conversation needed his input.

"Well, at least we wouldn't have to worry about buoyancy, would we, you fat fuck?"

"You will not speak to my king in that manner!" Julka pushed forward.

"Dude, the only way you could be more of a Red Shirt in this situation would be if I didn't know your name and was referring you to as Vin Diesel's less attractive brother. Settle down. Mummy and Daddy are talking."

"Will you all be quiet!" Arthur didn't shout, which I think was a sign of his growing authority over the small group. That we all did shut up, more so.

He turned to me, eyes flashing. "Morgan, you're sure there's nothing we can do to take on these Kraken?"

I had given them all the skinny on the beasts at the bottom of the lake. It would be fair to say this hadn't done much for morale.

"Merlin's pretty concerned about them. I'm largely up for anything - I think my record's pretty clear on that front - but I can't even look at pictures of these things without going slightly out of my mind; I'm not sure we've got much mileage in a straight-up battle."

Arthur stood on the treeline's edge, looking at the island in the middle of the lake. "I don't suppose you could, I don't know, just fly me over there?"

Owain and Mark shouted their disapproval of that plan. It was clear anything that didn't have them arriving simultaneously would be out. Not that my acting as some sort of flying delivery girl had much mileage, anyway.

Ingenious as the suggestion is, I am afraid that won't work, my dear. The sword produces a significant anti-Qi aura that affects all around it. Merlin had just kept the good news rolling.

"It's not too wide while it is in the stone, apparently, but it'd drop me and any passenger straight into the drink. Not that I've mastered flight anyway. From what the Big M tells me, it would be like hitting a brick wall, even if I was to take a big run-up."

"Could you throw me?"

That was not a terrible idea, actually. Since moving to Harry, I certainly had the strength to do it. But I was worried about the fairly high bar of consequences should I get it wrong. I didn't have a good track record for my aim. And playing Qi Coconut Shy with the Once and Future King over the top of ravenous sea monsters from the nether-most depths of Hell would be a vibe. "I'm not feeling that as a great idea, your majesty."

Arthur sucked air through his teeth in frustration. "We can, literally, see the object of our quest just there. I'm not turning around because we fear what's in the water."

"I'll take one," Lancelot had, hitherto, been silent during our discussion so far.

I turned to him, shaking my head. "You don't understand. These things are..."

"Matters not. In the way they are. Kill one, I will."

And with no further ado whatsofuckingever, he ran towards the lake.

***

Although he hid it well, Lancelot was excited.

He loved being part of Arthur's inner circle and had really enjoyed his time at Tintagel. However, the fight with the Shriket aside, he had not done anything recently to raise his heart rate.

Coming from a culture that measured its heroes' worth by great deeds, he was worried he was losing his edge. Even his skirmishes with the Fae lacked a certain something, as he could tell they were holding back.

But an... what did pretty hair call it? A Kraken? Well, that sounded like it would be something worth his time.

Lancelot had nearly reached the edge of the lake when he realised the wizard had jogged to follow him. Her lips were tight with fear, and her skin had gone even paler than usual, but he liked the firm resolve in her eyes. His mother would have torn the heart from this one and served it to him in a stew.

"You help?" he asked levelly.

"In lieu of a better plan, I'm your huckleberry. Still think a massive fuck off bridge would be a better solution."

He smiled and shook his head. He never understood much of what she said, but she was nice to look at. He sniffed, enjoying the odd spicey smell he had learned meant she was channelling her magic.

He was unusual amongst his tribe that he had not a a trace of... what did pretty hair call it? Chi? Qi? Something like that. Well, he did not have any of it within his spirit. His mother had explained that she had beaten the spark out of him to make him into a better warrior. He had no idea whether that was true, but he was certainly faster and stronger than any of his people who could make pretty lights or make it rain. In fact, until that big man who looked like Arthur's father, he had not come across anyone who could keep up with him.

That defeat still burned within him. He ached for another opportunity to attack that cheater. But until that happened, he could make do with one of these things.

"Look," pretty hair tugged at his sleeve, pulling him back from the edge of the lake. "We can't possibly take out three of these at once. We need to lure one out of the water but leave the other two behind."

Lancelot nodded understandingly. "Good plan," he said and then dived into the lake.

***

"Oh, for fuck's sake!"

I liked Lancelot. I liked his smile. I liked his muscles. And I liked the way his shirt fell off at a moment's notice. I liked him much more when he was nowhere near Guinevere, and I didn't have to worry about cockblocking him. I think I recognised we both had a similar sense of 'fuck it' running through our soul, and I certainly respected his fighting ability.

But, man. The motherfucker was stupid.

The second he dropped below the surface of the lake, I closed my eyes and reached out for him, seeking any connection I could try to mitigate the massive damage I knew he would be receiving from the freezing water.

But I couldn't get a hold on him. It was like the water itself, having been around Caeldfwch, had taken on some of its Qi rejection properties. Not entirely; I could just about track Lancelot's progress down towards one of the... nope, don't look, need to stay sane right now. However, I couldn't connect any of my Qi to him.

<Personal Space Invader>, my dear, and quickly.

I wasted a few seconds trying to work out what the Big M meant, but then I was on it, aiming a thin tunnel of concentrated air down into the water and around Lancelot. I hadn't tried to hold this technique for any length of time, usually using it as a quick blast of 'get the fuck away', but I could tell what was needed here.

The cone of air reached Lancelot, and then he was upright and walking forward, not swimming. If he thought anything odd about the transformation of his travelling medium, he didn't spare so much a backward glance. His skin, though...

Careful, my dear, Merlin cautioned as I tried to do something about the insane chilblains that covered the man's body. *You must maintain <Personal Space Invader> while healing his wounds. We have not experimented with holding multiple techniques at once before. If you are too heavy-handed, you could - at best - burn out all of your Qi and - at worse - burn your core entirely away.*

Awesome.

I did my best to reduce the amount of my paint flowing towards the pocket of air around Lancelot. This was easier than I had expected. I guess Merlin was right when he said I tended to waste colossal amounts of energy when I used techniques. It was like turning down a tap until just the right amount of water flowed out.

"Very nice, my dear. Now, can you remember what Melehan did to heal Arthur's burns?"

My mind flashed back to the Saxon wizard who had saved me on more than one occasion. He had been there when I accidentally cooked Arthur during our first meeting. I mean, I say 'I' as if I don't obviously mean Drynwyn. Melehan had used his Wood Qi in an interesting way to stabilise and then begin to heal the burning king.

I fumbled in my inventory for Melehan's Curing Rock, which I had created using the Saxon's Qi technique, and prepared to throw it to Lancelot.

No, my dear. Trust me when I say he will need both of his hands.

I glanced up and saw Lancelot was nearing one of the... things. I quickly looked away as the tunnel of air shook as I momentarily lost control of my technique.

You need to act quickly, my dear. That young man is astonishingly pig-headed, but even he cannot ignore the pain much longer.

I gripped the Rock and tried to feel how its power worked. The smells that I associated with Melehan came rushing back. Lavender, predominantly, and then the other herbs as secondary notes. I had bunches of all of them in my inventory. If there was one thing Alchemy levelling needed, it was millions of herbs. I grabbed hold of a massive bunch of them with my Qi.

Okay, my dear. Listen carefully. You have the shape of it, but you need to base it in a liquid. I know we've not had much luck with Water Qi, but this is... as you would say... my wheelhouse. Can you let me take charge for a moment?

I paused. It had been some time since I'd fully let the Big M take the reins. Although we hadn't really explored it, I knew he'd been up to something naughty with Melehan when I'd been stuck in the time loop in Aurelius' Dark Tower.

I think he was ashamed enough of what happened there not to try to elbow my consciousness aside and take permanent control but... fucking hell. It felt like a risk. But then I saw Lancelot stumble for a second; his skin blackened and peeling off. And I got over myself.

<Healing Wave> snapped into being the moment Merlin was in charge.

A beautiful, twisted coil of water - Wood Qi running through it - flowed down the centre of the air tunnel to strike Lancelot, driving him forward. My Qi levels dropped to the floor with the effort of maintaining two techniques at once, but the barbarian was looking pretty chipper in no time.

And not a moment too soon because, as I watched, he walked straight into a Kraken.

CHAPTER 46 – IN WHICH WE REALISE WE WERE GOING TO NEED A MUCH BIGGER BOAT

I found that as long as I kept my eyes fixed on Lancelot - and just let the Kraken exist in my peripheral vision - the sight of the thing only drove me partially out of my mind. Thus, what with with concentrating on maintaining the corridor of air for the barbarian to stand in, that was pretty much taking up all my mental space.

"Big M?" I gasped, feeling a wash of vertigo. "You're going to need to keep track of the other Krakens for me."

On it.

I remembered what Merlin had said about the necessity to focus on my cycling, and although this didn't necessarily feel like the most appropriate time — *the other two are on the opposite side of the lake. No sign they're bothered about Lancelot yet* - I would need to tap a mana stone if I planned to keep this up much longer.

Fixing the position of the Kraken in my mind - it blazed a horrible, pulsing blackness to my senses - I closed my eyes and tried to focus on the weft and wane of my Qi. Oddly, my sense of the monster's wrongness was helpful as it gave me something to push against. With each breath in, it was like my body pulled in little strands of ambient Qi, quickly converted them into paint and then pressed against the presence of the Kraken on my breath out.

To be honest, I felt like a bit of fraud standing on the edge of the lake meditating whilst Lancelot was in a fight to the death, but then if I ran out of Qi and dropped the tunnel of air he was fighting in, he'd be dead in seconds.

I was doing my bit.

"Any movement yet, Big M?"

Nothing. If you are interested, Lancelot is currently earning the title of 'Ballsiest Underwater Battle' since I accidentally sank Atlantis. I am rarely impressed with swordplay, but this young man is quite something. He is, nevertheless, being sliced into tiny little pieces.

I sent another wash of <Healing Wave> down the tunnel, hoping that would be enough to keep the barbarian in the game. That pretty much wiped out any Qi I'd been able to gather since the fight had started.

It kind of felt like we were just marking time until one of the other great beasts noticed us, and then the jig would be up.

"Dude, if you can hear me," I called out to Lancelot, "now would be the time to pull out any special moves you have."

"Your suggestion noted is!" Lancelot's voice sounded no different than if he were engaged in a little light warm-up. "Up your arse, you can stick it. Busy."

I guess that was fair enough.

I half-opened one eye and watched Lancelot move in a blur at the midpoint of the tunnel of air. He seemed to be fighting a spirited retreat, leading the creature back towards me. I somehow managed not to immediately run screaming, shortening the air tunnel to match his progress. At least that went some way to stop all my Qi flowing away.

"Is there a plan here?" There was probably more of a quaver to my voice here than I wanted, but - you know - I was the girl who hid behind the sofa when the Daleks appeared on the screen, so I think I was doing pretty damned well to be a going concern against this thing still.

"I'm killing it," he shouted back.

"Is he, Big M?"

There was a brief silence. *Hard to tell. Lancelot is still alive, which is causing the creature some significant surprise but... it is something like witnessing a battle between a mouse and tiger. I cannot help but think that the second the latter gets bored, it will be all over and done with.*

Almost at that very moment, there was an ear-piercing, stomach-churning shriek. *Good news and bad news, my dear.*

"Spill."

The tiger had lost one of its paws, if you will allow me to strain that metaphor a touch further. On the other hand, the largest of the other two Krakens is coming to find out what all the fuss is about.

"Shit! Lancelot, we got company!"

***

Arthur ground his teeth in frustration. There was little he could do to help either the wizard or his finest warrior. Watching Lancelot twist, turn, slice, and roll, the king was not too proud to recognise that he would just be in the way if he sought to join him at the bottom of the lake.

He wasn't even sure what it was that Lancelot was fighting.

As he watched, the colossal thing undulated and shivered like a giant leech, but one with a full complement of tentacles, teeth and claws. Arthur did not scare easily, but he was unsure he could stand, much less fight against such a thing.

And yet there was Lancelot, step-by-step kiting the monster to the surface. He felt such a wave of affection for the barbarian. He hadn't known him long but already counted him - alongside Bors - as his closest friend. If anyone was going to be able to defeat a nightmare monster single-handedly, he did not doubt it would be Lancelot.

Then the wizard called out and pointed towards the far side of the lake, where a massive fin was moving towards the battle. Due to the size of the body of water, it was easy to think the movement was slow, but after a moment, Arthur realised how quickly the distance was being eaten up.

An unfortunate turn of phrase.

Arthur needed to buy Lancelot some more time. He picked up his spear and began running around the lake's edge, away from the initial struggle and towards the approaching creature. The others in the party paused for a moment, then gathered up their own gear to follow him.

"Is this wise?" Owain had a surprisingly decent burst of speed for a big man.

"Compared to letting that thing double-team them?"

"Good point."

***

Lancelot wasn't exactly living his best life, but it sure wasn't a million miles away.

There was an art to fighting something where it would only take one substantial hit to wipe you out. It was all a matter of degrees. You accepted the lesser injuries to keep the catastrophic ones at bay. That's where most people got it wrong.

They thought fighting was about not getting hit.

Lancelot had discovered, when he was barely old enough to talk, that this was not the case. It was all about knowing how hard you could be hit and still be able to fuck the other guy - or girl - up. Warriors who were scared of a little pain didn't take chances. They didn't put themselves in a position to do damage.

You didn't have to not care if you died to win. But it certainly helped.

He let a flailing tentacle catch him on his chest, his skin bubbling at the contact, and chopped down, severing it with a spray of purple goo. But the shrieking from the monster, it had not enjoyed that exchange as much as he had.

Lancelot grinned and took another step backwards, leading the creature towards the shore. He didn't really have a plan beyond the next step, the next slice, the next blur of movement, but sometimes that's all you needed.

That, after all, was what life - and death - were about.

***

I felt Lancelot's presence vibrate in my mind - fuck, he's taken another massive injury - and let loose another <Healing Wave>. I wasn't sure how many more of those I had up my sleeve, especially if Lancelot wanted anything from me when he finally got this thing to the surface.

And particularly if the second Kraken reached us.

Running feet grabbed my attention, and I opened my eyes to see the rest of our little group quickstepping it around the lake. Fuck me. They were going to try to intercept the second creature.

"Big M, in the most charitable of terms, what chance do they have of being able to do what they're planning?"

Well, they seem to be aiming to grab the attention of the second beast. I am happy to confirm that they will likely be one hundred per cent successful in that endeavour.

"And then survive that success?"

Not so much, my dear.

"Fuckadoodledo."

I dropped into my Artist's Studio and took a deep, cleansing breath.

"I have absolutely no idea how we get out of this." At this stage, I hoped the Big M would have some thoughts for me. But, no. He was worryingly quiet. "I don't have enough Qi to keep the air tunnel open, the healing going, *and* to try something against the second creature. I can pull Lancelot out, I guess, but that's not going to help over much. Especially if Arthur and company get wiped. The water's stupidly cold, so I guess dropping Drynwyn in there on full blast will - eventually - piss them off. But it's a fucking huge pool of water, and we don't have the time. Feel free to chime in anytime you want, mate?"

I'm thinking, my dear. I just cannot figure out a course of action that leaves enough of you alive to be worth the effort. If you are looking for an upside, in most scenarios I envisage, you come out of them alive.

I licked my lips and reran the options.

"Fuck it," I popped back into real-time and yanked on my connection to Lancelot. As he was tethered in a <Personal Space Invader>, he flew backwards out of the water to land behind the treeline. A slightly disconcerting side-effect was that as he had a tentacle wrapped around his leg, he dragged the Kraken with him.

The weight of the pull, as I feared it would - even without the fucking monster on the other end of the line - sent me sprawling into the water.

As I hit the freezing liquid, I reached out to the bigger, uglier presence swimming towards Arthur and hit it with <Unnecessary Sequel Trilogy>, draining everything I had to give it the full beans.

You ever seen a toaster drop in a bathtub? It was a tiny, tiny bit like that.

I wasn't sure which caught up with me first: the Qi exhaustion or the devastating electric shock.

It was one of them.

CHAPTER 47 – IN WHICH NESSIE GETS FUCKED UP

Arthur skidded to a halt, narrowly avoiding being trampled by his pursuers. He had grown accustomed to Morgan's frequent displays of elemental power, but the sudden burst of light and energy that struck the figure in the water left him momentarily stunned.

"What was that?" Mark reached the rest of them, a little behind the others. "It was like a lightning storm, but the air is clear."

Arthur ignored him. If the King of Gwynedd still didn't understand the power of a cultivator, he wasn't going to waste his breath right now trying to re-educate him. The second monster he'd been running to distract had vanished towards the bottom of the lake. It was too much to hope his wizard had permanently put it out of action, but it had certainly dropped down the priority order right now.

He now just had two pressing problems.

Firstly, Morgan was adrift in that lake. He'd caught sight of her sling-shotting in the opposite direction to Lancelot and a terrifying being the size of one of Tintagel's towers.

Oh, and that led nicely into the second issue. Lancelot was one-on-oneing a Kraken on the land.

Arthur turned on a sixpence and started to run back to where he could see Morgan slowly sinking into the depths of the water. There was nothing he could do. Even reaching towards the water caused him to experience overwhelming pain. There was no way he could dive in there after her.

Get on with it, you fucking wet wipe.

Arthur looked down at the sword left on the water's edge as Morgan had been pinged into the lake. With only a minor hesitation, he bent down to pick it up. He was pleased not to be turned into a pillar of flame on this occasion.

Owain was at his side. "Figure out how to get her onto dry land, and we'll help your man with that one." With a roar, the King of Gwent raised his battle axe above his head and charged towards the Kraken, who was obviously disorientated by so suddenly being out of the water. He was followed - with various degrees of enthusiasm and brio - by Burford, Julka and Mark.

"Any ideas?" Another man might have felt embarrassed to seek advice from a sword. Another time, he might.

Give that fucker on land a nice quick fry, and then toss me at the wizard.

Arthur paused. "Wouldn't you be more use against the monster?"

The sword swivelled in his hand. **I'm her sword. I'll give you guys a leg up against that bastard, for old time's sake, but I'm not letting her freeze to death. Not on my watch.**

"Fair enough. How do I -" he raised the sword towards the creature that had righted itself and was finally fighting back against Lancelot. The barbarian had wasted no time of his advantage and had been slicing swathes off the beast. Worryingly, it didn't seem to be making as much impact on it as might have been hoped.

A blast of white-hot energy burst from the Drynwyn's tip to envelop the Kraken. Lancelot leapt backwards and out of the way of the fire and landed gracefully on his feet, sword raised to resume his attack.

Few more seconds, then yeet me at her. Make sure you get me close; I need to warm her up.

The flame's intensity increased even higher, with the monster shrieking outrageously as its skin crusted, burst and shrivelled. **Three. Two. One. And toss me.**

Arthur took careful aim and threw Drynwyn down into the water and towards Morgan's sinking body. He watched it for a moment and then went to join the attack on the Kraken.

"I hope you know what you're doing," he thought to the sword. "We need her back."

***

I'm so fucking over losing consciousness.

During my life, I've spent more time waking up in unfamiliar places with questionable liquids around me than I'd like to think. However, since my rebirth, my passing-out quotient seems to have gone through the roof.

Are you back in the land of the living, my dear?

I wasn't sure. From my memory, I'd gone all Qi-exhaustion (again) and fell into something like liquid nitrogen while simultaneously acting as some sort of lightning conductor.

My skin burned, my insides throbbed, and my head was splitting. It was Tuesday on the beach at Ayia Napa all over again.

"Mate, if you could scare up some S Club Seven, I'd be living my best life."

Excuse me, my dear?

"Don't worry about it. I assume I'm moments from death?"

To be honest, my dear, I have no idea how you are still alive. I'm theorising that your tempering with the Widow Weed has done something appalling to your constitution. You're really becoming quite a remarkable specimen.

Sure, I'm doing fuck-all here, I guess.

Considering the substance I was suspended in, I realised I was in an unusually warm bubble.

"That you, Drynwyn?"

Who else do you think it would fucking be? Ain't like Merlin was going to piss on you to keep you warm.

I opened my eyes and then closed them again quickly. It hurt. "I'm in the lake?"

Indeed. Someone appears to have neglected their reading on equal and opposite reactions. If you pull something that heavy out of the water, you better believe you will be dragged back the other way.

"Awesome. Is there any chance we can spare the lesson on Newtonian physics until I'm back on dry land? Just so I can pay proper attention, you understand." A thought hit me. "Where's the Kraken?"

I think you have put it into a nice little slumber. Well, the one that was about to attack Arthur, at any rate. However, I would recommend that we quickly introduce ourselves to Lancelot's confrontation.

I reached out with the pathetic amount of Qi that I'd recovered while unconscious and was alarmed at what a crappy state Lancelot's lifeforce seemed to be in.

"Fucking hell, this is a shit show. Which way is up?"

I groped around, grabbing hold of Drynwyn's handle as I tried to orientate myself. I kicked my legs - despite the bubble of warm air, the cold bit into me like acid - and started to move toward the surface. Then, having an idea, I pointed the sword downwards. "Give me what you've got, big guy."

An explosion of heat beneath me blasted me upwards. In seconds, I was breaching the waves.

***

Lancelot spat a mouthful of blood and jumped back into the fray.

He knew he only had a few more seconds before the damage his body had taken caught up with his brain. His arms were moving on pure instinct, and his footwork was just a stumbling disaster.

His mother would not be pleased. He guessed he'd be seeing her soon.

On the plus side, since a stray tentacle had taken out his eyes, he wasn't finding looking at the thing that much hassle anymore. It wasn't like he needed to see to hit the fucking thing.

He buried his sword up to the hilt and was gratified by the bloodcurdling scream that it caused. Since pretty hair's sword had bathed the monster in flame, its skin was much more responsive to damage.

And then he was back in the air again, a looping tentacle battering him away from his weapon. That was probably it, he thought. He'd given it a good go and was pleased with how he had conducted himself. He hoped his people would have a suitable song to commemorate his fall.

Then, a warm bath of healing hit, and everything reset.

Lancelot spared a moment to look towards the lake to witness the unusual sight of Morgan flying ten feet into the air, her sword spewing out fire beneath her. She was pointing towards him and yelling something. Lancelot did not always understand the words pretty hair used, but he was on board with the general gist of her sentiment on this occasion. He would indeed 'kill that motherfucker."

***

It took all of our combined efforts the rest of the afternoon to finally drop the beached Kraken. As I had suspected, Julka was the first of us to be dropped. One of the monster's mouths bit him in two when I was concentrating elsewhere. I hadn't really got enough headspace to care either way.

I was a bit more sad when Burford lost first an arm and then a leg. I managed to cauterise the first, and just didn't have enough Qi left to address the second. Owain had been able to pull him clear, and I'd doused him in a bunch of Elixirs. All being well, I'd have an opportunity to regrow his limbs later. Maybe.

Arthur probably got the official 'kill' listing.

We'd basically chopped, burned and speared the thing into so much sashimi, but it was still capable of sending Mark flying into a tree with a crunch. In response, Arthur took a running jump and piled his spear through its last remaining eye. I shoved on the end of it with the thinnest fucking whisp of <Personal Space Invader> I could squeeze out and drove it further into what counted as its brain.

It dropped to the ground, and we followed it, gasping and groaning. I didn't think anyone still alive was carrying an injury that needed my urgent attention, but there wouldn't have been much I could have done about it anyway.

I half-heartedly threw out a couple of Elixirs of Wellness just in case.

If we weren't all circling the drain, then at the very least squaring the sewer.

And we were still on the wrong fucking side of the lake.

Well done, my dear. Great effort. One down, two to go!

Fuck off, Big M.

CHAPTER 48 – IN WHICH WE HAVE A SLIGHT CHANGE OF PLAN

"I'm going to raise the prospect of a bridge again."

We were sitting under the shadow of a very dead Kraken. Drynwyn had done the honours on the remains of Julka, but no matter what we tried, it didn't appear a cremation was on the cards for the giant... whatever the fuck this thing was.

At least now that it was dead, I didn't feel like I was going to go mad every time I looked at it.

"Will you shut up about a fucking bridge!" Mark's temper had not improved since losing his bodyguard.

"Give me a better idea," I spat back. "We can't fight another two of these things!"

And that was true. We were a mess. For whatever reason, the wounds these fucking things inflicted didn't heal in the usual way. I was used to almost wiping the slate clean with my elixirs, so their inability to make it all okay was irritating. Worse than that, it seemed <Healing Wave> wasn't a free do-over.

What were you expecting, my dear? There's no such thing as a free lunch.

Honestly, that was almost exactly what I thought being a cultivator was. Seeing a cost to my new healing spell was a bit of a disappointment. The upshot was that Lancelot had lost a shedload of weight and looked like absolute shit.

Your spell is the catalyst for the subject's own resources to come into play. You speed up the process, for sure. However, the cost of healing must be paid. And Lancelot was wholly battered during that battle.

He hadn't been the only one. Don't even get me started on what remained of Burford . . .

Arthur stood and winced as he put the weight on a knee twice the size it should have been. "There is no conceivable way we're making it through anything like that again."

"So, the bridge?" I asked, hopefully.

The chorus of disapproval was unnecessarily loud and long, considering I was basically the human equivalent of an ICU unit at this point. I felt they could have let me down a little more gently.

Owain was nursing a deep gash that ran the length of his chest that, no matter what I tried, was proving resistant to healing. I'd had to stitch it up the old-fashioned way, and mamma did not raise no seamstress. "Do we need to discuss whether our quest has floundered?" he asked quietly.

"No," Arthur's voice was firm. "Should Gwent or Gwynedd wish to withdraw, there will be no hard feelings. My party will remain to claim Caeldfwch."

"Then you will die," Mark had not bothered standing. I couldn't help but notice he was in the best shape of any of us. All that padding, I assumed.

Lancelot cleared his throat. Man, he looked awful. His hair was lank and greasy, his cheeks were hollow and that indefatigable glow that surrounded him had vanished. He looked like nothing more than a smack addict who was in terminal decline. "My people," his chest was racked with coughs. I'd given him Melehan's Curing Rock to hold, but it didn't seem to be helping. That stone had helped bring Arthur back from Crispy City, what the fuck could be going on here for Lancelot to have it and still be in such a state?

The Kraken, my dear. As I said, I would have hesitated fighting one in my prime. Their attacks are not just physical. They inflict wounds on the soul.

Fuck me. And there were still two of them between us and the sword.

Lancelot had got his breath back. "My people raiders are. We know about boats. Canoes especially." He looked at me. "With help, I could guide making."

There was a general murmur of approval.

"Oh, sure. A bridge would be beyond our engineering capabilities. But a few boats, no worries. I think you guys just don't like it when a girl takes the initiative."

"Morgan?"

"Yes, my king?"

"Shut the fuck up."

***

It turned out that boat building wasn't an absolutely terrible idea. We were able to make use of the Kraken's rotting carcass to supplement any number of materials that Lancelot needed to direct the mocking up of a three-person canoe.

Of course, Muggins here was needed to do most of the work, which, suffering as I was from fairly substantial Qi exhaustion, was hardly a bowl of cherries and a slap on the arse from Di Caprio.

I basically poured out anything I had in the way of Qi to bring down the trees, turning them into serviceable shapes for Lancelot, Arthur and Owain to undertake some manual carpentry. Mark, noticeably, seemed to be doing much less.

I balanced out forestry with meditation, but I wasn't moving things on with anything like the sort of pace I wanted to. It was two full days before two serviceable-looking craft were made. I mean, we only had Lancelot's word for it that he knew what he was talking about, but as my bridge remained off the table and there wasn't any of us up for a scrap, I wasn't against giving this a shot.

We then started to play a game called 'Who doesn't want to share a boat with Mark?'"

"Look," Owain said, "me and him are the heaviest. You've got to have us in different boats."

This was a fair comment. It would have been an awful lot of work to simply send one of our ships to the bottom of the lake.

"That is fine, being. Arthur and I will go with Mark; Owain will go with Morgan."

"I'm not having that fucking lunatic anywhere near me. He killed a bunch of my men."

Arthur glanced at Mark. "Oh, come on! You attacked him first. In the middle of a battle!"

"I have spoken." And the fat fuck crossed his arms and closed his eyes.

196

"Okay," Arthur said. "How about Lancelot, Morgan and Owain? And I'll share with Mark?"

"No," it was Lancelot's turn to be belligerent. "He's not trustworthy. Alone with him, I will not leave you." Over the last day, the barbarian had begun to recover some of his vigour. He was still a long way from his Thor-best, but it was reassuring he was looking less like a walking skeleton.

"Boys, this is pathetic. Look, I'll go with Mark." Nothing like taking one for the team, was there?

"Can you tell where the Kraken are, Morgan?"

I shook my head at Arthur. "If you're wanting to use me as mobile radar, you'll need to give me at least another day. I'm fucking wrung out."

And that wasn't the half of it.

This was the longest I'd tried to operate in the Dark Ages without a fairly decent amount of Qi swishing through my channels. The lines connecting up all my hot spots – *meridians, my dear. You're not a baby cultivator anymore* - were looking pretty red and crusted again.

The last time something like this had happened, I'd been able to smooth them out again with a few hours of focused cycling. I worried that now I'd advanced, this level of damage would need a lot more effort to return things to normal.

"How long do you think you'll need?" Arthur's voice was just impatient enough to rub me up the wrong way.

"I don't know, mate. I'm not asking for a few minutes so I can reapply my fucking make-up. I've been doing the job of DPS, Healer and crafter for this party for the last few days and I'm fucking at the limit. If you want to kick off cruising over the Lake of Unspeakable Horror, feel free. But I won't have any goodies to bring to the party, and, as far as I can tell, I'm the only thing separating us from certain death. So, do the fuck what you want, but a 'thank you' every now and again would be nice!"

There was an awkward pause.

You know, sometimes, you sound like a very whiny bitch, my dear.

***

By general consent, we took the night off.

I found that mixing cycling from within my Artist's Studio with real-time exercise was the most efficient way to get myself fighting fit. There seemed to be a hard limit to how much Qi I could regenerate when time was paused, but if I came out and spent a good hour or so in the real world, I was able to click back in and start again.

It's only because you are not entirely operating at peak efficiency, Merlin explained. *You should not be able to cycle for anything more than mindfulness when you are here: you are still not automatically absorbing the ambient Qi when you drop in. But that will come in time.*

I'd been focusing on using my purple paint to repair the damage my overuse of Qi had caused. As long as I kept my mind entirely clear, each cycle of paint around my body reduced the inflammation by a tiny amount. It was like rubbing the thinnest layer of balm over sunburned skin.

By the time the rest of the party awoke in the morning, I was feeling less like a bear with a sore head and more up for another go at crossing the lake. Interestingly, the others seemed to be avoiding me.

197

It was Lancelot who girded his loins to risk my further displeasure.

"Feeling well, pretty hair?" He tossed me back Melehan's rock.

"Getting there, thank you. So, what's the plan?"

"We want to try crossing the lake," Arthur - now that Lancelot had tested the water, was walking over to me. "But we need you to track the Krakens for us."

"And was there a magic word?"

Arthur started back at me. "I don't know. You're the wizard. Shouldn't you know the word to use?"

"I mean, did you want to say 'please'?"

"I'm not sure you quite understand the King/Wizard dynamic at play here." Nevertheless, at Owain's discrete cough, he took a deep breath and plastered on a smile. "Morgan, I would be very grateful if you could, please, feel up to keeping an eye on the devastatingly destructive monsters that are likely to come and try to eat us the moment we step onto the lake. Such a huge favour would be peachy. Please."

"You only had to ask, boss. Let's rock and roll."

CHAPTER 49 – IN WHICH THERE IS A BETRAYAL OF ALL THAT IS GOOD

"'They're getting too far away from us!"

There were many things I did not like about King Mark. His whole aesthetic didn't help. Considering the paucity of junk food options in Dark Age South West Britain, it took a real commitment to gluttony to reach his level of corpulency. I mean, I don't want to fat shame, but I'd had to pack Earth Qi at one end of our canoe in order not to spend most of the early moments on the lake playing a game of seesaw.

However, my irritation with him went a bit further than just not wanting to spend much time with someone who was one wafer-thin mint away from explosion.

For a start, there was the whole issue with his son. Merlin had filled me in on the Tristain-Isolde-Mark love triangle. I had a dim memory that the whole Romeo and Juliet story had been based on those two kids, and it turned out that I wasn't too far away from the truth. I mean, I didn't remember the bit where Romeo's dad decided he fancied a bit of Juliet himself, arranged for his son to have a little 'accident' and then tried to turn Juliet into his own personal sex slave. That Tristian slaughtered the guys sent to kill him, beat seven bells out of his dad and then vanished into the land of the Fae - having faked both of their suicides - gave somewhat of a feel-good end to the whole thing.

If you ignored Mark ordering the immediate execution of Isolde's entire family line down to the dogs in the yard.

Dude had some issues with being told 'no'.

So, he was repellently fat, was clearly psychotic, and also a shit dad. Nevertheless, my most pressing issue right now was that the man wouldn't fucking row.

"Mate, you do get that I have a few more important things to do right now than ferry your fat arse across this lake, don't you? Remember those monsters I'm on the lookout for?" He just stared back at me.

"It is vital we reach the island at the same time as Arthur and Owain."

I looked significantly down at the oars lying in the water - trying to ignore that they were covered in frost and bits of wood were flaking away. Fuck knows what was happening to the bottom of the canoe. "Then. Start. Rowing."

To be honest, I wasn't delighted at how far Arthur, Owain and Lancelot were getting away from us. I was supposed to be our Early Kraken Detection System, but there was going to be little point if they couldn't hear me screaming 'We're fucking doomed!" Now I thought about it, I wondered if I should have come up with a more subtle signal.

I sent a light buzz of Qi across the water's surface. The smaller of the two remaining monsters was well over the far left of the lake. It hadn't moved in the time we'd been faffing around getting into the canoes, so I was assuming it was in the land of nod.

I was more worried about the bigger ball of malevolent energy that was cutting a wide circle around the perimeter of the lake. We'd watched it do this pass three times, carefully measuring how long it took to complete an entire circuit. As far as we could tell - okay, Merlin did the sums - we should be able to reach the middle of the lake before it noticed us.

I was worried about the amount of heavy lifting 'should' was doing in that sentence.

No matter how hard I tried, I couldn't get the fight with the first Kraken out of my head. It wasn't just that we'd been absolutely battered; it was that it was the first confrontation I'd had here that had properly left its mark on me. Even being tortured by Aurelius Ambrosius didn't feel as permanently debilitating as that terrifying mound of tentacles, claws and teeth.

It was all very well for me to 'keep an eye' on the two creatures, but fuck knows what we were planning to do if they came for us.

Tell you what, though, I'd be using Mark as a human shield.

I glanced ahead and agreed with the King of Gwynedd that the gap between us and the cool people boat was getting too big. "Dude, let's just work together and see if we can get out of this in one piece."

Mark looked at me, then the oar, and then back at me. "I'm not rowing. It's beneath me."

I may or may not have let a little spark of <Unnecessary Sequel Trilogy> drift across the canoe to singe his beard. "If we're stuck in the middle of the water when that big dude comes back round, you better believe I'm out of here faster than light. The only way you're making it to that island is if we work together."

We had a bit of stand-off before he took his oar in hand and, with a colossal amount of distaste, began to row.

We'd been going for a decent amount of time but were still nowhere near the first boat when I sent out another pulse of monster-searching-Qi. The big guy was still on track, lazily drifting around the outside of the lake, about a quarter of the way through his latest circuit. So far, so good.

And the little guy was... nowhere to be seen.

"Oh, shit!" I increased the power to the searching pulse and eventually found the missing Kraken. It had sunk to the very bottom of the lake and was now moving upwards towards Arthur's boat at a pace I would describe as "ramming speed."

***

Owain was the first to notice Morgan's panicked signalling. "I think we've got a problem."

Arthur paused his long, powerful strokes and looked at where the King of Gwent was pointing.

"Okay," he kept his voice calm—no point letting terror take over. "We knew this might happen. Let's push it!"

Lancelot began pulling his oar at a blinding speed. It took everything Owain and Arthur could do to keep up with him. They were not too far away from the island now. Arthur concentrated on his strokes - he would not let Lancelot outperform him. Not if this were the last thing he would do in this world.

Arthur fixed his eyes on the cairn rising in the middle of the island. They were close enough that he could see the handle of the blade sticking out from the top of it very clearly now. And, was that a woman sitting at the base of the stone? She was tall, as far as he could tell from her position, and had long, blonde hair cascading down her front and to the floor. She also appeared to be naked.

Any increase in Arthur's rowing output was obviously entirely coincidental.

Then, a dark shape breached the water ahead of them, and he had his mind very much on other things.

***

I watched, in horror, as the Kraken reared up in the water ahead of Arthur's boat.

It was directly between them and the island. My mind rebelled at the sight of the thing again, but I locked the madness down tight. Now was not the time. Funnily enough, I imagined years and years of pretending I wasn't about to have a horrible experience at the hands of one dealer or another made me pretty good at this sort of compartmentalisation.

"Hurry up," Mark hissed, "we can slip past while it is busy with them."

Surprisingly, he did not seem to be too worried about our companions.

I, on the other hand, was wrestling with a dilemma. Arthur becoming the Pendragon was the ball game. I'd only got into this to keep the timeline intact, so Zizzie wasn't wiped out of existence. Sure, I'd like to think I'd moved a bit past being Riggs in the first Lethal Weapon movie, but my personal survival remained far behind that key aim.

So, Arthur needed to get his Excalibur. That was a non-negotiable outcome of this quest. Me still being alive at the end? Well, that would be a bonus.

"What are you doing?"

I'd dropped my oar and stood unsteadily in the canoe, facing the monster towering over the other boat. We were probably four or five football fields away, but I could make out Lancelot pushing his way in front of the king, moving with far more poise and grace than I was managing. Did that dude do anything badly?

Mark, surprisingly, did not seem to be on board with Operation Noble Sacrifice.

To be honest, my dear, I'm not sure I'm over-delighted either.

"You have a better plan?" I'd filled my hands with Qi and gathered every joule of lightning I could hold at my fingertips. I had no illusions of taking this thing out at this range, but I figured I could piss it off.

Sadly not. Try not to hit Arthur when you attack. That would seem a touch counterproductive.

"Oh ye of little faith."

***

The sparkling, flashing lightning stream arced over Arthur's head, striking the creature with a sizzling hiss. It roared - the pressure of the sound dropping each man in the canoe beneath it to their knees - and dove back under the water, surging towards Morgan's boat.

201

"Fucking row!" Arthur grabbed his oar and began pulling against the water. The canoe lurched to the right. "What the fuck are you doing?"

Arthur turned to see why Lancelot was not doing his bit and was astonished to see Owain crash his own oar into the side of the barbarian's head and knock him into the water.

It was such an unexpected moment, Arthur's usual razor sharp reactions did not have chance to kick into action before the King of Gwent whipped out a dagger and plunged it straight into his stomach. He looked down uncomprehendingly at the hilt before toppling into the water after Lancelot.

Owain watched the surface of the water impassively for a few seconds until he was sure neither man was going to resurface. Then, grabbing an oar in each of his hands, he moved with smooth pulls towards Caeldfwch.

CHAPTER 50 – IN WHICH AN OBVIOUS FARTING JOKE IS MADE

"Owain killed Igraine?"

Guinevere's voice was shocked. She did not doubt Blæk's word – he had provided more than enough evidence of the King of Gwent's culpability in the crime for it to be incontrovertible. But she had liked the kindly old man. Thought he had liked her. She could not imagine the circumstances in which he had casually tossed Igraine through her window.

Blæk cocked his head as if trying to decide whether an answer was required. He appeared to determine it was not just a rhetorical question and that further commentary was needed. "Indeed, Your Majesty. It appears that the removal of his heir at the start of Uther's reign was a wound that has long festered in Owain's heart. Furthermore, I have reports of significant gold leaving to various guilds from which our most recent... incidents can be seen to originate. There can be no doubt that he himself tossed Queen Igraine from her tower."

"Motherfucker," Bors breathed. He had liked the Queen. And he liked Owain. He was finding the news challenging to process. "He just threw her out of the window after all these years? Why?"

Guinevere answered for Blæk. "Uther's death. Arthur seeking to become the Pendragon. Isca. Increased pressure from Aurelius. I guess we have never looked weaker. More ripe for assault." She put a hand to her mouth as the logical extension of this thought was reached. "And if he gets his hands on Caeldfwch, we won't even have the advantage of wizardry."

"Arthur won't let that happen," Bors answered confidently. "And he had Lancelot and Morgan with him. Owain won't be able to do anything about them."

Guienevre was not that sure. She thought back to the ease with which Morgan had spoken to the King of Gwent at the feast. The wizard had found him pleasant company, she thought. She wouldn't have any concerns about turning her back on him.

In a den of vipers that contained Beric and Mark, she doubted there would be a moment's suspicion wasted on the kindly grandfather with the twinkle in his eyes and the laugh in his voice.

"A cut is often more dangerous when it comes from a hidden place. Look at Igraine. Decades protecting the realm from the shadows and the moment her defences are down, Owain struck."

There was an uneasy silence.

Blæk had more pressing news, but he was unsure whether it was a polite moment to speak. He was much more comfortable giving his reports in writing—the way Igraine had preferred—than in these in-person meetings.

Paper was much more reliable than people. Easier to read too.

Bors had been watching him. "You have something more on your mind, little man?"

Guinevere turned her bright eyes towards him. "Sir Blæk?"

He swallowed. "Yes, indeed. Whilst I am confident we have now removed all traces of Owain's assassins from within our walls -" there had been five others that he had personally attended to since calling Bors and Guinevere to this meeting —"it strikes me that there is probably more to this. King Owain is aware Arthur and fifty of our men are not standing in defence of Tintagel. He likewise knows both our wizard and," Blæk's colourless eyes flicked to Bors. "*arguably*, our greatest warrior are also absent."

"No, that's a fair comment," Bors's face was entirely untroubled. "Lancelot can kick my arse from here to Frankia and back again. I'm not precious about that."

Blæk pressed on as if Bors had not spoken. "He can thus be reasonably confident - unaware of my existence nor that of the Grey - that his very expensive assassins will remove both the Queen and the remaining King's champion."

"All pretty sound assumptions. But what of it? Owain is away on the quest with Arthur."

Blæk blinked as if he was surprised he needed to continue. After a moment of consideration, he realised he was required to. "Why, I merely note that Gwent is in possession of extremely useful information should it be minded to test the walls of Tintagel. And, I am sure I do not need to remind anyone, the largest standing army of any of the British tribes."

Guinevere cursed. "Shit on a brick! Order the gates closed. How many men can we put on the walls?"

They were all standing now and moving with purpose into the courtyard. Bors was shaking his head. "A handful? More if you let me use competitors." He suddenly grinned. "You know, a proper war game could be just the ticket. Knocks all of this tournament bollocks into a cocked hat. We'll be able to see how much use each of them is in real time!"

Guinevere was not convinced that all the competitors who had turned up for a little light drinking, gambling and some friendly one-on-one fisticuffs would be quite so keen on defending Tintagel against the might of Gwent's spears.

But then there was a blasting of trumpets, and it seemed that theory was about to be tested.

Because the Prince of Gwent had arrived.

***

Just over a mile north of Tintagel is a small but perfectly formed valley into which the waterfall of Saint Nectan's Glen spills. The very high stone walls here have given it the name of Rocky Valley to those who knew where to find it. Which not many people did.

Ever since the feast on the eve of the quest for Caeldfwch, several hundred men of Gwent had found - as Cedric's Saxons had a few months earlier - that Rocky Valley was a pretty decent place for a hidden force to hide in easy marching distance from Tintagel.

Each man who lay in wait for the orders to attack felt pretty good about their chances of success in taking the castle. Although they had heard what Arthur and Morgan had done to the besieging Saxons - and none of them was too anxious to repeat the experience - the certain absence of these two from the forthcoming conflict was very much welcomed.

Concerns had been raised about trying to take the gates from Sir Bors, who—if rumour was to be believed—had pretty much single-handedly held the narrow strip of land that joined the island on which the castle stood with the mainland. However, their orders also made clear that both Bors and the new Queen would be well in their graves by then.

All things being equal, therefore, there was every prospect that one of the last great strongholds of the Britons would soon be flying the flag of Gwent.

Maelgwn ap Owain, the youngest son of the King of Gwent, strapped and restrapped his gauntlets nervously. "And we're confident the gates will be open when we arrive?"

The cold, dead eyes of Iorwerth, his father's chief advisor, rolled once again. "I said so, didn't I? There are more assassins at that damned tournament than there can be competitors. Your father has left nothing to chance. It is the fourteenth day since they rode out on that damned quest. It's time for the attack."

Maelgwyn was not sure. He didn't like this plan. He didn't like the idea of sneaking into another man's castle when he was off on a holy quest. He didn't like the use of assassins to kill that man's wife. And he didn't like skulking here with an army hoping to conquer a country by stealth.

He thought it was the kind of underhand deception that was likely to catch on.

"Your brother would not have had any qualms about his orders," Iorwerth added as if reading Maelgwyn's mind. "He could be relied upon to get his hands appropriately dirty."

Maelgwyn was too young to remember Kael properly. What he had heard about his brother in the intervening years since his... accident made him think whoever had brought that short, vicious life to an end via violent means had probably done the world a favour. "I do not have any 'qualms', Iorwerth. I just wonder about the advisability of publicly stabbing an ally in the back. It is the sort of thing that may make our other friends feel a touch less staunch in their support of us."

"Your father has long been clear that Dumnonia is an ally in name only. They murdered our country's heir, and this reckoning has been a long time coming. You are required to do your duty."

Maelgwyn ignored the older man. He had always been thus, so anxious to get redress for all manner of slights. Iorwerth may have his father's ear, but he had few other friends at court.

The prince drew his sword and looked over the rows of men who had formed up. Gwent was the workhorse of the remaining British kingdoms. Dumnonia might have the cultivator and the military geniuses, Powys had the mineral wealth, Gwynedd had the tactical position, and Dehuebarch had the links overseas, but Gwent had a big population. This meant lots and lots of raids for supplies by spearmen who quickly became veterans or became dead.

It made what they were about to do feel so distasteful to Maelgwyn.

He should make a speech. The prince knew he should. If he had been preparing for an assault that was this important anywhere else in Britain, he would have spoken of the joy of battle. In trusting to your shield mate. Of honouring the name of your father.

But none of that felt appropriate today. Instead, he signalled the men to begin their approach up the hill towards Tintagel.

***

The first thing that suggested to Maelgwyn that his father's plan may have come undone was when he saw the gates of Tintagel were barred to his approach.

Actually, that was the second thing.

The first thing was the sight of Bors' giant arse mooning him from the battlements. "This is the closest you are going to get to breaching these walls, you fuckers. Enjoy the smell!"

Iorwerth was beside him, wafting away the terrible stench that appeared to have enveloped the army. "What on earth is that?"

Maelgwyn redid the strap of his gauntlet. "I believe he has just farted in our general direction. Tell me, Iorwerth, is not that man supposed to be dead?"

"From the smell of that, he just might be."

"The best-laid plans, eh? Order the men to set up camp. We won't be sleeping behind those walls today."

As he stalked away, Maelfwyn offered up a little prayer. "Father, I hope you know what you are doing."

CHAPTER 51 – IN WHICH, ONCE AGAIN, OPERATION NOBLE SACRIFICE IS A GO

I will go out on a limb here and suggest that might just be the Betrayal of all that is Good, my dear.

I love a good understatement. Sadly, I was not in a position to fully appreciate it right now: my to-do list was suddenly a little busy. Kraken streaking towards me? Tick. Important mythical figures injured and sinking in below-freezing toxic sludge? Tick. Useless fat fucker crying in the boat behind me? Double tick.

But let's try to grab a few crumbs of comfort. The bigger of the two Krakens was not taking too much interest in us yet. I mean, that could change at any second, but it still seemed happy skirting around the edge of the lake like some sort of weird squid/Roomba hybrid.

Oh, and the fact that the smaller one was getting closer meant I was probably going to be able to hit it with my next blast of <Unnecessary Sequel Trilogy>. Of course, I'd probably be looking into the middle of its mind-bendingly ugly face at that stage. But I'm all about the upside right now.

Otherwise, I might just cry.

I lunged to the opposite side of the boat - fortunately, Mark's bulk kept it dead level - and dipped my hand into the water.

What are you doing, my dear? The Kraken is coming the other way.

"Yep. That's why we're out of here." I fired off a quick burst of <Personal Space Invader> and anchored myself to the boat by encasing my foot in a block of Earth Qi.

With a lurch, we shot forward as if I'd just switched on an outboard motor. "Where's the Kraken?" I yelled at Mark as we started cresting waves in a somewhat uncontrolled manner.

This was proving to be all a bit much for the King of Gwynedd, who vomited most of last week's supper up as we blasted along. "What the fuck is happening!!!"

"Can't talk right now, mate. Doing my best to defy the laws of physics. Where's the Kraken gone?"

"It was right ahead of us, but it dove under the... Oh shit!!!"

It didn't seem like Mark had good news for me. Without looking, I pointed my hand the opposite way and dramatically changed our direction, nearly throwing us both out of the canoe. There was a concerning creaking noise from the craft beneath us, but you know what, there is only so much worry I can hold in my heart at any one time. We were either going to be dead soon, or we weren't. There wasn't much more I could do than I was already trying.

A tentacle shot out just to my side, nearly knocking me into the water. "Mate, don't just sit there. Fucking hit it with something."

I changed direction again, lurching us to the opposite side. As Mark nearly toppled out, I also locked his feet to the base of the canoe. Losing the last king on the quest who wasn't a)dead, b)being fucked raw, or c) a fucking backstabbing bastard, would just be plain poor personnel management. More water crashed over the top of us, suggesting Nessie Mk II was still doing its best to ruin my day.

"Big M! Can you lock on to Lancelot and Arthur's position?"

Not a problem, my dear. Without wishing to add to the pressure, it appears Owain is about to reach the island. I am not sure you have time to both save your fellows and also intercept him from gaining Caeldfwch.

"Are they still alive?"

I performed another hairpin turn. It was difficult to tell whether all the accompanying noise was the Kraken's screaming, the canoe's seams about to give up the ghost, or Mark losing his shit. My money was on all three.

They are. For now. Arthur has a significant chest wound, but the cold of the water is actually keeping him from bleeding out. Lancelot...

"Nah, mate. I can't cope with ominous pauses right now."

Lancelot is still struggling with the aftereffects of his previous battle. I can sense he still lives, but...

"Dude!"

He is in a bad way.

"Drynwyn?"

What the fuck do you want now?

"I need you to let Mark hold you."

No fucking chance.

"Mate," another right-degree turn and more screaming, creaking and blubbering. A tentacle whipped across the side of the boat, catching me on the shoulder. "I'm so not up for this right now! Merlin, can you put some sort of waypoint up for me?"

He touches me, and it's Wicker Man time. That fucker is toxic.

A giant green triable appeared on the lake about a couple of hundred feet from our current position. I swung the canoe around, narrowly missing driving straight through the Kraken, which had suddenly crested the water and emerged in all its nightmarish glory.

"FUUUUUCCKKKK!" screamed Mark, swinging his oar at it. One of the creature's jaws snapped down, splintering it in two.

"Drynwyn! Wind your fucking neck in. I need him if we're going to survive this. I can't be an outboard motor, a Qi cannon, a lifeboat operator and provide adequate calamari protection. It would help if you stepped up."

Not a fucking chance.

In Drynwyn's defence, I don't think it was being deliberately difficult. Although it may have some discretion about its definition of a 'good man' who can safely hold it, I think the ship of Mark's goodness may have long since sailed.

To your left!

I turned the boat instinctively, missing a forest of tentacles by millimetres. "What the fuck, mate! You nearly sent me straight into it!"

I warned you it was on the left!

"I thought you meant to turn left! Oh, fuck this."

I dropped into my Artist's Studio.

"Okay. Okay. Let's take a beat here." If I thought it was a bit of a cheat code that I could essentially stop time and plan my next move, then that intrusive idea could bite me. The odds were more stacked against me than Pamela Anderson in her heyday. I'd be taking every advantage I could get my hands on, fuck you very much.

"Let's think through the next few seconds." I closed my eyes and tried to recapture the scene before me. I could feel my Qi refilling from soaking up the ambient essence in the air. It seemed to hit the hard limit much faster than it had been doing recently.

It might not be the appropriate moment, my dear, but this is significant progress. Suppose you can avoid being ripped apart by this first Kraken, somehow escape the notice of the second, reach Arthur and Lancelot before they expire and then prevent Owain from drawing Caeldfwch before he projects an aura of anti-Qi at you. In that case, you will be looking in pretty good shape.

"Well, thanks for the pep talk."

There were too many things to get done at once. I couldn't plot out a series of events that would continue to keep all the balls in the air. If I stopped using <Personal Space Invader> to drive the canoe, I could probably blast Arthur and Lancelot out of the water and onto the island. Maybe. It wasn't like I had much experience directing giant air jets. Knowing my luck, I'd overshoot and catapult them straight into the bigger Kraken.

On the other hand, I could ignore the men in the water and reach the island and royally fuck up Owain before he had a shot at the sword. I'd enjoy that, but I'm not sure the timeline would be so appreciative.

And then there was the Kraken hunting us down...

No. The only game in town was saving the two people whose existence kept Zizzie alive. That was the whole point of my resurrection.

"Big M, can you help me direct a blast of <Personal Space Invader> at Arthur and Lancelot? I need to get it just right to blow them out of the water and land them as close to Owain as possible."

I can, my dear, but if you stop using your Qi to drive the boat, you will immediately become Kraken food.

"Yep. Heard and understood. And if you have any solution to avoid that, which will also keep the Once and Future King alive, I'm all ears. But the timeline needs Arthur."

What does the future look like if Arthur has no cultivator by his side once he becomes the Pendragon, my dear? And that's assuming either of them will actually be in any shape to fight Owain when they land.

"It's a shitty situation. Give me another hand to play, and I'll run with it!"

The silence was the only answer I needed.

***

Things moved almost as if they were in slow motion when I popped back out into real-time.

I pulled my hand out of the water, immediately stopping our momentum. This was actually a net benefit as it momentarily wrong-footed - well, wrong-tentacled - the Kraken, which had incorrectly anticipated our course of direction.

"Why have we stopped!"

209

I was not at home to King Mark right now. I took aim at the green arrow Merlin had helpfully placed above my targets. I reached out with a gentle pulse and found them both, just barely alive. I pushed as much <Healing Wave> as I thought I could possibly spare their way. I was worried about the side effects, though. I needed them both to be able to function to take out Owain, or this wasn't going to be worth it.

"It's coming!"

Mark's voice was seriously getting on my tits.

"You're up, Big M."

My dear, are you sure? You could still get out of this. The Kraken will be upon you if you're stationary for much longer.

"Take the shot, mate."

I felt Merlin take control of my Qi. That feeling still made me retch, but it hardly mattered any longer. It was, briefly, interesting to watch how he shaped, controlled and executed the blast of <Personal Space Invader>. In my last moment, I recognised how far I still had to go before I was a millionth of the cultivator this man had been.

The stream of air shot out of me, plunging through the water and launching Arthur and Lancelot into the air. I didn't need to watch their progress to know they would hit dry ground.

A shadow fell over me. I turned to face a sight which, oddly, didn't seem so scary anymore.

"Big M? It's been emotional."

And my canoe was swallowed up.

CHAPTER 52 – IN WHICH BORS FEELS HIS AGE

"I'm no famed military strategist, but I have to wonder at the advisability of seeking to besiege a castle that has made significant preparations for a massive tournament. I mean, I'm probably eating as well as I have ever done." Bors stood on the narrow walkway that connected Tintagel to the mainland, ostentatiously eating a leg of pork.

A hail of arrows was launched towards him, which Blæk, hidden in the shadows of the gates, effortlessly batted aside by pushing on the metal at their tips.

"Again, just spitballing here, but isn't it seen as bad form to try to assassinate the commander of the opposing army when he is trying to discuss surrender? I'm sure I read that somewhere. Mind you, you guys are all about the fucking knives in the back, aren't you? Thrown any old women from windows recently?"

Maelgwn pressed his knuckles to his eyes in despair. Bors had been monologuing at his men for over an hour now, and there didn't seem to be anything he could do to stop it. He'd lost several elite units trying to storm the bridge to take the big man down before settling on trying to fill him full of holes. That wasn't being too successful, either.

If the men of Gwent had been feeling a touch uncertain about the honourability of the assault, Bors' lampooning was not doing much for morale. Although, if he was truly interested in surrender...

Maelgwn raised his hand to pause the pointless bombardment. "You wish to discuss terms?"

"Sure," Bors made a careless wave of the bones he was now pretty much gnawing.

"I presume you wish for safe passage?"

Bors frowned in faux confusion. "Sorry, why would I want safe passage?"

"For you and the Queen Guinevere. When you hand over the castle."

"Ah, with you. Sorry, I think what we're having here is a failure to communicate." Bors gesticulated towards the men of Gwent. "I was giving you a chance to call it quits. I mean, obviously, someone is going to need to be ritually fucked to death with a spikey stick for murdering Queen Igraine, but I'm not about visiting the sins of the father on his son. You're just being a good little prince, and it's not your fault your dad's a duplicitous shit. That everything is getting a tad humiliating is a bit more down to you, so I figure your best play is to surrender now - no harm, no foul - and fuck off back to Gwent to await your coronation on the news I've ripped Owain's head off and used it to fellate my horse."

"I don't think that will work," Guinevere appeared at Bors' side. The Gwent archers reloaded, waiting for the order to let loose.

"Sorry, your majesty?"

"From what I hear, Owain enjoyed sucking off the odd stallion. So, I doubt that would be as humiliating an end as could be hoped. I think it might just be better if we go old school and lop off his limbs and use his torso as a doorstop. You know, stick to the classics."

"Good point," Bors turned back to face Maelgwn. "So, what do we say? We'll even overlook all the assassination attempts. You good to fuck off now?"

The prince shook his head and retreated behind the front row of his shield wall. As he went, he swore under his breath. This was a disaster.

Iorwerth was immediately at his side. "They're both there. Give the order to attack now."

Maelgwyn lifted the man into the air by grabbing the front of his tunic. "What do you think we've been trying to do? There's a reason this castle is seen as fucking impregnable. They can hold that bridge until the end of the world. Our only chance of winning this was for the gatehouse to be open! And, guess what, that didn't fucking happen! Cheers, Dad!"

"So, you are just going to let them stand there and defame your father's name?" The advisor's face was turning purple.

"I can't take the gate, Iorwerth. The only option is to starve them out. And you heard him, they've got stores aplenty. We've got enough for a few more days before needing to resupply. This is a disaster!" The prince dropped the spluttering man to the floor.

"So what are we going to do?" Iorwerth rasped.

Maelgwyn shook his head. His father's command had been clear. When he returned from the quest for Caeldfwch, Owain wanted his men to be in control of Tintagel. There were to be no excuses. Maelgwyn was well aware of the many and various ways in which he regularly disappointed his father. He was not his brother, as Owain never tired of telling him.

But maybe it was time to channel a little bit of Kael. "Gather my guard; I will lead the next charge myself."

***

"You may want to consider getting up on the battlements," Bors growled, watching the troop movements across the bridge. "Find any archers you think will cut the mustard and see what cover you can provide. Did you speak to the merchants?"

Guinevere grimaced. "It seems they were running something called a 'confidence and supply' approach to provisions."

"What the fuck does that mean?"

"Basically, the cupboard is bare. They were waiting to make some more money to refresh our stores. They seemed to think you wanted them to pull out all the stops. This was how they were managing it."

"Fuck."

"Indeed. We'd normally evacuate the civilians in advance of a siege, but the castle is bursting with visitors. We're likely to be out of food this time next week - and that's if we start rationing now."

"We ration, and that dozy fucker out there will know he has us. We need to make him think we're set for the long term. Organise a feast or something."

"Even if that means we run out in days?"

"We can't just sit here and wait for Arthur to come back and pull our arses out of the fire. I need them to keep attacking."

Guinevere nodded towards an approaching group of spears led by the Prince of Gwent. "Say this for him, he's not slow coming forward."

"Nope. Go on, get up top. And if anyone in there fancies a heroic, suicidal last stand, let them know now would be a great time to find their balls."

***

Bors was good.

He knew that. The men watching from the walls knew that. The twenty-odd men of Gwent he had variously battered, smacked and launched off the bridge also knew that. However, that sort of knowledge was a more temporary sort of thing.

However, for all his strength, power and belligerence, he was still human. It had been said that three men could hold the bridge of Tintagel against ten thousand. But that assumed those three would occasionally get a break.

Sucking in huge gasps of air, Bors rested on his spear and did his best to plaster on a smile. Owain's kid - was it Maelgwyn? - was opposite him, flanked by some seriously solemn-looking motherfuckers.

"Enjoying yourself yet?"

The young man shook his head, and oddly, Bors believed him. He didn't know much about the heir to the kingdom of Gwent, but he did know he was decent. He couldn't imagine he was finding this any more of an edifying spectacle than Bors was. "Just let us pass, Sir Bors. You cannot possibly think you can hold out much longer."

"My king asked me to keep his castle safe. Until that moody twat stands where you are and tells me I should give it up, I'm going to do right by him. Now, where were we?"

Bors widened his stance, using the butt of his spear to take some of the weight off his sore knee. Mrs Bors was going to be pissed if he got himself killed today.

Two of Maelgwyn's men pushed forward, each on the edge of the bridge. Bors cursed. It was much easier when they came straight down the middle. These fuckers knew what they were about. Arrows streaked down from above, striking the men's shields. Irritatingly, that didn't seem to make much difference to them.

Veterans, then. Wonderful.

And then they were on him. It wasn't easy to engage two spearmen at once - especially ones not rushing at you in a fury - and Bors found himself shuffling backwards, trying to keep them both occupied.

He was used to his aggression spooking opponents, but these men weren't for turning. They were willing to accept his hay-maker blows, using an attack on one of them as the chance for the other to press for advantage. Bors cursed. He couldn't over-commit against one and risk being brought down by the other.

He felt the temptation to go all out, to let the red mist descend and fuck the consequences.

But no.

He had a job to do here.

The arrows continued falling, but the angle was becoming too acute. Soon, it was clear only one archer was still able to shoot. Guinevere, he assumed. She wasn't the type to accept that a shot couldn't be made.

He smiled and dropped a shoulder into the shield of the man to his left, pushing off the collision to pinball into the other one. He staggered them back a few steps but was unable to dislodge either from the bridge.

Unfortunately, that manoeuvre left him open to their counterattack. Oh well, it had been worth a try.

Bors braced himself for the return blow, hoping it'd be something non-essential that got skewered.

"Coming through, old man." Two figures ran past Bors, crashing into the men of Gwent and driving them backwards. It was two of the men from the melee - Galahad and Parsifal -, and they made short work of the attackers, both moving with the arrogance of youth. Bors remembered when his joints had been that flexible.

Thick, muscular arms pulled him back. "Don't worry about it, big guy. We've got this. Go put your feet up." He looked around into the ugliest face he had ever seen.

For once in his life, Bors didn't have it in him to argue, and he allowed himself to be guided back behind the gates.

Legend said three men could hold the bridge of Tintagel against three thousand. It was time to put the theory into practice.

CHAPTER 53 – IN WHICH WE DO THE TIMEWARP AGAIN

With one last surge, Owain pulled himself onto the shore of the island. He collapsed, his chest heaving with the effort, his arms aching from the unaccustomed rowing, his hands tingling with pins and needles.

A lesser man would have leapt from the canoe and run towards the cairn where the sword, the key to his revenge, rested. But you did not plan and execute a twenty-year delayed act of brutal revenge if you were a man given to hasty actions.

From the moment he had taken hold of Igraine and tossed her through her window, he had known he was living on borrowed time. His mind wandered - briefly - back to Tintagel. Did his son, even now, sit on Uther's throne? That would be sweet.

Owain sniffed and then spat a globule of green onto the shore. He was sorry for the deaths required to make that happen. He would find time to mourn Guinevere and, of course, Bors. But you didn't make an omelette without murdering your nemesis' friends and family in a bloody coup.

Or something like that.

And now Arthur...

The aching in his arms was increasing, but he pushed it down. He had needed to distract the wizard long enough to get his hands on the sword. What better way than to land her master in the drink?

This had been a difficult few weeks. Whilst not regretting the course of action he had put in place for a moment - the Dumnonians had killed his fucking son! - he recognised the fallout was going to be seismic. Owain knew his son had concerns about the plan and had subsequently packed his own men into the Gwent retinue to seek to influence the course of events. For that reason, he had no choice but to have led them into the Shriket's lair. After everything, he wasn't going to allow Maelgwyn to perform his own act of political decapitation.

Of course, getting himself trapped had not been part of the plan, but that had not worked out too badly after all.

Owain took a deep breath. He needed to get moving. The sooner he had the sword in his hand, the sooner he could get out of this place. And the sooner the men of Gwent - without fear of Aurelius Ambrosius - could take the attack to the Saxons.

"Are you the one who was promised?"

His head jerked to the side at the unexpected voice, and his eyes opened wide at the tall, willowy and entirely naked woman before him. Her blonde hair spilt down her front to below her knees, covering her modesty, and her startling green eyes were almost wholly serene.

He gawped at her for long enough that she took another step forward, smiling broadly. "Are you? Are you the one that was promised?"

Owain stood and stepped out of his canoe. He steeled himself not to look back at the lake. The wizard would save Arthur, or she wouldn't. It would not matter once he had the sword. "I am," he said, voice steady.

The Lady of the Lake held out her hand, which he took without hesitation. "About time. Come with me."

***

Funnily enough, the inside of a Kraken looks suspiciously like my Artist's Studio. "Big M? What's going on?"

Ah, excellent. I assumed I'd get the split-second timing just right, but it is always nice to have the reality of my excellence reconfirmed.

"Happy for you. So, I'm not dead yet? Or am I?"

Not quite, my dear. However, I would encourage you not to return to reality until we have developed a pretty solid plan that can instantaneously be put into action.

"How instantaneously?"

Let's just say our margin for error will be rather slim.

"Did Arthur and Lancelot make it?"

They're in the air, my dear. My calculations - which I flatter myself are likely to be correct to the millimetre - will have them hitting the island's edge eight seconds after you restart time.

"Are they okay?"

The Big M was a little slower responding this time. *You hit them with <Healing Wave> before I blasted them out of the water, so they have every chance.*

I chose not to parse those words too carefully. To be honest, it was taking me a beat to get used to still being alive. It felt a bit different than when I first woke up on the battlefield: then, I was more irritated than anything else. It had taken quite a bit of mental torment to move past that. But I had managed it, so I was sure I could do it again.

"What's our plan then, mate?"

No idea, my dear. I was working on the principle that being alive in here was a net benefit compared to being eaten by a Kraken.

"Good shout."

I thought so.

I stood up - I seemed to be lying on a chaise longue like some sort of Roman Princess - and stretched out. "How long can I stay in here?"

In theory, indefinitely, my dear. However, in my long experience, the quality of your internal landscape will start to degrade without any refreshing burst of Qi from the real world. This is, in and of itself, not a deal breaker, of course, but there are stories of cultivators going quietly - and not so quietly - insane when their soul space reduced down to nothingness.

"Got it. So, probably best to begin planning how to turn this frown upside down?"

The last picture I had in my head was of the maw of the Kraken expanding to encompass the entire span of the canoe. I had been able to see pretty much the whole way down its nightmarish throat: it hadn't looked like a good place to go. Although, saying that...

"Rhyddrech Hael was swallowed by one of these things, and he got out okay..."

I would redirect your attention to some of Drynwyn's stories of its previous owner. Under very few circumstances would I suggest Rhyddrech Hael was 'okay'.

"Fair point. So being swallowed and getting out *a la* Pinnochio is not an option?"

I would have that as an emergency backup plan.

I cast my eyes around the space. It was quite beautiful here: I could spend some happy hours just chilling. But, then, the fundamental problem wouldn't go away, would it?

I mentally cracked my knuckles. "Right. Let's A Team the shit out of this."

I have absolutely no idea what that means.

***

The Lady of the Lake was not living her best life.

As a neriad, she had not enjoyed being stuck on an island in the middle of a span of pseudo-water. What had seemed like a perfect place to set up and wait for the One Who Was Promised had rapidly turned into a nightmare. She couldn't set fin in the water without one of those bloody ugly things fawning all over her like a puppy. Their excretions had rapidly turned her lake into a morass of toxic sludge that brought her out in hives.

And now the man she had been waiting for turned out to be less than her expected aesthetic. But, she supposed, if she dropped her glamour for a moment, he probably wouldn't be too pleased to see the real 'her' either.

On the plus side, as soon as she could get rid of this bloody sword, she'd be free to fast-travel back home. Just the thought of having access to her power again made her beam with pleasure. Sure, it was nice to be entrusted with an important mission, but sometimes, you just wanted the familiarity of your own pond back.

With an act of conscious concentration, she kept putting one foot in front of the other - how did these bipedal things manage this for their whole lives? - leading the One Who Was Promised up the stone steps carved into the cairn where she had embedded Caeldfwch.

And then the old, fat man suddenly stopped, almost pulling her off her feet. She turned, ready to give him a piece of her mind - or turn him into a frog. Definitely one of those - and was surprised to see he was frozen in time.

Interesting. That suggested there was a cultivator in the near vicinity.

The Lady of the Lake looked back towards the water from which the human had emerged. She could see Kenneth frozen in the act of crashing down on another of those strange floating shapes in which the One Who Was Promised had arrived at her island. Two other humans were captured in time in the act of flying - did they fly? She hadn't realised that - towards her island. Neither of them was a cultivator, but each looked far more palatable than the big man who she was leading to the sword.

Interesting. Perhaps this wasn't going to be such a terrible assignment after all.

***

Tresaith continued to stare down the Fae war party that was trying to dislodge him from the crossroads to follow the fleeing humans.

217

Everyone involved knew this was all just for show and that, in an hour or so, honour would have been satisfied and they'd all make their way back to Moonglade, no more to be said. However, for now, both parties were giving it the full 'You Shall Not Pass / Yes, We Bloody Well Will'.

So, it was quite disconcerting to feel time lurch to a stop with such an overwhelming sense of panic.

Tresaith glanced down the road where the humans had disappeared. What was going on with that quest? The Fae had become used to Morgan dipping in and out of her soul space. The brief moments of time dilation were irritating, but that was simply the price of doing business with cultivators. It wasn't like it significantly inconvenienced the Fae, but it did mess up the thrill of the hunt when lesser beings became frozen in time.

This, however, felt different. The wizard had been dragged out of time and appeared to be staying there.

Maewyn appeared at his side. "Did you feel that?"

"I did." Tresaith's eyes flicked to the war party, which looked like it was gearing itself up for another faux charge. "I need to go and see what is occurring."

"You like these people, don't you?" His brother's face was flat, betraying no emotion.

Tresaith shrugged. "They're different. Short-lived beings who spend their time in high passion. What's not to like?"

Maewyn stared at him and then nodded slowly. "I'll stand your place, brother. Go and see what ails your pets."

Tresaith gripped Maewyn's shoulder. "Appreciated." He nodded towards the group of Fae. "You sure you can handle them?"

Maewyn drew his sword and planted his feet. "Let us say that I have a significant amount of respect to earn back."

CHAPTER 54 – IN WHICH I GIVE IT EVERYTHING I'VE GOT IN THE TANK

It turns out that given enough time, motivation, resources and 'what's the worst that can happen' energy, I am quite the MacGyver. Of course, it doesn't hurt having the combined might of a dragon hoard and a legendary wizard to suggest various tweaks and optimisations, but I was still feeling pretty damn good about myself.

I had no idea how long I spent pulling the plan together, but by the time I was ready, I had developed quite a collection of options.

"I'm feeling all Wile-E-Coyote here, mate!"

There was a pause. *From context, this suggests we're about to undertake a series of increasingly comedic challenges during which you will repeatedly fall off a cliff. And is the Kraken the very fast bird in this scenario?*

"You know what, Merlin?"

Fuck off?

"No, I was going to say you are making a really good point, and I really appreciate the feedback on my silly and irreverent commentary. I don't say it enough, but I'm so glad you are here to keep my feet on the ground."

Honestly, my dear? I am touched!

"No, of course not, you fucking helmet. Let's get on with it."

***

We'd decided to undertake a ten-second countdown before letting the chips fall where they may.

There was really not going to be much margin for error here, and if these were going to be my final moments on earth - again - I was damned if I was going out without a "Thunderbirds are go!"

Merlin had reached 'five' when I began to have second thoughts. I wasn't exactly someone you'd bet the rest of your continued existence on her ability to execute a complex plan with split-second timing. I wasn't even someone you would entrust with two quid to pop down the shops and buy a pint of milk.

However, I reflected as the Big M intoned 'three', you couldn't spend your life bemoaning the Damsel in Distress trope and then hope for a big strong guy to come and sweep you off your feet. Well, you could, but considering I'd just saved the arses of the two prime heroic beefcakes, I was going to need to take care of myself here.

And then it was launch time...

The millisecond I popped back into reality, I projected the most oversized version of <Zizzie's Gift> I could produce. Neither Merlin nor I thought the Wanderer

219

would likely last more than a few seconds against being eaten by a Kraken, but those earned moments would be the be-all and end-all.

As the painting swirled into being, I shoved out all the concoctions I'd spent my time in my Artist's Studio developing: for shits and giggles, I'd encased it all in a lovely big ACME crate. If I were going to die, I'd do so with whimsy in my heart and a smile on my face.

At the same time, I triggered the adapted version of <Personal Space Invader>, which pulled a bunch of little surprises to stick all over me. I held fire momentarily on triggering <I.E.D>; this would be the last of my cards to play.

My final bit of plotting was actually the most conceptually difficult. <Zizzie's Gift> was 99.9% formed when I made the critical change. With a delicate flick of my wrist, I smudged out the walking stick and gave my man something more useful to hold.

I'm not wild about this development, I hope you realise?

"You'll be swell, D. Just go to town. And remember, the more fire, the better."

Well, if you fucking insist...

***

You know the end of every Michael Bay movie you have ever seen?

This was now my life.

<Zizzie's Gift> formed fully, and I was sure the dude stood a little taller when he realised he was holding a sword of flaming death rather than facing a monster from nightmare armed with nothing more substantial than a stiff upper lip and an unearned sense of manifest destiny.

Drynwyn wasted no time and whipped upwards, firing a nice thick line of flame down the Kraken's throat.

And then shit got real.

It turned out that if you mixed together a few choice articles that a hoarding dragon had held on to, added in a couple of Pills of Agonising Death, suspended the whole thing in a pretty coating of Wood Qi (all stamped with the ACME seal of quality), and THEN hit it all with some legendary flame which despised the unrighteous, you had yourself quite the party.

<Zizzie's Gift> had already been reduced by something approximating a quarter of its initial size - fuck me, Krakens did not mess about - in the time it took for all this to go 'boom'.

The explosion vaporised my shield, dropping Drynwyn to the deck of the boat near my feet.

It would, however, be accurate to say the ensuing conflagration did little for the Kraken's health and temper.

Rather than swallowing the canoe—and Mark and I with it—the monster was rocked backwards, several massive, gushing wounds blown clear through it. This did not make it any prettier.

"What the fuck!" Obviously, as far as Mark was concerned, that had been a fairly incomprehensible series of events. I didn't really have the urge to fill him in right now.

"Just get behind me. This is going to get messy!"

The explosion, as well as royally fucking up the Kraken, had removed the front half of the canoe, so I was doing the best I could to keep us afloat with a thick wodge of Wood Qi. This was burning through my reserves like you wouldn't believe and wouldn't be anything like a long-term solution. However, considering the Kraken appeared to be preparing its ugly self for Round 2, I doubted neither drowning nor Qi exhaustion would be a central issue in my immediate future.

It screamed at us, opening its disgusting mouth wide. If you need a visual, think of Arnie standing above a de-helmed Predator. And times that by the Queen going in for a lick of Sigourney. Throw in a nice handful of Slimer flying down the corridor at Bill Murray and finish it off with lashings of every John Carpenter film you've ever seen.

You are aware, my dear, there have been films made outside of the 80s and early 90s?

I ignored him and reconstituted <Zizzie's Gift>. I didn't hold many hopes it would last any longer than it did last time, but it certainly couldn't hurt. I held <I.E.D> tight to my body, ready for the final play. What with my impromptu pseudo-canoe and that I was bleeding off all my spare Qi with bolt after bolt of <Unnecessary Sequel Trilogy>, I couldn't help but think I was multi-tasking like a fucking legend.

Then the Kraken reared up and launched itself at me, and I pushed out everything I was holding back in a concentrated direct blast of <I.E.D>.

The outcome was, I am afraid, rather underwhelming.

I'd geared up every piece of armour, weapon and general sharp implement I still possessed in my inventory. This was quite a lot. The gamble had been that, having weakened the monster through Drynwyn and all the other shit I'd thrown at it, this final explosion might just encourage it to fuck off and go away.

Unfortunately, all I seemed to have achieved was turning it into a massive, furious porcupine. Sure, it looked fucking ridiculous, but I didn't think I would be taking it down by crushing its sense of self-esteem.

That was my lot.

"Hey, it was worth a shot, mate. We gave it our best--"

And then Tresaith came.

***

There's a fun game you can play by adding the words "And then the Dragons came" after the first line of any famous novel to completely change its vibe. You should try it.

"It was the best of times; it was the worst of times. And then the dragons came."

"In the beginning was the word. And then the dragons came."

"Marley was dead, to begin with. And then the dragons came."

Trust me, there's not a work of literature that the timely appearance of giant, winged lizards in the second sentence cannot improve.

Tresaith appearing next to me with all the righteous, vengeful fury of a dad whose daughter's date just made her cry was of the same intensity.

The only way the moment could have been even more perfect was if he had whispered 'on your left' to me before stepping through a giant, yellow circle.

I won't be able to do the next few moments justice, so let's just say the boy had game. He literally walked on water to plunge both his hands straight through the

Kraken's carapace, ripping vast chunks of plating away, to thrust back in and start evacuating organs.

Tentacles whipped down on him, but he casually wrapped them around his arms and tugged, tearing them clear and then using their wet ends to beat the creature to death.

I felt his Qi move, and he did something pretty awesome with gravity. He squashed the thing flat and, in the next moment, stretched it out. Seriously, it was as if he had turned the thing into an accordion and was playing "How do you like me now?" At some stage, he even reconstituted the canoe and found time to push us out of what was increasingly becoming a Kraken splash zone.

I tried to follow the trail of destruction as we drifted away from the battle, but it was impossible. I'd have believed you if you'd told me five Tresaiths were stomping this thing into its constituent atoms. What was most impressive was the speed in which the Fae was linking and compounding techniques with just blasting out solid chunks of Qi straight through the monster.

"Fuck me!"

I know, my dear. This is why I tended to travel incognito through the Fae realm. I am not saying I could not compete with this, - Tresaith lifted the Kraken out of the water with one hand and took off for the sky like it was a nuclear bomb, and he needed to ram it through a portal to another universe – *okay, maybe I am.*

Several thoughts were competing in my rather exhausted brain. Firstly, if Tresaith fancied ramming his nuclear bomb in my – *My dear!* - sorry. Well, that was my first thought. Secondly, I was definitely going to be upping my studying. The dude was doing things with Qi I did not even know were possible.

But thirdly, and perhaps most pressingly, I needed to get to the island in the middle of the lake ASAP. Arthur and Lancelot had just crash landed on the shore, and Owain was doing his best to yank the sword free from its stone, cheered on by... I'm going to say Ariel without the strategically placed shells.

My life has gotten weird.

CHAPTER 55 – IN WHICH HELL HATH NO FURY LIKE A DARK AGE MONARCH SCORNED

Arthur and Lancelot hit the beach, rolled and came up running. Both had become used to healing from Morgan, in various forms, so neither was questioning still being in one piece despite Owain's attentions and a quick dip in the freezing, toxic water.

"He's up there!" Lancelot urgently pointed to the cairn and dashed towards it. However, as soon as his feet touched the bottom step, he was thrown backwards with a resounding 'boom' to land on his back. Arthur shot past him and took the stairs two at a time.

"Sorry! Must be a king thing. If he makes it past me, make sure he doesn't leave the island with the sword!"

Lancelot backflipped to his feet and kicked the sand in frustration.

***

The Lady in the Lake was starting to think she'd made a mistake.

Of all her various roles, transferring Caeldfwch to the One Who Was Promised should have been a cakewalk. I mean, how hard should it be to find a guy to give a magic sword to?

Apparently, more difficult than you'd think.

She raised an eyebrow at the fat man's effort to pull the sword from the stone. Contrary to popular opinion, pretty much anyone could bear Caeldfwch. Of course, whether they could control it once they had it was another matter entirely.

Or, indeed, draw it.

Who the fuck is this joker?

Oh, good. Now the fucking thing had woken up.

"The One Who Was Promised. Apparently," she sent silently to the sword.

You're fucking kidding me! This guy's one spoon of butter from stroking out. What is he? The One Who Was Promised A Massive Fucking Fried Breakfast?

"What can I tell you? He's here, and he wants you. It's not like this ritual is any more complicated than that."

I don't like him. He's sweating down my hilt. Tell him to go away.

The Lady in the Lake took a controlling breath. My word, she'd be glad to get this bitchy, whiney, self-obsessed blade off her hands. But for that, the One Who Was Promised needed to fucking do his bit.

"Are you making yourself deliberately too heavy so he cannot pull you out of the stone?"

...

"Caeldfwch? I'm talking to you."

I might be.

"Look, I know he might not be the most classically attractive man in the world, but he's here, you're here, and I want to get out of here. Can't you just play nice?"

It's not fair. You know I don't like to... hello, sailor!

The Lady in the Lake turned to see a second man reaching the top of the stone staircase. Well, that was new. The latest arrival was definitely easier on the eye than the first, even if he seemed to have no hair. Still, you couldn't have everything.

"Owain!" the bald man roared. Then he tackled the fat one, still wrestling with Caeldfwch, away from the stone and rolled with him on the floor.

"Well," thought the Lady in the Lake, "how thrilling." And with a wave of her hand, she turned the ground to mud.

***

I skidded to a halt on the island's shore, <Zizzie's Gift> melting into nothingness under my feet. Who knew a summer sleeping my way through a group of surfers would be helpful? "Who's the nasty skank that will never amount to anything now, Shelia?"

Who are you talking to, my dear?

"Just my youth, Big M. Where's Caeldfwch?"

Lancelot ran to meet me.

"Up there he's being. I can't follow!

I bounded forward but had the same issue. It was like there was a forcefield at the bottom of the cairn. "Big M? Any thoughts?"

I think, my dear, we will have to leave this one to Arthur.

***

The Once and Future King was embracing his central role in proceedings. "I. Thought. You. Were. My. Friend," he shouted, each word punctuated by a thudding blow to Owain's head.

However, bloodied, the King of Gwent had spent longer on the battlefield than Arthur had been alive. He took the punches, letting Arthur burn out his rage, then rolled, trapping the smaller man beneath him.

Owain would never be able to compete with sword or spear, but in an ugly grappling match in the mud, things were much more even.

The two wrestled for supremacy for a few moments before Owain grabbed a piece of driftwood and pressed it down on Arthur's neck, letting his whole weight fall on it.

Arthur's eyes bulged at the restriction, his biceps bunching as he tried to lever Owain off him. It was like trying to lift a mountain.

"I killed your mother. Did you know that?"

Now he had the upper hand - literally - Owain seemed to feel now was appropriate for some good old-fashioned villain monologuing. "And, by now, your wife will have joined her. My flag will be flying about Tintagel."

Arthur kicked and bucked, but he could feel darkness hovering at the edge of his vision. The debt from Morgan's healing was sucking at his strength, let alone being crushed by the king above him. In response, Owain just redoubled his efforts, feeling the body beneath him beginning to tire.

A few more moments were all it would take, and his long-cherished revenge would be complete—Uther's son for his son. And no trace of Uther's line would be left in this world.

*****

Is this really the best you can do?

Arthur thought the lack of oxygen had moved into the terminal stage. He was hearing things.

Are you still with me? It is polite to answer.

Arthur grunted a response. Twisting violently to the left earned him a quick breath, but then the crushing restriction was back on his throat. Fucking Owain. He'd been like family. He'd sat on the man's fucking knee. He'd marched at his side. He'd fucked the man's serving girls!

Seriously, what is wrong with men? Moments from death, and all you want to think about is getting squelchy. I have a good mind to leave you to it.

That grabbed Arthur's attention. "Help?"

If you ask me very nicely.

For a terrifying moment, Arthur thought he had no air left, but with a colossal effort, he forced out a "Please?"

Since you have been so polite, listen carefully. I will say this only once. The fat man who sweated all over me has a slightly loose grip on that piece of wood. He's readjusted it several times. I would calculate he will need to do it once before you die. If I were you, I'd get ready to give it all you've got at that moment—left hand.

It might have been uncharitable in the circumstances, but Arthur couldn't but compare that 'help' with Drynwyn's steaming, flaming death beams. Still, beggars could not be choosers.

He played dead, letting the wood crush down even further. The voice better be right about this. And then, when there was precious little 'playing' about it, he felt Owain readjust his left hand.

With every last bit of energy he possessed, Arthur exploded upwards, surprising the King of Gwent, throwing him off, and letting him suck in big lungfuls of air.

Excellent. I assume you can take it from here?

Wasting no time, Arthur got to his feet and then stamped down on Owain's knee, shattering it and - in the same movement - sweeping the piece of wood into his own hands. "Please let me let you know this gives me no joy," he said to the screaming man.

And then he went to town.

*****

Lancelot and I were feeling a little bit like spare cocks at an orgy.

After everything we'd been through to get here, I think we were both a touch underwhelmed by our roles in the grand finale.

Get used to it, my dear. Merlin had said. *You are not the lead character in the tales of King Arthur. Indeed, nothing says you are fulfilling your role more successfully than having done all you can to get the protagonist to the right place at the right time and then standing back with--*

And then a couple of things happened.

First, a pulped body of what may well have used to be Owain of Gwent hit the beach next to us. Some of his wounds may well have been caused by the fall from atop the cairn, but most looked like the king had been on the business end of a shellacking with a two-by-four. Owain may have had unbroken bones, but that would have needed a more thorough forensic examination than I was prepared to give.

Second, I realised all the little strings of Qi that I had got used to connecting me to everything around me had vanished. It was like suddenly going blind. Oh, and Merlin had gone.

Third - and I should probably have led with this, but the falling body was pretty damn visceral - a choir of angels was giving it some welly and a massive column of light had descended from the heavens to light on the figure of Arthur, stood atop the cairn, an enormous broadsword in his hand, stretching to the sky.

Apparently, someone had found Caeldfwch.

CHAPTER 56 – IN WHICH THE SIEGE OF TINTAGEL BEGINS TO BITE

"Are you sure this is the only way?"

Bors tightened the strap on his breastplate. He knew - intellectually - they'd only run out of food the day before, but he was certain his armour was feeling a little loose. "What?"

Guinevere sighed and shook her head. "I was just asking, for the hundredth time, whether there was truly no other option than to leave our impregnable fortress and engage an enemy in possession of overwhelming numbers."

"I'm hungry."

And, as if that was all that needed to be said, Bors pushed forward through the small group of men who, likewise, had decided that there was no state of being more horrific than feeling a touch peckish.

"You are being rather unfair," Blæk whispered at her side as the assault team approached the gate.

"No. No, I am not. This is dick-measuring, pure and simple. There's no need for him to lead an attack on them."

"Your Highness, we have run out of food. It is not going to be too many days before the warriors are not going to be in a position to fight. If we knew that relief was on the way, I am sure the last thing Sir Bors would risk would be a doomed sally beyond the walls to break the siege. However, as we are currently under assault by our single strongest ally, we must assume that if anyone is likely to receive extra troops soon, it will not be us."

"They're all going to be killed!"

"I don't think that is his plan, Your Majesty. I do not know Sir Bors well, but all of the Grey's reports suggest he is far more tactically astute than his public persona suggests. I am sure this is more than a forlorn hope to certain doom."

***

"And once we've killed as many as we can, we stop for a quick nap, then go again. All happy?"

"You're not being serious, are you?" Galahad said from Bors' side.

He looked down at the... he didn't want to call him a 'small boy' because that felt disrespectful to a warrior that had absolutely brought the thunder to the defence of the bridge for the last few days. There was something extraordinary fluent about the way Galahad moved in a fight - as if the air itself thought there was something forbidden about providing wind resistance.

The boy favoured sword and shield, which made sense. Considering his small stature, it allowed him far more freedom in the press than lugging a massive spear about. Bors had been impressed with how the shield was used more as an offensive weapon than to receive blows. He'd never tell a soul, but he'd been practising something similar in his downtime.

"Of course not. But you don't tell the men that. I have an image to maintain!" Bors flashed a big, toothy grin.

"So, we have a better plan than fight until either we or they are dead?"

"Of course we do."

Galahad nodded and fell back beside Parsifal and Archon. The three of them had formed an absolutely deadly trio that ensured the bridge's defence was far less spicey than it should have been. If Arthur ever made it back, the Marghekyon had its new core.

Palemedias cleared his throat and spat a bloody mouthful of spit to the ground. In common with most of the few men of Dumnonia, the siege had taken a toll. "There's no plan, is there?"

Bors winked at the last of his surviving childhood friends. "Of course not. You want to go out as you've lived, don't you? OPEN THE GATE!"

***

It took Maelgwn a moment to realise what was going on.

"The mad fucker!"

Unfortunately, it turned out that 'moment' was something he would regret.

The archers on Tintagel's walls, led - apparently - by Guinevere, launched a furious bombardment that carried far further than arrows had any right to travel. If he hadn't known for certain that the wizard had accompanied Arthur and his father on the quest for Caeldfwch, he would have assumed some cultivator shenanigans. But it just had to be luck, didn't it?

He was forced to reconsider that viewpoint when the rain of arrows didn't stop. Or he would have done, if he wasn't immediately occupied with pulling his men assaulting the bridge out of the way of the most lunatic-inspired charge he'd ever seen.

Bors bounded forward through Tintagel's gates, carrying a battering ram single-handedly. He struck the hastily assembled shield wall of the men of Gwent with all the inevitability of the setting sun. But didn't stop to admire his handy work. He pushed on through, punching a massive hole in the assembled force, allowing his own men to swarm through - was that a child with a sword and shield!!! - and continued onwards towards Maelgwn himself.

In normal circumstances, being outnumbered ten to one was a pretty straightforward calculation. And if anyone on the Gwent side had kept their heads, that would have seen that. But due to the spookily accurate, long-ranged arrows, a giant swinging a tree trunk to crush skulls left and right, and the fevered intensity of spearmen who didn't know where their next meal was coming from, things rapidly spun out of control.

Bors and company were clear of the bridge and halfway into the Gwent camp before Maelgwyn was able to pull things back in order. Then things got just that bit tougher for the Dumnonians.

***

"Ah."

Guinevere launched another arrow, which, empowered by Blæk, surged forward to take out a Gwent spear about to skewer Parsifal in the throat. There was no real power at such a distance, but it knocked the attacker off his stride, and the tall man could slip away from danger.

The queen rolled her aching shoulders and turned to the quiet man. "Is that a good 'ah' as in 'ah, now our problems are over!'"

"I'm afraid not, your highness. What Bors was attempting required significant momentum. They've done far better than I had possibly expected, but they are now getting bogged down. He would be wise to... Oh dear."

"I swear, Sir Blæk." Guinevere shot a further arrow at a spear flanking Bors' position, but the distance was too far, and it dropped short, even with Blæk giving it significant extra impetus. "If you keep making slightly panicked little noises without explaining yourself, I am going to be very unhappy indeed."

"Understood, Your Highness. At the risk of making you even more unhappy, I am afraid to say I rather think our men are getting cut off."

***

"Right. On to Plan B."

"We have a Plan B? Did we have a Plan A?" Palemedias was nursing a nasty cut to his arm that had Bors hoping Tasko had squirrelled away some of Morgan's elixirs back home. That, or he rather feared the Marghekyon would have its first-ever one-armed warrior.

"Of course we had a Plan A, Pally! And it went like an absolute dream, I will have you know. Textbook execution."

Bors stepped backwards from a determined surge from a heavily armoured Gwent spearman and clanked into the back of Archon, retreating the other way. Cursing, the big man looked around and saw his small expeditionary force was down to fifty - which sucked - and was also completely surrounded - which sucked that bit harder.

Bors glanced hopefully back towards Tintagel. Maybe in an act of astonishing perspicacity, he'd drawn the attack to a halt just inside Qi-empowered archery range? But no. They were too far out for support now. Either that or Gwin was saving her ammunition to cover the glorious and triumphant retreat he was doubtless about the lead, carrying those wagons of supplies that had been his principal target.

Yeah, he decided. It must be that.

Maelgwyn appeared opposite Bors, face like he'd been slapped with a wet fish whilst sucking a lemon. By the look of him, the Prince of Gwent hadn't been hiding at the back of the skirmished. His armour was fucked.

"Tell your men to lower their arms, Sir Bors. It's over."

"Counterpoint. Go fuck yourself."

Maelgwyn looked over at Iorwerth, who had made his position very clear on what needed to be the outcome of this tussle. He was already winching his crossbow.

"Sir Bors, you have done all that could have been asked of you. You held the bridge against appalling odds and your sally against our forces will live long in song. But we have you surrounded, you are cut off from any line of retreat and my men wish to revenge the hundreds that have fallen to you during the siege."

Bors looked around at some very grim faces. "Well, you shouldn't have been such pussies, should you?"

Maegywn shrugged and indicated for more men with crossbows to push their way forward. They lowered them to take aim at the small circle of spears that did its best to contract even tighter behind broken and damaged shields.

"Surrender, my lord. We have foes aplenty on this island. The British will be all the weaker should you force me to kill you."

"I mean, that sounds all very reasonable and grown up. However, your king murdered our queen, you tried to have Guinevere assassinated, and *you* have invaded *us*. If there's a moral high-ground of 'let us all unite against the Saxons,' you could probably make it more powerfully if you weren't full of shit. Worst case scenario for me here is you kill us all - "

Bors heard Palemedias whisper "I mean, that's a pretty bad downside... "

"- and you STILL will not be able to take Tintagel. However, with us dead, Arthur will be even more pissed with you all than he's already going to be. Angry Pendragons are rarely especially forgiving."

Maelgwyn shook his head. Damn his father for forcing him into this position. "Sir Bors, King Arthur will not return to avenge your deaths. As we speak, Owain of Gwent will have claimed Caeldfwch, dispatched your wizard and removed the heads of your warriors. Believe me when I say nothing can be achieved by further bloodshed. For the final time, lower your arms."

Bors glanced at his small ring of men just for forms' sake. All of them had set, resolute expressions. He fucking loved these guys.

"Sir Bors? Your answer, please." Maelgwyn's tone was grim.

"On behalf of the men of Dumnonia, go fuck - "

The men of Gwent fired.

CHAPTER 57 – IN WHICH ARTHUR KEEPS IT IN HIS PANTS

The Lady of the Lake looked at the saturnine face of the new bearer of Caeldfwch. He certainly had more the bearing of the One Who Was Promised. And the sword had just slid out of the stone for him, whereas the fat man had been huffing and puffing like a giant hog at a trough.

I am content. You may leave, the sword said imperiously.

Yeah, sure. Because a crucial aspect of this ceremony is whether you are happy about the whole thing. The Lady of the Lake was not going to miss her latest burden. Instead, she addressed her attention to the swordsman.

"I now transfer ownership of Caeldfwch to you, my lord. Is there anything you would like to ask before I bid you farewell?"

Arthur turned his intense eyes on the beautiful, naked woman before him. She felt herself, well not exactly blush - this wasn't her first rodeo - but she certainly was not used to quite such an appraising glance.

"How strong is the blade's Qi-disruption field?"

"It is total. Caeldfwch was forged to directly counter cultivators. When drawn, all of the Qi within its range will be annulled." From thin air, the neriad produced a scabbard and handed it to Arthur. "When sheathed in this, the effect is deadened. It is only when it is drawn that you will be protected."

I am right here. It is the height of rudeness to speak about a lady and not to her.

"My apologies, my lady. I did not want to waste your time with trivialities." Arthur winked at the Lady of the Lake. "I will finish with your guardian and then be with you shortly."

That is fine, the sword giggled, *I appreciate your consideration.*

The Lady of the Lake decided she needed to be somewhere else. It was one thing to be stuck on an island with this bloody thing; it was quite another to have to watch it play the coquette.

"When worn, my lord, the scabbard will provide you with significant healing properties, with none of the after-effects which I sense you are currently labouring under. I would suggest wearing it as soon as possible."

Arthur strapped the scabbard around his waist and, after a moment, sheathed the sword. "One final question, if I may. How wide a shadow does she cast?"

The Lady of the Lake was already beginning to go transparent. "It is something you will learn to control. Initially, it will simply provide you with a small personal shield, but as your mastery of Caeldfwch increases, you will find that aura grows. It has been rumoured that the sword has an unlimited reach. Of course, no one has ever survived its curse long enough to discover its true range.

The smile on Arthur's face vanished as his brain caught up with his ears. "Its what now?!"

The Lady of the Lake was entirely see-through now. "Ensure you return her to me when you fall. She will be your ticket to Avalon."

And with that, the neriad vanished, leaving Arthur standing on top of the cairn with more questions than he would like.

Where to now, big boy?

Where to, indeed...

***

"What the fuck was that, Big M?"

I think you've just experienced your first Qi-disruption field, my dear. Caeldfwch completely blocks all capacity for cultivators to reach their techniques. When Arthur has her drawn, until he learns to direct the sword's annulment field, you will - effectively - be entirely normal.

"Well, I'm not too wild about that, to be honest."

No, I can understand that. But imagine how much less Aurelius is going to enjoy the experience.

That put a smile on my face. "Okay. So that would be pretty sweet."

Tresaith sauntered onto the shore, dragging a very sorry for himself Mark behind him. I tossed out a quick <Healing Wave> as it kind of seemed that four kings going into the woods and only one returning might cause questions.

"There is a larger Kraken circling this position," Tresaith said in his lovely musical voice. "I'd rather not kill another one of these beautiful creatures if I can avoid it."

"Beautfiul creatures? Mate!"

Tresaith shrugged. "They are exactly as they were created to be. It is not their fault they have been set to guard this artefact. In the normal run of things, they would not be within a thousand leagues of humans."

I tried. I really did. I gave all my considerable empathy over to the task of giving two fucks about the poor monster from the deep that had been shanghaied to swim around a massive lake, eating anything that came across. Sad to say, I just didn't have it in me. Fuck 'em.

Mark stirred and sat up. "I need to get to the sword!"

"Dude, that ship has sailed. Arthur's claimed it, and Owain..." We all looked at the battered corpse lying near us. "Well, Owain no longer has a vote on the next Pendragon."

I squatted down next to him. "You may want to consider your own position on that. I'm not against leaving you here to find your own way back."

I wasn't sure whether I really had that in me. It felt a little different to abandon someone to starvation and worse on a desert island than to just blast them out of existence - but the fat twat didn't know that.

He noticeably quailed. I could get used to that reaction.

Arthur was coming down the last few steps of the cairn to join us on the beach. He had a very snazzy red scabbard around his waist from which emerged a long, jewelled-encrusted handle.

"Why don't you have some pretty decoration like that?"

Why don't you go fuck yourself with that piece of driftwood? I sensed I may have touched a bit of a nerve there.

232

"What's up, D? Bit of hilt envy?"

It didn't reply. I switched my attention to the scabbard itself. A gentle push towards it with my Qi was slapped back pretty hard. I'd utilised that particular slap when waitressing around handsy men.

"Big M?"

Hardly surprising, my dear. The scabbard covers a blade whose sole purpose is the negation of Qi. I would not expect you to be able to determine its makeup. From my reading, it is theorised it possesses significant healing properties.

I kept a nervous eye on the sword as Arthur drew near me. I hadn't enjoyed the experience of being 'normal' again. "All okay, mate?"

Arthur ignored me, kicking Owain's body as if to reassure himself the man was dead and then turned his attention to Mark, his face even grimmer than usual. "King Mark, are you hale?"

The King of Gwynedd struggled his way to his feet - I quite enjoyed that - and squared up to Arthur. "No thanks to you. You abandoned me to die, just as you did with Beric. Now you have killed Owain. What is it? You wish to gather all of our kingdoms under your thumb?"

Arthur simply stared back. This did little to calm Mark who took another step forward, finger pointing. "The men of Gwynedd will never follow you. Neither will anyone else. Sure, you have your pretty sword, but that won't wash. You won't even have a castle by the time we get back. Let's see if anyone supports a homeless Pendragon."

Then, he made the mistake of prodding Arthur in the chest.

Lancelot moved faster than could have been perceived outside of a slow-motion reply. His fist closed around Mark's stubby finger and dragged it downwards with an audible snap. Mark was on his knees, face white, Lancelot holding the finger aloft. I heard Tresaith give a soft murmur of approval at the speed of the takedown.

"King Mark, I offer you a choice. I began this quest with four British kings and in the spirit of mutual agreement, we all swore oaths to recover Caeldfwch and to do so under the banner of brotherhood. At every turn, I have been undermined and betrayed by those who once swore fealty to my father. And I am sick of it."

He whipped out the sword and held it to Mark's neck. I was once again changed back into an entirely normal person, standing on a beach with a bunch of superhuman beings. I hadn't felt that vulnerable since my first night at a young offender's institute. The raised voices, sense of imminent violence and, oddly, giant threatening octopus (probably another story) completed my *deja vu*.

"I will give you one chance and one chance alone. You swear fealty and recognise me as the Pendragon, or you lose your head, and I renew negotiations with one of your sons. I am sure, eventually, I will find one willing to make that deal."

Oh, isn't he masterful?

We all ignored the breathy voice coming from the sword.

"You would not dare. You are not your father; we all know that."

Arthur's eyes darkened. I have heard people say that before, but never seen it happen before. It was like a different Arthur suddenly peaked out from behind a mask. I was reminded what Bors had said had taken place in the weeks following the destruction of Isca: Arthur going all Heart of Darkness. Suddenly, I could believe it.

"King Mark. I think you should consider your next words very carefully. I am currently in possession of not only the only cultivator of real quality amongst our allies but also the only tool capable of mitigating her power. I am perfectly able - as I am sure you will agree – of causing any amount of chaos and destruction to your lands simply by invading using conventional forces. Along with Morgan, well, it hardly bears thinking about, does it? Particularly if she actually does what I ask her to. You can choose to pledge your fealty, or I will make it my life's work, once I have removed your head, to put Tristian on your throne."

Mark went to stand, and in a flash, Lancelot broke another of his fingers.

"No more words other than 'Hail the Pendragon,' from you, please."

For a moment, I didn't think he would fold, which was interesting. I was idly wondering how many hacks it would actually take to get through his walrus-like neck, but then he muttered something under his breath, and Arthur hauled him back to his feet.

"Serve me as honourably as you did my father and I will have no complaints. And now, wizard," he resheathed Caeldfwch and my powers pinged back on. I was absolutely not wild about this change in our dynamic, "you need to fast-travel us home. Owain revealed that great danger was approaching Tintagel."

Dude didn't need to ask me twice.

With what I hoped was a 'see you soon, big boy' smile to Tresaith, I grabbed Arthur, Lancelot, Mark, Owain's body and, for good measure, lassoed in what was left of Burford too, and triggered for the return journey.

We popped back into existence into quite a shit show.

CHAPTER 58 – IN WHICH ALL'S WELL THAT ENDS WELL

There are various ways in which I am very comfortable bringing a confrontation to a messy, violent conclusion.

If my encounter with the Kraken had taught me nothing else, throwing every possible explosive technique at the problem was, sometimes, the only way forward.

Hang on, my dear. I'm sure one of the key learning points of the last few weeks has been learning the 'less is more' approach in the way in which you use your Qi...

"Can't talk, Big M. Being the GOD OF HELLFIRE!"

With little fanfare, we'd popped back into the human realm in the general vicinity of Tintagel. By which, I mean the five of us - well, six if you count a dead King of Gwent - landed in the middle of a hail of crossbow bolts.

This was disconcerting. However, a cultivator of my quality and experience had no issue activating < I.E.D.> and quickly sucking in all the projectiles to stick to an outer shell of Qi.

Just so we are clear, you are aware that I activated that technique, aren't you?

"Not now, Big M. Too busy being an absolute legend."

"Arthur?" a nicely familiar voice boomed out behind us.

I held on to < I.E.D.> for a few more moments to get the lay of the land.

We appeared surrounded by a large warband of somewhat surprised men with unloaded crossbows. Lying all around us were groaning and moaning bodies, which bore all the hallmarks of a particularly big and belligerent friend of mine going loco down in Acapulco.

"Bors, my old mucker! Surrounded by overwhelming numbers again?"

"Morgan! Nice to see you. Still a manic pixie bitch?"

"You betcha!"

I'd have hugged him, but felt like skewering him with all the crossbow bolts I was currently bristling with would have been counterproductive to the accidental rescue I seemed to have just pulled off.

And Bors was already not at his best. He had about twenty guys at this back who likewise looked like the 'after' video of a particularly brutal cage fight.

He and Arthur had an emotional reunion—you know, in that manly way whereby guys give each other a little nod that carries the weight of years and years of pent-up, repressed love—and I got a better look at what was occurring.

The guys attacking Bors hadn't wasted much time reloading their crossbows, which suggested they weren't easily spooked by magically manifesting warriors in the mix. I reckoned I could probably catch another volley in < I.E.D.> before needing to unload, but maybe there was another way forward.

"By what right do you fire on my men whilst standing on my land." Arthur's voice was at its most, 'Don't fuck with me.' His hand was resting on Caeldfwch's hilt, which gave me pause.

"If he draws that, Big M, which way are these arrows going when my Qi vanishes? Will they release outward? Because my hold on them is removed, or do they continue towards us because I'm not controlling them anymore?"

There was the sort of confused silence you were not really looking for when the distribution of several hundred crossbow bolts was concerned. *Just to be safe, my dear, I might suggest letting go of them. Gently.*

I didn't need to be told twice. Using all of my expertise and hard-earned experience—*once again, my dear, let's be clear, I am in control of this technique*—I released the bolts over the heads of the men surrounding us.

As much as Arthur's stern expression, I like to think this sharpened the men of Gwent's attention.

An attractive twenty-something pushed himself forward. He spared me a somewhat concerned glance - that's right, dude, Big Dog in the house - and then fixed his eyes on Arthur. I mentally added thirty years and seven stone to him and realised we were probably looking at Owain's son.

"Arthur. We did not expect to see you here."

"I bet you didn't, Maelgwn. Give me one reason I don't have my wizard vapourise you where you stand."

I'm not going to lie, I quite liked how everyone looked at me when he said that. I may or may not have let a little ripple of electricity shimmer across my body.

You are such a fucking drama queen.

"Was your quest successful?"

I had to admire this man's chutzpah. He must know he was in all sorts of shit and was still managing to keep his voice pretty matter-of-fact. An older guy giving off distinct Grand Vizier vibes was suddenly stood at his shoulder, looking like he was about to have a coronary.

Arthur nodded. "I am now the bearer of Caeldfwch, and Mark of Gwynedd has acknowledged me as the Pendragon."

Lancelot shoved the fat man forward. He didn't look up, merely nodded his head.

Maelgwyn's face remained still. "And the other kings? Did they follow suit?"

"Beric was eaten by goblins, and Corys is probably still doing his own eating out about now." I might be wrong, but I sensed my contribution was not universally welcomed.

"And my father?"

Lancelot threw the corpse of Owain at Maelgwyn's feet.

"He betrayed us," he said Arthur. "He took an oath to join us in a quest for Caeldfwch whilst all the time plotting to steal my throne. He murdered my mother, sent assassins to kill my wife and clearly charged you to steal in under cover of that chaos to claim my castle. And he has paid for his presumption. The question is, does anyone else need to die this day?"

Both men looked at each other.

I didn't think Maelgwyn looked hugely devastated, considering the still oozing body of his father was at his feet.

"I guess," continued Arthur, "the only question is whether you wish to re-establish relationships with Dumnonia or if avenging your father's death is foremost in your mind."

I couldn't get a read on the new King of Gwent. He certainly had the numbers to be a pain in the arse, particularly if Arthur forgot himself and drew Caeldfwch. No matter how impressed these dudes had been with my little game of catch and throw, it would go very differently if I didn't have any Qi at my disposal. I really hoped Arthur's brain had considered that before upping the ante.

The red-faced older man stepped forward. "Murderer!"

We all turned to look at him.

"Twice you have bathed your hands in the blood of the royal line of Gwent. First, your bitch of a mother ordered the murder of Prince Kael to bring us to heel, and now you seek to intimidate King Maelgwyn in the same way! The men of Gwent will not bow their heads to tyranny!"

I'm not sure who was more surprised when the dude's head hit the ground—him or Maelgwyn, who had decapitated him.

Nah. It was the dead guy.

Maelgwyn resheated his sword and took a knee. I giggled at the thought that two entirely shit series of my favourite T.V. shows would probably have been avoided if another twenty-something with curly black hair had done something similar.

"King Arthur, the men of Gwent reconfirm our long alliance with the men of Dumnonia and acknowledge your right to hold the title of Pendragon."

His men followed his lead, and the tension noticeably dropped.

With them all now on their knees, I could make out the towers of Tintagel reaching up into the sky.

Weirdly, I felt like I'd come home.

***

"And we are sure he now possesses the sword?"

Several pairs of eyes did their best not to meet the gaze of the Bretwalda. If any of them had any qualms about a Briton being their supreme leader, they had long since learned to keep such thoughts to themselves.

There used to be an awful lot more senior Chieftains of the Saxons. Those left were canny enough to see which way the wind was blowing.

And Aurelius Ambrosius was a veritable hurricane.

Cedric of the West Saxons was the first to speak. "Our spies were clear that, on his return, both Gwent and Gwynedd acknowledged Arthur as the Pendragon. I cannot see any other circumstances where that would have occurred unless he held the sword."

Aurelius took another of his little vials from a satchel and crunched down on it. The men who stood before him did their best to ignore the smell as the flesh of his face was eaten away - and then rebuilt - by the vitriolic poison.

"And Powys and Dehuebarch?"

"Unclear," Hansad, a newly arrived warlord from the east, was a bit trigger-happy when offering Aurelius bad news. The others shuffled away from him surreptitiously. "Neither Corys nor Beric appear to have returned from the quest."

237

Aurelius stood, causing the others to immediately take a knee. He did not acknowledge this and walked to the window of his newly reconstructed tower. When he spoke, none of them were clear about whether it was to them or to himself.

"Arthur Pendragon will be feeling invulnerable. He has pushed us from his lands, his wizard is growing in power, and he now possesses an ancient artefact capable of negating my magic. He has reconfirmed his alliances and, if we understand true, has even managed to rebuild his relationship with his wife. I imagine he is feeling pretty damn smug at this moment."

From his high vantage point, he could see the teeming mass of Saxons beneath him. Boats had been arriving steadily since the turn of the year, and, if possible, there was an even greater mass of men at the Bretwalda's disposal than before the fall of Isca.

"What would you have us do, High King?" Hansad really wasn't going to be long for this world.

Aurelius turned around, eyes blazing with power. All heads dropped to the floor, the leaders of the Saxon race on the island of Britain full-on genuflecting.

"But a Pendragon cannot squat behind his walls, weathering our storm. We may not be able to prise him free from Tintagel, but let us see how firmly his allies stand with him when we slay their people and sow their fields with salt. This will be a summer of slaughter, the like of which the land has never seen before. By the time we are finished, Arthur will be alone. Let us see how much a pretty sword and pair of shapely tits help him when Britain is on fire around him."

<u>EPILOGUE</u>

Life had been relatively peaceful since our return from the quest.

Surprisingly so, as, by hook or by crook, the events of our journey had led to a number of succession crises amongst the remaining British kingdoms that winter.

Gwent had transitioned to King Maelgwyn in a reasonably smooth manner. Who knew, but it seemed that when you dedicated yourself to plotting revenge for twenty years, there were aspects of governmental administration that fell by the wayside. That the new king was interested in actually ruling rather than secret blood-feuding made things a bit easier for him. Most importantly, Dumnonia's connection to the kingdoms across the Severn was secured.

Unfortunately, that was where the good news about the other kingdoms dried up. Mark had fucked off the second the last of his men found their way back to Tintagel. He'd reconfirmed his support for Arthur, and with Maelgwyn on board - and no one else alive to dissent - there was now a very snazzy red dragon flying above Tintagel again.

The news from Powys and Dehuebarch was less than ideal. Corys was still not back from his shagathon, and his kingdom had descended into a very uncivil civil war. Arthur had expressed no preference as to which of his sons we wanted to come out on top but earnestly wished they would get themselves sorted out before the campaign season against the Saxons opened in earnest.

Of Powys we heard nothing, and our messengers were returned without their heads. Lancelot had offered to attend to the matter 'personally', but we all agreed that it might be wise to let some time pass before renewing diplomatic relations. After all, "Sorry we let goblins eat your king" was not the strongest of opening gambits.

Winter had come, buying us all some much-needed respite from the incessant fighting that had marked my time thus far in the Dark Ages. I enjoyed taking the opportunity to round out some of my skills and to spend much longer in meditation.

Which was why I was standing on the roof of my tower, freezing my tits off. Merlin had said it was good for my resilience or something. I think he just liked seeing my nipples turn into bullets.

My dear!

Given the weather, it was somewhat surprising to hear the noise of training coming from the courtyard below. But, then again, considering who was doubtless down there, it probably shouldn't.

Lancelot's Rangers had become a 'thing' with all of the original survivors signing up, alongside a fair number of those who attended the Grand Tournament. If Arthur was concerned about the commitment a large section of his elite warriors were showing to someone who wasn't him, he didn't mention it.

At least not to me.

Mind you, Arthur Pendragon was not exactly lacking in men flocking to his banner. I was secretly pleased to hear a few names I recognised from the stories. There's no easy way to tell someone you've just met that you've heard all about them and they're ballers in the future, but I've done my best to pull it off with subtlety and flair.

You spectacularly embarrassed them, my dear. Especially Galahad. No one needs to know they are one of the most famous virgins in history.

I ignored him

Due to the success of the tournament, the coffers of Tintagel were now overflowing, and a fuckton of money was sunk into gearing Arthur's men up for the spring. I tried to find out from Bors the secret to making quite so much cash out of what I assumed would have been a money pit, but he'd just shrugged.

From Guinevere, I'd heard that the two weeping merchants I'd seen leave the castle had been responsible for the epic financial success of the venture. From what we could ascertain, they'd taken no payment for their hard work and - bizarrely - seemed to have self-funded a considerable amount of the event at their loss. They'd oddly fled in terror from Bors when he'd been to see them to 'discuss their bill'—strange pair.

Speaking of Guinevere...

One of the little-known side-effects of wearing Caeldfwch's scabbard at his waist was to repair whatever damage Drynwyn had caused Arthur's love juice.

It's been mentioned I have somewhat of a hard heart, but even I felt a little flutter of happiness at a very undignified "I'M PREGNANT!" coming from the Queen's chamber shortly after the old witch, Nimue, made her customary post-coital examination.

Unfortunately, that led to a slightly awkward few days after it became clear that King Leodegrance's dowry of 'ten thousand spears' might have been a touch hyperbolic. When three hundred horsemen of dubious quality showed up, it was hard not to feel a bit disappointed. I mean, everyone was welcome to the anti-Saxon party, but it put an ever-so-slight black cloud over what should have been a time of joy.

"We don't have enough men."

Bors had taken to joining me in meditation on the roof of Merlin's tower. He was slowly recovering from his injuries but was walking far more stiffly than I remembered. Guinevere thought he wanted to work on his recovery away from Lancelot and Arthur, but I was fairly sure he was on Team Merlin when it came to gawping at my frost-enhanced ladies.

Honestly, my dear...

"You say that every day, mate," I answered Bors. "And I still say you are being pessimistic."

"We've narrowly fought back armies at our gates twice in the last six months. I don't think it happened once in the last century. Do you think we've got a third siege in us?"

"I think we've fought off Saxons, wyverns, goblins, demonic cultivators, magical forests and giant fucking sea monsters. The smart money is on us in any confrontation."

Bors sat up a bit straighter and winced at the pain in his back. "He's talking about going on the offensive in the spring. Of taking the fight to the Saxons."

I didn't need to ask who 'he' was.

"I've heard worse ideas. Get us out into Saxon territories. Doing what we do best. Could be interesting."

"I worry it's all too fragile. We were in the best shape we'd ever been before Isca fell. Merlin, armies, allies, strongholds. We had it all, and it felt like there was a sense of destiny behind what we were about to achieve. I look at us now, and it feels like we're always one battle away from a wipeout. It scares me that it will only take one bad call, one strategic error, and that could be it. I can't comprehend stakes like that."

I decided not to take offence at the comparison. Everyone knew I was doing my best, but I wouldn't be Merlin anytime soon.

"This isn't like you, mate. You okay?"

Bors puffed out his cheeks. "Mrs Bors is pregnant again."

I high-fived him. "You and Arthur are both going to be daddies at the same time! That's so cool!"

"It just makes you think." I thought that was it, but - after a few moments - he continued. "I never knew my own dad, you know? He died fighting the Saxons before I was born. I always promised myself that my kids wouldn't grow up like that."

A billion jokes lined up in my head to break the dark mood that was settling on us. But I couldn't make any of them come out.

Because, in a few months or so, the Saxons would be coming.

And we weren't ready.

THANK YOU

Hi everyone! Thant brings the first arc of 'Morgan and Merlin's Excellent Adventures' to a close. I hope you've enjoyed this irrelevant take on the Arthurian Mythos - or at least have had half as much fun reading it as I've had writing it! You can catch up with Morgan's latest adventures, as we move inexorably towards Mordred and the Battle of Camlann, over on Royal Road..

If you've enjoyed the ride so far, I'd love for you to leave a review or spread the word. It's one of the best ways to keep this circus rolling, and it means a lot.

As my first trilogy comes to a close, I wanted to take a moment to thank everyone at Legion Publishing. It is quite a thing to be told that, not only do people want to *read* something you've written, but that they're going to *pay* you for it, too. This last year has been, genuinely, life-changing for me, and I cannot thank Jez, Chrissy and Geneva enough for everything they have done for me. Thank you for inviting me into the Legion family.

Hopefully, there's plenty more where this comes from.

Cheers,

Malory

28/1/2024

RISE OF MANKIND 6: AGE OF GLASS

By Jez Cajiao

The Age of Glass dawns, a fragile era balanced on the edge of oblivion. Will it shatter beneath the relentless hammer of fate?

From the depths of despair to the pinnacle of power, Matt's ascension to Dungeon Lord has been a crucible of blood and terror. But the higher he climbs, the more precarious his perch becomes. As winter's icy fingers close around his hard-won domain, Matt and his beleaguered allies yearn for respite. Instead, they face a nightmare beyond imagining.
The Coronaught infection sweeps through the land like wildfire, twisting human flesh into abominations that defy sanity. Grotesque mutations stalk the shadows, their hunger insatiable. In this maelstrom of horror, Matt must be more than a leader – he must become a legend.

With each agonizing decision, the weight of command threatens to crush his spirit. Can he salvage the humanity of the infected, or will the price of compassion be too steep? Nuclear fire looms on the horizon, a cleansing inferno that promises annihilation. How much of his soul will Matt sacrifice to shield his people from the coming storm?

In the bowels of the earth, Matt labors to transform his dungeon into an impregnable fortress. But in a world where loyalty shatters like spun sugar, yesterday's allies may become tomorrow's executioners. Survival exacts a terrible toll, paid in blood and betrayal.

Step carefully into the Age of Glass, where every triumph balances on a knife's edge, and a single misstep can leave you bleeding in the dark.

Buy now!

THEFT OF DECKS

By Lars Machmüller

When the deck is stacked against you? Change the game!

In the frontier town of Isarn, Chase will never be more than the lowly Darkborn thief he is. Banned from training, banned from acquiring better cards, if the Lightborn had their way, he'd be banned from life itself.

He's not alone though, and the one thing he and his friends have is determination. Losing a hand to a brutal punishment only fueled his obsession to get access to his own amazing, reality-bending cards.

That is the path to power and a future for them all. Nobody cares where you came from when you're rich enough. For now, though, they're facing both established powers, churches and age-old prejudices. It's time to get to work, and if the Lightborn won't share and play nice?

Sometimes the only way to get dealt a better hand is to steal the whole damn deck!

Buy on Amazon

QUEST ACADEMY

By Brian J. Nordon

A world infested by demons.
An Academy designed to train Heroes to save humanity from annihilation.
A new student's power could make all the difference.

Humans have been pushed to the brink of extinction by an ever-evolving demonic threat. Portals are opening faster than ever, Towers bursting into the skies and Dungeons being mined below the last safe havens of society. The demons are winning.

Quest Academy stands defiantly against them, as a place to train the next generation of Heroes. The Guild Association is holding the line, but are in dire need of new blood and the powerful abilities they could bring to the battlefront. To be the saviors that humanity needs, they need to surpass the limits of those that came before them.

In a war with everything on the line, every power matters. With an adaptive enemy, comes the need for a constant shift in tactics. A new age of strategy is emerging, with even the unlikeliest of Heroes making an impact.

Salvatore Argento has never seen a demon.
He has never aspired to become a Hero.
Yet his power might be the one to tip the odds in humanity's favor.

Buy on Amazon

<u>WANDERING WARRIOR</u>

By Michael Head

A divine quest to deliver justice.
One year to accomplish his mission.
After nineteen planets, there's something different about this one.

James Holden has reached the maximum level there is for a human. That's perfect, since he's the only one of his kind. A wandering warrior, without control of his destination, tossed between universes by gods who've failed to tell him why. James is the lone Judge on a new world in need of someone to balance the scales. He isn't afraid to do so with extreme prejudice. As the Chief Justice, he has to right the wrongs the innocent can't fix themselves.

As James quickly discovers, the roots of corruption run deep. Guilds choose to protect themselves rather than the people. Monsters roam the wilderness unchecked. Judgment is usually a decision between right and wrong, but nothing is ever that simple. This time, being the strongest human won't be enough to punish the guilty. James might have to recruit some new blood, even if he prefers to work alone.

On his twentieth world, he is going to win, no matter the cost. James will have to find a way to break past the limits of the system if he's going to have a chance at making a difference.

<u>Buy on Amazon</u>

KNIGHTS OF ETERNITY

By Rachel Ní Chuirc

When Zara awoke in chains she thought she'd gone mad.

She was Zara the Fury - mistress of flame and fear. Her name was whispered across the land, from ramshackle taverns to the royal court. Even the heroic Gilded Knights thought twice before crossing her path.
She was feared—*respected.*
Now she was curled up on a dirt floor on her fiancé's orders. Valerius, leader of the Gilded, mocks her cries for help. And the kingdom is on the brink of war over the missing Lady Eternity…
But that wasn't why Zara thought she had gone mad.
The reason why is that the last thing she remembered was blood, an arcade screen, and the gun that changed everything.

But no chains can hold the Fury, and when she gets out?
The world is going to *burn.*

Buy on Amazon

SCARLET CITADEL

By Jack Fields

Gormon Hughes is 19, thin as a broom, and has—not for the first time in his life—been swept into the path of trouble. Poor, recently heartbroken, and indebted to the sort of people who file their teeth into needle points and devour wriggling bloated spiders for fun, Hughes sets his sights on salvation.

That salvation is the Scarlet Citadel, a wealthy organization of pageant fighters, monster hunters, and secret keepers. With the aid of strange oracles, rare good fortune, and a unique power that bubbles like champagne in the core of Hughes' being, he must join the Citadel and advance himself.

But the ladder of progression is harsh and dark. The rungs are slippery.

And falling means disaster…

Buy on Amazon

<u>LITRPG!</u>

To learn more about LitRPG, talk to other authors including myself, and to just have an awesome time, please join the LitRPG Group

www.facebook.com/groups/LitRPGGroup

FACEBOOK

There's also a few really active Facebook groups I'd recommend you join, as you'll get to hear about great new books, new releases and interact with all your (new) favorite authors! (I may also be there, skulking at the back and enjoying the memes…)

https://www.facebook.com/groups/LitRPGlegion/

https://www.facebook.com/groups/GamelitSociety

https://www.facebook.com/groups/LitRPG.books

https://www.facebook.com/groups/LitRPGforum/

MALORY